PENGUIN BOOKS

The Realist

Hermann Broch was born in Vienna in 1886. He managed his father's textile firm and was almost forty before he studied philosophy and mathematics at Vienna University. He published the three parts of *The Sleepwalkers* trilogy (*The Romantic, The Anarchist* and *The Realist*) in 1931–2, and *The Unknown Quantity* in 1933. He was briefly imprisoned by the Nazis when they invaded Austria in 1938, but the help of friends such as James Joyce and Willa and Edwin Muir led to his emigration to America that year, where he remained until his death in 1951. *The Death of Virgil* was published to great acclaim in 1945, and *The Guiltless* in 1950. His last work, *The Spell*, an incomplete fragment, was published posthumously in 1953.

During his lifetime Broch's work brought him great praise as an innovative visionary writer, comparable to Joyce, Thomas Mann and Robert Musil. He was admired by Aldous Huxley, who wrote of *The Sleepwalkers*, 'We are haunted by the strange and disquieting feeling that we are at the very limits of the expressible ... Broch performs with an impeccable virtuosity.'

The Sleepwalkers is a trilogy whose component novels can be read completely independently of one another.

Each novel is set in a different year – *The Romantic* in 1888, *The Anarchist* in 1903 and *The Realist* in 1918.

HERMANN BROCH

The Realist

Translated by Willa and Edwin Muir

With a Biographical Note by John White

PENGUIN BOOKS

PENGUIN BOOKS

Published by the Penguin Group
Penguin Books Ltd, 27 Wrights Lane, London w8 5tz, England
Penguin Putnam Inc., 375 Hudson Street, New York, New York 10014, USA
Penguin Books Australia Ltd, Ringwood, Victoria, Australia
Penguin Books Canada Ltd, 10 Alcorn Avenue, Toronto, Ontario, Canada m4v 3b2
Penguin Books (NZ) Ltd, Private Bag 102902, NSMC, Auckland, New Zealand

Penguin Books Ltd, Registered Offices: Harmondsworth, Middlesex, England

First published in German as *1918. Huguenau oder die Sachlichkeit* 1932
This translation first published in the USA by Little, Brown, and Company, 1932

Published in Penguin Classics 2000
1 3 5 7 9 10 8 6 4 2

Copyright © The Estate of Hermann Broch
Biographical note copyright © John White 2000

Translation by Willa and Edwin Muir used by permission of Alfred A. Knopf, Inc.
All rights reserved

The cover shows a detail from *The Engineer Heartfield*, 1920, by George Grosz.
Watercolour and collage of pasted postcard and halftone on paper, 16½″ × 12″.
The Museum of Modern Art, New York. Gift of A. Conger Goodyear © DACS
2000 (Photo © 1999 The Museum of Modern Art, New York). The back cover
shows the painting in its entirety

The moral right of the author of the biographical note
has been asserted

Printed in England by Clays Ltd, St Ives plc

Contents

The Realist (1918)

CHAPTER I

HUGUENAU, whose forefathers might well have been called Hagenau before Alsace was occupied in 1692 by Condé's troops, had all the characteristics of the town-bred Alemanni. He was thick-set, inclined to be fat, and had worn glasses since his boyhood, or, to be more precise, since the time when he had attended the commercial school in Schlettstadt, and now that he was approaching his thirtieth year at the outbreak of the war he retained no trace of his youth either in face or behaviour. He did business in Baden and Württemberg, partly in branch establishments of his father's textile firm, André Huguenau, Colmar, Alsace, partly on his own account and as a representative of various Alsatian factories for which he acted as agent in that section of the country. In these provincial circles his reputation was that of an energetic, prudent and reliable man of business.

There is no doubt that with his capabilities he would have done better at smuggling, which the times made more profitable, than at soldiering. But he submitted without further ado when in 1917 his extreme shortsightedness was summarily ignored and he received a call to arms, as the phrase went. True, even while he was being trained in Fulda he did manage to wind up a tobacco business here and there, but soon enough he dropped everything. Not only because his military duties made him tired or inapt for other things. It was simply so pleasant not to have to bother about anything at all, and it reminded him vaguely of his schooldays; the boy who was once at school, Huguenau (Wilhelm), could still remember his last Speech Day in the Schlettstadt Academy, and how he and his class-mates had been dedicated by the Head to the serious issues of life, serious issues which hitherto he had coped with well enough and now had to abandon again in favour of a new schooling. Once more he was pinned down to an endless succession of duties that had been forgotten in the course of years, once more he was treated as a pupil and shouted at, had a similar attitude to the common lavatories as in his boyhood, and attached the same importance to food, while the ceremonies of respect and the ambitious competition in which he found

3

himself involved gave a completely infantile stamp to the whole. As if
that were not enough, he was quartered in a school building, and before
falling asleep could see the two rows of lights with their green-and-
white shades and the blackboard that had been left where it was. All
this confused his schooldays and his soldiering days in an inextricable
tangle, and even when the battalion set off at last to the Front, singing
childish songs and bedecked with little flags, crowded into primitive
sleeping-quarters in Cologne and Liège, Huguenau the fusilier could
not get rid of the notion that he was on a school excursion.

It was evening when his company moved into the front line. They
were posted in a fortified trench which was approached by long covered
passage-ways. Unexampled filth reigned in the dug-outs, the floors were
covered with spittle both fresh and dry, there were streaks of urine
on the walls, and it could not be determined whether the prevailing
stench was that of fæces or of corpses. In any case Huguenau was too
tired to realize the actual sights and smells around him. Even while
trotting in single file through the approach trenches all the men already
had the feeling of being outcasts from the sheltering warmth of comrade-
ship and common life, and hardened as they were to the complete lack
of cleanliness, little as they missed the conventions of civilization with
which humanity seeks to banish the stench of death and corruption,
however surely the repression of their disgust advanced them one step
towards heroism (a step that links heroism most strangely with love),
long as most of them had been accustomed to live among horrors during
the years of war, so that they merely joked and swore as they made their
beds, yet there was not one among them who did not know that he
was posted there as a solitary creature to live alone and to die alone
in an overwhelmingly senseless world, so senseless that he could not
comprehend it or rise beyond describing it as " this bloody war."

It was at a time when the various general staffs had reported that in
the Flanders section complete quiet prevailed. The company that had
just been relieved also asserted that there was nothing doing. And yet
as soon as darkness fell the artillery on both sides began a cannonade
that was severe enough to banish their weariness from the newcomers.
Aching in every bone, Huguenau sat on a kind of camp-bed, and only
after a fair length of time did he remark that his limbs were all trembling
and twitching. The other men were in no better case. One of them was
weeping. Some of the old soldiers, indeed, were merely amused: this

was just a game the batteries played every night, it meant nothing, one soon got used to it; and taking no further notice of their weaker brethren they were actually snoring in a minute or two.

Huguenau would have liked to remonstrate with somebody: this was not at all what he had bargained for. Sick and faint as he was, he yearned for fresh air, and when his knees began to tremble less he tottered to the entrance of the dug-out, sat down there on a box and stared with vacant eyes at the firework display in the sky. Time and again he thought he saw the figure of a man flying up to Heaven with one hand raised in an orange cloud. Then he remembered Colmar, and that his school class had been taken one day to be lectured on art in the Museum; it had been rather boring, but there was one picture, standing like an altar in the middle of the floor, that had terrified him. It was, moreover, a Crucifixion. He detested crucifixions. That reminded him that years ago he had had to put in a Sunday in Nürnberg, between visits to customers, and had gone to see the torture chamber. Now that had been interesting. There was a fine collection of pictures too. One of them showed a man chained to a kind of camp-bed, a man who, the inscription said, had murdered a clergyman in Saxony by stabbing him repeatedly with a dagger, and now had to lie on that bed waiting to be broken on the wheel. To be broken on the wheel was a punishment sufficiently explained by other exhibits in the place. The man had a good-humoured expression, and it was just as unimaginable that he had stabbed a pastor and was doomed to be broken on the wheel, as that Huguenau himself should have to sit where he was, on a camp-bed in a stench of corpses. No doubt the man had ached all over too, and was bound to befoul himself since he was chained down. Huguenau spat, and said " Merde! " He went on sitting at the door of the dug-out like a sentry; he leaned his head against a post, he had turned up his coat-collar, he was no longer cold, he was not asleep, but neither was he awake. The torture chamber and the dug-out blended and sank more profoundly into the sordid and yet brilliant colours of Grünewald's altar-piece, and while in the palpitating orange light of the distant cannonade and the shooting rockets the boughs of naked trees stretched their arms towards Heaven, a man with uplifted hand soared through the illuminated vault of the sky.

When the first grey light of dawn came cold and leaden Huguenau noticed the tufts of grass at the lip of the trench and a few daisies that had survived from last year. So he simply crawled out and made off. He knew that he might be picked off at any moment by the English, and that similar attentions would be paid to him by the German outposts; but the world lay as if under a vacuum glass—Huguenau could not help thinking of a glass cover over cheese—grey, worm-eaten and completely dead in a silence that was inviolable.

CHAPTER II

Bathed in the limpid air that heralds the spring, the deserter made his way unarmed through the Belgian landscape. Haste would have served him little, prudent caution served him better, and weapons would not have protected him at all; it was, one might say, as a naked man that he slipped through the armed forces. His untroubled face was a better protection than weapons or hurried flight or forged papers.

For the Belgians were suspicious fellows. Four years of war had not improved their disposition. Their corn, their potatoes, their horses and cows had all had to suffer. And when a deserter came to them looking for sanctuary they examined him with twofold suspicion, lest he might be one of the men who had beaten on their doors with a rifle-butt. And even if the fugitive spoke passable French and gave himself out as an Alsatian, in nine cases out of ten that would have availed him little. Woe to the man who strayed into a village merely as a fugitive timidly imploring help! But a man who came like Huguenau with a ready jest on his lips, with a beaming and friendly face, found it easy enough to have beer smuggled to him in the barn, or even to sit with the family of an evening in the kitchen and tell tales of the Prussians' brutality and violence in Alsace; such a stranger was welcomed and got his share of the hoarded provisions; with luck he might even be visited in his bed of hay by one of the maids.

It was still more advantageous, of course, to get into the parsonages, and Huguenau soon discovered that he could manage this by way of the confessional. He made his confessions in French, skilfully grafting an account of his miserable plight on to the admission of his sin in breaking his oath of allegiance. To be sure, the results were not always pleasant. Once he hit upon a priest, a tall lean man so ascetic and passionate in appearance that Huguenau almost shrank from presenting himself at the parsonage on the evening after confession, and when he saw the severe figure busy at spring work in the orchard he felt inclined to turn tail. But the priest came quickly towards him. " Suivez-moi," he said harshly, and led him indoors.

For nearly a week Huguenau stayed there on meagre rations with a bed in the attic. He was given a blue blouse and set to work in the garden; he was awakened for Mass and permitted to eat in the kitchen at the same table as his silent host. Not a word was said of his escape, and the whole affair was like a penance that sat but ill on Huguenau. He had even made up his mind to quit the relative security of his asylum and continue his dangerous flight, when one day—eight days after his arrival —he found a suit of civilian clothes laid out in his attic. He was to accept the suit, said the priest, and he was free to go or to stay as he chose; only he could no longer be boarded there, for there was not sufficient food. Huguenau decided to go on farther, and as he embarked on a lengthy speech of thanks the priest cut him short: " Haïssez les Prussiens et les ennemis de la sainte religion. Et que Dieu vous bénisse." He lifted two fingers in benediction, made the sign of the Cross, and the deep-set eyes in his peasant face gazed with burning hate into a distant region inhabited, presumably, by Prussians and Protestants.

When Huguenau quitted that parsonage it became clear to him that he had to think out a definite plan of escape. Formerly he had often enough hung about in the neighbourhood of various corps headquarters where he passed without comment among the other soldiers, but that had now become impossible. He was really depressed by his civilian clothes; they were like an admonition to return to the work-a-day world of peace, and that he had donned them at the command of the priest seemed now a lapse into stupidity. The priest's offer was an unauthorized interference with his private life, and he had paid dear enough to secure his private life. Besides, even if he did not regard himself as belonging to the Kaiser's forces, yet as a deserter he had a peculiar, one might almost say a negative connection with them, and in any case he belonged to the war and he did not disapprove of the war. For instance, he had not been able to stomach the way in which men in the canteens abused the war and the newspapers, or asserted that Krupp had been buying up newspapers in order to prolong the war. For Wilhelm Huguenau was not only a deserter, he was a man of business, a salesman who admired all factory-owners for producing the wares that the rest of the world used. So if Krupp and the coal barons bought newspapers they knew what they were doing, and had a perfect right to do it, as much right as he had to wear his uniform as long as he pleased. There was no reason, therefore, why he should return to that background of civilian life which the priest with his suit of clothes had obviously destined for him, nothing to induce him to return to his native country in which there were no holidays, and which stood for all that was commonplace.

So he remained in the base lines. He turned southwards, avoiding towns and calling at villages, came through the Hennegau and penetrated to the Ardennes. The war by that time had lost much of its formality, and deserters were no longer closely hunted—there were too many of them, and the authorities did not want to admit their existence. Still, that does not explain how Huguenau got out of Belgium undiscovered; one can attribute it rather to the somnambulistic sureness with which he picked his way through the dangerous zone; he walked along in the clear air of early spring, walked light-heartedly as if under a glass bell, cut off from the world and yet in it, and he was untroubled by reflections. From the Ardennes he crossed into German territory, coming out on the bleak plateau of the Eifel where winter still prevailed and it was difficult to make headway. The inhabitants did not bother about him, they were surly, silent people, and they hated every extra mouth that sought a share of their scanty provender. Huguenau had to take to the train and break into his savings, hitherto untouched. The serious issues of life threatened him again in a new and different guise. Something had to be done to secure and prolong his holiday.

CHAPTER III

The little town lay girdled by vineyards in a tributary valley of the Moselle. The heights above were crowned by woods. The vineyards were all in trim, with the vine-stocks set in straight lines interrupted at places by outcrops of reddish rock. Huguenau observed with disapproval that many of the owners had not weeded their plots, and that the neglected patches stood out like rectangular yellow islets among the reddish grey soil of the others.

After the last days of winter in the Eifel highlands Huguenau had come down all at once into the real springtime. Like a promise of inalienable order and comfort the sun radiated gay well-being and light security into his heart. Any anxiety that might have lurked there could be thrown off. It was a satisfaction to him to see in the forefront of the town the stately District Hospital with its long façade lying in the morning shadow, he approved the fact that all its windows were open as if it were a southern sanatorium, and he found it pleasant to imagine the light spring airs blowing through the white wards. He approved, too, the large red cross marked on the roof of the hospital, and as he passed by he cast a benevolent glance at the soldiers in their grey hospital uniform, who were convalescing, some in shadow and some in the sun of the garden. Across the river lay the barracks, recognizable by its style of architecture, and a building resembling a monastery which he later discovered to be the prison. But the road sloped down towards the town in a friendly and comfortable manner, and as Huguenau passed through the mediæval town gate, a small fibre case in his hand just like the case of samples he used to carry, it did not even ruffle him that his entry reminded him strongly of similar entries into Württemberg towns which once upon a time—and how long ago it seemed—he had visited on his business rounds.

The streets, too, were so old-fashioned that they reminded him of his compulsory day of rest in Nürnberg. Here in Kur-Trier the war of the Palatinate had not raged with such ruthlessness as in the other regions west of the Rhine. The old fifteenth- and sixteenth-century houses were still intact, and so was the Gothic Town Hall in the market-place, with its Renaissance outworks and the tower before which stood the old pillory. And Huguenau, who had visited many a lovely old town on his commercial rounds, but had remarked none of them, was seized by a novel emotion which he could not have given a name to or traced to any known source, but which made him feel curiously at home in this town: if it had been described to him as an æsthetic emotion or as an emotion springing from a sense of freedom, he would have laughed incredulously, with the laughter of a man who has never had even an inkling of the beauty of the world, and he would have been right, in so far as nobody can determine whether it is freedom that opens the eyes of the soul to beauty, or beauty that gives the soul its vision of freedom, but yet he would have been wrong, for there was bound to be even in him a deeper human wisdom, a human longing for that freedom in which all the light of the world has its source and that finally creates the Sabbath that hallows life; and since this is so and cannot be otherwise, a gleam of the higher light may well have fallen on Huguenau in that very moment when he crawled out of the trench and shook himself free of human obligations, a gleam of that light which is freedom and which entered even into him and for the first time dedicated him to the Sabbath.

Far removed from speculations of this nature, Huguenau engaged a room in the hotel in the market-place. As if to assure himself that he was still on holiday, he set out to have a jolly evening. The Moselle wine was not rationed and in spite of the war had retained its quality. Huguenau treated himself to three pannikins full and sat long over them. There were citizens all round at the various tables; Huguenau was an alien among them, and here and there hasty questioning glances were directed at him. They all had their business and their pre-occupations, and he himself had nothing. None the less he was happy and contented. He was himself amazed: no employment and yet happy! so happy that he found pleasure in recapitulating to himself all the difficulties that would incontestably arise should a man like himself, a stranger without identification papers and without any connections in the town, attempt to set up business and obtain credit. It was extra-ordinarily funny to imagine the fix he would be in. Perhaps the wine was responsible. Huguenau, at any rate, as he climbed into bed with a somewhat addled head, did not feel like a worried commercial traveller, but like a merry and light-hearted tourist.

CHAPTER IV

When Gödicke, a bricklayer in the Landwehr, was unearthed from the ruins of his trench, his mouth, gaping as if for a scream, was filled with earth. His face was a blackish blue, and he had no discernible heart-beat. Had not the two ambulance men who found him made a bet about his survival he would simply have been re-buried immediately. That he was fated to see the sun again and the sunny world, he owed to the ten cigarettes which the winner of the bet was due to receive.

He could not be said to have revived under artificial respiration, although both men toiled and sweated over him, but they carried him off and observed him closely, abusing him from time to time because he so obstinately refused to solve the riddle of his life, the riddle of his death; and they were tireless in shoving him under the doctors' noses.

So the object of their bet lay for four whole days in a field hospital without moving and with a blackened skin. Whether during this time a dim flicker of infinitesimal slumbering life began to glimmer and was fanned with pain and anguish through the wreck of the body, or whether it was a faint and ecstatic pulsing on the verge of a great beyond, we do not know and Gödicke of the Landwehr could not have told.

For it was only piecemeal, half a cigarette at a time, so to speak, that the life returned to his body, and this slow caution was both proper and natural, since what his crushed body demanded was the utmost immobility. For many long days Ludwig Gödicke must have fancied himself the child in swaddling-clothes that he had been forty years before, constricted by an incomprehensible restraint and feeling nothing save the restraint. And if he had been capable of it he might well have whimpered for his mother's breast, and as a matter of fact he soon did begin to whimper. It was during the journey, and his whimpering was like the incessant mewling of a newly born child; nobody was willing to lie next to him, and one night another patient even threw something at him. That was during the time when everyone believed that he would have to die of hunger, since it was impossible for the doctors to find a way of introducing nourishment into him. That he went on living was inexplicable, and the Surgeon-Major's opinion that his body had nourished itself on all the bruised blood under the skin was scarcely worth calling an opinion, let alone a theory. The lower part of his body in especial was terribly injured. He was laid in a cold pack, but whether that alleviated his sufferings at all could not be determined. But it was possible that he had ceased to suffer so much, for the whimpering gradually died away. Until a few days later it broke out again more strongly: it was now—or one may imagine that it was—as if Ludwig Gödicke were recovering his soul only in single fragments, and as if each fragment came to him on a wave of agony. It may be that that was so, even though it cannot be proved; it may be that the anguish of a soul that has been torn and pulverized into atoms and must join itself together again is greater than any other anguish, keener than the anguish of a brain that quivers under renewed spasms of cramp, keener than all the bodily suffering that accompanies the process.

Thus Gödicke of the Landwehr lay in his bed on rubber air-cushions, and while it was impossible to nurse his battered body, while food was slowly injected in minute doses, his soul collected itself; to the bewilderment of Doctor Kühlenbeck, the Senior Medical Officer, to the bewilderment of Doctor Flurschütz, to the bewilderment of Sister Carla, his soul collected itself with agony around the core of his ego.

CHAPTER V

Huguenau woke up early. He was an energetic man. A decent bed-room; no garret such as he had had with the priest; a good bed. Huguenau scratched his leg. Then he tried to find his bearings.

A hotel; the market-place; and the Town Hall was facing him.

There were really many inducements for him to go back and take up the threads of his life again in the place where they had been dropped; there were many reasons why he should do his duty as a business man and pick up easy money as an agent for butter and textiles. Yet the very idea of casks of butter and sacks of coffee and bales of textiles was so repugnant to him that he was himself surprised,—and the repugnance was really a matter for surprise to a man who since his boyhood had thought and spoken of nothing but money and trading. And the thought of being on holiday from school came up again most amazingly. Huguenau found it pleasanter to meditate on the town he happened to be in.

Behind the town were the vineyards. And in many of them were weeds. The owner had probably been killed in the war or was a prisoner. His wife could not manage the work alone, or was running round with another man. Besides, the price of wine was controlled by the State. Unless one could sell wine on the sly it wasn't worth while to tend the vineyard. But the wines were of fine quality; they actually went a little to one's head.

A war widow like that would really be glad to sell her vineyard cheap.

Huguenau began to think of possible buyers for stocks of Moselle. One should be able to find them. One could make a good bit of com-mission on the deal. Wine-shippers were the people. Friedrichs' in Cologne, Matter & Co. in Frankfort. He had delivered pipes of wine to them before.

He jumped out of bed. His plan was made.

He tidied himself before the looking-glass. Combed his hair back. It had grown long since the company's barber had shaved it. Now when had that been? It seemed to be in a former life; if it weren't that hair grew slowly in winter he would have had a fine mane. When a man is dead his hair and nails go on growing. Huguenau took a strand of his hair and pulled it down over his forehead. It reached almost to the point of his nose. No, a man couldn't go about in that state. One always had one's hair cut just before a holiday. True, this wasn't a holiday. But it wasn't so very unlike one.

The morning was bright. A little chilly.

There were two yellow armchairs with black-leather seats in the barber's shop. The barber himself, a shaky old man, tied the not-very-clean overall round Huguenau's neck, and tucked a roll of paper into his collar. Huguenau moved his chin a little to and fro; the paper rasped him.

There was a newspaper hanging on a hook and Huguenau asked for it. It was the local *Kur-Trier Herald*, with a supplement on " Farming and Viniculture in the Moselle District." That was exactly what he needed.

He sat motionless, studying the paper, and then he looked at himself in the glass; he could easily have passed for one of the more solid citizens in the place. His hair was now cut as he liked it, short, respectable, and German. On top of his head a few strands of longer hair were left to make a parting. The next thing was to be shaved.

The barber whipped up a thin lather that spread cold and sparingly over Huguenau's face. The soap was no good.

" The soap's not up to much," said Huguenau. The barber made no reply, but stropped his razor. Huguenau was offended, but after a while said excusingly: " War goods."

The barber began to shave. With short, scraping strokes. He did it badly. Still, it was pleasant to be shaved. Shaving oneself was one of the conditions of war. Cheaper, too; but for once in a while it was pleasant to have it done for one. More like a holiday. There was a picture of a girl hanging on the wall with a lavish display of bosom, and beneath her were the words " Lotion Houbigant." Huguenau had laid back his head and let the paper hang in his idle hands. The barber was now shaving his chin and throat; was he never going to finish? Well, Huguenau didn't care; he had plenty of time. And to put off time a little longer he ordered a " Lotion Houbigant." What he got was eau-de-Cologne.

Freshly shaved, a clean-shaven spruce man with the scent of eau-de-

Cologne in his nose, Huguenau walked back to the inn. When he took off his hat he sniffed at the lining. It smelt of pomade, and that too was satisfactory.

There was no one in the dining-room. Huguenau got his coffee and the maid brought out a bread-card from which she snipped a portion. There was no butter, only a blackish syrupy kind of jam. Nor was the coffee real coffee, and while he sipped the hot liquid Huguenau reckoned up how much profit the manufacturers were making on their coffee-substitute; he reckoned it up without envy and approved it. In any case buying wine cheap in the Moselle district was just as profitable a venture, an excellent investment. And when he had finished his break-fast he set about drawing up an advertisement offering to buy wines of good quality. Then he took it along to the office of the *Kur-Trier Herald*.

CHAPTER VI

The District Hospital had become entirely a military hospital. Dr Friedrich Flurschütz was making his round of the wards. He was wearing a military cap with his doctor's white overall; a combination which Lieutenant Jaretzki characterized as absurd.

Jaretzki had been put into Officers' Room III. That had been pure chance, for these double-bedded rooms were supposed to be reserved for Staff Officers, but once he was in he stayed there. He was sitting on the edge of his bed with a cigarette in his mouth when Flurschütz came in, and his arm in its unwrapped bandage was lying on the bedside table.

" Well, how are we, Jaretzki? "

Jaretzki indicated his arm:

" The Surgeon-Major's just been in."

Flurschütz looked at the arm and touched it cautiously here and there:

" A bad business . . . gone a bit further? "

" Yes, an inch or so . . . the old man wants to amputate."

The arm lay there inflamed and reddish, the palm of the hand swollen, the fingers like red sausages, and round the wrist a ring of purulent blisters.

Jaretzki regarded his arm and said:

" Poor thing, look at it lying there."

" Don't worry about it, it's only the left."

" Yes, all you want to do is to cut things off."

Flurschütz shrugged his shoulders:

" Can't be helped; this century has been devoted to surgery and rewarded by a world-war with guns . . . now we're beginning to find out about glands, and by the time the next war comes along we'll be able to do wonders with these damned gas-poisonings . . . but for the present the only thing we can do is cut."

Jaretzki said:

" The next war? Don't tell me you believe that this one's ever going to come to an end."

" I don't need to be a prophet to do that, Jaretzki, the Russians have given it up already."

Jaretzki laughed bitterly:

" God preserve you in your childish faith and send us decent cigarettes. . . ."

With his sound right hand he had drawn a packet of cigarettes from the open shelf under the drawer of the table and now offered it to Flurschütz.

Flurschütz pointed to the ash-tray full of cigarette-butts:

" You shouldn't smoke so much. . . ."

Sister Mathilde came in.

" Well, do we bind it up again . . . what's your opinion, Doctor? "

Sister Mathilde was looking well. She had freckles on her forehead. Flurschütz said:

" It's a bad business, this gas."

He stayed to watch the Sister binding up the arm and then he went on his rounds again. At both ends of the broad corridor the windows were wide open, but no current of air could blow away the hospital smell.

CHAPTER VII

The house lay in Fischerstrasse, one of the side-streets leading down to the river, a timbered edifice in which, it was obvious, all sorts of handicrafts had been carried on for centuries. Beside the door there was a black battered tin plate with the words in faded gold-lettering: " *Kur-Trier Herald*, Editorial and Business Office (in the courtyard)."

Penetrating through the narrow passage-like entry, where in the darkness he stumbled over the trap-door leading down to the cellar, and passing an opening that gave on the stairs leading to the dwelling-house, Huguenau found himself in an unexpectedly spacious courtyard shaped somewhat like a horseshoe. A garden adjoined the courtyard; there a few cherry-trees were in blossom, and beyond the garden one's gaze was lost in the lovely mountain country.

The whole place witnessed to the semi-peasant character of its former possessor. The two wings had certainly served as granaries and stables; the left one had two storeys, and there was a steep and narrow wooden ladder on the outer wall; probably the top floor had once been the servants' quarters. The upper storey of the stable buildings on the right was a hayloft, and one of the stable doors had been displaced by a large business-like barred window, behind which a printing-press could be seen at work.

From the man at the printing-press Huguenau learned that Herr Esch was to be found on the first floor opposite.

So Huguenau climbed the wooden steps and found himself plump before a door with the inscription, " Editorial and Business Office," behind which Herr Esch, owner and publisher of the *Kur-Trier Herald*, exercised his functions. He was a lean man with a clean-shaven face in which, between two long and deep furrows running down the cheeks, a mouth as mobile as an actor's grimaced sarcastically, showing a set of strong yellowish teeth. He had something of the actor about him, something of the clergyman, and something of the horse.

The advertisement which Huguenau handed to him he scrutinized with the air of an examining magistrate considering a document. Huguenau took out his pocket-book, from which he extracted a five-mark note, as a hint, so to speak, that he was prepared to allot that sum for the insertion of the advertisement. But the other, paying not the least attention to this, asked abruptly: " So you're out to exploit the people round about here, are you? I suppose the poverty of our wine-growers is common talk already—heh? "

It was an unprovoked attack, and Huguenau decided that its purpose was to force up the price for inserting the advertisement. He produced therefore another mark, but that merely had the opposite effect from what he had wished: " Thanks . . . you can keep your advertisement. . . . Evidently you don't appreciate what it means to corrupt the Press

. . . let me tell you, you won't corrupt me with your six marks, nor with ten, nor with a hundred! "

Huguenau became more and more certain that he was dealing with a sharp business man. But simply for that reason it was imperative that he should not give way; perhaps the man was waiting for him to suggest going shares in the venture, and after all that arrangement would not be without its advantages.

" Hm, I've heard that these advertisement deals are sometimes made on a percentage basis—how about a half-per-cent commission on the results? Of course in that case you would have to insert the announcement three separate times at least . . . still, you're quite at liberty to insert it oftener than that, when it's a matter of generosity I impose no limits . . ." he risked a confidential laugh and sat down beside the rough kitchen table which served Herr Esch as a desk.

Esch paid no attention to him, but with a morose and suffering face walked from side to side of the room in a heavy awkward step which did not go with his lank appearance. The scrubbed floor creaked under his clumsy tread, and Huguenau contemplated the holes and loosened plaster between the two rooms, as well as Herr Esch's heavy black shoes, which were fastened, instead of with laces, with queer thongs that reminded one of saddle-straps; over the tops of the shoes bulged an expanse of grey darned sock. Esch communed aloud with himself: " The vultures are hovering over those poor people already . . . but when you try to draw public attention to all the misery, you find yourself up against the censorship."

Huguenau had crossed his legs. He regarded the things scattered on the table. An empty coffee-cup with brown stains, now dry, a bronze replica of the Statue of Liberty in New York (aha, a paper-weight), a paraffin lamp whose white wick behind the glass funnel reminded one distantly and dimly of a fœtus or a tapeworm preserved in spirits. Now Esch's voice boomed from the opposite corner:

" The censorship people should be made to look at all the misery and the distress themselves . . . it's to me that the people come . . . it would be simple treachery if . . ."

On a rickety shelf some manuscripts were lying, along with piles of newspapers tied together. Esch had resumed his prowling. In the middle of one of the walls, which were distempered in yellow, hung on a fortuitous nail a small faded picture in a black frame, " Badenweiler and the Schlossberg "; probably it was an old picture postcard. Huguenau reflected that a picture or a bronze statuette like that would look very well in his office. But when he tried to recall to his memory that office, and what he had done in it, he was unsuccessful, it seemed so remote and strange that he gave up the attempt, and his eyes sought again the excitable Esch, whose brown-velvet jacket and light cloth trousers went just as badly with his clumsy shoes as the bronze statuette on the kitchen table. Esch must have felt his glance, for he shouted:

" Damn it all, why do you go on sitting here? "

Of course Huguenau could have gone away—but where? it was not so easy to hit on another project. Huguenau felt that unknown powers had launched him on these new rails, and that he could not afford to leave them without a struggle, nor indeed without suffering for it. So he remained quietly sitting and polished his eyeglasses, as he was in the habit of doing during difficult commercial negotiations to maintain an air of composure. Nor did it fail of its effect this time, for Esch, exasperated now, planted himself in front of Huguenau and burst out anew:

" Where have you come from, anyway? Who sent you here? . . . you don't belong to this part of the country, and you needn't tell me that you intend to set up here as a wine-grower yourself. . . . You're just here to spy. Locked up, that's what you should be! "

Huguenau gazed at Esch's brown-velvet waistcoat, which was just at the level of his eye and showed a strip of leather belt beneath it, gazed at the light-coloured trousers spotted with grease. Past dry-cleaning, thought Huguenau, he'll have to have them dyed black, I should tell him so; what is he really after? if he really wants to throw me out he has no need to provoke a quarrel first . . . so he wants me to stay, then. There was something queer about it. Somehow Huguenau felt a sort of fellow-feeling with this man, and at the same time divined that there was some profit to be made. So returning to the attack he resolved to make certain:

" Herr Esch, I've offered you an honourable deal, and if you decide to refuse it that's your business. But if you merely want to swear at me, then there's no point in continuing our conversation."

He snapped his eyeglasses together and raised his bottom slightly from the chair, indicating by this movement that he was ready to go away—Esch had only to say the word.

But now Esch seemed really to have no wish to break off the conversation; he raised his hand propitiatingly, and Huguenau, once more using his bottom as an indicator, signified that he would remain:

"To tell you the truth, it's unlikely that I'll set up as a wine-grower here myself; perhaps you were quite right there—although even that isn't out of the question; a fellow longs for a quiet life. But I'm not here to exploit anyone," he wrought himself up, "a middleman has as much title to respect as anybody else, all that he's concerned with is to bring two parties together in a deal and satisfy them both, for then he has his reward too. Besides I must ask you to be a little more careful in the way you fling about expressions like ' spy,' that's a dangerous game in war-time."

Esch was put to shame:

"Come, come, I didn't intend any offence . . . but sometimes your disgust at things rises into your throat, and then you can't keep it from bursting out. . . . A Cologne builder, a thorough swindler, has been buying up land here for a mere song . . . driven the people out of their homes . . . and the chemist here has been following his example . . . what use can Paulsen the chemist have for vineyards? can you tell me that, perhaps?"

Huguenau said again in an offended voice:

"A spy. . . ."

Esch had once more resumed his prowling:

"One should emigrate. Somewhere or other. To America. If I were younger I would fling everything up and start all over again . . ." once more he halted before Huguenau, " but you're a young man—why aren't you at the Front, eh? how do you come to be wandering about here?" Suddenly he had become aggressive again. Well, Huguenau had no desire to enter into that question; he evaded it; it was quite incomprehensible to him, he said, that a man in a distinguished position, the proprietor and editor of a newspaper, living amid lovely surroundings and enjoying the esteem of his fellow-citizens, and no longer young besides, should cherish thoughts of emigrating.

Esch grimaced sarcastically:

"Esteem of my fellow-citizens, esteem of my fellow-citizens . . . they snarl at my heels like a pack of curs. . . ."

Huguenau glanced at the picture of the Schlossberg, then he said:

"I can hardly believe that."

"Indeed! perhaps you're on their side? that wouldn't surprise me. . . ."

Huguenau steered his craft into safer waters:

" Again these vague accusations, Herr Esch. Won't you at least express yourself more precisely, if you have anything against me? "

But Herr Esch's desultory and irascible mind was not so easy to curb: " Express myself precisely, express myself precisely, it's very easy to talk like that . . . as if a man can give a name to everything . . ." he shouted in Huguenau's face. " Young man, until you know that all names are false you know nothing; not even the clothes on your body are what they seem to be."

An uncanny feeling came over Huguenau. He didn't understand that, he said.

" Of course you don't understand it . . . but when a chemist snaps up land for a song, you can understand that all right . . . and it's quite understandable to you that a man who calls things by their real names should be persecuted and slandered as a communist . . . and be set upon by the Censor, what? that seems quite right to you? . . . and I suppose you think too that we're living in a just country? "

It was a disagreeable position to be in, said Huguenau.

" Disagreeable! One should emigrate . . . I'm sick of struggling against it."

Huguenau asked what Herr Esch thought of doing with the paper.

Esch waved his hand contemptuously: he had often said to his wife that he would like to sell the whole show, but he would keep the house —he had thoughts of opening a bookshop.

" The opposition must have damaged the paper a good deal, I suppose, Herr Esch? I mean to say, the circulation can't amount to very much now? "

Not at all, the *Herald* had its regular subscribers, the restaurants, the hairdressers, above all the people in the villages round about: the opposition was confined to certain circles in the town. But he was sick of squabbling with them.

Had Herr Esch any idea as to the price he wanted?

Oh yes . . . the paper and the printing-office were worth 20,000 marks, and a bargain at the price. In addition he would let the buyer have the use of the buildings rent-free for an extended period, say five years: and that would mean a big advantage for the buyer too. That was how he had figured it out, it was a decent offer, he didn't want to overreach anybody, he was simply sick of the whole business. He had often said so to his wife.

" Well," said Huguenau, " I didn't ask out of idle curiosity . . . as I said before I'm a middleman, and perhaps I may be able to do something for you. Mark my words, my dear Esch," and he patronizingly clapped the newspaper proprietor on the bony shoulder—" we'll do a little business deal together yet; you should never be in too great a hurry to throw anyone out. All the same you must put the thought of twenty thousand out of your head. Nobody pays fancy prices nowadays."

Self-assured and in excellent spirits Huguenau clattered down the wooden steps.

A child was squatting in front of the printing-shed.

Huguenau contemplated the child, contemplated the entrance to the printing-shed; he saw " No Admittance except on Business " on the door-plate.

Twenty thousand marks, he thought, and the little girl thrown in.

Well, he had no business in there yet, but from now on they could not refuse him admittance; if you were trying to sell a concern you had a right to see it. Esch would be obliged to show him round the printing-shed. Huguenau considered whether he should shout to him to come down, but then he decided, no: in a couple of days he would be returning here in any case, perhaps even with concrete proposals for buying the place,—Huguenau was quite certain of it, and besides it was dinner-time now. So he betook himself to his hotel.

CHAPTER VIII

Hanna Wendling was awake. She did not open her eyes, however, for there was still a chance that she might catch her vanishing dream. But it glided slowly away, and finally nothing remained but the emotion in which it had been immersed. As the emotion too drained away, Hanna voluntarily abandoned it just an instant before it completely vanished and glanced across at the window. Through the slats of the venetian blinds oozed a milky light; it must still be early, or else the sky was overcast. The striped light was like a continuation of her dream, perhaps because no sound entered with it, and Hanna decided that it must be very early after all. The venetian blinds stirred with a soft swaying motion between the open casements; that must be the dawn wind, and she inhaled its coolness by sniffing delicately, as if her nose could tell her what time it was. Then with closed eyes she reached out her hand to the bed on her left; it was not occupied; the pillows, the blankets and the eiderdown quilt were methodically piled up and covered by the plush counterpane. Before she drew back her hand, so as to return it along with her naked shoulder beneath the warm sheets, she ran it again over the yielding and slightly cold plush, and the action was like a corroboration of the fact that she was alone. Her thin nightgown had slipped up over her thighs and formed an uncomfortable bunch. Ah, she had slept badly again; as a sort of indemnification, however, her right hand was lying on her warm smooth body, and her finger-tips stroked softly and almost imperceptibly the soft downy curve of her bosom. She could not help thinking of some French rococo picture of dalliance; then she remembered Goya's portrait of the disrobed Maya. She remained lying in this position for a few minutes longer. Thereupon she smoothed down her nightgown—strange that a film-thin gown could warm one immediately like that—considered whether she should turn on her left or her right side, decided for the latter, as though she were afraid that the piled-up bed beside her would cut off the air, listened for a little longer to the silence of the street, and gave herself up to another dream, sought refuge in another dream, before any sound could reach her from outside.

When an hour later she once more found herself awake, she could no longer conceal from herself that the forenoon was already far advanced. For anyone who is bound only by very frail threads, threads that are scarcely palpable to him, to what other people or he himself calls life, getting up in the morning is always a hard task. Perhaps even a slight violation. And Hanna Wendling, who felt the unavoidable day once more approaching, got a headache. It began at the back of her head; she crossed her hands behind her neck, and when she tugged at her hair, which softly coiled round her fingers, for a moment she forgot her headache. Then she pressed against the place where the pain was; it was a throbbing which began behind her ears and ran down to the top of her spine. She was used to it. When she was in company, sometimes it seized her so violently that she became quite dizzy. With sudden resolution she flung back the bedclothes, slipped her feet into her high-heeled bedroom slippers, opened the venetian blinds without pulling them up, and holding her hand-glass behind her head contemplated the painful area at the back of her neck in the large mirror on her toilet-table. What was hurting her there? nothing could be seen. She turned her head from side to side; she could see the play of her spine under the skin; really she had a pretty neck. And her shoulders were pretty too. She would have liked to have had her breakfast in bed, but it was war-time; bad enough to have stayed in bed so late. Really she should have got up and taken her little son to school. Every day she made up her mind to do it. Twice she had actually done it, and then had left it again to the maid. Of course the boy should have had a French or an English governess long ago. Englishwomen made the best governesses. Once the war was over they would have to send the boy to England. When she was his age, yes when she was seven, she spoke French better than German. She searched for the flask with the toilet-vinegar, rubbed her neck and temples, and examined her eyes attentively in the mirror: they were golden-brown, in the left one a tiny red vein could be seen. That came from her restless night. She threw her kimono round her shoulders. And then she rang for the maid.

Hanna Wendling was the wife of Dr Heinrich Wendling, advocate. She was a native of Frankfort. For two years Heinrich Wendling had been in Roumania or Bessarabia or somewhere at the back of beyond.

CHAPTER IX

Huguenau sat down at his table in the dining-room. At a table not far from him a white-haired gentleman was sitting, a major. The waitress had just set down a plate of soup before him, and the old gentleman now went through a curious pantomime; with his hands folded and his reddish face piously composed he bowed his head a little over the table, and only after having ended this unmistakable grace did he break his fast.

Huguenau gaped at this unusual spectacle; he beckoned the waitress and asked without much ceremony who the strange officer was.

The waitress put her mouth to his ear; that was the Town Commandant, a high-born landowner from West Prussia who had been re-called to service for the duration of the war. His family were still living on the estate at home, but he got letters from them every day. Oh, and the Commandant's office was in the Town Hall, but the Herr Major had lived in the hotel ever since the beginning of the war.

Huguenau nodded, his curiosity satisfied. But then he suddenly felt a cold contraction in his stomach, and it struck him that the man sitting over there embodied the power of the army, that the man needed only to stretch out the hand now gripping a soup-spoon and he would be done for, and that therefore he was, so to speak, living next door to his own executioner. His appetite was gone! hadn't he better countermand his order and take to flight?

But meanwhile the waitress had brought his soup, and as he mechanically spooned it up the paralysing coldness relaxed, passing over into an almost comforting cool lassitude and defencelessness. Besides, he daren't run away, he had to finish the deal with the *Kur-Trier Herald*.

He felt almost relieved. For although every man believes that his decisions and resolutions involve the most multifarious factors, in reality they are a mere oscillation between flight and longing, and the ultimate goal of all flight and all longing is death. And in this wavering of the soul and the spirit between the positive and the negative poles, Huguenau, the same Wilhelm Huguenau who a moment before had dreamt of flight, now felt himself strangely drawn to the old man sitting at the other table.

He ate mechanically, not even noticing that to-day was meat day; he drank mechanically, and in the extreme and as it were more clairvoyant state of awareness to which he had had access for the past weeks, all things fell asunder, flew apart and receded to the poles, receded to the frontiers of the world where things once more regain their oneness and distance is annihilated,—fear was changed to longing, and longing to fear, and the *Kur-Trier Herald* coalesced into an extraordinarily indissoluble unity with the white-haired Major. The matter cannot be put much more precisely or rationally than this, for Huguenau's actions now developed in a world where all measurable distance was annihilated, they were in a way short-circuited into irrationality without any time for reflection; so while he waited for the Major to finish his meal, it was not really waiting, it was a sort of simultaneity of cause and effect that made him rise at the very moment when the Major, after another silent grace, pushed back his chair and lit his cigar; forthwith and without the slightest embarrassment Huguenau approached the Major, walked up straight to the Major, quite unembarrassed although he had no pretext whatever for such an intrusion.

Yet hardly had he duly introduced himself than he sat down without being asked and the words began to flow effortlessly from his lips: he took the liberty of respectfully announcing that he was from the Press

Bureau and had been sent here at its instructions. It seemed that there
was a local sheet here called the *Kur-Trier Herald*, about whose policy
all sorts of doubtful rumours were going round, and he had come,
furnished with the fullest powers required, to study the position on
the spot. Yes, and—what shall I say now? thought Huguenau—but his
stream of eloquence flowed on; it was as though the words took shape
in his mouth—yes, and seeing that the question of censorship fell to a
certain degree and in a certain sense within the Town Commandant's
province, he had considered it his duty to wait on the Herr Major and
report himself.

In the course of this announcement the Major, drawing himself up
with a little jerk, had assumed a formal attitude, and attempted to make
the objection that the usual official channels were better suited to deal
with such an affair; Huguenau, however, who could not afford to let
his fluent stream of words run dry, scarcely listened to him, and summarily dismissed the objection by pointing out that he had approached
the Herr Major not in an official, but merely in a semi-official capacity,
since the full powers he had mentioned were not from the Government,
but rather from the patriotic big industrialists—he need mention no
names, they were well enough known—who had entrusted him with the
mission of eventually purchasing doubtful newspapers if the price were
reasonable, for they must of course prevent suspicious ideas reaching
the people. And Huguenau repeated again the words, " suspicious ideas
reaching the people," repeated them as though this return to his starting-
point had given him absolute assurance, as though the phrase were a
soft bed on which he could lie in comfort.

Apparently the Major did not understand what all this was leading
to, but he nodded and Huguenau continued to revolve in his orbit:
yes, it was a question of suspect newspapers, and in his own opinion,
as indeed according to general opinion, the *Kur-Trier Herald* was a
suspect paper, whose purchase he would unconditionally recommend.

He looked at the Major triumphantly, drummed with his fingers on
the table, and it was as though he were awaiting the Town Commandant's
admiration and praise for a successfully achieved feat.

" Very patriotic, no doubt," the Major at length agreed. " I thank
you for the information."

With that Huguenau could have taken himself off, but it was necessary
that he should achieve something more, and so he thanked the Herr

Major warmly for the good will he had shown him and, in view of that good will, begged to add one more request, a small request:

" My employers naturally regard it as important that in buying a newspaper such as this, which of course must be looked on more or less as a local paper, local people interested should share in the transaction: that of course is quite understandable, for the sake of local control and so forth. . . . The Herr Major sees that? "

Yes, that was understandable, said the Major, not understanding in the least.

Well, said Huguenau, the request he had to make was that the Herr Major, who of course had the greatest prestige of anyone in the town, should give him the names of a few reliable moneyed gentlemen among the residents—of course in the strictest confidence—who might be interested in the plan.

The Major remarked that the whole business really fell within the province of the civil authorities and not of the military command, yet he could give Herr Huguenau one piece of advice: to be here on Friday evening, for on that evening he would always find a few town councillors and other influential gentlemen in the place.

" Splendid! but the Herr Major will be here too, I hope," said Huguenau, who was not to be put off so easily. " Splendid! If the Herr Major will take the transaction under his patronage I can guarantee that everything will go smoothly, especially as the capital required is relatively small, and many of the gentlemen here will be interested no doubt in the idea of getting into touch with the large industries, in being admitted to partnership with them, so to speak. . . . Splendid! really splendid! . . . May I smoke, Herr Major? " . . . and he pulled his chair nearer, took a cigar out of his cigar-case, polished his eyeglasses, and began to smoke.

The Major observed that certainly the auspices were very favourable, and that he was sorry he was not a business man.

Oh, that didn't matter, said Huguenau, that didn't affect the matter at all. And as he felt a need to repeat his performance again, perhaps out of pure virtuosity, perhaps to establish his newly won confidence, perhaps out of sheer wantonness, he pulled his chair yet a little nearer to the Major, and begged permission to add a further piece of information, but only for the Herr Major's personal ear. In his dealings thus far with the publisher of this newspaper—his name was Esch, the Herr

Major must certainly have heard of him—well he had got the definite impression that behind the paper there was a—how could he put it? a whole subterranean movement going on, a movement composed of suspicious and subversive elements. Something of this seemed to have leaked out already: but when the plan of buying the paper was actually realized, he would of course be in a position to get that insight into these obscure activities which it was desirable and necessary to have in the interests of the whole people.

And before the old gentleman could reply, Huguenan got up and said in conclusion:

" Please, oh, please, Herr Major! . . . it's simply my duty as a patriot . . . not worth mentioning. . . . So I'll take the liberty, then, of accepting your most flattering invitation for Friday evening."

He clicked his heels and went back with a light, almost jaunty step to his own table.

CHAPTER X

The fact that Herr August Esch's editorial duties filled him with such impatience and exasperation, and that he felt so strangely uncomfortable in his position, may be comprehensively referred back to the other fact that all his life he had followed the vocation of a book-keeper, having been, indeed, a head book-keeper for many years in a large industrial concern in his Luxemburg home, before—it was already in the middle of the war—he took possession of the *Kur-Trier Herald* and the buildings attached to it, as the result of an unexpected legacy.

For a book-keeper, and a head book-keeper in particular, is a man who lives within a strict and extraordinarily exact system of rules, rules so exact that he will never be able to apply them in any other kind of occupation. Supported firmly by such rules, he grows acclimatized to an all-powerful and yet modest world in which everything has its place, in which he himself is the point of reference, and where his glance remains unerring and undisturbed. He turns the pages of the ledger and compares them with the journal and the daybook; without a break numberless bridges stretch from the one to the other, giving security to life and the day's work. Each morning the janitor or the office girl brings the new book-keeping entries from the order office, and the head book-keeper summarizes them, so that the junior clerks may enter them in the daybook. This done, the head book-keeper is at liberty to reflect in peace on the more difficult problems, to examine the books and give his decisions. Then if in his head he has disentangled and straightened out a particularly difficult book-keeping problem, he sees new and approved bridges once more stretching reciprocally from continent to continent, and this intricate maze of established connections between account and account, this inextricable and yet so clearly woven net, in which not a single knot is missing, is symbolized at last in a single figure which he already foresees, though it may not go into the balance sheet for months to come. Oh, sweet agitation of the final balance! no matter whether it show a gain or a loss; for to the book-keeper all transactions bring gain and satisfaction. Even the monthly trial balances are triumphs of power and skill, yet they are nothing when compared with the general settlement of the books at the end of the half-year: during those days he is the captain of the ship, and his hand never leaves the helm; the young clerks in his department stick to their posts like galley slaves, and no one heeds the dinner-hour, or thinks of sleep, until all the accounts are balanced; but the drawing up of the profit and loss account and the final balance sheet he reserves for himself, and when he has achieved his task, and ruled the last line beneath the account, he seals his labours with his signature. But woe if the balance is out even by so much as a penny! A new, but bitter pleasure follows. Aided by his chief assistant he goes through the suspected accounts with the eye of a detective, and if that is of no avail all the entries of the last half-year are ruthlessly scrutinized yet again. And woe to the young man in whose books the error is found,—wrath and cold contempt will be his portion, yea dismissal. If meanwhile, however, it is discovered that the error has occurred not in the books but in the stocktaking in the storeroom, then the head book-keeper simply shrugs his shoulders, and his lips wear a pitying or sarcastic smile, for the stocktaking lies outside his province, and moreover he knows that in the store, as in life, that perfect order can never be achieved which he maintains in his books. With a contemptuous wave of the hand he returns to his office, and when presently the days become more tranquil, not seldom it may be the head book-keeper's good fortune, while flinging open a ledger, smoothing out the page rapidly with his thumb, running down a column of figures to check it, proud meanwhile of his skill which in spite of the sureness of his smoothly proceeding calculations permits his thoughts to stray freely to distant things—it may be his good fortune to realize with delighted surprise, expected and yet enchanting surprise, that the miracle of calculation still exists like a sure rock in an incalculable world. But then, it may be, his hand slips down from the page, and sadness steals into his heart as he thinks of the new system which it is one of the duties of a modern book-keeper to inaugurate; and reflecting that the new system is an affair of matter-of-fact cards instead of imposing and massive tomes, superseding personal skill by adding-machines, he is filled with bitterness.

Outside their work book-keepers are irritable. For the frontier between reality and unreality in life can never be clearly drawn, and a man who lives within a world of precisely adjusted relations will refuse to allow that there can be another world whose relations are incomprehensible and inscrutable to him: so when he steps out of his firmly established world or is torn from it he becomes impatient, he becomes an ascetic and passionate fanatic, even a rebel. The shadow of death has touched him, and the one-time book-keeper—if he has grown old—is really fit for nothing but the petty existence of the superannuated, and, impervious to accident and all the life round him, can be content to water his garden and attend to his fruit-trees; but if he is still vigorous and eager for work, his life becomes a galling combat with a world of reality which to him is unreal. Especially if fate or a legacy has deposited him in such an exposed position as that of a newspaper editor, even though it may be only a small provincial newspaper that he controls! For there is certainly no occupation so dependent on the uncalculability and uncertainty of the world's affairs as that of an editor, particularly in times of war when report and counter-report, hope and despair, heroism and misery, tread so closely on one another's heels that any methodical keeping of the books becomes a sheer impossibility; only by referring to the Censor's office can one establish what is to pass for truth and what must remain in the realm of untruth, and each nation lives enclosed in its own patriotic reality. Here a book-keeper is very much out of place, for he may easily be tempted to write that our brave troops are still posted on the left banks of the Marne awaiting orders for a further advance, while in reality the French, on their side, have long since pushed forward to the right bank. And if the censorship should reprimand him for such falsehoods, the book-keeper, especially if he is a man of impetuous moods, will inevitably get into a rage and point out that while General Headquarters had indeed reported the fortification of the bridgehead on the left bank, nothing at all had been said of the withdrawal of the troops. This is only one instance among many, one may even say among hundreds, and they are sufficient to show amply how impossible it is to apply to entries in the annals of history that scrupulosity which is accepted as the first and absolute condition of the registration of business events, and how the inaccuracy of a war which it has become impossible to survey as a whole may nourish a spirit of rebellion, for which a precise and scrupulous man might have found excuse enough even in times of peace, but which now must develop of necessity into an inevitable struggle between authority and justice, between two unrealities, two violent forces, a struggle that is eternal, a renewal of Don Quixote's crusade against a world which refuses to submit to the demands of the law-bringing spirit. For ever the book-keeper will do battle for the right, since if a penny is out he will go over every item again should the integrity of his books require it, and without being actually a good man himself, he will rise as the advocate of oppressed justice as soon as he has recognized and registered the existence of injustice and wrong; unyielding and wrathful he will rise to give battle, a lean knight with lance in rest who must charge again and again for the honour of the accurate book-keeping that ought to be able to account for everything on earth.

So Herr Esch's editorial labours were by no means so easy as one might have supposed. True, the material for his half-weekly sheet was delivered by a Cologne news and article agency, and all that the editor really needed to do was to extract from among the sensational reports the most sensational, to choose from the elegant serials and articles the most elegant, and there was nothing left for him to deal with personally but the local news, which moreover consisted chiefly of paragraphs " from a correspondent." But simple as this looked, and simple indeed as it really was so long as Esch confined himself to the book-keeping, which he had established on a new basis (not of course on the American, but on the more modest Italian model), all sorts of complications set in when the acting editor was called up and Herr Esch found himself compelled, partly by his natural and book-keeping parsimony, partly by the increasing difficulty of the general situation, to take the editorship of the paper into his own hands. Then the fight began! the fight for precise evidence of the world's doings, and against the false or falsified book-keeping

entries which people tried to fob off on him, the fight against the
authorities who were indignant that the *Kur-Trier Herald* should give
public currency to abuses at the Front and behind the lines, to sailors'
revolts and unrest in munition factories, more, who refused to listen even
to the paper's proposals for genuinely fighting these evils, but on the
contrary found it suspicious—although only an ill-wisher could have
found it suspicious—that such reports should be confided to Herr Esch,
and already were seriously considering whether they should interdict
him the exercise of his editorial calling, on the ground that he was a
foreign subject (a Luxemburger) ; he had been repeatedly warned, and his
relations with the Censor's office in Trier were becoming more uncomfortable from week to week. Small wonder, then, that Herr Esch, himself
at odds with the world, should begin to feel a brotherly sympathy for his
oppressed and downtrodden fellow-creatures, and should become an
obstructionist and a rebel. But he did not actually admit it to himself.

CHAPTER XI

STORY OF THE SALVATION ARMY GIRL IN BERLIN (1)

Among the many intolerances and limitations which were so common
in pre-war days, and of which we are now rightly ashamed, there must
be reckoned our total lack of understanding when faced with phenomena
that lay even a little way outside the confines of a seemingly rational
world. And since we were then accustomed to regard only Western
thought and culture as valid, and to depreciate all else as inferior, we
were easily disposed to class as inferior and infra-European all phenomena
that did not accord with simple reason. So when a phenomenon of that
nature, such as the Salvation Army, made its appearance in the unimpres-
sive garb of peace and fervent petition, it was met with endless ridicule.
People demanded simplicity and heroism, something æsthetic in other
words, believing as they did that such were the attributes of European
man; for they were entangled in a misapprehension of Nietzsche's ideas,
even although most of them had never heard his name, and the bogy
which obsessed them was never laid until the world produced so many
heroes that the sheer prevalence of heroism kept them from noticing it.

To-day, if I encounter a Salvation Army meeting in the street, I join
it and am glad to put some money on the collection plate, and often I

enter into conversation with the soldiers. Not that I have been converted by their somewhat primitive doctrine of salvation, but I feel that we who were once given over to prejudice are morally bound to repair our past errors wherever possible, even though these errors could be palliated as mere æsthetic decadence and had moreover the excuse of our extreme youth. Of course one's realization of these things came only gradually into consciousness, especially as during the war one seldom saw a Salvation Army soldier. I had indeed heard that they were developing a widely spread charitable organization, but I was almost surprised to meet a Salvation Army girl in one of the outlying streets in Schöneberg.

I suppose I must have looked somewhat lost and helpless, but my smile of friendly surprise encouraged her to accost me under a tactful pretext: she offered me a paper from the bundle under her arm. Perhaps she would have been disappointed if I had merely bought one, so I said: " I'm sorry, but I have no money." " That doesn't matter," she said, " come to us."

We traversed several typical suburban streets, passing derelict bits of ground, and I groused about the war. I believe she took me for a shirker, or even a deserter, who was forced by a kind of obsession to return to that theme, for she openly did her best to divert me to other topics. But I stuck to the war, I cannot now tell why, and went on grousing.

Suddenly we found that we had missed our way. We had taken a narrow road skirting a block of factory buildings, and as we rounded a corner we discovered that the block went on and on. So we turned left into a little path bounded by a slack and forlorn wire fence—it was incomprehensible why the path should be fenced off, since there was nothing on either side but rubbish-heaps, broken crockery, battered water-cans, and piles of jugs and pots that had been carted out to this remote and inaccessible spot for no discoverable reason—and the path finally came to an end in an open field, not a real field, for there was nothing growing in it, but a field that had at any rate once been ploughed, either before the war or in the previous spring. That was indicated by the hard-baked furrows, which looked like frozen waves of clay. But obviously nothing had ever been sown there. In the distance a train puffed slowly across the countryside.

Behind us lay the factories and the great city of Berlin. So our case was not desperate, although the afternoon sun blazed pitilessly down upon us. We debated what we were to do. Go on walking to the next village? " We're not fit to appear anywhere like this," I said, and she obediently tried to shake the dust off her dark uniform. It was of the same coarse stuff as the uniform of the tram-conductors, shoddy stuff with threads of paper woven through it.

Then I noticed a wooden post rammed into the earth like a boundary mark. We made for it. We sat in turn in the narrow shadow of the post, speaking little, except of my thirst. And when it grew cooler we found our way back to the city.

CHAPTER XII

DISINTEGRATION OF VALUES (I)

Is this distorted life of ours still real? is this cancerous reality still alive? the melodramatic gesture of our mass movement towards death ends in a shrug of the shoulders,—men die and do not know why; without a hold on reality they fall into nothingness; yet they are surrounded and slain by a reality that is their own, since they comprehend its causality.

The unreal is the illogical. And this age seems to have a capacity for surpassing even the acme of illogicality, of anti-logicality: it is as if the monstrous reality of the war had blotted out the reality of the world. Fantasy has become logical reality, but reality evolves the most a-logical phantasmagoria. An age that is softer and more cowardly than any preceding age suffocates in waves of blood and poison-gas; nations of bank clerks and profiteers hurl themselves upon barbed wire; a well-organized humanitarianism avails to hinder nothing, but calls itself the Red Cross and prepares artificial limbs for the victims; towns starve and coin money out of their own hunger; spectacled school-teachers lead storm-troops; city dwellers live in caves; factory hands and other civilians crawl out on reconnoitring duty, and in the end, once they are back in safety, apply their artificial limbs once more to the making of profits. Amid a blurring of all forms, in a twilight of apathetic uncertainty brooding over a ghostly world, man like a lost child gropes his way by the help of a small frail thread of logic through a dream landscape that he calls reality and that is nothing but a nightmare to him.

The melodramatic revulsion which characterizes this age as insane, the melodramatic enthusiasm which calls it great, are both justified by the swollen incomprehensibility and illogicality of the events that apparently make up its reality. Apparently! For insane or great are terms that can never be applied to an age, but only to an individual destiny. Our individual destinies, however, are as normal as they ever were. Our common destiny is the sum of our single lives, and each of these single lives is developing quite normally, in accordance, as it were, with its private logicality. We feel the totality to be insane, but for each single life we can easily discover logical guiding motives. Are we, then, insane because we have not gone mad?

The great question remains: how can an individual whose ideas have been genuinely directed towards other aims understand and accommodate himself to the implications and the reality of dying? One may answer that the mass of mankind have done nothing of the sort, and were merely forced towards death—an answer that is perhaps valid in these days of war-weariness; yet there undoubtedly was and still is, even to-day, a genuine enthusiasm for war and slaughter! One may answer that the average man, whose life moves between his table and his bed, has no ideas whatever, and therefore falls an easy prey to the ideology of hatred—which is in any case the most obviously intelligible of all, whether it concerns class hatred or national hatred—and that such narrow lives were bound to be subsumed in the service of any superpersonal idea, even a destructive one, provided that it could masquerade as socially valuable: yet even allowing for all that, this age was not devoid of other and higher super-personal values in which the individual, despite his narrow mediocrity, was already a participant. This age harboured somewhere a disinterested striving for truth, a disinterested will towards art, and had after all a very definite social feeling; how could the men who created these values and shared in them " comprehend " the ideology of war, unresistingly accept and approve it? How could a man take a gun in his hand, how could he march into the trenches, either to die in them or to come out again and take up his work as usual, without going insane? How is such adaptability possible? How could the ideology of war find any kind of response in these men, how could they ever come even to understand such an ideology and its field of reality, not to speak of enthusiastically welcoming it, as was not at all impossible? Are they insane because they did not go insane?

Is it to be referred to a mere indifference to others' sufferings? to the indifference that lets a citizen sleep soundly next door to the prison yard in which someone is being hanged by the neck or guillotined? the indifference that needs only to be multiplied to produce public indifference to the fact that thousands of men are being impaled on barbed wire? Of course it is that same indifference, but it goes further than that; for here we have no longer merely two mutually exclusive fields of reality, that of the slayer on one side and of the slain on the other; we find them co-existing in one and the same individual, implying that one single field can combine the most heterogeneous elements, among which, however, the individual apparently moves with the utmost naturalness and assurance. The contradiction is not one between supporters and opponents of war, nor is it a horizontal split in the life of the individual, on the supposition that after four years' semi-starvation he " changes " into another type and stands in complete contrast to his former self: it is a split in the totality of life and experience, a split that goes much deeper than a mere opposition of individuals, a split that cuts right into the individual himself and into his integral reality.

We know too well that we are ourselves split and riven, and yet we cannot account for it; if we try to cast the responsibility for it on the age in which we live, the age is too much for our comprehension, and so we fall back on calling it insane or great. We ourselves think that we are normal, because, in spite of the split in our souls, our inner machinery seems to run on logical principles. But if there were a man in whom all the events of our time took significant shape, a man whose native logic accounted for the events of our age, then and then only would this age cease to be insane. Presumably that is why we long for a " leader," so that he may provide us with the motivation for events that in his absence we can characterize only as insane.

CHAPTER XIII

Looked at from the outside, Hanna Wendling's life could have been described as idle passivity within a perfectly ordered system. And, curiously enough, this description would have fitted it from the inside view also. Probably she herself would have agreed with it. It was a life that from her uprising in the morning to her lying down at night hung like a slack silken thread, slack and curling through lack of tension. In her particular case life, which has so many dimensions, lost one dimension after another, it barely sufficed even to fill the three dimensions of space: one could safely assert that Hanna Wendling's dreams were more plastic and more alive than her waking states. But however closely this opinion might have accorded with Hanna Wendling's, it leaves the heart of the matter untouched, for it illumines only the large-scale view of that young woman's existence, leaving almost unguessed-at the microscopic detail which is alone significant: there is no one who knows anything about the microscopic structure of his own soul, and unquestionably it is better that he should not. Behind the visible slackness of Hanna Wendling's life, then, there was a constant tension of its separate elements. If one could have snipped off a small but sufficient portion of that apparently slack thread, one would have discovered in it an extreme torsion, as if every molecule, so to speak, were spasmodically cramped. The external symptoms of this condition could best be covered by the popular term " nervousness," in so far as that implies the exhausting guerrilla warfare which during every second of its existence the ego has to wage against even the minutest encroachments of the empirical world with which its surface comes into contact. But although this term might account for much in Hanna Wendling, the peculiar tension in her life did not arise from nervous impatience with chance annoyances, such as dust on her patent shoes, or the pressure of the ring on her finger, or even the mere fact that a potato was not thoroughly cooked; it did not arise from that kind of thing, for all such disturbances were an infinitesimal rippling of the surface, like the shimmering of restless water in sunshine, and she would have regretted their absence, since they kept her somehow from being bored; no, it did not arise from that, but from the discrepancy between this infinitely modulated surface and the still, immovable profundity of her soul, which like the bottom of the sea was extended at a depth which no eye could ever penetrate: it was the discrepancy between the visible limited surface and an invisible limitlessness, that discrepancy which is the eternal setting for the most exciting drama ever played by the soul; it was the immeasurable gulf that stretches between the obverse and the reverse sides of darkness, a tension without equilibrium, a fluctuating tension, one might say, since on the one side there was life, but on the other that eternity which is the sea-bottom of the soul and of all life.

Hanna Wendling's life was one largely emptied of all substance, and perhaps for that reason purposeless. That it was the life of the insignificant spouse of an insignificant provincial lawyer makes very little difference. For the significance of any one human life is not particularly great. And even if the moral value of a slacker in a time of deadly war is not to be rated very highly, one must not forget that not one single person who voluntarily or under compulsion fulfilled the heroic duties of war-time would have been sorry to exchange his ethically valuable activities for the ethically valueless existence of a slacker. And perhaps —although only perhaps—the increasing paralysis that gripped Hanna Wendling as the war progressed in severity was nothing but the expression of a highly moral revulsion from the horror to which mankind saw itself committed. And perhaps that revulsion, that horror, had already grown so strong in her that Hanna Wendling herself did not dare to be aware of it.

CHAPTER XIV

On one of the following afternoons Huguenau again visited Herr Esch. " Well, Herr Esch, what do you think: the thing's as good as done! "

Esch was correcting proofs and raised his head: " What thing? "

Imbécile, thought Huguenau, but he said:

" Why, the sale of your newspaper."

" Depends on whether I agree to it."

Huguenau became suspicious:

" Now, look here, you can't let me down . . . or are you negotiating with someone else? " Then he noticed the child whom he had seen outside the printing-office in the morning:

" Is that your daughter? "

" No."

" Indeed . . . well, then, Herr Esch, if I'm to sell your paper for you, you must at least show me round the premises. . . ."

Esch waved his hand to indicate the room in which they were sitting; Huguenau tried to draw a smile out of him:

" So the little girl's included, is she? . . ."

" No," said Esch.

Huguenau pressed his point; he did not really know why he was so interested:

" But the printing-shed, that's included . . . you must at least show me round the printing-shed. . . ."

" I don't mind," said Esch, getting up and taking the child by the hand, " let's go into the printing-shed, then."

" And what's your name? " asked Huguenau.

The child said:

" Marguerite."

" Une petite française," said Huguenau.

" No," said Esch, " only her father's French."

" Interesting," said Huguenau, " and her mother? "

They were clambering down the ladder. Esch said in a low voice:

" Her mother's dead . . . her father was an electrician here in the paper factory, but now he's interned."

Huguenau shook his head:

" A sad business, very sad . . . and you've taken the child? "

Esch said:

" You're not inquisitive, are you? "

" I? no . . . but the child must surely live somewhere. . . ."

Esch said gruffly:

" She lives with her mother's sister . . . she only comes here sometimes for dinner . . . her people aren't well off."

Huguenau was content, now that he knew everything:

" Alors tu es une petite française, Marguerite? "

The child looked up at him, a glimmer of recollection played over her face, she let Esch go and took Huguenau's finger, but she made no reply.

" She can't speak a word of French . . . it's four years since her father was interned. . . ."

" How old is she, now? "

" Seven," said the child.

They went into the printing-shed.

" This is the printing-room," said Esch, " the press and the setting-plant alone are worth several thousands."

" A bit old-fashioned," said Huguenau, who had never seen a printing-press before. The composing-room was to the right. The grey-painted type cases did not interest him, but the printing-press took his fancy. The tiled floor, strengthened here and there with great patches of concrete, was saturated and brown with oil all round the press. The machine stood there heavy and stolid, its cast-iron parts lacquered black, its steel bars shining, and its joints and supports bound with rings of brass. An old workman in a blue blouse was rubbing up the steel bars with a handful of waste, paying no heed to the intruders at all.

Esch said:

" Well, that's all, let's go . . . come, Marguerite."

He went out without another word, leaving his visitor simply standing. Huguenau stared after the unmannerly lout, but was quite pleased; he could now examine things at his leisure. There was a pleasant effect of quietness and solidity. He took out his cigar-case, selected a cigar that was somewhat frayed, and offered it to the workman at the machine.

The printer looked at him incredulously, for tobacco was rare and a cigar at the best of times an acceptable gift. He wiped his hands on his blue garment, took the cigar, and because he was at a loss for adequate words of thanks he said:

" One doesn't often see these." " Yes," replied Huguenau, " it's a bad look-out for tobacco nowadays." " It's a bad look-out for everything," asserted the printer. Huguenau pricked up his ears: " That's just what your chief says." " It's what everybody says." The answer was not quite what Huguenau would have liked. " Well, light up," he ordered. The man bit off the end of the cigar with strong brownish teeth, somewhat as if he were cracking a nut, and lit up. His working blouse and his shirt were wide open, showing the white hair on his chest. Huguenau felt that he should get some return for the cigar; the man owed him something; so he encouraged him, saying: " A fine little machine." " It'll do," was the laconic answer. Huguenau's sympathies were with the machine, and he felt hurt by this grudging approval. And since he could think of no other way of breaking the silence, he asked: " What's your name? " " Lindner." Then silence settled definitely upon them, and Huguenau wondered if he shouldn't go away,—but suddenly his finger was clasped again by a childish hand; Marguerite had run in noiselessly on her bare feet.

" Tiens," he said, " tu lui as échappé."

The child looked up incomprehendingly.

" Oh, of course, you don't speak French . . . tut, tut, you'll have to learn it."

The child made a contemptuous gesture, the same gesture that Huguenau had already remarked as characteristic of Esch:

" The one upstairs can speak French too. . . ."

She said: the one upstairs.

Huguenau was pleased and said in a low tone:

" Don't you like him? "

The child's face grew sullen and her lower lip protruded, but then she noticed that Lindner was smoking.

" Herr Lindner's smoking! "

Huguenau laughed and opened his cigar-case.

" Would you like one too? "

She pushed the case away and answered slowly:

" Give me some money."

" What! It's money you want, is it? What do you want money for? "

Lindner said:

" They begin young nowadays."

Huguenau had drawn out a chair for himself; he sat down and took Marguerite between his knees:

" I need money myself, you know."

" Give me some money."

" I'll give you some sweets."

She was silent.

" What do you want money for? "

And although Huguenau knew that " money " was a very important word, and although he could not get it out of his head, yet he was suddenly incapable of seeing any meaning in it, and had to ask himself with an effort:

" What does anybody want money for? "

Marguerite had braced her arms on his knees and stood very rigid. Lindner growled:

" Oh, send her away," and to Marguerite, " out you get, the printing-room is no place for children."

Marguerite gave him an angry side-glance. She clutched Huguenau's finger again and began to pull him to the door.

" More haste, less speed," said Huguenau, rising up. " It's quietly that does it, eh, Herr Lindner? "

Lindner was polishing his machine again without a word to spare, and all at once Huguenau felt that there was some vague kinship between the child and the machine, almost as if they were sisters. And as if his assurance might comfort the machine he said quickly to the child before he reached the door:

" I'll give you twenty pfennigs."

When she thrust out her hand he was again aware of that curious doubt about the value of money, and cautiously, as if the affair were a mystery that concerned only the two of them and must not be overheard by anyone, not even the machine, he pulled the child close to him and whispered in her ear:

" What do you want the money for? "

The little one said:

" Give it to me."

But as Huguenau still delayed, she drew down reflective brows. Then she said: " I'll tell you," escaped from his arm and pulled him out through the door.

It had grown really cold by the time they were out in the courtyard. Huguenau would gladly have carried in his arms the little girl whose warmth he had so lately felt; it was not right of Esch to let a child run round barefooted at this time of the year. He was a little embarrassed, and polished his eyeglasses. Only when the child again thrust out her hand and said " Give it to me," did he remember about the twenty pfennigs. But he forgot to ask again what she wanted them for, opened his purse and extracted the two coins. Marguerite grabbed them and ran off, and Huguenau, left alone, could think of nothing else to do but to run his eye once more over the yard and the buildings. Then he too departed.

CHAPTER XV

As soon as Ludwig Gödicke of the Landwehr had gathered the most essential parts of his soul round his ego, he discontinued the painful struggle. It could be argued that all his life Gödicke had been a primitive kind of creature, and that a further struggle on his part would not have availed to increase the dimensions of his soul, since not even in the most dramatic moments of his life had there been many elements at the disposal of his ego. But that Gödicke was ever a primitive creature is a mere assertion that cannot be proved—and this alone invalidates the objection—nor could his new personality have been described as primitive; least of all, however, can one assume that the soul of a primitive and the world he sees are meagre and, so to speak, rough-hewn. One has only to remember how much more complicated is the structure of a primitive language than that of civilized peoples, in order to see that such an assumption is nonsensical. It is impossible to determine, therefore, whether Gödicke's choice among the elements of his soul was comprehensive or not, how many he admitted into his new personality, and how many he excluded; all that can be said is that Gödicke went about with the feeling of having lost something that formerly belonged to him, something that was not absolutely essential to his new life, but something nevertheless that he missed and yet dared not find again lest it should kill him.

And that there really was something missing was easily discernible from the economy of his utterances. He could walk, although with difficulty, could eat, although without appetite, and his very digestion, like everything connected with the crushed lower part of his body, gave him severe trouble. Perhaps his difficulty in speaking was in the same category, for it often seemed to him that the same oppression lay on his breast as on his bowels, that the iron rings constricting his belly were also bound round his chest and hindered him from speaking. Yet his incapacity to bring out even the shortest of words certainly sprang from that very economy with which he had composed his ego, and that provided for only the minimum of activity, so that any further demand upon it, let it be only the breath required for a single word, would have meant an irreplaceable loss.

So he hobbled about the garden on two sticks, his brown beard down on his chest, and his brown eyes above the deeply pitted hairy furrows on his cheeks gazing into vacancy; he wore the hospital overall or his soldier's cloak according as the Sister laid out one or the other for him, and he was certainly unaware that he was in a hospital or living in a town the name of which he did not know. Ludwig Gödicke the brick-layer had, so to speak, built a scaffolding for the house of his soul, and as he hobbled about on his sticks he felt himself to be merely a scaffolding with supports and stresses on all sides; meanwhile he could not decide, or rather, it was a sheer impossibility for him, to assemble the tiles and bricks for the house itself, and all that he did, or more precisely all that he thought—for he did nothing—was concerned with the mere scaffolding, with the elaboration of that scaffolding and all its ladders and gangways, a scaffolding that grew more perplexing daily and needed careful underpinning: a scaffolding that existed in itself and by itself, though none the less its purpose was a real purpose, since invisibly in the centre of the scaffolding, and yet also in every single supporting beam, the ego of Ludwig Gödicke was precariously suspended and had to be preserved from dizziness.

Dr Flurschütz often thought of handing the man over to a mental hospital. But the Senior Medical Officer, Surgeon-Major Dr Kühlenbeck, was of the opinion that the patient's state of shock was merely the result of his experiences, and not organic, and so would pass off in the course of time. And since he was a quiet patient, easy to deal with, they agreed to keep him until he had completely recuperated from his bodily injuries.

CHAPTER XVI

STORY OF THE SALVATION ARMY GIRL IN BERLIN (2)

There's much that can't be said except in verse,
despite the sneers of men who stick to prose;
the bonds of verse are less tight-drawn than those
of logic; song is fitter for a curse
or a lament, when day like a dark hearse
out-glooms the night, summoning ghostly woes,
and in a hymn the sad heart overflows,
even at a loud Salvation Army Meeting,
nor smiles when drums and tambourines are beating.—
Marie walked Berlin streets like a bold jade
and haunted drinking-dens in her poke-bonnet;
her girlhood was in flower, and yet upon it
the ugly uniform like a blight was laid;
her singing, when she sang before the Lord,
was a thin, empty piping—yet it soared.
Salvation Army Homes were Marie's setting,
where corridors were grey and reeked of stoves
burning foul coal, and old men sat in droves
with stinking breath and dirty feet a-sweating,
where even in summer chills played on one's back
and yellow soap stank strong from every crack.
Here was her dwelling-place, within that gate,
here in a brown deal alcove stood her bed
with a brown crucifix set at its head,
and here she knelt and thanked God for her fate,
waiting with rapt eyes for His heavenly grace,
and here she slept, and glory filled the place.

But she must rise at dawn and wash her face
with ice-cold water—hot water is forbidden
in such a house—while yet the sun is hidden,
while the expectant air is still and grey,
and sometimes heavy, as if the sky were chidden,
or a tarpaulin blotted out the day,
and that's an hour when one may be hag-ridden,
when hope may fail; for in the lonely dawn
how can one think that day will bring a friend?
or that the precious yesterday that's gone
will be affirmed again before day end?
Marie has no misgivings; she must fend
for all her charges; she puts coffee on,
she sweeps and scours; then, at the window dreaming,
she sees the grace of God on all things gleaming.

CHAPTER XVII

It was very seldom that Hanna Wendling went into the town. She hated the way there, not only the dusty main road, which would have been quite understandable, but the path along the river as well. Yet the path took barely twenty-five minutes, and the main road only a quarter of an hour. She had always had a deep dislike for the road into the town, even at the time when she was still daily calling for Heinrich at the office. Later there had been the car, but only for a few months, for then the war broke out. To-day it was Dr Kessel who had taken her to the town with him in his buggy.

She made some purchases. Her new frock reached only as far as her ankles, and she felt as if people were staring at her feet. She had an intuitive feeling for fashions, and had always had it; she anticipated a coming fashion somewhat as certain people know that they will awaken at a certain time without having to look at the clock. Fashion journals for her had always been merely a belated corroboration. And the fact that people were staring at her feet now was also a sort of corroboration. There are of course lots of people who are able to waken to the minute, and many women with an intuitive feeling for the immanent logic of fashion, yet the man or woman who possesses a gift of this kind generally regards himself or herself as unique. So Hanna Wendling was feeling a little proud of herself now, and even if she had only a vague inkling that her pride was unjustified, yet a slight feeling of guilt assailed her when she saw the haggard women standing in queues before the bakers' shops. But when she reflected that any woman with the smallest sense of fashion could quite well shorten her skirt, for it could be done practically without expense—the housemaid had fixed hers up in an hour in spite of the new edging—then her pride did not seem unjustified after all, and as pride puts one in a good humour Hanna Wendling was not irritated by the greengrocer's dirty finger-nails, nor by the flies buzzing round his shop, and for the moment even the fact that her shoes were covered with dust scarcely troubled her. As she strolled through the streets, stopping now at one shop window, now at another, she had incontestably that virginal or nun-like appearance—it was often to be remarked during the war— that is to be seen in women who have been parted from their husbands for a long time and have remained faithful to them. Yet simply because Hanna Wendling felt a little proud at the moment, her face had opened out, and that indefinable soft veil which can fall over such women's faces like a stealthy premonition of approaching age was drawn aside by some invisible hand. Her face was like the first spring day after a long and severe winter.

Dr Kessel, who had to make several visits to patients in the town and thereafter to drive out to the hospital, had promised to set her down again at her door; she had arranged to meet him at the chemist's. When she reached it the buggy was already standing before the door, and Dr Kessel was chatting with Paulsen the chemist. Hanna Wendling had no need to be told what to think of Paulsen; indeed, she probably possessed the knowledge, extending far beyond his particular case, that all men who know that they are betrayed by their wives are wont to display a conspicuous and curiously empty gallantry towards other women; and yet she felt flattered when he rushed up to her with the words: "What a charming visit! Like a fresh spring day." For ruthlessly as Hanna Wendling was accustomed to avoid and cut people in general, to-day, because she felt free and unconstrained she was susceptible even to the empty compliments of the chemist,—it was an oscillation from one extreme to the other, a vacillation between complete reserve and complete lack of it, an immoderation of bearing such as often appears in cramped natures and is not in the least the immoderation of the Renaissance popes, but simply the instability and insignificance of an ordinary bourgeois who lacks a sense of values. At least it may be asserted that it was the lack of a sense of values which now made Hanna Wendling, as she sat on the red plush-covered settle in the shop, shower dazzling and friendly glances on the chemist, and supply his lyrical phrases with a content in which she at once believed and did not believe. Indeed she felt quite cross with Dr Kessel, whose duty called him back to the hospital, when he was forced to suggest that they should leave, and when she sat beside him in the buggy the veil was once more drawn over her face.

She was monosyllabic on the way, monosyllabic at home. Once more she could not comprehend why she had refused so absolutely to return to her father's house in Frankfort for the duration of the war. The objection that food was easier to procure in the little town, that she could not leave the house standing empty, that the air here would be better for the boy; these were subterfuges which merely served to cloak the curious state of estrangement into which she had fallen, and to which she could not shut her eyes. She was shy of people, she had said so to Dr Kessel; "Shy of people," she repeated the words, and as she uttered them it was as though she were putting the responsibility for her shyness on Heinrich, just as she had blamed him when the brass pan in the kitchen had to be given up to be melted down for the war. Even with regard to the boy she was not immune from this mysterious feeling of estrangement. When she woke up in the night she found it difficult to realize that he was sleeping in the next room, and that he was her son. And when she struck a few chords on the piano, it was no longer her hands that did it, but unfeeling fingers which had become strange to her, and she knew that she was losing even her music. Hanna Wendling went to the bathroom to wash away her morning in the town. Then she contemplated herself carefully in the mirror, looking to see whether the face there was still hers. She found it, but she found it curiously veiled, and although she was in reality pleased by this, nevertheless she blamed Heinrich for it.

Moreover she often discovered now that his name did not come to her at once, and then even to herself she called him by the same name that she employed before the servants: Dr Wendling.

CHAPTER XVIII

STORY OF THE SALVATION ARMY GIRL IN BERLIN (3)

I had lost sight of Marie, the Salvation Army girl, for some weeks. Berlin at that time resembled—well, what did it resemble? the days were hot; the asphalt soft, even gaping in places, for nothing was repaired; women were everywhere in charge as conductresses and the like; the trees in the streets wilted in the very spring-time, looking like children with old men's faces, and whenever the wind blew, dust and scraps of paper went whirling; Berlin had grown more countrified, more natural, as it were, and yet that made it all the more unnatural, as if it were an imitation of itself. In the house where I lodged there were two rooms occupied by Jewish refugees from the neighbourhood of Lodz, whose number and relationship to each other I was never able to make out; there were old men in Russian boots and ritual curls, and one that I happened to meet had buckled shoes and white stockings to the knee under his caftan, in the fashion of the eighteenth century; there were men who merely wore their coats rather long to suggest the caftan, and young men of remarkably mild appearance with woolly blond beards growing like false theatrical beards. Now and then a man in service grey uniform turned up, and even his uniform had a hint of the caftan about it. And sometimes there came a man of indefinite age, in ordinary town clothes, and his brown beard was shaven to a square fringe like Oom Paul Kruger's, and left unshorn only at the temples. He always had a stick with an old-fashioned crook handle, and a pince-nez on a black cord. I took him at once for a doctor. Of course there were women too, and children, matrons with false fronts, and young girls dressed, curiously enough, in the height of fashion.

In time I picked up a few words of the Yiddish German they spoke. But I never, of course, really understood it. Still, they seemed to think that inconceivable, for whenever I drew near they broke off the guttural gibberish that came so queerly from the mouths of such dignified ancients, and regarded me with sidelong shyness. In the evenings they mostly sat together in their unlighted rooms, and when in the mornings I came into the hall that was always crammed with garments of all kinds, in the middle of which the maid brushed shoes, I often used to find one of the older men standing at the window. He had his phylacteries bound on brow and wrists, he swayed his torso in time to the shoe-brush, and from time to time kissing the fringes of his cloak, recited at passionate speed with his faded lips faded, passionate prayers out of the window. Perhaps because the window faced east.

I was so fascinated by the Jews that I spent many hours daily quietly observing them. In the hall there hung two chromolithographs of rococo scenes, and I could not help wondering if the Jews could really see these pictures and many other things with the same eyes as ours, and read the same meaning into them. And obsessed by such preoccupations I completely forgot Marie of the Salvation Army, although in some way I felt that she was not unconnected with them.

CHAPTER XIX

Lieutenant Jaretzki's arm had been amputated. Above the elbow. When Kühlenbeck did a thing he did it thoroughly. What was left of Jaretzki sat in the hospital garden beside the shrubbery, regarding the blossoming apple-tree.

A round of inspection by the Town Commandant.

Jaretzki rose to his feet, felt for his diseased hand, felt nothing but emptiness. Then he stood to attention.

" Good-morning, Herr Lieutenant: well on the road to recovery, I see ? "

" Yes, sir, but there's a good bit of me missing."

It almost seemed that Major von Pasenow felt himself responsible for Jaretzki's arm as he said:

" It's a terrible war . . . won't you sit down again, Herr Lieutenant ? "

" Thank you, Herr Major."

The Major said:

" Where were you wounded ? "

" I wasn't wounded, sir . . . gas."

The Major glanced at the stump of Jaretzki's arm:

" I don't understand . . . I thought gas suffocated a man. . . ."

" It can do this kind of thing too, sir."

The Major thought it over for a while. Then he said:

" An unchivalrous weapon."

" Quite so, sir."

Both of them remembered that Germany too was employing that unchivalrous weapon. But they did not mention it.

The Major said:

" How old are you? "

" Twenty-eight, sir."

" When the war began there wasn't any gas."

" No, sir, I believe not."

The sun illumined the long yellow wall of the hospital. A few white clouds hung in the blue sky. The gravel of the garden-path was firmly embedded in the black earth, and at the edge of the lawn crawled an earthworm. The apple-tree was like an enormous nosegay.

The Senior Medical Officer in his white overall came out of the house towards them.

The Major said:

" I hope you'll be all right soon."

" Thank you very much, sir," said Jaretzki.

CHAPTER XX

DISINTEGRATION OF VALUES (2)

The horror of this age is perhaps most palpable in the effect that its architecture has on one; I always come home exhausted and depressed after a walk through the streets. I do not even need to look at the house-fronts; they distress me without my raising my eyes to them. Sometimes I fly for consolation to the so highly commended " modern " buildings, but—and here I'm certainly at fault—the warehouse designed by Messel, who is none the less a great architect, strikes me only as a comic kind of Gothic, and it is a comic effect that irritates and depresses me. It depresses me so much that looking at buildings in the classical style scarcely suffices to restore me. And yet I admire the noble clarity of Schinkel's architecture.

I am convinced that no former age ever received its architectural expressions with dislike and repugnance; that has been reserved for ours. Right up to the development of classicism building was a natural function. It is possible that people never even noticed new buildings, much as one scarcely notices a newly planted tree, but if a man's eye did light upon them he saw that they were good and natural; that was how Goethe still saw the buildings of his time.

I am not an æsthete, and unquestionably never was one, although I may unwittingly have given that impression, and I am just as little addicted to the sentimentality that yearns for the past, transfiguring dead-and-gone epochs. No, behind all my repugnance and weariness there is a very positive conviction, the conviction that nothing is of more importance to any epoch than its style. There is no epoch in the history of all the human race that divulges its character except in its style, and above all in the style of its buildings; indeed no epoch deserves the name except in so far as it possesses a style.

It may be objected that my weariness and irritation are the results of my under-nourishment. It may be pointed out that this age has its own very suggestive machine-and-cannon-and-concrete style, and that some generations must pass before it will be recognized. Well, every age has some stylistic claim; even the experimental ages in spite of their eclecticism had a kind of style. And I am even willing to admit that in our day technique has simply outrun creative effort, that we have not yet wrested from our new material its adequate forms of expression, and that all the disquieting lack of proportion arises from imperfectly mastered purpose. On the other hand, no one can deny that the new kind of building, whether because its material is recalcitrant or its builders incapable, has lost something, has even quite deliberately abandoned something that it could not help abandoning, the lack of which distinguishes it fundamentally from all previous styles: the characteristic use of ornament. Of course that renunciation can be praised as a virtue, on the assumption that we are the first to discover principles of structural economy that enable us to dispense with ornamental excrescences. But is not that term " structural economy " merely a modern catchword? Can it be maintained that the Gothic or any other style was not built with structural economy? To regard ornament as merely an excrescence is to mistake the inner logic of structure. Style in architecture is logic, a logic that governs the whole building from the plan of its foundation to its skyline, and within that logical system the ornament is only the last, the most differentiated expression on a small scale of the unified and unifying conception of the whole. Whether it is an inability to use ornament or a renunciation of it makes no difference; the result is that the architectural structures of this age are sharply distinguished from all previous styles.

But what does it avail to recognize this? Ornament can neither be fashioned by eclecticism nor artificially invented without falling into the

comic absurdities of a Van der Velde. We are left with a profound dis-
quiet and the knowledge that this style of building, which is no longer
a style, is merely a symptom, a writing on the wall proclaiming a state
of the soul which must be the non-soul of our non-age. Simply to look
at it makes me tired. If I could, I would never leave my house again.

CHAPTER XXI

Apart from the fact that the food at the hotel was expensive and that
Huguenau was unwilling to allow himself such a luxury until he had
established himself in a new position, he had the distinct feeling that
it might endanger his impending transactions if the Major saw too much
of him. Further discussions would only spoil the effect he had made and
gain nothing, and it seemed more advantageous that the Major should
forget about him until they met again on Friday. So Huguenau took
his meals in a humbler establishment, and appeared in the dining-hall
again only on the Friday evening.

He had not reckoned in vain. There sat the Major, and he looked
completely surprised when Huguenau approached him briskly and
cordially and thanked him anew for his very friendly and flattering
invitation. " Oh yes," said the Major, who now remembered at last.
" Oh yes. I'll introduce you to the gentlemen."

Huguenau once more thanked him and sat down modestly at another
table. But when the Major had finished his supper and looked up,
Huguenau smiled over at him and rose slightly, to show that he was
at the Major's disposal. Thereupon they went together into the little
adjoining room, where was held the Friday gathering of the gentlemen
of the town.

The gentlemen were present in full force, even the burgomaster himself was there. Huguenau was quite unable to catch all their names. As
soon as he entered he had a feeling of being greeted with warm sympathy,
and a premonition of complete success. This feeling did not deceive
him. The majority of the company already knew of his presence in the
town and the hotel; obviously he had become a theme for speculation,
and they now evinced the warmest interest in his proposals, as he
later informed Esch. The evening ended with unexpectedly positive
results.

That was indeed nothing to be surprised at. The company had the impression that they were taking part in a secret conventicle, which was moreover at the same time a sort of summary court held on the rebel Esch. And if Huguenau got such an exceptionally gracious hearing from his listeners, that was not merely because of his intense desire to win it, nor because of his somnambulistic sureness, but also because he was not in the least a rebel, being rather a man fending for himself and his own interests, and speaking consequently a language which the others understood.

Huguenau could with ease have got the gentlemen to the point of subscribing the 20,000 marks demanded by Esch. But he did not do so. A secret fear admonished him that everything must remain tentative and no more than just plausible, because real security always hovers beyond or above the actual, and any too great solidity is dangerous and like an inexplicable oppression. This may appear meaningless, yet as every absurdity admits of some shred of reasonable explanation, so Huguenau's explanation here was perfectly reasonable and led strangely enough to the same conclusion: it was that if he demanded or accepted too much money from these people, one of them might be struck with the idea of inquiring into his credentials; but if he was standoffish and declined large subscriptions, retaining for his own legendary group the greater share of the invested capital, then they could not doubt that they beheld in him the genuine representative of the most highly capitalized industrial group in the Empire (Krupp's). And indeed no one doubted this, and in the end Huguenau himself finished by believing it. He declared that he was not in a position to offer his esteemed friends a greater share of the proposed 20,000 marks than a third—in other words 6600 marks in all; nevertheless he was prepared to enter into negotiations again with his group to find out whether instead of the two-thirds majority they would be content with a simple one of 51 per cent., and he would be glad also to accept suggestions in advance for later capital expansion; for the moment, however, the gentlemen must content themselves with the small sum mentioned.

The gentlemen were naturally disappointed, but there was no help for it. It was agreed that they should receive interim share certificates in return for their payments as soon as Huguenau had completed the purchase of the *Kur-Trier Herald*, and that after further sounding of the central group the consolidated undertaking would be established as a limited liability company or perhaps even as a syndicate. The prospective shareholders dreamed of future meetings of directors, and the evening closed with cheers for the allied armies and His Majesty the Kaiser.

CHAPTER XXII

When Huguenau awoke he put his hand under the pillow; there he was accustomed to keep his pocket-book for safety of nights. He had a pleasant sense of owning 20,000 marks, and although he knew that his pocket-book did not contain even the 6600 marks which he would receive from the local gentlemen only when the purchase of the *Herald* was completed, but that all that was left in it was a balance of 185 marks, yet he stuck to it that he had 20,000. He possessed 20,000 marks, and that settled the matter.

Against his usual custom he remained lying in bed for a little. If he had 20,000 marks it would be a piece of madness to give them to Esch, simply because the man asked so much for his measly rag. Every price allowed for give-and-take, and he would be able to beat Esch down a bit, Esch could depend on that. At 14,000 marks the paper would still be too dear, and that left a private profit of 6000. The matter had merely to be cleverly managed, so that nobody might know that Esch was not getting his full 20,000. One could put it down as capital reserve, or give out that the industrial group were content with a bare majority instead of the decisive two-thirds preponderance, or something like that. Something was certain to occur to him! and Huguenau leapt cheerfully out of bed.

When he appeared at the office of the *Herald* it was still quite early. And he fell upon the dumbfounded Herr Esch with the most violent reproaches for having let his paper fall so low. It was shocking, the things that he, Wilhelm Huguenau, who after all was not in the least responsible for Herr Esch, had had to listen to about the paper during those last two days. As a middleman, of course, that might have left him quite indifferent, but it broke one's heart, yes, it was heart-breaking to look on and see a good business wantonly being ruined; a newspaper lived by its reputation, and when its reputation was bankrupt, then it was itself bankrupt too. As things stood, it seemed that Herr Esch had managed things so that the *Kur-Trier Herald* was now a wretched unsaleable proposition. "You must see yourself, my dear Esch, that you should actually pay something to anyone who'll take over the paper, instead of demanding money from him."

Esch listened with a woebegone face; then he grimaced contemptuously. But Huguenau was not to be put out of countenance by that: " It's not a smiling matter, my dear friend, it's deadly serious, apparently far more serious than you think." The idea of making a profit was out of the question, and if one nevertheless did not give up all hope of that, it would be made possible only with the help of tremendous sacrifices, yes sacrifices, my dear Esch. If among his friends, as he hoped and believed, there were some self-sacrificing men prepared to take up this quite sense-less, because idealistic scheme, then Herr Esch could simply call it luck, a piece of luck such as one did not encounter more than once in a lifetime; for thanks to singularly favourable circumstances, and his own very efficient abilities as a negotiator, he might eventually get together in spite of everything a round sum of 10,000 marks for Esch, and if Esch didn't snatch at that, then he was only sorry that he had thrown away his time on Esch's affairs, which didn't concern him in the least, no, not in the very least.

" Then leave them alone!" shouted Esch, striking the table with his fist.

" Pardon me, of course I can leave them alone . . . but I don't quite see why you should jump into a rage when a man doesn't accept straight off your fantastic ideas of what the paper's worth."

" I haven't made any fantastic demands. . . . The paper's a bargain at twenty thousand."

" Well, but don't you see that I actually accept your valuation? For you'll admit that the buyer will have to spend a further ten thousand at least in getting the paper on its legs again . . . and thirty thousand would really be exorbitant, don't you agree? "

Esch became thoughtful. Huguenau felt that he was on the right lines:

" Now, I see that you're going to be reasonable . . . I don't want to press you, of course. . . . You should just sleep on it. . . ."

Esch paced up and down the room. Then he said:

" I would like to talk it over with my wife."

" Do that by all means . . . only don't be too long in considering it . . . money talks, my dear Herr Esch, but it doesn't wait."

He got up:

" I'll call on you again to-morrow . . . and meanwhile please give my respects to your good lady."

CHAPTER XXIII

Dr Flurschütz and Lieutenant Jaretzki were walking from the hospital towards the town. The road was pitted with holes made by the motor-lorries, which ran on iron tyres now, for there was no rubber left.

A closed-down roofing-asphalt factory stretched thin black-zinc pipes up into the still air. Birds twittered in the woods.

Jaretzki's sleeve was fastened by a safety-pin to the pocket of his army tunic.

" Extraordinary," said Jaretzki, " since I've got rid of my left arm, the right one hangs down from my shoulder like a weight. I almost feel as if I would like it amputated too."

" You're a symmetrical fellow, it seems . . . engineers have a feeling for symmetry."

" Do you know, Flurschütz, sometimes I forget altogether that I ever was an engineer. . . . You won't understand that, for you've stuck to your profession."

" No, one can hardly say that . . . I was really more of a biologist than a doctor."

" I've sent off an application to the General Electric, there's a shortage of skilled workers everywhere now of course . . . but I simply can't picture myself sitting at a drawing-board again . . . what do you really think, how many have been killed altogether? "

" Can't say, five millions, ten millions . . . perhaps twenty before it comes to an end."

" I'm quite convinced that it can never come to an end . . . it will go on like this for all eternity."

Dr Flurschütz stopped:

" Look here, Jaretzki, can you understand how we can be walking about so peacefully here, how life itself can run on so quietly here, while only a few miles away they're blazing away merrily at each other? "

" Well, there's lots of things I don't understand . . . besides we've both done our bit out there. . . ."

Dr Flurschütz mechanically felt under the peak of his cap for his bullet scar:

" That wasn't what I meant . . . that was at the start, when one rushed into it because one felt ashamed to be left . . . but now one should by rights be going off one's head."

" It hasn't come to that yet . . . no, thanks, better to drink oneself blind. . . ."

" Well, you follow the prescription rather thoroughly."

The wind carried a smell of tar to them from the closed-down factory.

Thin and bent, with his fair pointed beard and his eyeglasses, Dr Flurschütz looked somewhat awkward in his uniform. They were silent for a while.

The road descended. The scattered bungalows that had sprung up outside the town gates during recent years presently drew together in a continuous line; they looked very peaceful. In all the front gardens wretched-looking vegetables were growing.

Jaretzki said:

" Not very pleasant to live all the year round in this smell of tar."

Flurschütz replied:

" I was in Roumania and Poland. And do you know . . . everywhere the houses had just the same peaceful look . . . with the same trade signs as here, master-builder, locksmith, and so forth . . . in a dug-out near Armentières I once saw a shop sign, it was one of the roof props, ' Tailleur pour Dames ' . . . perhaps it's silly, but the complete madness of the whole war really only dawned on me then for the first time."

Jaretzki said:

" With my one arm I suppose I could get myself taken on for some job in the army as an engineer."

" You would like that better than the General Electric? "

" No, I'm past liking anything better . . . perhaps I'll just report for service again with my remaining arm . . . for throwing hand-grenades one arm would be enough . . . lend me a hand to get this cigarette lit."

" What have you been drinking to-day, Jaretzki? "

" Me? nothing worth speaking of, I've kept sober for the sake of the wine I'm presently going to introduce you to."

" Well, how about the General Electric? "

Jaretzki laughed:

" To be quite honest, merely a sentimental attempt to get back into civilian life, with a career to look forward to, no more of this drifting about, perhaps get married . . . but you believe as little in that as I do."

" Why on earth shouldn't I believe in it? "

Jaretzki punctuated his reply with his cigarette:

" Because . . . the . . . war . . . can . . . never . . . come . . . to . . . an . . . end . . . how often must I tell you that? "

" That too would be a solution," said Flurschütz.

" It is the only solution."

They had reached the town gate. . . . Jaretzki put up his foot on the curbstone, drew his handkerchief out of his pocket, and, his cigarette aslant in his mouth, flicked the dust of the road from his shoes. Then he stroked his dark moustache smooth, and passing through the cool arch of the gate they stepped into the still and narrow street.

CHAPTER XXIV

DISINTEGRATION OF VALUES (3)

The primacy of architectural style among the things that characterize an epoch is a very curious phenomenon. But, in general, so is the uniquely privileged position that plastic art has maintained in history. It is after all only a very small excerpt from the totality of human activities with which an age is filled, and certainly not even a particularly spiritual excerpt, and yet in power of characterization it surpasses every other province of the spirit, surpasses poetry, surpasses even science, surpasses even religion. The thing that endures through thousands of years is the work of plastic art; it remains the exponent of the age and its style.

This cannot be due merely to the durability of the material employed; the bulk of the printed paper from the last few centuries has survived, and yet any Gothic statue is more " medieval " than the whole of medieval literature. No, that would be a very inadequate explanation,—if there should be one, it must be found in the intrinsic nature of the concept of style itself.

For certainly style is not a thing confined to architectural and plastic art merely; style is something which uniformly permeates all the living expressions of an epoch. It would be against all reason to regard the artist as an exception among mankind, as a man leading a sort of peculiar existence within the style which he himself produces, while the others remain excluded.

No, if there is such a thing as style, then all human manifestations are penetrated by it, so that the style of a period is as indubitably present in its thought as in every other human activity of the period. And only by starting from this fact, which must be so, because it is impossible that it should be otherwise, can we find an explanation for the remarkable fact that precisely those activities which manifest themselves in spatial terms have become of such extraordinary and in the real sense of the word visible significance.

Perhaps it would be idle to consider this too curiously if behind it there did not stand the problem which alone justifies all philosophizing: our dread of nothingness, our dread of Time, which conducts us to death. And perhaps all the disquietude which bad architecture evokes, causing me to hide in my house, is nothing else than that dread. For whatever a man may do, he does it in order to annihilate Time, in order to revoke it, and that revocation is called Space. Even music, which exists only in time and fills time, transmutes time into space, and it is in the utmost degree probable that all thought takes place in a spatial world, that the process of thought represents a combination of indescribably complicated many-dimensional logically extended spaces. But if that be so, then it also becomes clear why all those activities which are immediately related to space achieve a significance and an obviousness that can never be achieved by any other human activity. And in this also can be seen the peculiar symptomatic significance of ornament. For ornament, detached from all purposive activity, although produced by it, becomes the abstract expression, the " formula " of the whole complex of spatial thought, becomes the formula of style itself, and with that the formula of the entire epoch and its life.

And in this, it seems to me, lies the significance, a significance that I might almost call magical, of the fact that an epoch which is completely under the dominion of death and hell must live in a style that can no longer give birth to ornament.

CHAPTER XXV

Had it not been for the prospect of building the new house they were to live in, Hanna Wendling might perhaps never have become engaged to the young provincial advocate. But in 1910 all young girls in the better-class bourgeois families read *The Studio*, *Interior Decoration*, *German Art and Decoration*, and owned a work called *English Period Furniture*, and their erotic preconceptions of marriage were in the most intimate manner bound up with problems of architectonics. The

Wendlings' house, or " Rose Cottage," for such the quaint lettering on its gable designated it, conformed in a modest degree to these ideals; it had a deep roof with low eaves; majolica cherubs at either side of the front door displayed symbols of love and fertility; there was an English hall with a rough tiled stove, and a chimneypiece with brass knick-knacks standing on it. It had given her a great deal of labour and pleasure to find for every piece of furniture its appropriate position, so that a general architectonical equilibrium might be inaugurated; and when all was finished Hanna Wendling had the feeling that she and she alone was aware of the perfection of that equilibrium, even though Heinrich too had a share in the knowledge, even though a great part of their married happiness consisted in this mutual awareness of the secret harmony and counterpoint exemplified in the arrangement of the furniture and pictures.

Now the furniture had not been moved since that time, on the contrary, strict care had been taken not to alter the original arrangement by an inch; and yet it had become different: what had happened? can equilibrium suffer depreciation, can harmony become threadbare? In the beginning she was not conscious that apathy was at the back of this,— her positive emotion simply relapsed into neutrality, and only when it transformed itself into a negative condition did it become perceptible: it was not that the house or the arrangement of the furniture had now become repellent to her, for that might have been got over at a pinch by changing the disposition of the furniture; no, it was something that went deeper; the curse of the fortuitous and the accidental had spread itself over things and the relations between things, and one could not think out any arrangement that would not be just as fortuitous and arbitrary as the existing one. In all this there lay doubtless a certain confusion, a certain darkness, indeed almost a danger, particularly as there seemed no reason why this insecurity in architectonics should stop at other matters of sentiment, even for instance at questions of fashion: this thought was particularly alarming, and although Hanna Wendling knew very well that there were far more important and difficult problems, yet perhaps nothing was more alarming to her than the thought that even the fashion journals might lose their attraction for her, and that one day she might regard without delight, without interest, without comprehension, the English journal *Vogue* itself, which she had missed so sorely during these four years of the war.

When she caught herself indulging in those thoughts she told herself that they were fantastic, although in fact they were far more essentially sober than fantastic, filled with a kind of disenchantment which was only fantastic in so far as no intoxication had preceded it, rather indeed a subsequent and additional disenchantment supervening on a state that was already sober and almost normal, so that in a sense it became still more normal and landed in negation. Such evaluations must always of course be relative in a certain degree; the border-line between sobriety and intoxication cannot always be established, and whether for instance the Russian love for humanity should be regarded as an intoxication, or whether it is to be taken as a standard for normal social relations, indeed whether the whole panorama of existence is to be regarded as drunk or sober; all these questions in the final resort are not to be resolved. Nevertheless it is not impossible that sobriety implies an ultimate state of entropy or an absolute zero, an absolute zero towards which all movement perpetually and of necessity strives. And there were many indications that Hanna Wendling was moving in this direction, and in essentials perhaps she was simply as usual anticipating a coming fashion; for the entropy of man implies his absolute isolation, and that which hitherto he has called harmony or equilibrium was perhaps only an image, an image of the social structure, which he made for himself, and could not help making, so long as he remained a part of it. But the more lonely he becomes, the more disintegrated and isolated will things seem to him, the more indifferent he must become to the connections between things, and finally he will scarcely be able any longer to see those connections. So Hanna Wendling walked through the house, walked through her garden, walked over paths which were laid with crazy-paving in the English style, and she no longer saw the pattern, no longer saw the windings of the white paths, and painful as this might well have been, it was scarcely even painful any more, for it was necessary.

CHAPTER XXVI

Huguenau now turned up daily in Fischerstrasse to see Herr Esch. Often, employing a well-tried business ruse, he did not even mention the transaction that had brought him, but waited for his opponent's move, talking meanwhile about the weather, the crops, and the latest victories. When he saw that Esch did not want to hear anything about the victories, he dropped the victories and confined himself to the weather.

Sometimes he found Marguerite in the courtyard. The child was confiding, clung to his finger, and begged him to take her into the printing-room again. Huguenau said:

" Aha! you're after another twenty pfennigs, are you? But Uncle Huguenau isn't rich enough yet, everything takes its time."

Nevertheless he gave her ten pfennigs for her money-box:

" Well, what will we do when we're both rich . . . ? "

The child stared at the ground and did not reply. At last she said hesitatingly:

" Go away."

For some reason Huguenau felt pleased by this:

" So that's what you need the money for . . . well, when we're rich we can both go away together. . . . I'll take you with me."

" Yes, do," said Marguerite.

Whenever he went up to see Esch she generally stole up after him, sat down on the floor and listened. Or if she did not do this she would at least put her head in at the door and laugh. Huguenau would say then, because it was an unfailing topic for conversation:

" I'm fond of children."

Esch seemed to like that; he smiled complacently:

" A little ruffian . . . she would do one in if it came up her back."

Haïssez les Prussiens, Huguenau could not help thinking, although Esch was not a Prussian at all, but a Luxemburger. Esch went on:

" I've often thought of adopting the little rascal . . . we haven't any children of our own."

Huguenau was surprised:

" Another man's child. . . ."

Esch said:

" Another's or your own . . . it's much the same . . . a pretty thin life without one."

Huguenau laughed:

" Well, yes, you can't be too sure even of your own children."

Esch said:

" Her father's interned. . . . I've talked over the question of adopting her with my wife . . . after all she's practically an orphan."

Huguenau said reflectively:

" Hm, but then you would have to provide for her."

" Of course," said Esch.

" If you had any spare cash, or could get hold of some, by selling out, for instance, you could take out a life insurance policy for your family. . . . I have connections with several insurance companies."

" Indeed," said Esch.

" I'm still a single man, thank God, in difficult times like these that's an immense advantage . . . but if I should ever set up house, I'll safeguard my family by a settlement of capital or something of the kind . . . well, you're in the enviable position of being able to do that. . . ."

Huguenau went away.

Marguerite was waiting for him in the courtyard.

" Would you like to stay here always? "

" Where? " asked the child.

" Why, here, with Uncle Esch."

The child gazed at him with hostility.

Huguenau winked at her and wagged his head:

" Rather not, what? "

Marguerite laughed too.

" Well, you would rather not . . .? "

" No, I don't want to."

" And you don't care much for him either . . . he's very strict with you, eh? " and Huguenau brought his arm down as if smacking someone.

Marguerite made a contemptuous grimace:

" No. . . ."

" And the other one . . . Aunt Esch . . .? "

The child shrugged her shoulders.

Huguenau was satisfied:

" Well, you won't need to stay here . . . we'll run away, the two of us, to Belgium . . . come, let's go and see Herr Lindner in the printing-room."

Together they went up to the printing-press and watched Herr Lindner as he fed it with sheets of paper.

CHAPTER XXVII

STORY OF THE SALVATION ARMY GIRL IN BERLIN (4)

The feeling that the Jews had been taking stock of me proved to be justified. For two days I had felt rather out of sorts, had scarcely touched my breakfast and gone out for only half-an-hour. On the evening of the second day there came a knock at the door of my room, and to my surprise the little man entered whom I had always taken to be a doctor. And indeed he actually revealed himself as one.

" You must be ill," he said.

" No," I said, " and if I am it's nobody's business."

" It won't cost you anything, I haven't come for the sake of the money," he said timidly, " one must help."

" Thanks," I said, " I'm quite well."

He stood before me, holding his walking-stick tightly pressed to his bosom.

" Fever? " he asked imploringly.

" No, I'm quite well, I'm just going out."

I got up and we left the room together.

In the hall one of the young Jews was standing, one of those with the downy stage beards.

The doctor now introduced itself:

" My name is Dr Litwak."

" Bertrand Müller, doctor of philosophy," I gave him my hand; the young Jew also offered me his hand. It was dry and cool, and as smooth as his face.

They attached themselves to me as though it were the most natural thing in the world. I wasn't going anywhere in particular, but I walked very fast. The two of them, one on my right and the other on my left, kept step with me and conversed with each other in Yiddish. I became seriously annoyed:

" I don't understand a word you're saying."

They laughed:

" He says he doesn't understand a word."

After a while:

" Really, you don't know any Yiddish? "

" No."

We reached the end of Reichenbergerstrasse, and I set my course for Rixdorf.

Well, and then we encountered Marie.

She was leaning against a lamp-post. It was already quite dark, but the gas was being used sparingly. All the same I recognized her at once.

Moreover the windows of the restaurant opposite gave a little light.

Marie recognized me too; she smiled to me. Then she asked:

" Are these friends of yours? "

" Neighbours," I replied.

I suggested a visit to the restaurant, for Marie seemed to be exhausted and in need of something to eat. But the two Jews refused to enter the restaurant. Perhaps they were afraid that they might be forced to eat pork, perhaps they were afraid of being jeered at or something or other. In any case one could have made it a pretext for getting rid of them.

But an extraordinary thing happened: Marie ranged herself on the side of the Jews, said that she was not in the least hungry, and as though it were an unavoidable arrangement, she went on in front with the young Jew, while I followed with Dr Litwak.

" Who is he? " I asked the doctor, pointing at the young Jew, the tails of whose grey coat swung in front of me.

" He's called Nuchem Sussin," said Dr Litwak.

CHAPTER XXVIII

Dr Kühlenbeck and Dr Kessel had been in the operating-theatre. Generally Kühlenbeck spared Dr Kessel as much as possible, for Dr Kessel, although at the disposal of the hospital, was overworked attending to his panel patients; just now, however, the new offensive had brought in fresh material for treatment, and Kühlenbeck had no choice. It was fortunate that only lighter cases had been sent. Or at least what were called lighter cases.

And because the two men were genuine doctors, they sat talking over their cases later in Kühlenbeck's room. Flurschütz too had come in.

" A pity that you weren't there to-day, Flurschütz, you would have enjoyed it," said Kühlenbeck. " It's astonishing how much you learn . . . if we hadn't operated, the man would have been a cripple for the rest of his life . . ." he laughed, " but now he'll be able to go out and be shot at again in six weeks' time."

Kessel said:

" I only wish my poor panel patients were as well looked after as the men here."

Kühlenbeck said:

" Do you know the story of the convict who swallowed a fish-bone and had to be operated on so that they might be able to hang him next morning? That's our job at the moment."

Flurschütz said:

" If the doctors in all the combatant countries went on strike, the war would soon be over."

" Well, Flurschütz, you can make a beginning."

Dr Kessel said:

" I feel jolly well inclined to send the ribbon back . . . you should feel ashamed of yourself, Kühlenbeck, playing an old colleague such a dirty trick."

" What could I do? I had to give you your medicine . . . the civilians are all wearing the black-and-white now."

" Yes, and you're just running round palming it off on them. . . . You've been down on the list too for a long time now, Flurschütz."

Flurschütz said:

" At bottom it just comes down to this, that we all sit about here discussing cases that are more or less interesting, without thinking of anything else . . . we haven't time as a matter of fact to think of anything else . . . and it's the same everywhere. You get swallowed up, swallowed up by what you're doing . . . simply swallowed up."

Dr Kessel said:

" Damn it all, I'm fifty-six, what is there left for me to think about? . . . I'm glad when I get into bed at night."

Kühlenbeck said:

" Would you care for a drink at the regiment's expense . . .? We'll be getting another twenty men or so in by two o'clock . . . will you stay to receive them? "

He had got up and walked over to the medicine cabinet beside the window, from which he now took a bottle of cognac and three glasses. As he stood in profile against the window reaching up his hand to the shelf in the cabinet, his beard was outlined against the light and he looked gigantic.

Flurschütz said:

" We're all being pumped dry by the profession we're stuck in . . . and even soldiering and patriotism are nothing more than professions . . . we're simply past understanding what is happening in any province but our own."

" Thank God for that! " said Dr Kühlenbeck, " doctors don't need to be philosophers."

Sister Mathilde entered. She smelt of scented soap. Or at least one felt that she must smell of it. Her narrow face with the long nose contrasted with her housemaid's red hands.

" Dr Kühlenbeck, the station people have rung up to say that the transport train has arrived."

" Good, one more cigarette before we go . . . you're coming too, Sister? "

" Sister Carla and Sister Emmy have gone to the station already."

" Excellent . . . well, shall we be going, Flurschütz? "

" Straining at the leash," remarked Dr Kessel, but without real gusto.

Sister Mathilde had remained standing at the door. She liked to dawdle in the doctors' room. And as they all went out, Flurschütz's eye caught the gleam of her white throat, noted the freckles where her hair began, and he felt a little touched.

" 'Day, Sister," said the Chief.

" Good-day, Sister," said Flurschütz too.

" Gott mit uns," said Dr Kessel.

CHAPTER XXIX

Trees and houses appeared before the eyes of the bricklayer Gödicke, the weather changed, sometimes it was day and sometimes night, people moved about and he heard them speaking. Food was brought and set before him on objects, mostly round, made of tin or earthenware. He knew all this, but the way that led to a knowledge of these things, or by which they reached him, was a laborious one: the bricklayer Gödicke had now to work harder than he had ever done in his hard-working life. For it was by no means a simple and self-evident action to lift a spoon to one's mouth when one was not clear in one's mind who it was that was being fed, and the frightful strain of making this clear turned it into a torment of despairing labour and impossible duty; for nobody, least of all Gödicke himself, could have provided a theory to explain the

structural elements that composed his personality. For of course it would
have been erroneous to assert that the man Gödicke was made up of
several Gödickes, including for instance a boy Ludwig Gödicke who
had played in the street with his friends and made tunnels in the ash-
heaps and sandpits, a boy who was called in every day to dinner by his
mother and made to carry his father's dinner afterwards to the building
where he was working, since he too had been a bricklayer; to assert that
that boy Ludwig Gödicke represented a constituent part of the man's
present self would have been just as erroneous as to recognize another
constituent part of it, say, in the apprentice Gödicke who had envied the
Hamburg carpenters so intensely on account of their broad-brimmed
hats and the mother-of-pearl buttons on their waistcoats that he had not
rested until, to spite them all, he had seduced the bride of the carpenter
Gürzner among the bushes by the riverside, although he was merely a
bricklayer's apprentice; and it would be erroneous again to assert that
yet another part was the man who during a strike had put the concrete-
mixing machine out of action by unscrewing the cylinders, and in spite
of that had left the union when he married the servant-girl Anna
Lamprecht, and that simply because she cried so much on account of
the baby that was coming: no, such a longitudinal splitting as this, such
a quasi-historical section, can never give the constituent elements of a
personality, for it cannot go beyond the biographical. The difficulties
with which the man Gödicke had to contend, then, were certainly not
caused by the fact that he felt this whole series of persons living within
him, but rather sprang from the sudden interruption of the series at a
certain point, from the fact that there was no connection between the
earlier biography and himself, though he himself should obviously have
been the last link in the chain, and that being cast adrift in this way from
something which he could hardly any longer describe as his life, he had
lost his own identity. He saw these figures as through smoked glass, and
although when he lifted the spoon to his mouth he would have liked well
enough to be feeding the man who had lain with Gürzner's fiancée under
the bushes—indeed, that would have given him great pleasure—nevertheless he simply could not bridge the gap, he remained as it were on
the farther bank and could not lay hold of the man on the other side.
And yet perhaps in spite of all that he might have bridged the gap if he
could only have known for certain who it really was that remembered
Gürzner's girl: for the eyes that had looked at the bushes by the riverside

then were not the same eyes that gazed at the trees along the avenue now, nor again were these quite the same as those which looked round the room. And beyond doubt there was one Gödicke who could not bear that that other man should be fed, and who refused to feed him, that man who was even now still prepared to sleep with Gürzner's girl. And the Gödicke who was enduring these pains in his abdomen might be with equal probability either the one who issued the refusal, or the one against whom it was directed, but he might just as well be a quite different Gödicke altogether. It was a highly complicated problem, and the bricklayer Gödicke could not see his way through it at all. It had probably arisen through his reluctance to resume all the scattered fragments of his soul in returning to consciousness, but perhaps it might also have been the cause why he was not in a condition to do so. True, if he could have peered within himself now, one could not exclude the possibility that in each fragment of his ego which he had admitted he might have recognized a separate Gödicke, somewhat as though each of those fragments were an independent nucleus. For it may be that the same thing happens with the soul as with a piece of protoplasm, in which by dissection one can produce a multiplication of nuclei and therewith new regions of autonomous, intact and separate life. However that may be, and however it may have come about, in Gödicke's soul there existed several autonomous and integral separate existences, to each of which one might have ventured to give the title of Gödicke, and it was a laborious and almost impossible task to subsume them all in one personality.

This task the bricklayer Gödicke had to accomplish entirely by himself; there was no one who could help him.

CHAPTER XXX

When after a politic interval of two days Huguenau once more appeared in Esch's office, he found a broad-hipped person of uncertain age, devoid equally of sex and charm, sitting in the basket-chair beside Esch's desk. It was Frau Esch, and Huguenau knew that now the game was his. He had only to make a favourable impression on her:

" Oh, your good lady is going to give us the benefit of her assistance in these difficult negotiations. . . ."

Frau Esch drew back a little:

" I know nothing about business matters, that's my husband's affair."

" Ah, yes, your husband, he's a real business man *comme il faut*; he's a tough nut to crack, I can tell you, and lots of people will break their teeth on him yet."

Frau Esch smiled faintly, and Huguenau felt encouraged to go on:

" A splendid idea of his to take advantage of the market and get rid of the paper, which brings him only worry and annoyance, you might say, and business going from bad to worse."

Frau Esch said politely:

" Yes, my husband has a great deal of worry with the paper."

" I'm not going to give it up, all the same," said Esch.

" Come, come, Herr Esch, if your health is of no account to yourself, I'm sure that your good lady will have a word or two to say about that . . . besides," Huguenau considered, " . . . if you don't want to sever your connection entirely with the paper, you can make your further collaboration a condition of the deal, the group I represent will only be too glad if I secure them such valuable assistance."

Well, that might be considered, Esch thought, but under 18,000 marks it couldn't be done, he and his wife had just come to that decision.

Well, it was a hopeful sign that Herr Esch had already somewhat qualified the fancy price he had asked; still, if he wanted to retain his connection with the business, he must surely make some allowance for that too.

To what extent, asked Herr Esch.

Huguenau felt that something concrete was demanded:

" The simplest way, really, would be to draw up a trial contract and go over the different points by the way."

" All right, I don't mind," said Esch, taking out a sheet of paper, " dictate."

Huguenau seated himself in the appropriate posture:

" Well, right then; Heading: Memorandum of Contract."

After much desultory discussion, which took up the whole forenoon, the following contract resulted:

> *1. Herr Wilhelm Huguenau, as representative and executor of a group of combined interests, hereby enters into partnership with the private company owning the* Kur-Trier Herald *on the following terms, the property of the firm to be allocated as follows:*
>
> *10 per cent. to remain in the possession of Herr August Esch.*

60 per cent. to be held by the " Industrial Group " represented by Herr Huguenau.

30 per cent. to be held by the group of local interests also represented by Herr Huguenau.

Esch's original claim to half-ownership was turned down by Huguenau: " That would be against your own interests, my dear Esch, the bigger your share, the less you'll realize in cash . . . you see, I'm keeping an eye on your interests."

2. The firm's assets consist of the publishing and other rights, together with the office furnishings and complete printing plant. Interim share certificates shall be issued, covering the new distribution of share capital.

The Statue of Liberty and the view of Badenweiler were claimed by Herr Esch as his private property and not included among the firm's assets. " Certainly," said Huguenau magnanimously.

3. The net profits shall be distributed among the shareholders in proportion to the number of share certificates held, except for any sum that may be carried to the reserve fund. The losses shall be borne in the same proportion.

The clause regarding the losses was inserted in the contract at Herr Esch's request, as Herr Huguenau had not entertained the possibility of losses. The reserve fund too was Esch's suggestion.

4. As representative and executor of the new group of shareholders Herr Huguenau brings into the firm capital amounting to 20,000 marks (say twenty thousand marks). One-third of this amount to be paid up immediately; the two further instalments of one-third may be paid, if the shareholders desire, within the next six months or twelve months respectively. On deferred payments the firm shall charge interest at the rate of 4 per cent. per half-year. The share certificates shall be allotted in proportion to the money paid in.

As the share certificates were to be issued immediately on payment, and the high rate of 4 per cent. was a grave deterrent, Huguenau was not greatly afraid of the local subscribers taking advantage of the deferred payment; but even if they did, some means or other would easily enough be found of tiding over the emergency. Nor was he worried by the question of how he himself was to get together the deferred pay-

ments of his legendary industrial group—the first instalment did not
fall due for another half-year, at the beginning of 1919, that was to say,
and it was a long time until then, and lots of things might happen; the
war conditions created a great deal of confusion, perhaps peace might
have come by then, perhaps the paper itself might have brought in the
sum required, in which case it would of course be necessary to conceal
those gains by the creation of imaginary losses and thus wipe them
off, perhaps Esch would be dead by that time—one would find some
way of getting over the difficulty and coming out on top.

> 5. *The payments made by Herr Wilhelm Huguenau, in all 20,000
> marks, shall be allocated to two accounts: viz. 13,400 marks to the
> account of the Huguenau " Industrial Group," and 6600 marks to the
> account of the local subscribers.*

But now came the most difficult point in the negotiations. For Esch
insisted on his 18,000 marks, while Huguenau maintained that first of all
10 per cent., that was 2000 marks, had to be deducted on account of the
shares retained by Esch, but that in addition the rebate had to be doubled
in consideration of the increased capital put into the business, thus
making in all 4000 marks; so that Esch, even accepting his own valuation, would have only 14,000 coming to him; but even that was still far
too much; he, Huguenau, as a middleman, had to be unbiassed, and he
would never be able to get such a price as that out of his group, delighted
as he would be to do so for Esch and his charming wife's sake; no, that
would be simply impossible, for he must have a serious proposal to lay
before his clients, and he had no wish to be laughed out of court; in this
matter he was not in the least a partisan, but quite objective, and as an
impartial judge he could offer 10,000 marks for the remaining 90 per
cent. of the business, but not a penny more.

No, Esch shouted, he wanted his eighteen thousand.

" How can anyone be so hard of hearing? " Huguenau turned to
Frau Esch, " I've just proved to him that according to his own valuation
all that he can ask is fourteen thousand."

Frau Esch sighed.

Finally they agreed on 12,000 marks and on the following clause:

> 6. *As former sole proprietor Herr August Esch shall receive:*
> (a) *A final quittance of 12,000 marks, of which a third, that is
> to say, 4000 marks, shall be paid immediately to Herr Esch by the*

*company, and the two further instalments of 4000 each on 1st January
and 1st July 1919 respectively. Interest at the rate of 4 per cent. will
be charged on the two outstanding instalments;*

(b) *A contract engaging him for a period of two years as assistant
editor and head book-keeper with a monthly salary of 125 marks.*

Perhaps Esch might not still have given in, even though Huguenau
adroitly diverted the dispute to the subordinate concession of the interest
payable to Esch, intending only after a hotly contested sham fight to
allow the 4 per cent. to be wrung from him; no, Esch might not even
then have given in, had not the prospect of such complicated book-
keeping so dazzled and enchanted him that it never entered his head
that the outstanding instalments—and he had not the slightest idea
that their payment presupposed nothing less than a miracle—might
never be settled, or that the difference between the 12,000 marks and the
20,000 marks might flow, in spite of all those book-keeping prospects
which so allured him, into Huguenau's fraudulently open pockets. To
tell the truth, Huguenau thought just as little of such sordid matters,
so unconscious was he that once the payments were made by the local
subscribers the *Kur-Trier Herald* became *via facti* a pure gift to him;
he fought with all sincerity for the interests of his hypothetical clients
and said at last in an exhausted tone: " Ouf, well, as far as I'm concerned, let us make it 12,000 marks and 4 per cent. as you say, to settle
the matter for good. I'll take the responsibility on my own shoulders . . .
but I must get something out of it too. . . ."

7. *Reciprocal rights and duties:*

(a) *Herr Huguenau shall act as publisher and editor. The commercial
and financial conduct of the enterprise rests exclusively in his hands.
He has furthermore the right to accept and reject articles for the paper
as he thinks fit. In return for these services the firm guarantees him
a minimum salary of 175 M. per month, that is to say, 2100 M. yearly.*

(b) *During the period covered by his contract Herr Esch shall for
his part keep the books of the firm and act as assistant editor.*

Esch had to agree to the limitation of his editorial powers out of consideration for the industrial group; his book-keeping powers represented
a sort of compensation.

8. *The rooms in Herr Esch's house hitherto employed in the production of the paper shall be placed at the disposal of the firm for a*

period of three years. Furthermore Herr Esch shall put at the dis-
position of the editor for the same period two comfortably furnished
front rooms with breakfast in the aforesaid house. Herr Esch shall
receive from the firm's revenues a reimbursement of 25 marks per month
for these services.

9. Should the company be converted at a later stage into a limited
liability or joint stock company, the gist of the aforesaid conditions
shall be respected.

With this projected conversion of the business into a company compelled to audit its accounts, Huguenau's house of cards of course would
fall to pieces. But Huguenau did not worry his head about such trifles;
for him the whole thing was a perfectly legitimate piece of business,
and the only item that struck him as verging on sharp-practice was the
one giving him a present of free quarters with his breakfast thrown in,
but he was elated at bringing it off. Esch, on the other hand, was grieved
because the contract had not run to ten clauses. They thought for a
while and then they found the tenth:

10. Any difference of interpretation which may arise out of this
contract shall be decided by public arbitration.

So in an astonishingly short time—it was the 14th of May—Huguenau
was able to report that the purchase had been smoothly settled. The
local subscribers did not hesitate to pay up their full capital investment
of 6600 marks; of this 4000 was allotted to Herr Esch in accordance with
the terms of the contract; as a prudent and solid business man Herr
Huguenau allocated 1600 marks for working expenses, while as for the
remaining 1000, he embellished it with the title of floating capital and
employed it for his own uses. The interim share certificates were issued
to the shareholders, and in a few days it was duly announced that from
the first of June the paper would appear under its new editorship and
in a new make-up. Huguenau had managed to induce the Major to
inaugurate the new era with a leading article, and the festal number was
also embellished partly with patriotic, partly with political-economical,
but in greater part with patriotic-economical pronouncements from the
pens of the local subscribers.

But to celebrate the new epoch Huguenau installed himself in the
two rooms prepared for him in Esch's house.

CHAPTER XXXI

DISINTEGRATION OF VALUES (4)

The style of an epoch, it is certain, affects not merely the artist; it penetrates all contemporary activities, and crystallizes itself not only in works of art but in all the values which make up the culture of the age, and of which works of art constitute only an insignificant part; yet one is fairly at a loss when confronted by the concrete question: in how far is the style of an age incarnated in the average man, in a business man, for example, of the type of Wilhelm Huguenau? Has the man who deals in pipes of wine or textiles anything in common with the feeling for style that is evident in the shops built by Messel, or Peter Behrens's turbine power-houses? His private taste will certainly run to pinnacled villas and rooms cluttered with knick-knacks, and even if it should not, he remains a member of the public, which, however it may comport itself, is separated by a great gulf from the artist.

Yet when one regards more closely a man such as Huguenau, one sees that the gulf between him and the artist does not affect the real point at issue. One may certainly assume that in epochs which had a supreme feeling for style the lack of understanding between the artist and his contemporaries was less strongly marked than it is to-day, that for instance a new picture by Dürer in the Sebaldus Church excited general joy and admiration among even the Huguenaus of the time; for there is plenty of evidence that at that period the artist and his public were bound together in a very different kind of community, and that the painter understood the clothier and the saddler at least as profoundly as they enjoyed looking at his pictures. Of course this cannot be verified, and it may be, too, that many revolutionary spirits received but little recognition from their contemporaries; perhaps that was the case with Grünewald. But such exceptions are not particularly relevant, and in any case whether an understanding between the artist and his contemporaries ruled in the Middle Ages or not becomes a matter of indifference in face of the fact that misunderstanding and understanding alike are just as truly expressions of the legendary " Time Spirit " as a work of art in itself or any other contemporary activity.

But if this be so, then it is also a matter of indifference what direction is taken by the architectural or other taste of a business agent of

Huguenau's type, and the fact that Huguenau had a certain æsthetic pleasure in machinery is likewise without importance; the sole question of any moment is whether his ordinary actions, his ordinary thoughts, were influenced by the same laws that in another sphere produced a style devoid of ornament, or evolved the theory of relativity, or led up to the philosophical conclusions of neo-Kantianism,—in other words, whether even the thought of an epoch is not a vehicle for its style, governed by that same style which attains visible and palpable expression in works of art; which amounts to the assertion that truth, the ultimate product of thought, is equally a vehicle for the style of the epoch in which it has been discovered and in which it is valid, precisely like all the other values of that epoch.

And indeed it cannot be otherwise. For it is not merely that, seen from a certain standpoint, truth is just a value among other values; truth also governs all the actions of mankind, which are, one may say, steeped in truth : whatever a man does is plausible to him at every moment, he justifies it to himself with reasons which in his eyes represent the truth, he proves it to himself logically, and—at least in the very moment of action —his actions are always justifiable. If his actions, then, are dominated by the style of his age, so must his thoughts be; we need not decide (from the practical or epistemological standpoint) whether the act has preceded the thought or the thought the act, the motion of life the motion of reason, the *sum* the *cogito*, or the *cogito* the *sum*—all we can take into account is the rational logic of thought, for the irrational logic of action, in which style is embodied, can be perceived only in the finished product, in the result.

But with this extremely intimate connection between the substance of logical thought and the positive and negative values which action embodies, the scheme of thought which governs a man like Huguenau and compels him to act in one particular way, which determines his business methods for him and makes him draft contracts from a certain standpoint—that is to say, all the inner logic of a man like Huguenau—is given its own place in the whole logical framework of the epoch, and brought into essential relation with whatever logic permeates the productive spirit of the epoch and its visible style. And even although that rational thought, that rational logic, may be nothing but a thin and as it were one-dimensional thread which has to be wound round and round the multiplicity of dimensions presented by life, nevertheless that thought, projected in the abstraction

of logical space, is an abbreviated expression of life's multiplicity and
prevailing style, much in the same way as ornament is an abbreviated
spatial expression of the visible style-product,—a projected abbreviation
of all the works that embody style.

Huguenau is a man who acts with singleness of purpose. He organizes
his day with singleness of purpose, he carries on his business affairs with his
eye singly on his purpose, he evolves and concludes his contracts with
his eye singly on his purpose. Behind all his purposefulness there lies a
logic that is completely stripped of ornament, and the fact that this logic
should demand the elimination of all ornament does not seem a too daring
conclusion to draw; indeed it actually appears as good and just as every
other necessary conclusion. And yet this elimination of all ornament
involves nothingness, involves death, and a monstrous dissolution is
concealed behind it in which our age is crumbling away.

CHAPTER XXXII

The rebel must not be confused with the criminal, though society may
often stigmatize the rebel as a criminal, and though the criminal may
sometimes pose as a rebel to dignify his actions. The rebel stands alone:
the most faithful son of that society which is the target of his hostility
and rejection, he sees in the world he combats a totality of living
relationships whose threads have merely been tangled in confusion by
some diabolical wickedness, and it is his chosen task to disentangle them
and order them according to his own better ideas. Thus did Luther make
his protest against the Pope, and so Esch might with justice be called a
rebel.

This is by no means, however, a sufficient cause to asperse Huguenau,
on the other hand, as a criminal. That would be not only to slander him, but
also to do him grievous injustice. From the military standpoint a deserter
is of course a criminal, and undoubtedly there are convinced militarists
who loathe the deserter with the same intensity as, let us say, a farmer
loathes a chicken thief, and like the farmer they will recognize nothing
less than the death penalty as a just punishment for such a transgressor.
Nevertheless there is here a principal and objective distinction: the
essence of a crime lies in the fact that it can be repeated; and the fact
that it can be repeated characterizes it as nothing else than a social profession. Criminalism is directed only in a very loose sense against the

existing social order, even when its battle against law and order assumes American forms; to the thief and the coiner the slogans of communism cannot mean very much, and the burglar who goes about his work of nights on noiseless rubber soles is a handworker like any other handworker, he is conservative like all handworkers, and even the profession of the murderer, who with his knife between his teeth climbs up the unaccommodating wall, is not directed against the whole community, but is simply a private affair which he has to settle with his victim. There is no attempt to upset the existing regime. Proposals for the improvement or amelioration of the penal laws have never emanated from the criminal classes, closely as these things may concern them above all others. If it had been left to the criminals, we should still be hanging thieves and coiners on the gallows, and we should not even have got to the point of distinguishing murder from manslaughter, in spite of the fact that criminals usually show a fine feeling for the nuances of their professional exploits, and are delighted when the penal code adapts itself to their fine-drawn distinctions and exactions; but the very fact that they demand a corresponding distinction of penalties, the gallows for one crime, the wheel and the red-hot brand for another, the cat-o'-nine tails or the stocks for a third,—this simple and clumsy desire for recognition, in reality nothing but the groping aspiration of uneducated men who cannot express themselves properly, and who awkwardly, in symbol as it were, demand something that represents only a small fraction of what their hearts are set on, though they scarcely know what it is; this very fact betrays the goal of their aspiration: which is that the border-land they live in, that border-land on the frontier of a world full of good ordinances, should be admitted into that greater, that good, that almost beloved order which they do not want to alter; and if criminals can conceive of such an admittance and acknowledgment only within a framework of regulated and severe penalties, yet that proves them to be aspiring and social by nature, men who are moved simply by the desire to avoid frontier friction, to go about their vocation in peace and quiet, and to accommodate themselves more and more uncomplainingly, inconspicuously and sensitively to their calling, whose point of reference is the whole structure of society and the existing order.

Rebel and criminal, they both bring their own order, their own conceptions of value into the existing regime. But while the rebel wants to subjugate the existing regime, the criminal seeks to fit himself into it.

The deserter belongs neither to the one category nor the other, or perhaps he belongs to both. Huguenau may have felt this, now that he was faced with the task of setting up his own little world of reality on the outposts of that greater order and of adapting the one to the other, and even if he agreed that deserters should be sentenced to death by rifle fire, that was irrelevant for the time being, and the fact that the *Kur-Trier Herald* represented in his eyes a part of a great machine, say, a brass-plated joint where the bars met and were clamped together, a point at which the country where his own law ruled met that other one whose laws he reverenced and loved, into which he was resolved to make his way and in which he wished to dwell; this fact was not merely nonsensical; it was no more nonsensical than the language of his dreams. And all these motives were jointly responsible for the need that Huguenau felt to get hold of the *Kur-Trier Herald*; they also provide an explanation for the complete success of his transaction.

CHAPTER XXXIII

(Leading Article in the *Kur-Trier Herald* of 1st June 1918.)

THE TURNING-POINT IN THE DESTINY OF THE GERMAN PEOPLE.

Reflections by
Town Commandant Major Joachim von Pasenow.

Then the devil leaveth him, and, behold, angels came and ministered unto him.—MATTHEW iv. 11.

Although the change in the editorial policy of this paper is but a trifling occurrence compared with the mighty event whose anniversary we may soon be seeing for the fourth time, yet it seems to me that, as so often is the case, we must here too regard the smaller event as a mirror of the greater.

For we too and this paper of ours stand at a parting of the ways, we too have the desire to take a new and better path which will lead us nearer to the truth, and we nurse the faith that as far as it is permitted to human powers we shall . . . . .

where is the devil whom we must drive out from amidst us, where the angel whom we can call to our aid?

It beseems an old soldier to speak his mind bluntly, even at the risk that what he says may seem untimely to many people   .   .

.   .   .   .

.   .   .   .

.   .   .   .

to free ourselves from the iron embrace of the enemy nations, but also to release the Fatherland and with it the whole world from the unclean spirit which   .   .   .   .   .   .

.   .   .   .

.   .   .   .

.   .   .   .

not to be wondered at that the nations should be visited with hundred-fold dissension and thousandfold disunion. For in the member with which you have sinned shall you be punished.

I hear someone objecting that in that case we should simply submit to the punishment, endure the scourge, and turn the other cheek to the persecut-

.   .   .   .

.   .   .   .

.   .   .   .

just as Luther's struggle against a Popedom which had grown corrupt was a justified struggle. And does not our master Clausewitz teach us that the spirit of righteousness is one of the weapons of war, which

.   .   .   .

.   .   .   .

.   .   .   .

it shall be said of our struggle: " His foes fled in terror before him, the evil-doer was abashed, and salvation was in his hands " (Maccabees iii. 6), yet we must not fix our thoughts on the pursuit of the flying foe, but on salvation, the salvation of our own as of other nations. We have been shortsighted, and in very truth all our sacrifices will have been in vain, if they are regarded frivolously, and God's   .   .

.   .   .   .

.   .   .   .

.   .   .   .

possesses that outward freedom which we have to fight for, only when at the same time that inward and truly divine freedom is vouchsafed to it. And we shall achieve that freedom not on our battlefields, victorious as we may be there, but we shall find it only in our hearts. For that inward freedom is commensurate with the faith which the world stands now in danger of losing. So the war is not only

according to the Scriptures? " Good and pious works will never make a man good and pious, but a good and pious man will do good and pious works," asserted Luther, writing of Christian freedom, and he goes on: " But if works can make no man pious, and a man must be pious before he can do good works, then it is evident that only the faith granted us by infinite grace through Christ . . .

and John says (iii. 30) " He must increase, but I must decrease," and so it was with the war, which had to increase that our faith might decrease, and until our faith is re-born to blossom anew, until that happens this war may not be able to come to an end. Evil for the mere sake of evil

and it almost seems to us that first the black hordes will have to be let loose on the whole world, so that out of the fires of the Apocalypse the new brotherhood and fellowship may arise, so that once more the kingdom of Christ may be established, and new and glorious

the black troops, armed with unchivalrous weapons, sent out against us, yet these are only the vanguard. They shall be followed by the black hosts, by the terrors of the Johannine Apocalypse. For as long as the white races are incapable of overcoming this inertia of feeling, and casting from them

embraces honour, it is a lost generation and the dreadful darkness will be
round it, and no one will come to help it and its   .   .   .

.   .   .   .

.   .   .   .

the venom of the blasphemer and the adventurer, which infects not
only the insolent capitals of the enemy, but has not spared our
Fatherland. Like an inextricable network it lies invisibly over our cities

.   .   .   .

.   .   .   .

just as first our glorious campaign of 1870 had to come so as to unite
the dispersed tribes of the German people, so it will be the glory of this
far greater and more dreadful war not merely to have united whole
races in brotherhood, but in a sense   .   .   .   .

.   .   .   .

.   .   .   .

and the Christian faith and the grace of freedom be ours again. Then
we shall be able to say: " A Christian is a faithful servant of all things
and subject to every man," no less than: " A Christian is a free master
over all things and subject to no man "; for both will be true, and that
is how we should think of true freedom.

I do not know whether I have been able to make myself thoroughly
understood, for I myself have had to wrestle for a long time in order to
arrive at these truths, and am convinced that they are still fragmentary.
But here too the words of General Clausewitz may apply: " The
heart-rending spectacle of danger and suffering may easily make our
feelings prevail over our reasonable convictions, and in the twilight
of appearance it is so hard to gain a profound and clear insight
into things that vacillation is understandable and excusable. *It is
always out of a mere inkling and foreboding of the truth that man
acts.*"

Thus did Major von Pasenow come to grips with the problem of the
war and the future of Germany, and he found it hard work. War, for
which his upbringing had been a preparation, war, for whose sake he
had worn a uniform during the years of his youth and donned it again

four years ago, war had suddenly become no longer a matter of uniform, no longer a matter of red regimentals or blue regimentals, no longer an affair between gallant enemies who chivalrously crossed swords; no, war had proved neither the crown nor the fulfilment of a life in uniform, but had invisibly and yet more and more palpably shaken the foundations of that life, had worn threadbare the ties of morality holding it together, and through the meshes of the fabric grinned the Evil One. Spiritual forces trained in the cadet school of Culm were not adequate for the subjugation of the Evil One, and that was not surprising, since the Church itself, although much better equipped, has failed to overcome once and for all the antinomy of original sin. But the idea that once hovered before Augustine's mind as the salvation of the secular world, the dream that the Stoics had dreamed before him, the idea of a religious State embracing within it all that bears the lineaments of mankind, this exalted idea shone through the picture of heart-rending danger and suffering, and had awakened—more as a feeling, it is true, than as a reasoned conviction, rather a vague divination than a profound and clear intuition—it had awakened in the soul of the old officer too; and so a connection, hazy, indeed, and sometimes misconceived, but continuously traceable, ran from Zeno and Seneca, perhaps even from the Pythagoreans, to the thoughts of Major von Pasenow.

CHAPTER XXXIV

DISINTEGRATION OF VALUES (5)

Logical Excursus.

Although it cannot be denied that the style of thinking prevailing, say, in the Royal Prussian Cadet School at Culm is quite different from that in a Roman Catholic seminary, yet the concept " style of thinking " is so vague that it reminds one of the vagueness of those philosophical and historical tendencies which find the crux of their methodology in the word " intuition." For the *a priori* unambiguity of thought and logic permits of no stylistic gradations, and so cannot countenance any other intuition than the mind's *a priori* apprehension of itself, discarding everything else as empirical and pathological abnormality more fitted for psychological and medical research than for philosophy. An argument for the insufficiency of the human brain's work-a-day and empirical thinking in face of the absolute logic of the self, the absolute logic of God.

Or it could be argued that the absolute formality of logic is unassailable and cannot be changed even by human agency; all that changes being the content of its propositions, their interpretation of the nature of the world; so that the question of style is at most an epistemological question and can never be a logical one. Logic, like mathematics, is devoid of style.

But is the form of logic actually so independent of its content? For somewhere, curiously enough, logic itself is identified with content, and nowhere more clearly than in so-called formal concatenations of proof; for not only are the links of these chains axioms or axiomatic propositions —such as the principle of non-contradiction—which form an impassable limit to plausibility (until one fine day that limit is passed, all the same, as for instance in the principle of the excluded middle), and whose evidence is no longer based on formal proof but only on actual content, but more than that, there would be no syllogisms at all, the whole logical machinery of drawing and proving conclusions would not even work, without the application of extra-logical principles to set the whole in motion, principles that in the long run, however far one pushes the limit of definition, are ultimately metaphysical and substantive. The structure of formal logic thus rests on substantive foundations.

The idealism of intuitional psychologizers presupposes a " feeling for truth " which provides the resting-point in which every line of inquiry, beginning with the wondering question: " What is that? " and proceeding by posing reiterated " whys? " finally comes to an end with the assertion of an axiomatic plausibility: " That is so and not otherwise." Now although in reference to the immutability of an *a priori* and purely formal logic this feeling for truth is a superfluous importation, yet in reference to the substantive element in logical proof it has claims to more reasonable respect. For the resting-points of evidence at the end of the lines of inquiry and chains of proof have detached themselves from formal immutability and yet are supposed to have a determining influence on the process of logical proof itself and on its form. The problem which this raises: " In what way can substantive content, be it a logical axiom or non-logical in its nature, so affect formal logic as to admit of variation in style of thinking while maintaining intact the invariability of form?" this problem is no longer empirical and psychological, but methodological and metaphysical, for behind it stands in all its *a priority* the first question of all ethics: How can God permit error, how is it that a madman is allowed to live in God's world?

One can imagine a line of inquiry that never comes to a conclusion at all. All inquiries into ultimate origins obviously have this peculiarity; the problem of matter, which advances from one fundamental concept to another, from primal substance to the atom, from the atom to the electron, from the electron to the quantum of energy, and each time reaches only a temporary resting-place, is an example of such an infinite line of inquiry.

Now the point at which such a line of inquiry terminates is obviously conditioned by a feeling for truth and evidence, conditioned, therefore, by whatever axioms prevail. The doctrine of Thales, for instance, that the terminal point, the point of plausibility for the inquiry into the origin of matter, was the substance " water " permits us to infer that for Thales there was an accepted system of axioms within which the watery nature of matter seemed probable. Here it is substantive and not logically formal axioms that stop the line of inquiry, axioms of the prevailing cosmogony,—but these substantive axioms must have some relation to those of formal logic, they must at the very least be incapable of formal contradiction, for if the substantive development of the evidence did not agree with the formal there would be no plausibility in the conclusion. (And yet the possibility of disagreement between substantive and logical axioms can be discovered in the doctrine of twofold truth.) Moreover, even if one were to take up a position of complete scepticism and say *Ignorabimus*, and, denying the existence of a plausibility depending on cosmogony and of its concomitant axioms, were to assume the non-terminable nature of inquiries and regard their termination at any fixed point as a purely purposeful and yet fictitious piece of arbitrariness, still it is clear that even the plea *Ignorabimus* as such possesses a definite attribute of plausibility, which again is supported by a definite frame of logic and a definite system of logical axioms.

Perhaps the number of axioms implicit and effective in any view of the world could provide some kind of conception of these relationships, a reasonable conception extending beyond the limits of pure intuition.

Naturally the precise quantity could neither be produced nor enumerated —one could only indicate the comparative multiplicity or dearth of axioms in extreme cases. The cosmogony of a primitive people, for instance, is of the utmost complexity; every object in the world has a life of its own, is in a sense *causa sui*; each tree is inhabited by its own god, each thing by its own demon; it is a world of an infinite number of things, and every line of inquiry relating to the objects in that world advances only a few steps, perhaps one step only, before stopping short at one of these axioms. In contrast with such a multiplicity of short chains of ontological reasoning, mostly chains of only one link, the chains of reasoning in a monotheistic world are already much lengthened, although not lengthened into infinity; they are lengthened, that is, to the point where they all converge in the sole First Cause, God. So that if one considers merely the ontological axioms of cosmogony—leaving out of account the others, those that are purely logical—in the two extreme cases represented by the polarized cosmogonies of primitive magic and of monotheism, the number of axioms varies from infinity to one.

In so far as language is an expression of logic, in so far as logic appears to be immanent in the structure of language, one could draw from the language of a people a conclusion about the number of its ontological axioms, the nature of logic and the variability of its " style." For the complicated ontological system of a primitive race, its widely distributed system of axioms, is what is reflected in the extraordinary complication of the structure and syntax of its language. And just as little as the change in our metaphysical view of the world can be explained on practical grounds—nobody would maintain that our Western metaphysic is more " practical " than, say, the Chinese, which stands at least on an equally high pinnacle of development—just as little can the simplification and fundamental changes in the style of languages, including their tendency to obsolescence, be explained exclusively by practical considerations, quite apart from the fact that no practical explanation suffices to account for a great number of changes and syntactical peculiarities.

But the part played by a system of axioms, whether ontological or logical, in relation to a purely logical structure, the manner in which it stamps a particular " style " on a formal logic that yet remains immutable, can be made conceivable by reference to a diagram. In certain geometrical figures an infinitely distant point is arbitrarily assumed to lie within a given finite plane, and then the figure is constructed as if this assumed point were really at an infinite distance. The relation of the various parts to each other in such a figure remain the same as if the assumed point were really at an infinite distance, but all the masses are distorted and foreshortened. In somewhat similar fashion we may conceive that the constructions of logic are affected when the logical point of plausibility is moved from the infinite to the finite: the purely formal logic as such, its methods of inference, even its substantive associative relations, remain unaltered,—what is altered is the shape of its masses, its " style."

The farther step taken beyond the monotheistic cosmogony has been taken almost imperceptibly, and yet it is of greater significance than any preceding one: the First Cause has been moved beyond the " finite " infinity of a God that still remained anthropomorphic, into a real infinity of abstraction; the lines of inquiry no longer converge on this idea of God (they no longer converge on any point, one may say, but run parallel to each other), cosmogony no longer bases itself on God but on the eternal continuance of inquiry, on the consciousness that there is no point at which one can stop, that questions can for ever be advanced and must for ever be advanced, that there is neither a First Substance nor a First Cause discoverable, that behind every system of logic there is still a meta-logic, that every solution is merely a temporary solution, and that nothing remains but the act of questioning in itself: cosmogony has become radically scientific, and its language and its syntax have discarded their " style " and turned into mathematical expressions.

CHAPTER XXXV

Esch and Huguenau were crossing the market-place; it was Tuesday, the fourth of June, and a rainy day. Plump and rotund, Huguenau swaggered along with his overcoat thrown open. Like a conqueror, thought Esch venomously.

When they turned the corner by the Town Hall they met a melancholy procession; a German soldier, handcuffed and escorted by two men with fixed bayonets, was being conducted—probably from the railway station or the courts of justice—to the prison. It was raining, the drops were splashing on the man's face, and to wipe them away he had to lift his fettered hands every now and then and rub them against his face; it was both a clumsy and a pathetic gesture.

"What's he been doing?" said Esch to Huguenau, who seemed to be as affected as himself.

Huguenau shrugged his shoulders and muttered something about murder and robbery and child violation:

"Or he's stabbed a parson perhaps . . . with a kitchen knife."

Esch repeated:

"Stabbed with a knife."

"If he's a deserter he'll be shot," said Huguenau, closing the subject, and Esch saw the court martial sitting in the familiar court of justice, saw the Town Commandant sitting in judgment, heard him pronouncing the pitiless sentence, and saw the man being led out into the prison yard in the spattering rain, and while he faced the firing squad wiping for the last time with his fettered hands his face, down which ran in a mingled stream rain, tears and icy sweat.

Esch was a man of impetuous moods; he saw the world divided into black and white, he saw it dominated by the play of good and evil forces. But his impetuosity often made him see an individual where he should have seen a system, and he was already on the point of blaming the Major instead of a cold and brutal militarism for the inhumanity presently to be wreaked on the poor deserter, and was just going to say to Huguenau that the Major was a swine, when suddenly it ceased to be valid; suddenly he did not know what to think, for suddenly it was quite incomprehensible that the Major and the author of that article should be the same person.

The Major wasn't a swine, the Major was something superior, the Major had suddenly moved from the black to the white side of the world.

Esch saw the leading article quite clearly before him, and the Major's somewhat hazy but noble thoughts seemed clear and great to him, like an exposition of man's high duty to strive for freedom and justice in the world; and that was all the more remarkable as he found in it a restatement of his own task and his own aims, though transmuted, indeed, into such lofty, radiant and soaring language that all that he himself had hitherto thought or done appeared now dull, narrow, ordinary and purblind.

Esch stopped.

"One must pay for things," he said.

Huguenau was disagreeably affected by the words:

" It's easy for you to talk, you aren't going to be shot."

Esch shook his head and made a disdainful and slightly despairing gesture with his hand:

" If it was only a question of that . . . it's a question of one's self-respect . . . do you know that at one time in my life I wanted to join the Free-thinkers? "

" And what of it? " said Huguenau.

" You shouldn't talk like that," said Esch, " there's something in the Bible, all the same. Just you read the Major's article."

" A fine article," said Huguenau.

" Well? "

Huguenau considered:

" He's not likely to write any more articles for us . . . we must look out for something else. . . . But of course I'll have to attend to that myself as usual, you never think of anything. And yet you fancy yourself at bringing out a paper! "

Esch gazed at him despairingly; quite obviously you could not get any further with a lump of flesh like that, the fellow couldn't understand or didn't want to understand. Esch would have liked to thrash him. He shouted at him:

" If you're to set up as the angel sent to serve him, then I would rather be the devil."

" We're none of us angels," replied Huguenau sagely.

Esch gave it up; they had reached the office in any case.

In the entry Marguerite was playing with a few boys from the neighbourhood. She looked up crossly at being disturbed, but Esch, paying no attention, seized her and set her on his shoulders, holding her fast by the legs.

" Look out for the doors! " he shouted, bending low at the threshold.

Huguenau entered behind them.

As they climbed the steps and Marguerite, teetering high above the banister, looked down on the courtyard, now so strangely enlarged, and on the garden that swayed before her eyes, she was seized with fear; she grabbed Esch's forehead with her hard little hands and tried to fix her fingers in his eye-sockets.

" Be quiet up there," Esch ordered, " look out for the door." But it was in vain that he stooped; Marguerite made herself rigid, threw her body back, bumped her head against the lintel of the door and began to howl. Esch, from old habit accustomed to comfort weeping women with physical caresses, let the child slide down to kissing height, but now she struggled with all her strength and flew again at his eyes, so that willy-nilly he had to set her down and let her go. Marguerite wanted to escape, but Huguenau blocked the way, making signs as though to catch her. He had looked on with pleasure as she tried to struggle away from Esch, and if she had now stayed with him instead, it would have been a great satisfaction. All the same when he saw her darkened face he did not dare to hold her back, but straddled his legs and said: " Here's the door." The child understood him, laughed, and crept on all-fours through the door.

Esch followed her with his eyes: " She could do you in like a shot," it sounded as if he were moved to tenderness, " the little black rascal." Huguenau sat down opposite him: " Well, she seems to suit your taste pretty well . . . but I'll have to get a desk of my own installed here fairly soon now." " I can't prevent you," Esch growled, " and anyhow, it's about time you began to do some editorial work." Huguenau's thoughts were still with the child: " That kid's always about the place too." Esch smiled slightly: " Children are a blessing and a trial, Herr Huguenau, but you don't understand that yet." " I understand well enough that you're crazy about her . . . otherwise why should you want to adopt somebody else's brat?" " Your own or somebody else's, it doesn't matter: I've already told you that." " Oh, it matters all right, when another man's had the pleasure." " You don't understand that," shouted Esch, jumping up.

He prowled up and down the room a few times, then went to the corner where the files of newspapers were piled up, pulled out a paper—it was the special issue—and began to study the Major's article.

Huguenau regarded him with interest. Esch held his head clasped in his hands, his short grey brush of hair escaped from between his fingers, —he had a passionate, almost an ascetic appearance, and Huguenau, desirous of banishing some vague, unpleasant memory, said cheerfully: " You just see, Esch, we'll make a great thing of the paper yet." Esch replied: " The Major is a good man." " That may be," said Huguenau, " but it would be better for you to be thinking of what we can make out of the paper," he had stepped up to Esch, and, as though to waken him up, tapped him on the shoulder, " The *Herald* must be asked for in Berlin and Nürnberg, and it must be on show in the Hauptwache Coffee

House in Frankfort too, you know Frankfort, don't you? . . . it must become a paper for the whole world."

Esch paid no attention. He indicated with his finger a passage in the article: " But if works can make no man pious, and a man must be pious before he can do good works . . . do you know what that means? it means that the child doesn't matter, but only your feeling about it; another's or your own, it's all one, do you hear, it's all one! "

Huguenau felt disappointed somehow: " All I know is that you're a fool and that you've brought the paper to ruin with your feelings," he said and left the room.

The door had slammed long since, but Esch still sat there staring at it, sat and thought. It was not by any means clear, but Huguenau might be right all the same about one's feelings. Nevertheless it looked as if there was some hope of order at last. The world was divided into good and evil, debit and credit, black and white, and even if a book-keeping error should happen to creep in, then it must be expunged, and it would be expunged. Esch had grown calmer. Peacefully his hands rested on his knees, he sat placidly staring through closed eyelids at the door, saw through closed lids the whole room, which now strangely transformed itself into a landscape—or was it a picture postcard?—and was like a kiosk among green trees, the trees of the Schlossberg at Baden-weiler; he saw the Major's face, and it was the face of a greater and higher being. And Esch sat for so long that at last, filled with wonder, he knew no longer where he had got to, and only with an effort did he manage to return to his reading. True, he could have recited the article by heart, word for word, yet he forced himself to read on, and now he knew once more what side he belonged to in this world. For the reflections which the Major had addressed to the German people had made an impression on one part of the German nation, even if it was not a very important part; they had made an impression on Herr Esch.

CHAPTER XXXVI

Four women were scrubbing the hospital ward.

Surgeon-Major Kühlenbeck entered and looked at them for a moment.

" Well, how are things with you? "

" What can you expect, Herr Surgeon-Major . . . ? "

The women sighed, then they went on scrubbing again.

One of them raised her head:

" My man's coming home on leave next week."

" Great, Tielden . . . the bed will fairly bounce then."

Frau Tielden blushed under her brown leathery skin. The others laughed heartily. And Frau Tielden laughed with them.

All at once a noise, somewhat like a bark, was heard from one of the beds. It was not so much a bark, however, as a breathless, heavy and very painful expulsion of something that was scarcely a sound and came from far within.

Gödicke of the Landwehr sat up in his bed; his features were painfully distorted, and it was he who had laughed in such a strange fashion.

It was the first sound that had been got out of him ever since his arrival in the hospital (if one does not take into account his first whimperings).

" A lewd rascal," said Surgeon-Major Kühlenbeck, " why, he can laugh! "

CHAPTER XXXVII

STORY OF THE SALVATION ARMY GIRL IN BERLIN (5)

The sickly spring-time of an adamant law,
The sickly spring-time of a Jewish bride,
The sickly din of the city, that yet tongue-tied
Lies trapped and netted in invisible snares,
A summer day of stone no warmth can thaw,
A sickly sky looks down on asphalt squares,
On streets like chasms, on a stony waste that wears
Out like a scabby sore the earth's grey hide.
O city of lying light, O city of lying prayers,
The penitent desires no verdant tree,
He seeks but penitential caves, where he
Implores the Law to yield him holiness
Uprising like a fountain from deep thought,
From holy words, from doubts, from fear distraught.
It is the city of exiles, of penitents in distress,
The city of the people chosen by God,
A race that breeds for duty, passionless,
And only counts its sons, whose old men nod

Praying at windows, a monk-bearded race
Bound ever to its God with fasts and thongs,
The while its women knead the unleavened bread
And votive oil flames raise their pallid tongues:
A race that marries to beget in bed
The pallid youth with the actor's beard and face,
The youthful Jacob to whom angels bend,
Whom truth guides on a journey that will end
At that far well by which the angels sank,
At that far well where Rachel's wethers drank.
Grey city, the pallid nomads' halting-place
Upon their road to Zion, their way to God,
A godless city in an invisible net,
A vacant mass of stone with curses laden
And sorrow; where the Salvation Army maiden
Tinkles her tambourine, so that the sinner yet
May find the true way and return to grace,
The way to Zion, to love's holy place.—
In this town of Berlin, in these spring days
Did Nuchem Sussin meet the girl Marie,
And for a while they felt a sweet amaze
And each fell down in spirit on one knee;
The uplifted hand of Fate they did not see,
Zion they saw; their hearts were filled with praise.

CHAPTER XXXVIII

For almost two years Heinrich Wendling had not been home on leave.
Yet in spite of this Hanna was surprised, as surprised as though some
irrational and incomprehensible event had burst in upon her, when the
letter arrived in which he announced his homecoming. The journey
from Salonika would take six days at least, probably even longer, but
in any case it was only a matter of days. Hanna dreaded his arrival as
though she had a secret lover to conceal from him. Every day's delay
was to her like an act of grace, yet every evening she went through
her night toilet even more scrupulously than usual, and she lay in bed
each morning too even longer than usual, waiting, dreading lest the
returning wanderer might take possession of her immediately, filthy and

unshaven as he was. And even though she felt she should be ashamed of such fancies, and for that very reason hoped that some offensive or other accident might cancel his leave, yet she felt as well the presence of a still stronger, a very strange hope that lurked somewhere, a vague presentiment that she did not want to acknowledge and indeed did not acknowledge, and which was like one's sensation before a grave operation: one had to submit to it in order to be protected from something fatal towards which one was involuntarily striving; it was like a last terrifying refuge, and dark as it was, yet it rescued one from a profounder darkness. To dismiss as masochism such an attitude of hopeful dread and terrified waiting would be to leave unexplored all but the mere surface of the spirit. And the only explanation that Hanna could find for her state, in so far as she was aware of it at all, was very like the fatuous conviction of old women that marriage is the sole means of putting an end once and for all to the various sufferings of anæmic girls. No, she could not dare to examine it more closely, it was a tangle into which she had no wish to penetrate, and though with one part of her she expected that as soon as Heinrich came in everything would be the same again, quite naturally, yet she divined with equal intensity that never would things be the same again.

Summer had really come at last. " Rose Cottage " did honour to its name, although in deference to the times vegetables were cultivated rather than flowers, and although the semi-invalid jobbing gardener was incapable of attending properly to his business. But the crimson ramblers did not allow even the war to restrain them and had climbed up to the cherubs at each side of the door; the beds of peonies were pink and white, and the rows of heliotrope and stock on the border of the lawn were in full blossom. In front of the house the green landscape stretched peacefully, the spacious sweep of the valley held one's gaze and carried it to the edge of the woods; the forester's house, exposed to the eye in winter so that every one of its windows could be seen, was again smothered in green; the vineyards too had greened over, the woods lay dark, darker than ever now that black clouds were approaching from the mountains.

In the afternoon Hanna had taken her chair outside. She lay back in it beneath the chestnut-trees and gazed at the advancing clouds, whose shadows marched across the fields, transforming the bright clear green into a dark and strangely restful greenish violet; as the shadow stretched across the garden and the air suddenly became cool and cellarlike, the flowers, until now sealed up by the heat, began all at once to exhale their perfumes as though their breath had been released. Or perhaps it was the sudden coolness that now gave Hanna leisure to feel their scent; yet it was so sudden, so unique, so vehement, this breaking wave of sweet perfume, cool and magical as an evening in a southern garden, as the falling dusk on the rocky beach of a Tyrrhenian sea. So the earth lay on the shore of a sea of cloud that broke in waves of rain, the soft, thick rain of thunder-showers, and Hanna, standing at the open veranda door, could smell the south; and even though she breathed in almost greedily the soft humidity that felt so cool and fresh in her nostrils, yet with the memory of that southern fragrance there had also been wafted to her the fear which she had felt for the first time during her honeymoon, standing on the seashore one rainy evening in Sicily; the hotel lay behind her, the flowers in the hotel garden perfumed the air, and she did not know who the strange man was that stood beside her —he was called Dr Wendling.

She started; the gardener had hurried across the path to put the garden implements in a place of safety out of the rain; she started, because she could not help thinking that it was a burglar who had broken in, although she knew quite well what the man was about. If Walter had not come out to her she would have fled into the house and locked the door. Walter had seated himself on the door-step; he stretched out his naked legs into the rain and occupied himself in cautiously loosening the dried crust of a scar on his knee, afterwards contentedly stroking the new pink skin. Hanna too sat down on the door-step; she clasped her hands round her legs, her beautiful slender legs—she too wore no stockings when she was in the house or the garden—and her smooth shins felt cool to the touch.

By now the rain had beaten down the scent of the flowers which it had awakened at first, and the air smelt only of moist earth. The brown-flecked tiled roof of the garden-house gleamed with wet, and when the gardener once more trudged down the path the gravel no longer crunched dryly under his feet, but rattled its wet and separate pebbles. Hanna put her arm round her son's shoulders,—why couldn't they remain always sitting like this, calmly at rest in a cool and cleanly world? only a very little of her fear was left. All the same she said: " If there's more thunder like this during the night, Walter, you can come in beside me."

CHAPTER XXXIX

When Surgeon-Major Kühlenbeck and Dr Kessel entered the dining-room of the hotel, the Major was already sitting at his accustomed place. He was reading the *Cologne News*, which had just arrived. The two gentlemen said good-evening, and the Major rose and invited them to sit at his table.

The Surgeon-Major most tactlessly referred to the newspaper:

" Are we to have the pleasure, Herr Major, of reading you in other papers too? "

The Major simply shook his head, handed the paper across the table, and indicating the column containing the reports from the Front said: " Bad news."

Dr Kühlenbeck glanced over the reports:

" Really no worse than usual, Herr Major."

The Major looked up questioningly.

" Herr Major, all news is bad except one thing, and that is—peace."

" You're right there," said the Major, " but it must be an honourable peace."

" Right," said Kühlenbeck, lifting his glass, " then here's to peace."

The other two gentlemen clinked glasses with him and the Major repeated again:

" To an honourable peace . . . otherwise what should all those sacrifices have been made for? " As though he wanted to say something more, he still held his glass in his hand but remained silent; at last, however, he shook off his immobility and said: " Honour is by no means a mere convention . . . once upon a time poison-gas would have been rejected as a weapon of warfare."

The gentlemen made no reply, and went on drinking their wine.

Then Dr Kessel said:

" What's the good of all those beautiful theories about war-time food? . . . When I come home at night I can scarcely stand on my legs; for a man well on in years the food simply isn't enough."

Kühlenbeck said:

" You're a defeatist, Kessel: it's been demonstrated that diabetes has been reduced to a minimum, and with carcinoma it seems to be the same . . . it's only your personal misfortune that you're not a diabetic . . .

besides, my dear chap, if you do feel pains in your legs . . . we're none of us getting younger."

Major von Pasenow said:

" Honour isn't mere inertia of feeling."

" I don't quite understand, Herr Major," said Dr Kühlenbeck.

The Major gazed into vacancy:

" Oh, it was nothing . . . as you know . . . my son fell at Verdun . . . he would be twenty-eight now. . . ."

" But he wasn't your only son, Herr Major ? "

The Major did not reply at once, it may be that he regarded the question as an indiscretion. Finally he said:

" Yes, there's my younger son . . . and the two girls . . . the boy will soon be called up too . . . one must render unto Cæsar the things that are Cæsar's . . ." he stopped, then he went on: " You see, the cause of all the evil is that we don't render to God the things that are God's."

Dr Kühlenbeck said:

" We don't even render to human beings the things that are theirs . . . it seems to me we should begin with that first."

" God first," said Major von Pasenow.

Kühlenbeck threw out his chin; his dark grey beard jutted out into the air:

" We doctors are blatant materialists, I'm afraid."

The Major said deprecatingly:

" You mustn't say that."

Dr Kessel too dissented; a true doctor was always an idealist. Kühlenbeck laughed:

" It's true, I forgot your panel patients."

After a while Dr Kessel said:

" As soon as I have half a chance I'll take up my chamber music again."

And the Major remarked that his wife too loved her playing. He thought for a little and then he added: " Spohr, an excellent composer."

CHAPTER XL

Since it had been rumoured that Gödicke had laughed, his room-mates had tried everything possible to make him laugh again. The grossest stories were dished up to him, and as he lay in bed hardly anyone passed without hopefully shaking the bed until it bounced up and down. But it was of no avail. Gödicke did not laugh again. He remained dumb.

Until one day Sister Carla brought him a postcard: " Gödicke, your wife has written to you . . ." Gödicke did not stir, " I'll read it to you." And Sister Carla read out to him that his faithful wife had heard nothing from him now for a long time, that she and the children were well, and that they all hoped he would soon be coming back. " I'll answer it for you," said Sister Carla. Gödicke gave not a sign of comprehension, and one might have thought that he had really understood nothing. And probably he would actually have succeeded in concealing from any eye-witness the tempest in his soul, that tempest which jumbled together the constituents of his ego and in rapid succession heaved them to the surface to submerge them just as rapidly again in the dark waves, he might have succeeded in calming the storm and gradually laying it altogether, had not the practical joker of the ward, Josef Settler the dragoon, passed by at that moment and as usual caught hold of the foot of the bed to make it oscillate a little. At that Gödicke of the Landwehr gave a cry which by no means resembled the laugh that was expected of him and that he was really under an obligation to provide; he gave an angry and heavy cry, sat up, by no means so slowly and laboriously as he was accustomed to do, and he snatched the postcard from Sister Carla, and he tore the postcard to pieces. Then he sank back, for the violent move-ment had started his pains again, and clasped his abdomen with his hands.

So there he lay looking up at the roof, and tried to reinstate a minimum of order among his thoughts. He was conscious of having acted rightly; he had with full justification turned away the intruder. That this intruder was the servant-girl Anna Lamprecht with her three children was almost immaterial, and could be quickly forgotten again. Indeed he was very glad that the Gödicke who had made an honest woman of the servant-girl Lamprecht had been so expeditiously called to order and relegated to his place behind the dark barrier,—there he would have to wait until he was summoned. Nevertheless with that the matter was not settled; an intruder who comes once may come again, even though he is not summoned, and once one door is opened, then every other door may fly open of itself. With terror he felt, though he could not have formulated it, that this intrusion into one part of his soul had affected all the other parts by sympathy, indeed that through it they were all being changed. It was like a humming in his ears, a humming of the soul, a humming of the ego that hummed so violently that he could feel it in all his body; but it was also as though a clod of earth had been pushed under one's tongue, a stifling clod that deranged all one's thoughts. Or perhaps it was something else, but in any case it was something beyond one's power, something before which one felt helpless. It was as though one wanted to spread the mortar before laying a brick, and the mortar hardened on the trowel. It was as though a foreman were there driving one to work at an illegal and impossible speed, and causing the bricks to be piled with furious haste on the scaffolding, so that they towered in great heaps and could not be worked off. The scaffolding must collapse if one did not at once put the winch and the concrete-mixing machine out of action to stop the whole business. Best of all if one's eyes could grow together again and one's ears be sealed again: the man Gödicke must see nothing, hear nothing, eat nothing. If the pain were not so bad now he would go into the garden and fetch a handful of earth to stop up all the holes. And while he clasped his sore abdomen, from which his children had issued, while he pressed his hands down on it as though never again must anything issue from him, while he clenched his teeth and bit his lips so that not even a sigh of pain might escape them, it seemed to him that thus his powers were increased, and that those waxing powers must raise the scaffolding to ever higher and airier heights, that he himself was omnipresent on every level and storey of that scaffolding, and that at last he would manage to stand quite alone on the topmost storey, at the summit of the scaffolding; that he would be able to stand there, dare to stand there, released from all pain, singing as he had always sung when he was up aloft. The carpenters would be working beneath him, hammering and driving in nails, and he would spit down, as he had always spat, spit down in a wide arc over them, and where the spittle struck and rebounded trees would grow up, which, no matter how high they grew, would never reach the height where he stood.

When Sister Carla came with the washing basin and the towels, he was lying peacefully, and peacefully too let himself be packed into the compresses. For two whole days he again refused meat and drink. And then an incident happened that made him begin to speak.

CHAPTER XLI

STORY OF THE SALVATION ARMY GIRL IN BERLIN (6)

To my own surprise I had again begun to occupy myself with my thesis on the disintegration of values. Although I hardly ever left the house, my work proceeded but slowly. Nuchem Sussin often came to see me, seating himself on the grey tails of his frock-coat. He never unbuttoned it; it was probably a kind of shame that prevented him. I often asked myself how these people could put any trust in Dr Litwak, whose short jacket flouted all their prejudices. Until I came to the conclusion that the walking-stick he carried before him might represent a sort of substitute for his lack of coat-tails. But that, of course, was a mere assumption.

It took me a long time to find out what Sussin was really after. When he seated himself he never neglected to say " With your kind permission," and after a short embarrassed silence he would then bring up some juristic problem: whether the Government was empowered to confiscate food or fat that was already in one's house or on one's plate; whether the maintenance allowance received by soldiers' wives could be applied to taking out a life insurance policy . . . one simply could not tell what he was trying to get at, he seemed to be pulling wires at random, and yet one had the feeling that out of all this real problems were emerging, or that in his mind a juridical landscape lay outspread, which one was challenged to survey through these artificial and distorted lenses.

Even when he took up a book and held it in front of his shortsighted eyes, he seemed to be reading quite other things out of it. He had an immeasurable respect for books, but he could laugh uproariously over a few lines of Kant, and was astonished when I did not join in. So it seemed to him an extraordinarily good joke when he found this maxim while looking over Hegel: *The principle of magic consists in this, that the connection between the means and the effect shall not be recognized.* He certainly despised me for not seeing the funny side of things as he did, and strangely enough I was inclined to ascribe to him a truer, if also more complicated, insight than I myself possessed. In any case it was only at things such as these that I had ever seen him laugh.

And he had some feeling for music. A much-beribboned lute hung in my room. I imagine that it had belonged to my landlady's son: he was either in captivity or missing. Every time he came Sussin begged me to "play something" and would not believe me when I said I couldn't. He thought I was too shy. But by way of this he managed at last to reach his real theme:

"Have you ever heard the people playing . . . the ones in uniform? . . . very beautiful."

He meant the Salvation Army, and smiled guiltily at my guessing it.

"I'm going this evening to listen. Will you come too?"

CHAPTER XLII

Huguenau's delight in the paper had not lasted long, not even for a whole month. It was still June, and Huguenau was sick of the whole business. In his first enthusiasm he had succeeded in bringing off the great idea of the special number and the Major's leading article; but as nothing fresh had immediately occurred to him he had lost interest. It was as though he had flung a toy into the corner; he no longer liked it. And even although this dislike perhaps masked an intuition that one really could not make a great newspaper out of a provincial rag, yet he was merely aware of boredom, he simply did not want to hear anything more about it, and felt the independent reality of the newspaper routine as an interference with himself. If at one time he could not get quickly enough to his work, he now loved to linger in bed, dawdled unconscionably over his breakfast, and only with repugnance could drag himself to the backyard where the office was; indeed quite often it happened that he got no farther than the kitchen, where he discussed the price of food with Frau Esch. And if he finally did reach the editorial office, generally he clattered down the steps again in a little while and stole in to look at the printing-press.

Marguerite was playing in the garden. Huguenau shouted across the courtyard to her: "Marguerite, I'm in the printing-shed."

The child came running, and they went in together. "'Morning," said Huguenau curtly, for since Lindner and the assistant compositor had become his subordinates he had set himself to be as curt as possible with them. The two men, however, did not seem to worry much about that, and he had once more the feeling that they looked down on him as a man who knew nothing about machines. At present they were working in the case-room, and Huguenau, with the child hanging on to his hand, did his best to look over their shoulders with the air of an expert, but was relieved when he was out of the case-room again and back beside his printing-press.

For he still loved the printing-press. A man who all his life has sold commodities produced by machines, but for whom factories and the possessors of machines remain in a class above him, a class he can never attain, such a man will assuredly regard it as a wonderful experience if he himself suddenly becomes the possessor of a machine; and it may well be that there will dawn in him that affectionate attitude to machines which one almost always finds in boys and in young races, an attitude that glorifies the machine and projects it into the exalted and free plane of their own desires and of mighty and heroic deeds. For hours the boy can watch the locomotive in the station, deeply content that it should shunt the trucks from one line to another; and for hours Wilhelm Huguenau could sit before his printing-press and watch it affectionately with the serious and vacant gaze of a boy behind his glasses, quite satisfied because it was in motion, because it ate up paper and gave it out again. And the ardour of his love for that living entity filled his being so completely that it left room neither for ambition nor even for any desire to understand that incomprehensible and marvellous mechanical function; admiringly and tenderly, almost timidly, he accepted it as it was.

Marguerite had crawled up on to the paper bales, and Huguenau sat on the rough bench which stood beside them. He gazed at the machine, gazed at the child. The machine was his property, it belonged to him, the child belonged to Esch. For a while they tossed to each other a sheet of paper rolled into a ball; then Huguenau grew tired of the game, he crossed his legs, wiped his glasses, and said:

" Something more could be made out of the advertising side."

The child went on playing with the paper ball.

Huguenau continued:

" It's worse even than I imagined. The paper was too dear at the price . . . all the same, we own the press; you like the printing-press, don't you? "

" Yes, let's play at printing-presses, Uncle Huguenau! "

Marguerite came down from her paper bales and climbed on to his knee. Then they took each other by the arms, threw their bodies rhythmically backwards and forwards, and punctuated the motion with: " Pum, pum."

Huguenau put on the brake. Marguerite remained sitting stridelegs on his knees. Huguenau was a little short of breath:

"The paper was too dear . . . if things go well, we'll bring the circulation up to four hundred . . . but if we can get two pages of advertisements it will pay and we'll grow rich. Won't we, Marguerite?"

Marguerite jumped up and down on his knee, and Huguenau set her in brisk trotting motion; she laughed, for it made her words come in jerks:

"Yes, you'll get rich, you'll get rich."

"Are you glad, Marguerite?"

"Then you'll give me lots of money."

"Oho?"

"Lots of money."

"I tell you what, Marguerite, we'll hire some boys, they'll collect the advertisements . . . in the villages . . . all over the place. For a commission."

The child nodded gravely.

"I've thought it all out already, marriage announcements, sales, and so forth and so forth . . . just fetch the lay-outs from Herr Lindner," and he shouted across to the case-room: "Lindner, the advertisement lay-outs."

The child ran over and brought them back.

"Look here, we'll give our agents a copy of these . . . you'll see what a draw that'll be." He had taken her on his knee again and they studied the lay-outs together. Then Huguenau said:

"So, you want the money so as to run away from them . . . where do you want to go?"

Marguerite shrugged her shoulders:

"Anywhere."

Huguenau considered:

"If you go through the Eifel country you'll come to Belgium. There's good people there."

Marguerite asked:

"Will you come too?"

"Perhaps . . . yes, perhaps later."

"When later?"

She snuggled against him, but Huguenau said suddenly and brusquely: "That's enough," lifted her up and set her on the press. Strangely clear there rose up again the picture of that murderer, that violator of children chained to his pallet, and it disturbed him. " Everything in its time," he said, contemplating the girl, who sat, slender and animated, on the solid inanimate machine, and yet in some way belonged to it. If the machine were set in motion it would swallow up Marguerite just as it did the paper, and he made quite certain that the belt was not on. Almost fearfully he repeated: " Everything in its time, the time will come all right . . . he doesn't disturb us here at any rate."

And while he was wondering what it was that the time would come for, he remembered Esch with his big teeth, that lean insufferable pedagogue who would never leave him in peace and was always insisting on the terms of the contract and trying to push editorial duties upon him,—insisting on the terms of the contract and demanding that he should sit there all day and work, probably expecting him, too, to put on a blue overall. Stand on his rights, the fellow could do that, but as for ideas, he hadn't a single one! And now Huguenau was filled with extraordinary satisfaction at the thought that his schoolmaster had not once yet succeeded in forcing him to work.

As he folded up the advertisement lay-outs he said:

" We'll pay out the schoolmaster yet, Marguerite—what do you say? "

" Lift me down," said the child.

Huguenau went up to the printing-press, but when the little girl put her arm round his neck he remained standing for a moment in silent reverie, for now he had found what he had been looking for: in secret he was actually set above the schoolmaster! for he had himself offered to exercise a surveillance over the dangerous fellow, and the Major had approved of it! It dawned on Huguenau that he had been led here simply in order to find his real goal in life, and that his life would be completely fulfilled if he could succeed in completely unmasking Herr Esch's secret machinations. Yes, that was it, and Huguenau gave Marguerite a hearty kiss on her cheek that was smeared with printing-ink.

But Herr Esch sat upstairs in the editorial office, relieved that he could continue his labours and not give them up to Huguenau. For among other things he was convinced that Huguenau would never be capable of running the paper on the lines laid down by the Major, and he was bent on doing so himself, for in that way he might serve the Major and the good cause.

CHAPTER XLIII

Dr Flurschütz was examining Jaretzki's arm stump in the operating-theatre:

" Looks splendid . . . the chief will be sending you off one of these days . . . if you agree to it . . . to a convalescent home."

" Of course I agree to it; high time one was out of this."

" I think so too, or we'll have you on our hands next with delirium tremens."

" Well, what is there to do but drink? . . . it's here that I really learned to do it."

" Didn't you ever drink before? "

" No . . . well, a little, just like everybody else. . . . I was in the polytechnic in Brunswick, you know . . . where did you get your degree? "

" Erlangen."

" Oh well, you must have drunk a bit in your time too . . . one always does in small towns . . . and what with sitting about as one has to here, it comes back of itself . . ." Flurschütz was still probing and fingering the arm stump " . . . look there, that one bad spot simply won't heal . . . how about my artificial arm? "

" Been ordered . . . we shan't send you off without the arm."

" Right, but see that it comes soon . . . if you hadn't your work to do here, you would start drinking again too."

" Couldn't say . . . I might find something else to do . . . really, I've never seen you with a book yet, Jaretzki."

" Look here, tell me honestly: do you actually read all those piles of books that you keep lying about in your room? "

" Yes."

" Extraordinary . . . and has that any meaning or object? "

" Not the slightest."

" That's a relief . . . look here, Dr Flurschütz . . . all right, I'll keep still . . . you've dispatched a good few people in your time, that's part of your job of course, but when one has deliberately done in a few . . . well it seems to me one hasn't any need to look into a book for all the rest of one's life . . . it's a sort of feeling I've got . . . one has achieved everything . . . and that's the reason too why the war will never end. . . ."

" A daring speculation, Jaretzki; what have you been drinking to-day? "

" I'm as sober as a new-born babe. . . ."

" Well, that's finished . . . we'll give the artificial arm a trial in a fortnight at latest . . . then you must really go into one of those schools where they teach you to use it . . . you want to draw, don't you? "

" Yes, I suppose so, only I simply can't imagine it to myself."

" And what about the General Electric? "

" Oh, very well, let it be the artificial-arm school . . . sometimes it seems to me that you snicked off the thing quite unnecessarily . . . simply out of a sense of justice, so to speak, because I once flung a hand-grenade between a Frenchman's legs. . . ."

Flurschütz looked at him attentively:

" I say, Jaretzki, pull yourself together. You're quite alarming . . . how many have you really had to-day? "

" Nothing worth speaking of . . . besides I'm really grateful to you for your sense of justice, and the operation was very well done . . . I feel on much better terms with the world now . . . on bloody good terms, every-thing settled . . . and the General Electric's simply pining for my arrival."

" Seriously, Jaretzki, you should go there."

" But I just want to tell you . . . it was the wrong arm you took . . . this one here," Jaretzki tapped with two fingers on the plate-glass cover of the instrument-case, " this one here was the one I flung the hand-grenade with . . . probably that's why I feel it hanging from my shoulder like a dead weight."

" That will soon be all right, Jaretzki."

" Oh, everything's all right as it is."

CHAPTER XLIV

DISINTEGRATION OF VALUES (6)

The logic of the soldier demands that he shall throw a hand-grenade between the legs of his enemy:

the logic of the army demands in general that all military resources shall be exploited with the utmost rigour and severity, resulting, if necessary, in the extermination of peoples, the demolition of cathedrals, the bombardment of hospitals and operating-theatres:

the logic of the business man demands that all commercial resources shall be exploited with the utmost rigour and efficiency to bring about the destruction of all competition and the sole domination of his own business, whether that be a trading house or a factory or a company or other economic body:

the logic of the painter demands that the principles of painting shall be followed to their conclusions with the utmost rigour and thoroughness, at the peril of producing pictures which are completely esoteric, and comprehensible only by those who produce them:

the logic of the revolutionist demands that the revolutionary impulse shall be pursued with the utmost rigour and thoroughness for the achievement of a revolution as an end in itself, as, indeed, the logic of politicians in general demands that they shall obtain an absolute dictatorship for their political aims:

the logic of the bourgeois climber demands that the watchword "enrichissez-vous" shall be followed with the most absolute and uncompromising rigour:

in this fashion, in this absolute devotion to logical rigour, the Western world has won its achievements,—and with the same thoroughness, the absolute thoroughness that abrogates itself, must it eventually advance *ad absurdum*:

war is war, *l'art pour l'art*, in politics there's no room for compunction, business is business,—all these signify the same thing, all these appertain to the same aggressive and radical spirit, informed by that uncanny, I might almost say that metaphysical, lack of consideration for consequences, that ruthless logic directed on the object and on the object alone, which looks neither to the right nor to the left; and this, all this, is the style of thinking that characterizes our age.

One cannot escape from this brutal and aggressive logic that exhibits itself in all the values and non-values of our age, not even by withdrawing into the solitude of a castle or of a Jewish dwelling; yet a man who shrinks from knowledge, that is to say, a romantic, a man who must have a bounded world, a closed system of values, and who seeks in the past the completeness he longs for, such a man has good reason for turning to the Middle Ages. For the Middle Ages possessed the ideal centre of values that he requires, possessed a supreme value to which all other values were subordinate: the belief in the Christian God. Cosmogony was as dependent on that central value (more, it could be scholastically deduced from it) as man himself; man with all his activities formed a part of the whole world-order which was merely the reflected image of an ecclesiastical hierarchy, the closed and finite symbol of an eternal and infinite harmony. The dictum " Business is business " was not permitted to the medieval merchant, competitive struggle being forbidden to him; the medieval artist knew nothing of *l'art pour l'art*, but only that he must serve his faith; medieval warfare claimed absolute authority only when it was waged in the service of the faith. It was a world reposing on faith, a final not a causal world, a world founded on being, not on becoming; and its social structure, its art, the sentiments that bound it together, in short, its whole system of values, was subordinated to the all-embracing living value of the faith: the faith was the point of plausibility in which every line of inquiry ended, the faith was what enforced logic and gave it that specific colouring, that style-creating impulse, which expresses itself not only in a certain style of thinking, but continues to shape a style characterizing the whole epoch for so long as the faith survives.

But thought dared to take the step from monotheism into the abstract, and God, the personal God made visible in the finite infinity of the Trinity, became an entity whose name could no longer be spoken and whose image could no longer be fashioned, an entity that ascended into the infinite neutrality of the Absolute and there was lost to sight in the dread vastness of Being, no longer immanent but beyond the reach of man.

In the violence of this revolution caused by the radical application, one might even say by the unleashing, of logic, in this removal of the point of plausibility to a new plane of the infinite, in this withdrawal of faith from concrete life, the simple sufficiency of existence was also destroyed. The style-creating force seems to vanish from concrete expression at this point, and beside the mass of the Kantian structure and the flames of revolution all that we find is rococo and an Empire degenerated overnight into Biedermeyer. For even although the Empire, and shortly after it the romantic movement, recognizing the discrepancy between this spiritual revolution and the existing forms of concrete expression, looked to the past for help, calling in the antique and the Gothic, yet the new development could not be checked: immanent Being had been analysed into pure function, the physical world itself had been analysed into such abstraction that two generations later even Space could be eliminated from it; the decision for pure abstraction was already irrevocable. And the infinite remoteness, the inaccessible noumenal remoteness of that point towards which all lines of inquiry and chains of probability were now destined to strive, rendered impossible at one stroke the binding of all single value-systems to a central value; the abstract ruthlessly invaded the logic of every single value-making activity, stripping its content bare, and not only forbade it to deviate at all from the form determined by its function, insisting on purely functional structure whether in architecture or in any other constructive activity, but has also radicalized so thoroughly the single value-systems that these, being thrown back on themselves and referred to the Absolute, have separated from one another, now run parallel to each other, and, since they can no longer combine in the service of a supreme value, claim equality one with the other: like strangers they exist side by side, an economic value-system of " good business " next to an æsthetic one of *l'art pour l'art*, a military code of values side by side with a technical or an athletic, each autonomous, each " in and for itself," each " unfettered " in its autonomy, each resolved to push home with radical thoroughness the final conclusions of its logic and to break its own record. And woe to the others, if in this conflict of systems that precariously maintain an equilibrium one should gain the preponderance and overtop all the rest, as the military system does in war, or as the economic system is now doing, a system to which even war is subordinate,—woe to the others! For the triumphant system will embrace the whole of the world, it will overwhelm all other values and exterminate them as a cloud of locusts lays waste a field.

But man, who was once the image of God, the mirror of a universal value created by himself, man has fallen from his former estate: he may still have some dim remembrance of his one-time security, he may still ask himself what is this superimposed logic that has perverted his life; yet he is driven out into the horror of the infinite, and, no matter how he shudders at the prospect, no matter how romantically and sentimentally he may yearn to return to the fold of faith, he is helplessly caught in the mechanism of the autonomous value-systems, and can do nothing but submit himself to the particular value that has become his profession, he can do nothing but become a function of that value—a specialist, eaten up by the radical logic of the value into whose jaws he has fallen.

CHAPTER XLV

Huguenau had arranged with Frau Esch that she should give him his midday meal every day. That suited his convenience in all sorts of ways, and Frau Esch did her best for him, she had to be given credit for that.

One day when he went up for his dinner, he found Esch sitting at the newly laid table absorbed in a black-bound book. Huguenau looked inquisitively over his shoulder and recognized the woodcuts of a Bible. As he seldom allowed himself to be surprised at anything, except perhaps when someone overreached him in business, and that happened rarely enough, he merely said: " Aha! " and waited for his food to be served up.

Frau Esch, broad-hipped, sexless, dowdy, passed through the room; her indeterminately fair hair was caught untidily in a knot. But in passing she touched her husband's bony shoulder with an uncalled-for gesture, and Huguenau suddenly had the feeling that of nights she must know very well how to avail herself of her conjugal state. The thought was unpleasant, and so he asked:

" Well, Esch, are you preparing to go into a monastery? "

Esch glanced up from his book:

" That's just the question, whether any escape is permissible," adding with his accustomed rudeness, " but you don't understand that."

Frau Esch brought in the soup, and Huguenau's disagreeable thoughts would not leave him. The two of them lived together like lovers, without desiring children, and it was probably to cloak this that they wanted to adopt the girl Marguerite. Actually he was sitting on the chair where their son should have been. So with simple guile he took up the joke again and told Frau Esch that her husband was going into a monastery. Whereupon Frau Esch asked whether it was true that in all the monasteries there were suspicious goings-on among the monks. And she laughed over some dissolute fancy that rose in her mind. But then her eyes turned slowly and suspiciously towards her husband:

" Yes, you're capable of anything."

This was obviously painful to Herr Esch; Huguenau noted that he flushed and returned her glance with anger. Nevertheless, resolved not to lose his prestige in front of his wife but rather to enhance it, Esch declared that after all it was simply a matter of habit, but that everybody knew well enough that even in a monkery there wasn't the slightest need to take refuge in these practices, on the contrary, he flattered himself that even if he wore a cowl he would be able to give a good account of himself.

Frau Esch had stiffened into expressionless gravity. She mechanically patted her hair to rights and said at last:

" Is the soup good, Herr Huguenau ? "

" Splendid," said Huguenau, supping it up.

" Would you like another plateful ? " Frau Esch sighed. " I've nothing very grand to follow to-day in any case, only a tart."

She nodded in satisfaction when he let his plate be filled again. But meanwhile Huguenau stuck to his theme: apparently Herr Esch was already sick of the war rations; there were no meat and flour cards in the monasteries, one could still live there as if it were peace-time; but considering how much land the priests owned that wasn't surprising. They still stuffed their bellies full in these places. When he was in Maulbronn an employee of the monastery had told him . . .

Esch interrupted him: if the world became really free again, there would be no need for anyone to eat prison fare. . . .

" Turnips and cabbages," said Frau Esch.

" But not fresh cabbage," said Huguenau, " what do you call being really free ? "

Esch said:

" The freedom of a Christian soul."

" By all means," said Huguenau, " but I would like to know what that has to do with cabbage."

Esch seized the Bible:

" My house shall be called the house of prayer; but ye have made it a den of murderers."

" Hm, and murderers are given stale cabbage," grinned Huguenau; then he became serious: " So you think the war is a kind of murder, murder with robbery in a way, as the Socialists say."

Esch paid no attention to him; he went on turning over the leaves:

" And besides it's stated in Chronicles second book . . . sixth chapter, eighth verse . . . here it is: ' Forasmuch as it was in thine heart to build an house for my name, thou didst well in that it was in thine heart: Notwithstanding thou shalt not build the house; but thy son which shall come forth out of thy loins, he shall build the house for my name.' " Esch's face had grown red: " That's a very important passage."

" It may be," said Huguenau, " but why? "

" Murder and counter-murder . . . many must sacrifice themselves that the Redeemer may be born, the son who shall build the house."

Huguenau asked cautiously:

" Do you mean the future Socialist State? "

" Trade unions alone can't do it."

" I see . . . that's from the Major's article, I suppose? "

" No, that's in the Bible, only nobody has gathered its meaning yet."

Huguenau threatened Esch with an upraised finger:

" You're a sly dog, Esch . . . and you fancy that the old Major will never notice what you're up to now under cover of the Bible? "

" What's that? "

" Why, communistic propaganda."

Esch grinned, showing his strong yellow teeth:

" You're an idiot."

" It's easy to be rude . . . what's your idea of the future state, then? "

Esch thought hard:

" It's impossible to make you understand anything . . . but one thing I can tell you: when people begin again to understand how to read the Bible, then there won't be any more need of Communism or Socialism . . . and there won't be any French Republic or German Emperor either."

" Well, but that's plain revolution . . . just tell that to the Major."

" I'd tell him, too, without any hesitation."

" He'll be delighted to hear it, no doubt . . . and what will happen next, after you've got rid of the Emperor? "

Esch said:

" The Redeemer will reign over all men."

Huguenau winked across at Frau Esch:

" Your son, do you mean? "

Esch too gazed at his wife: it looked almost as if he were startled:

" My son? "

" We have no children," said Frau Esch.

" But you said that your son would build the house," Huguenau grinned.

That, however, was too much for Esch:

" You're blaspheming, sir . . . you're so dense that you can't help blaspheming or twisting one's words. . . ."

" He doesn't mean it like that," said Frau Esch appeasingly, " the food will grow quite cold if you two quarrel."

Esch sat in silence and accepted his portion of tart.

" Oh, I've often sat at table with a silent parson," said Huguenau.

Esch still made no reply, and Huguenau challenged him again:

" Well, what about this reign of the Redeemer, then ? "

Frau Esch assumed an expectant look:

" Tell him."

" It's a symbol," growled Esch.

" Interesting," said Huguenau, " do you mean the priests are to reign ? "

" God in Heaven . . . it's hopeless to get anything into your head . . . the sovereignty of the Church is something you never heard of, I suppose . . . and yet you call yourself an editor."

Now Huguenau on his side was honestly indignant:

" So that's what your communism is . . . if that's what it really is . . . you want to hand everything over to the priests. That's why you want to go into a monastery . . . so that the priests may live still better . . . then there won't be even stale cabbage for us . . . to throw the hard-earned money of this company into the maw of these gentry . . . no, I much prefer my honest business to your communism in that case."

" Devil take it, then go about your business! but if you refuse to learn anything you shouldn't persist in wanting to run a paper with your narrow-minded—yes, I repeat, narrow-minded views. It can't be done."

Whereupon Huguenau triumphantly retorted that Esch should be jolly glad to have found him; the advertising side of the paper, as a certain Herr Esch had run it, would have brought the *Herald* to ruin within a year, anybody could prove that in his sleep. And he blinked expectantly at Frau Esch, assuming that she would give him support on this practical question. But Frau Esch was clearing the table and seemed in a softened mood: once more Huguenau was forced to note with disapproval that she had laid her hand on her husband's shoulder; she did not listen to what was said, but simply stated that there were things which you and me, dear Herr Huguenau, find it difficult to grasp. And Esch, rising from the table in apotheosis, closed the discussion:

" You must learn, young man; learn to open your eyes."

Huguenau left the room. Priests' gabble, he thought. *Haïssez les ennemis de la sainte religion.* Oh, yes, merde, blagueurs, he was willing enough to hate, but he refused to have it laid down for him whom he was to hate. D'ailleurs je m'en fous. The clattering sound of washed plates and the stale smell of dishwater accompanied him down the wooden stairs and reminded him with strange vividness of his parents' house and his mother in her kitchen.

CHAPTER XLVI

A few days later the following epistle flowed from Huguenau's pen:

To the TOWN COMMANDANT MAJOR JOACHIM VON PASENOW. *Local.*

Secret Report No. 1.

MOST ESTEEMED HERR MAJOR,

With reference to the conversation which I was privileged to have with you regarding above, I respectfully beg to report that I was present yesterday at a meeting between the said Herr Esch and several suspicious elements. As already mentioned, Herr Esch meets certain subversive elements several times every week in the Palatine Tavern, and yesterday he kindly invited me to accompany him. In addition to a foreman in the paper factory, a certain Liebel, there were present a worker in the aforesaid factory whose name was uttered with intentional indistinctness so that I did not catch it, also two inmates of the military hospital who had been given leave to go out—viz.: a corporal of the name of Bauer and an artilleryman with a Polish name. Somewhat later there arrived a volunteer belonging to a bomb-throwing section. He was called Betge, Betzge, or something resembling that, and was addressed by the aforesaid Herr E. as " Herr Doctor." The conversation soon switched on to the war even without my suggesting it, and a great deal was said especially about the possibility of the war ending. The aforesaid volunteer in particular asserted that the war was nearing its end, because the Austrians were slackening. He had heard from some of our allies passing through in an armoured train that a great munition factory near Vienna had been blown into the air by Italian fliers or by treachery, and that the Austrian fleet had gone over to the enemy after murdering their officers, and that they were only prevented from doing this by German submarines. The artilleryman replied that he could not believe this, because the German sailors too were sick of the war. When asked by me who had informed him of that he said that he had learned it from a girl in the town brothel, who had been told it by a naval paymaster here on leave. After the glorious Skagerrak sea-fight she said, as reported afterwards by the artilleryman, the sailors had refused to obey further orders, claiming also that the men's food was bad. Every one agreed thereupon that an end must be made of the war. In this connection the works foreman maintained that the war brought profit to nobody except the big capitalists, and that the Russians had been the first to recognize this. These subversive ideas were also advocated by E., who drew his support in doing so from the Bible, but from my experiences with Herr E., I think I can say with certainty that he is pursuing hypocritical ends by such means, and that the properties of the Church are a thorn in his flesh. Obviously to serve as a cloak for the plot that is being hatched, he proposed that a Bible Society should be founded, but all the same this was greeted with scorn by most of those present. So as to learn more of him on the one hand, and of the paymaster on the other, we visited the brothel at my suggestion after the two inmates of the hospital and the factory worker had left. I could not gather much information, however, about the paymaster at the brothel, but on the other hand the conduct of Herr E. seemed more and more suspicious to me. For the " Doctor," who beyond doubt is a regular customer of the house, introduced me with the words: " This is a gentleman from the Government, you must treat him gratis," from which I deduced that E. had certain suspicions regarding me, and accordingly had warned his accomplices to be cautious in my presence. Consequently I was unsuccessful in my attempt to induce Herr E. to drop his reserve, and although he drank a great deal at my invitation and my expense, he refused in spite of every encouragement to go upstairs, but remained apparently quite sober, which state he employed to make noisy harangues in the waiting-room on the unChristian and blasphemous nature of such establishments. Only when the volunteer " Doctor " explained to him that these houses were allotted to the army on sanitary grounds by the military authorities, and consequently must be regarded as military institutions, did he give up his antagonistic standpoint, which he once more took up, however, on the way home.

As I have nothing further to report to-day, I beg to send you my profoundest respects and to declare myself eagerly willing for further service.

Yours respectfully,

WILH. HUGUENAU.

P.S.—I beg respectfully to add that during our conversation in the Palatine Tavern Herr Esch made mention of the fact that in the prison in this town one or more deserters are lying at present, preparatory to their being shot. Thereupon everyone, including Herr Esch, loudly expressed the opinion that there was no object in shooting deserters now that the war is nearing its end (which these people seem to count on), seeing that enough blood had already been shed without that. Herr Esch was of the opinion that steps should be taken for this purpose. Whether by this he meant violent or other steps he did not say. I should like once more to respectfully insist that I consider the said E. as a wolf in sheep's clothing, who conceals his subversive aims behind pious phrases. Once more with profoundest respects,

W. H.

After concluding this report Huguenau gazed into the mirror to see whether he could bring off an ironical grimace like that which had so often exasperated him in Esch. Yes, his letter was a masterly achievement; it did one good to put a spoke in Esch's wheel, and Huguenau was so delighted with this pleasant thought that he could not help picturing the satisfaction which the Major would feel on receiving the letter. He considered whether he should deliver it personally, but then it seemed more fitting to him that it should reach the Major's hands by the official postal delivery. So he sent it by registered post, not however without first writing in huge letters on the envelope " Personal," and underlining it thrice.

Huguenau had deceived himself, however; the Major was by no means pleased when he found the letter among the correspondence lying on his desk. It was a dull thundery morning, the rain poured down the window panes of his office and the air smelt of sulphur or of soot. Something ugly and violent was concealed behind this letter, something subterranean, and even though the Major did not know, and even though it was not his duty to know, that there must always be violence and violation when one man tries to force his way into the reality of others and to graft his own on to it, yet the word " Night-birds " came into his mind, and it seemed to him that he was called upon to protect himself, to protect his wife and children from something which was not of his world, but belonged to the pit. Hesitatingly he took up the letter again; at bottom one could not blame this man, whose violence was only, so to speak, an insignificant kind of violence, who merely fulfilled his duty as a patriot and made his report, and if he did it in the loathsome and dishonourable manner of an *agent provocateur*, yet one could not take that amiss in an uneducated man. Yet because all this was really incomprehensible and beyond his grasp, the Major felt only a rush of shame at having reposed confidence in a man of low mind, and his face under his white hair became a little redder with shame. Nevertheless the Town Commandant could not consider himself justified in simply relegating the communication to the wastepaper-basket; rather did his office oblige him to continue to regard the suspicious Herr Esch with due mistrust, to keep watch on him, so to speak, from the distance, so that any danger that might possibly threaten the Fatherland from Herr Esch's activities might be prevented.

CHAPTER XLVII

Surgeon-Major Kühlenbeck rang up Dr Kessel on the telephone:

" Can you come at three this afternoon to operate, a small bullet extraction . . .? "

Dr Kessel thought he could hardly manage it, his time was so taken up.

" Too simple for you, I suppose, fishing out a bullet, for me too . . . but one mustn't ask too much . . . this isn't a life or the type of work a man can stand for long, I admit, and I'll throw it up some day or other, too . . . but to-day there's no help for it. . . . I order you to come. I'll send a car for you, it won't take longer than half-an-hour."

Kühlenbeck put back the receiver and laughed:

" Well, that's two hours of his time accounted for."

Flurschütz was sitting beside him:

" I had been wondering, I must admit, why you asked Kessel to come for such a trifle."

" Poor old Kessel is always trying to give me the slip. We'll take out Kneese's appendix at the same time."

" You really intend to operate on him? "

" Why not? The man must be allowed his pleasures . . . and me too."

" Why, does he want to be operated on? "

" Come, Flurschütz, you're becoming as naïve as our old friend Kessel—have I ever asked anybody that? Afterwards they were all thankful enough. And the four weeks' sick-leave that I get for every one of them . . . well, just think for yourself."

Flurschütz made to say something. Kühlenbeck put up his hand:

" Oh, leave me in peace with your secretion theories . . . my dear chap, if I can look into a man's belly I have no need of theories . . . follow my example and become a surgeon . . . the only way of keeping young."

" And am I to throw up all the work I've done on glands? "

" Throw it up with a good conscience . . . you operate quite neatly as it is."

" Something must be done about Jaretzki, sir . . . the man's going to pieces."

" Suppose we try a trepanning operation on him."

" But you've already discharged him . . . with his nerves in the condition they're in he should be sent to a special institution."

" I've reported him for Kreuznach, he'll soon pull himself together there. . . . You're a fine generation! a little boozing and you break down and must be sent to an institute for neurotics. . . . Orderly! "

The orderly appeared in the doorway.

" Tell Sister Carla that we shall operate at three . . . oh yes, and Murwitz in room two and Kneese in room three are to be given nothing to eat to-day . . . that's all . . . what do you say, Flurschütz, we won't really need poor old Kessel, we'll manage quite nicely by ourselves . . . it's hardly worth while calling in Kessel, he only complains that his legs are paining him: real sadism of me to drag him out . . . well, what do you say, Flurschütz? "

" With all respect, sir, I can act for Kessel this time, but this can't go on indefinitely . . . and then it won't be possible any longer simply to order a medical man to operate."

" Insubordination, Flurschütz? "

" Merely theoretical, sir . . . yes, it seems to me that in no very long time medicine will have specialized itself so completely that a consultation between a physician and a surgeon or a dermatologist will lead to no result at all, simply because there will be no means of making one specialist understand another."

" Wrong, quite wrong, Flurschütz, very shortly there will be nothing but surgery . . . that's the only thing that will be left of this whole wretched art of medicine . . . man is a butcher and whatever he may do he remains a butcher, he can't understand anything else . . . but he understands that to a T." And Dr Kühlenbeck regarded his great hairy skilful hands with the nails cut quite short.

Then he said reflectively:

" Do you know, a man who refused to come to terms with that fact might actually go off his head . . . one must take the matter as it is and get what pleasure one can out of it . . . so be advised, Flurschütz, swop horses and become a surgeon."

CHAPTER XLVIII

One had to fight for every bale of paper that one asked to be delivered, and although Esch was furnished with a certificate from the authorities empowering him to receive the supply required by the *Kur-Trier Herald*, he had to go out to the paper factory every week. And almost every time there was a row with old Herr Keller or the factory manager.

The men were just leaving for the day when Esch left the factory. He overtook the foreman Liebel and the mechanic Fendrich on the road. He really couldn't stand Liebel, with his fair-haired conical head and the thick vein across his brow. He said:

" 'Evening."

" 'Evening, Esch, have you been praying all this time with the old man ? "

Esch did not understand.

" Why, to get him to deliver your paper."

" Bloody nonsense," said Esch.

Fendrich stopped and showed the soles of his shoes; they were in holes:

" That'll cost six marks . . . that's how your rises in wages go."

This provided Esch with a starting-point:

" You can't do much by simply raising your wages, that's the mistake all the unions make."

" What's this, Esch? Are you thinking of mending Fendrich's boots with the Bible too? "

" Bloody nonsense," repeated Esch.

Fendrich's eyes glowed feverishly in their dark cavities; he was tuberculous and could not get enough milk to drink. He said:

" Religion too is probably a luxury that only the rich people can afford."

Liebel said:

" Majors and newspaper editors."

Esch said somewhat apologetically:

" I'm only an employee of the paper, like yourself," then he flared up, " besides that's all nonsense, as if the unions had ever taken the vow of poverty! "

Fendrich said:

" It would be all very fine if one could believe."

Esch said:

" I've discovered something: religion has to renew itself too, and get a new life . . . it says in the Bible that only the son can build the house."

Liebel said:

" Of course the next generation will have a better time, that isn't news to me. . . . I simply can't live now on my hundred and forty marks, even reckoning in the bonus . . . the old man won't admit that . . . and I'm supposed to be foreman, too."

" I haven't any more than that myself," said Esch, " counting in the house and all. . . . I've two tenants, but I can't decently ask anything from them, poor devils . . . my rent account is passive."

The evening wind freshened. Fendrich coughed.

Liebel said:

" Well? Any news? "

Esch admitted:

" I've been seeing the priest. . . ."

" What for? "

" About that passage in the Bible, the idiot didn't even listen . . . mumbled something about prayer and the Church, and that was all. The bloody priest . . . one must help oneself."

" That's right," said Fendrich, " nobody helps you."

Liebel said:

" If you stick together, you help one another . . . that's the advantage of the unions."

" The doctor says I must go to the mountains, and he's applied ten times already to the sick-fund . . . but if you don't come from the Front you've got to want, these days, and my cough just goes on and on."

Esch put on his ironical expression:

" With your unions and your sick-funds you won't get much further on than me with my priests. . . ."

" You have to die by yourself," said Fendrich, coughing.

Liebel asked:

" What really are you after? "

Esch considered:

" I used to think that one only had to clear out . . . to America . . . across the wide ocean on a ship . . . so as to begin a new life . . . but now . . ."

Liebel waited for the end of the sentence:

" And now? "

But Esch answered unexpectedly:

" Perhaps the Protestants are nearer it . . . the Major is a Protestant after all . . . but one must think the matter over first oneself . . . one must get together with other people and read the Bible to get some clear light . . . when one's alone, one keeps on doubting, no matter how much one broods on the subject."

" When one has friends, everything's easier," said Fendrich.

" You come and see me," said Esch, " I'll show you the passage in the Bible."

" All right," said Fendrich.

" And what about you, Liebel? " Esch felt obliged to ask.

" You must tell me first what you've concocted together."

Fendrich sighed:

" Everybody can only see things through his own eyes."

Liebel laughed and went away.

" He'll come yet, all right," said Esch.

CHAPTER XLIX

STORY OF THE SALVATION ARMY GIRL IN BERLIN (7)

My memory has not retained much of the evening that I spent with Nuchem Sussin at the Salvation Army meeting. I was occupied with more important things. No matter how one may estimate philosophical activity, it has at any rate the effect of making the external world insignificant and less worthy of notice. And apart from that even the most noteworthy things escape one's notice while one is experiencing them. In short, all that I can remember is Nuchem Sussin walking along beside me with his grey frock-coat buttoned up, his trousers flapping about his legs, they were so short, and his absurdly small velour hat perched on his head. All these Jews, when they're not rigged out in black caps, wear those velour hats that are too small for them, even the ostensibly fashionable Dr Litwak does this, and I could not forbear asking Nuchem the rude question where he had got that hat of his. " I just got it," was the answer.

Besides, the whole affair was not worth mentioning. It took on some colour of importance only because of Dr Litwak, who came in to see me yesterday. He has the unpleasant habit of simply walking in on me; he did the same thing on the occasion of my so-called illness. So he appeared before me again as I lay on the chaise-longue; he had the indispensable walking-stick in his hand and the absurd little velour hat on his head. That is to say, the hat itself was by no means small, it had a broad brim, but it sat on the very top of his skull without covering it. It occurred to me at that moment that Dr Litwak too must have had a milk-white complexion in his youth. Now it reminded one unquestionably of yellow cream.

" You will be able to tell me about Sussin."

I said, because it conformed with the truth:

" He is my friend."

" Friend, very good . . ." Dr Litwak pulled over a chair for himself, " his people are anxious, they asked me to come . . . you understand? "

In reality I was under no obligation to understand him, but I wanted to shorten the proceedings:

" He has a right to go where he likes."

" Oh, who has the right, who hasn't the right. . . . I'm not reproaching you of course . . . but why is he running about with this goy girl? "

It dawned on me only then that on that evening I had asked Marie and Nuchem into my room. People who haven't money can't sit about in restaurants.

I could not help laughing.

" You laugh, and his wife is sitting up there crying."

Well, that was certainly news to me; all the same I might have remembered that these Jews get married at fifteen. If I had only known which was Nuchem's wife: one of the stylish girls? or one of the matrons with their hair parted in the middle? the latter seemed the more probable.

I held Dr Litwak by the cord of his eyeglasses:

" Has he children as well? "

" Why, what do you expect him to have? Kittens? "

Dr Litwak put on such an indignant expression that I had to ask him what his first name was.

" Dr Samson Litwak," he introduced himself anew.

" Well then look here, Dr Samson, what do you really want of me? "

He reflected for a while:

" I'm an enlightened man . . . but this is going too far . . . you must stop him."

" Stop him from what? from wanting to go to Zion? Leave him that harmless pleasure."

" He'll get himself baptized yet . . . you must stop him."

" But whether he reaches Jerusalem as a Jew or a Christian is surely a bagatelle."

" Jerusalem," he repeated, as if a bonbon had been put into his mouth.

" Well, then," said I, hoping that he would retire now.

He was still obviously rolling the name on his tongue:

" I'm an enlightened man . . . but nobody ever got there by singing songs and beating drums . . . that's for a different kind of people. . . . I must visit everybody, I'm a doctor, it needn't matter to me whether one is a Jew or a Christian . . . there's decent people everywhere, will you stop him? "

This persistence got on my nerves:

" I'm a great Anti-Semite," he smiled incredulously, " I'm an agent of the Salvation Army, I'm quartermaster in Jerusalem."

" A joke," he said appreciatively, although he was visibly disconcerted, " a joke, *nebbich*."

There he was certainly right; a joke, *nebbich*, that was for the time being the attitude to life into which I had fallen. What could be held responsible for it? The war? I did not know, and probably do not know even to-day, although many things have changed since.

I still held Dr Litwak by the cord of his eyeglasses. He said:

" But you're an enlightened man too. . . ."

" Well? "

" Why don't you leave people their . . ." he brought out the word only with difficulty, ". . . their prejudices? "

" So, you call such things prejudices! "

Now he was quite thrown into confusion.

" They're not really prejudices of course . . . what do you mean by prejudices? . . . " and finally becoming calm again: " but in reality they're not prejudices."

When he had gone I went over in my mind that evening of the Salvation Army meeting. As I have said, it had passed without making the slightest impression on me. Now and then I had regarded Nuchem Sussin as he sat there with a somewhat lifeless smile round the curved Jewish lips in his milk-white face, listening to the singing. And then I had asked them both up to my room, or more correctly Marie only, for Nuchem of course lived in the house,—well, and then they had both sat in my room silently listening while I talked. Until Nuchem once more pointed to the lute and said: " Play something." Then Marie had taken the lute and sung: " We're marching on to Zion's gate, A host so great and true, All cleansed in the Redeemer's blood, And there is room for you." And Nuchem listened with a somewhat lifeless smile.

CHAPTER L

Huguenau waited for eight days, expecting some sign of approval or at least a reply from the Major. He waited for ten days. Then he became uneasy. The report had obviously not come up to the Major's expectations. But was it his fault that that cretin Esch provided him with no material? Huguenau considered whether he should follow up the first report with a second, but what was he to say in it? That Esch was colloguing as usual with the vine-growers and the factory workers was nothing new; that would only bore the Major!

The Major mustn't be bored—Huguenau racked his brains to find some proposal to lay before the Major. Something simply must be done; Esch reigned supreme in the office and acted as though the real editor of the paper were non-existent, and in the printing-shed everything was dreary beyond endurance. Huguenau looked through the great newspapers for stimulation, and found it when he made the discovery that all these journals were labouring in the service of national charities, while the *Kur-Trier Herald* had undertaken nothing, absolutely nothing at all. So that was what Herr Esch's warmth of heart amounted to, that warmth of heart which could not endure the spectacle of the misery among the vine-growers. But as for himself he knew now what to do.

On Friday evening, after a long absence, he appeared again at the hotel and proceeded at once to the room where the notabilities sat, for that was his place by right. The Major was sitting at his table in the outer dining-room, and Huguenau greeted him formally and curtly in passing.

By good luck the gentlemen were already there in force, and Huguenau announced that he was glad to find so many of them, for he had an important matter to discuss, and at once, before the Major came in. And in a fairly long speech he pointed out that the town lacked, painfully lacked, any proper charitable organization such as had already existed for years almost everywhere else for the alleviation of hardships caused by the war, and he moved that such an organization should be established at once. As for its objects, he would content himself with mentioning, among other things, the preservation of soldiers' graves, the provision for soldiers' widows and orphans and so on; further, he would like to point out that the money for these lofty objects must be raised, and that in this connection an " Iron Bismarck," [1] for instance, could be erected in the market-place, nails at ten pfennigs per nail, besides it was a crying scandal that this town alone should lack such a monument—and finally that charitable appeals of various kinds, not to speak of public collections, would always help to increase their funds. And that this organization, for which he begged to suggest the title of " The Moselle Memorial Association " should appear under the patronage of the Town Commandant. He himself and his paper—of course within the limits of their modest powers—stood at all times and free of cost at the disposal of the association and its lofty aims.

It need scarcely be said, of course, that the proposal was greeted with universal applause and was accepted unanimously and without discussion. Huguenau and Herr Paulsen the chemist were nominated as delegates to convey the proposal to the Herr Major, and smoothing down their coats they strode with a certain solemnity into the dining-room.

The Major looked up with some surprise, then he drew himself up with a little jerk as though on parade and listened attentively but without understanding to the phrases of the two gentlemen. These phrases crossed one another and raced one another, and the Major heard something about an Iron Bismarck and war widows and a " Moselle Memorial " and did not understand. At last Huguenau was intelligent enough to resign all speech to the chemist; it seemed to him also that that was the more modest course, and so he sat still and regarded the clock on the wall, the picture of *The Crown-Prince Friedrich after the Battle of Gravelotte*, and the Spatenbräu sign (with the spade) which hung on a cord beside the picture of the Crown-Prince. Where could one get Spatenbräu now! Meanwhile the Major had grasped what Paulsen was saying: he thought, he said, that there were no military grounds against

---

[1] A wooden statue, into which the public were encouraged to hammer nails until the wood was covered.

his acceptance, he welcomed this patriotic proposal, he could only thank them most cordially, and he rose in order to convey his thanks to the gentlemen in the next room. Paulsen and Huguenau followed, proud of their accomplished achievement.

They sat for a long time together, for it was in a sense an inaugural celebration. Huguenau waited for an opportunity to get hold of the Major, and it came presently when they drank to the health and success of the new association and its patron, not forgetting, of course, the man who had originated the splendid idea, Herr Huguenau.

Huguenau, his glass in his hand, went the round of the table and in this manner reached Major von Pasenow:

" I hope Herr Major is satisfied with me to-night."

He had never had any cause for dissatisfaction, replied the Major.

" Come, Herr Major, my report seems to have rather missed fire . . . but I hope you'll take into consideration that the circumstances were very difficult. And then I have been working early and late reorganizing the paper; I hope you will not set it down to negligence that I haven't been able to send you a second report. . . ."

The Major said firmly:

" I think it is scarcely worth while pursuing the matter any further; you have done already all that you were in duty bound to do."

Huguenau was taken aback.

" Oh, not at all, not at all," he muttered, and assured the Major that he would take up his work of surveillance really in earnest now.

As the Major made no reply to this, Huguenau went on:

" We'll print the appeal for ' The Moselle Memorial ' at once, to-morrow . . . in honour of the occasion will not the Herr Major pay our concern the honour of a visit, after so graciously standing god-father to it . . . that would be the most splendid propaganda for the new association."

The Major replied that he would be only too delighted to pay the *Kur-Trier Herald* a visit; for the next day, however, all his arrangements were already made, but he presumed any day would suit equally.

" The earlier the better, Herr Major," Huguenau ventured. " The Herr Major won't find anything very remarkable to inspect . . . every-thing quite modest . . . and of course there aren't many outward signs of the work that has been put into reorganizing it, but I can say with all modesty that the printing arrangements are in perfect order . . ."

Suddenly he had a new idea:

"The printing-press, for instance, would do splendidly for any printing required by the military authorities," he caught fire, he would have liked to seize the Major by the coat-button. "You see, Herr Major, you see how Esch has neglected the business . . . it needed me to hit on that idea. We must get the custom of the army authorities, now that the paper is, so to speak, under your direct patronage, and we have put so much money into it . . . how else am I to squeeze a dividend out of it for the shareholders . . . considering the state I found the business in?" he said in despair, and he felt honestly embittered.

The Major replied somewhat helplessly:

"But that isn't my province . . ."

"Quite, quite, Herr Major, but if the Herr Major seriously desired it . . . and once the Herr Major has seen the printing-office, he will certainly desire it. . . ."

He gazed at the Major alluringly and seductively and despairingly all in one. But then he pulled himself up, wiped his glasses, and cast a glance round the table: "It is obviously in the interests of all the gentlemen sitting here too . . . all you gentlemen are invited to inspect the place, of course that's understood."

But most of them knew Esch's den already. Only they did not say so.

CHAPTER LI

Since Heinrich Wendling had announced that he was coming home on leave, more than three weeks had passed. And although she still lay long in bed of mornings, Hanna scarcely believed now that Heinrich would really come. He suddenly arrived, however, neither in the evening, nor in the morning, but in the broad light of day. He had spent half the night in Coblenz station, and then had come on with a dawdling transport train. And as he was telling her this they stood opposite each other on the paved garden-path; the noonday sun shone down, and in the middle of the lawn a red garden-umbrella glowed warmly beside the camp-chair on which she had been lying; they could smell the hot, red cotton, and the leaves of her book, which had slipped down, fluttered in the light wind. Heinrich did not touch her, he had not even reached out his hand to her, but stared immovably in her face, and she, knowing that he must be searching for a picture which he had carried in his mind for more than two years, kept quite still under his searching glance; and she too looked into the face turned towards her, seeking in her turn not, indeed, for a picture she had harboured, for there was no longer any picture in her mind, but for the traits because of which she had once been compulsively drawn to love that face. Strangely unaltered that face seemed to her now, she knew and recognized again the line of the lips; the arrangement and shape of the teeth, the dimple on the chin had remained unchanged, and the space between the eyes was a little too wide on account of the breadth of the skull. " I must see your profile," she said and he turned his head obediently. And it was the same straight nose and long upper lip that she saw again, only every trace of softness had vanished, that was all. One had really to acknowledge that he was a handsome man, yet she did not find what had once so intensely delighted and attracted her. Heinrich asked: " Where's the boy? " " He's at school . . . won't you come in? " They went into the house. Yet even now he still did not touch her, still did not kiss her, but simply gazed at her. " I must have a thorough wash first of all . . . haven't had a bath since leaving Vienna."

" Yes, we'll turn on a bath."

The two maids appeared to bid the master welcome. Hanna did not quite like that. She went up with him to the bathroom, and herself laid out the bath towels.

" Everything's still in its old place, Heinrich."

" Oh, everything's still in its old place? "

She left the bathroom; there were all sorts of things to arrange and rearrange; she attended to them wearily.

She cut roses in the garden for the dinner-table.

After a while she returned softly to the bathroom door and listened to the splashing inside. She could feel her usual headache coming on. Supporting herself on the banister she descended once more to the hall.

At last the boy returned from school. She took him by the hand. At the bathroom door she cried: " May we come in now? " " Of course," the reply came in a somewhat astonished voice. She opened the door a little, and peeped in through the opening: Heinrich was standing half dressed before the mirror, and she thrust one of the roses into the unwillingly opened hand of the child, pushed him in and ran away.

She waited for the two of them in the dining-room, and could not help averting her eyes when they entered. They looked absurdly alike, with the same eyes set wide apart, the same movements, the same crop of brown hair, except that Heinrich wore his quite short now. It was as though she had had no share at all in the child. A terrible mechanism; oh, it was terrible to have been loved. And at that moment her life seemed to her like one long imbecility, a despairing imbecility, which nevertheless she would never be able to change.

Heinrich said: " Home again " and sat down at his old place. Perhaps his words seemed stupid to him; he smiled uncertainly. The boy regarded him attentively and distantly.

There he sat, the father of the family, and spoilt everything.

The maid too could not keep her eyes off him; there was a hint of admiration and envy in her glance; and when she entered again Hanna said very distinctly:

" Should I telephone to Röders . . . about this evening? "

The advocate Röders was Wendling's colleague in the office; he was over fifty and exempt from military service.

The English clock in its mahogany case struck a deep gong-like stroke.

With her little finger Hanna lightly touched the back of Heinrich's hand, as though by the caress she were begging forgiveness for thinking of spending the evening with Röders, but warning him at the same time that she desired to avoid physical contacts.

Heinrich said:

" Of course, I'll have to ring up Röders . . . I'll fix it up, then."

Hanna said:

" We'll go out walking with papa in the afternoon and show ourselves."

" Yes, let's do that," said Heinrich.

" Isn't it lovely to have papa sitting here with us again? "

" Yes," said the boy after some hesitation.

" You must look over his school books . . . he can write and count already. He wrote his letters to you quite by himself."

" They were splendid letters, Walter."

" They were only postcards," said Walter shyly.

That they were appealing to the child between them, so as to find each other across his brown head, seemed to them both like an abuse of the child. Certainly it would have been more honest to say: we will not kiss each other until our longing has become intolerable. But that longing was not really longing, it was only intolerable expectation.

They went up to the nursery, on whose panelled walls a childish fresco, intentionally gay, was painted. And with that second and clearer and somewhat wry intelligence which can arise from intensified expectation or from an agonizing headache, Hanna knew that all these lacquered furnishings and all this whiteness was also an abuse of the child, knew that it had nothing to do with his own life and nature, but that a symbol had been set up in this room, a symbol of her white breasts and of the white milk which they would produce after successful embraces. It was a very remote and very vague thought, and yet in it lay the reason why she had never been able to stay long in the nursery and had preferred that the boy should come to her. She said: " You must show papa your new toys too." Walter brought the new box of bricks and the soldiers in field-grey. There were twenty-three men and an officer, who with one knee bent waved his drawn sword towards the enemy. None of the three noticed that Dr Heinrich Wendling also wore the field-grey uniform of an officer; each, it is true, had a different motive for not noticing it: Walter, because he felt that his father was an intruder, Heinrich, because it was impossible for him to identify the heroic gestures of the tin soldiers with real war, Hanna because, to her own horror, she suddenly saw this man naked before her, naked, and isolated in his nakedness. It was the same isolation as she had remarked in the pieces of furniture about her, that stood as though naked, with no connection with their surroundings, no relation to each other, strange and disturbing.

He too could not but feel it. And when they went out walking they took the child between them, and although Hanna held the boy's hand and swung it gaily, and Heinrich often took the other hand, he was a barrier separating them. They did not look at each other, they were embarrassed, as if ashamed, they gazed straight ahead or at the fields where dandelions and purple clover, wild pinks and lilac scabious, were growing in the grass. The day was warm and Hanna was not used to walking in the afternoon. Yet it was not solely the heat that made her feel such an urgent need for a bath when she returned; every wish of hers now reached down in the most curious way to a deeper stratum of consciousness: it was as though the immersion of her body in the water would spread a great solitude around her, as if she had visions of that magical rebirth which one experiences in the isolation of the water. More definite, certainly, than these thoughts was her repugnance at the idea of visiting the bathroom at bedtime in Heinrich's presence. On the other hand the maid would think it queer if she were to take a bath in the middle of the day, and on the pretext that she had to change for the evening she asked Heinrich if he would order a car meanwhile and look after Walter. Then she went to the bathroom, intending to have a shower-bath at least. But when she got into the tub, to which a few drops from the midday bath still clung, for the douche was dripping, her knees grew weak and she had to let the cold water run over her until her skin was like glass and the points of her breasts grew quite hard. After that it was more endurable.

It was late when they drove over to Röders'; Heinrich dismissed the car since it was such a lovely evening, and Hanna was thankful for the suggestion that they should walk home—the later that happened, the better. And it was actually midnight when they left Röders! But when they were crossing the silent market-place on which nobody was to be seen except the sentry on duty at military headquarters, when the empty place surrounded by the dark houses, in which scarcely a light was burning, lay before them like a crater of isolation, like a crater of silence out of which recurring waves of peace flowed over the sleeping town, then Heinrich Wendling took his wife's arm, and at that first physical contact she closed her eyes. Perhaps he too had closed his eyes and saw neither the deep summer night sky nor the white ribbon of the road that stretched in front of them as they walked in its dust, perhaps each of them saw a different firmament, both of them sealed like their eyes, each in a separate isolation, and yet united in the renewed knowledge of their bodies, which yielded at last to a kiss; and the veils dropped from their faces, that were lascivious in the consciousness of sex, yet chaste in the pain of a separation that could never end, that could never be abolished again no matter how tender they were with each other.

CHAPTER LII

After Samwald's funeral Gödicke of the Landwehr began to speak.

Samwald, a volunteer, was the brother of Friedrich Samwald the watchmaker, who had a shop in Römerstrasse. After a mass attack accompanied by a heavy bombardment, young Samwald had suddenly begun to cough and collapsed. He was a nice brave lad of nineteen, everybody liked him, and so he had managed to get sent to the hospital of his native town. He did not arrive even in a hospital transport, but alone, like a man on leave, and Surgeon-Major Kühlenbeck said: " Well, as for you, my lad, we'll soon put you to rights." And although Dr Kessel never came to the hospital without looking up young Samwald, and although Samwald seemed quite restored to health, he was suddenly seized with another hæmorrhage and in three days he was dead. In spite of the brilliant sun smiling down from the sky.

Since the hospital was one only for light cases, death was not hushed up there as in larger hospitals. On the contrary it was treated as a solemn event. Before the coffin was borne to the cemetery it was laid on the bier in front of the entrance to the hospital, and there consecrated. Those patients who were not confined to bed put on their uniforms and formed up in order, and there were a good many people from the town. The Surgeon-Major pronounced a stirring eulogy, the priest stood beside the coffin, a boy in a red soutane with a white tunic swung the censer. Then the women knelt, many of the men too, and once more they told over their rosaries.

Gödicke had remained in the hospital garden. When he noticed the crowd assembling he hobbled up on his two sticks and joined it. The spectacle he now saw was familiar to him, and consequently he refused to countenance it. He thought deeply; he wanted to destroy what he saw, to tear it to bits as one tears to bits a piece of paper or cardboard—and how that was to be done had to be vigilantly and keenly thought out. When the women plumped down on their knees like charwomen, a laugh rose into his throat, but he dared not make a sound, that was forbidden him. Supported on his two sticks, he stood in the midst of the kneeling women, he stood there like a scaffolding, and rammed his supports into the ground and pressed the sound back into his throat. But now the women had finished their Paternoster and their three Aves and came to the passage, " descended into Hell, and rose again from the dead on the third day "; then—it seemed in a lower storey of the scaffolding, and as though spoken by a ventriloquist he had once heard—words began to form just above his tortured and compressed abdomen, and instead of roaring them out, so reluctantly did the words emerge that it was perhaps inaudibly that the bricklayer Gödricke said: " Arisen from the dead," and immediately fell silent again, so terrified was he at what had taken place in the lower storey of his scaffolding. No one was regarding him; they had raised the coffin; the coffin with the crucifix fastened to it swayed on the bearers' shoulders; the watchmaker Samwald, small and a little bent, fell in with the other relatives behind the bearers; then followed the doctors; then came the rest of the procession. Last of all hobbled the bricklayer Gödicke on his sticks, wearing his hospital overall.

Sister Mathilde caught sight of him as they were going along the boulevard. She made straight for him: " But, Gödicke, you can't come like this . . . what are you thinking about, in your overall . . ." but he paid no attention to her. Even when she fetched the Surgeon-Major to support her he refused to be shaken, but simply stared steadily through them both and went straight on. At last Kühlenbeck said: " Oh, let him come, war is war . . . if he gets tired one of the men must stay with him and take him back."

It was a long road that Ludwig Gödicke travelled in this way; the women round about him were praying, and there were bushes beside the road. When one group reached the end of their Aves, another took them up, and from the wood came the cry of a cuckoo. Some of the men, the little watchmaker Samwald among them, wore black suits like carpenters. Many things came nearer and closed up, especially when at the turnings the procession slowed down and the mourners' bodies were pressed closely together; and the women's skirts were like his own overall; their skirts struck against their legs when they walked; and a woman away in front was walking with her head bowed and her handkerchief before her face. And even if Gödicke did not look at anything, but held his eyes immovably fixed on the wheel tracks in front of him, trying, indeed, every now and then actually to keep his eyes closed just as firmly as his teeth were clenched, so that the parts of his soul crowded together still more closely, threatening to stifle his ego; yes, though he would actually have preferred to come to a stop, to ram his crutches into the ground and force all these people to keep still and say nothing, or to scatter them all to the four winds; nevertheless he was drawn on, borne on, and he swam and floated, himself a swaying coffin, on the wave of ever-recurring prayer that accompanied him.

In the cemetery, when the body had once more been consecrated, and over the opened grave into which it was lowered the litany once more began: "Arisen from the dead," and while the little watchmaker Samwald stood rigid, gazing into the hole and sobbing, and one by one the people went up to fling a spadeful of earth on the dead warrior and to shake the watchmaker by the hand, suddenly, uplifted before the eyes of all, the gigantic form of Gödicke, supported on his two sticks, in his long grey hospital overall, his long beard waving, appeared on the edge of the grave beside the little watchmaker and ignored the hand offered him, but said with a great effort, yet clearly enough for everybody to understand, his first words: " Arisen from the dead." And thereupon he laid his sticks aside, yet not to take the spade and throw a little earth down into the grave; no, he did not do that, he did something quite different and unexpected; he addressed himself to the task of climbing down into the hole, he began laboriously and systematically to clamber down into it, and already by good luck had one leg over the edge. Naturally his intentions were incomprehensible to all the bystanders; they thought that without the support of his sticks he had simply fallen down out of sheer weakness. The Surgeon-Major and a few others rushed across, pulled him out of the hole and carried him to one of the benches. Perhaps by now the man Gödicke was really forsaken by his strength; in any case he offered no resistance, but sat there quite quietly with his eyes shut and his head a little to one side. But the watchmaker Samwald, who had run to him with the others and would have gladly helped to carry him, now stayed beside him; and as a great sorrow may sometimes shake up a man's soul, Samwald divined that something very strange had happened to his companion; sitting beside the bricklayer Gödicke, he spoke to him comfortingly as to one who was bearing a sorrow, a heavy sorrow, and he spoke too of his own dead brother, who had had a beautiful and early and painless death. And Gödicke listened to him with his eyes shut.

Meanwhile the local celebrities advanced to the grave, among them, as was fitting, Huguenau in a blue suit, a stiff black hat in one hand, a wreath in the other. And Huguenau looked about him in extreme indignation because the deceased's brother was not at hand to admire the wreath, a beautiful garland of oak-leaves sent by " The Moselle Memorial Association," a really beautiful wreath with a ribbon on which could be read: " From the Fatherland to its brave soldier."

CHAPTER LIII

STORY OF THE SALVATION ARMY GIRL IN BERLIN (8)

Like the quick sperm of future shining seas
the iridescent foam holds, one by one,
these quivering golden shafts cast by the sun—
a spirit moving on the water's face—
and to the far horizon's edge they gleam
where the bright sky begets itself again,
itself a mirror of the glassy plain,
sinking to rest in Aphrodite's dream:
was this the hour in which he was beset?
was this the hour in which the anguish fell,
twisting him in the throes and pains of hell,
bringing forth natural need's unnatural get?
Was it a wood like this, beside a field,
that sank beneath his feet so that he reeled?
for in a blinding rain of fire there spoke
a voice of thunder; headlong he was hurled,
nor did his senses waken till he whirled
far down in sulphurous chasms of glowing rock,
dashed on the stones, the void beneath his feet,
breaking himself as, impotent, he strove
to rise again to that lost land above,
to that lost land of shade and cypress grove,
where tangled bushes dip in waters fleet,
where night and day in one green twilight meet,
where delicate sharp odours drift and twine
along the glimmering aisles of beech and pine,—
this was the hour he sought and seeks for ever
to win again, the hour for ever lost,
ere like a leaf by sudden tempest tossed
that dread voice whirled him off, the hour for him
of new-won knowledge, filling to the brim
his cup of being, even while it drained
all meaning from the draught, and nought remained
but knowledge big with doubt in a waste land,

a land unending: did the cypress stand
beside him? Was there sea? He cannot tell.
He only knows he heard the voice resound,
the voice that hurled him headlong into hell,
the voice that masters him and holds him bound.
Were that hour once re-won, then, purged of sin,
he would find long-forgotten things break in,
bringing the tang of brine on grass and tree,
the mirrored shore beside the shining sea.—
But new-born knowledge drives him on from doubt
to doubt in anguish, hounds him through the wastes
to seek the voice that he can never find,
the voice he flees when it pursues behind
yet conjures still to stop, as on he hastes,
by that great oath he falsely swore to One
who in days past once chose him as a son,
him, the betrayer; and a shriek bursts out
from his despairing mouth, a shriek that wrongs
and deafens knowledge, a cry from the abyss,
a cry that shivers into nothingness,
cry of the helpless animal at bay,
cry of the wild beast trapped by fiery tongues;
O cry of amazement! cry of dire dismay!
Do I feel it, this wonder of amazement? or is it myself
    that is amazed?
From what far country comest thou by right
to me, O thought, profoundest Almost-but-not-quite?
in the blankness of death I hover,
Ahasuerus, crying in despair for ever!
In hell's sleepless, bloodshot, yellow light
my hands are withered and blinded my sight,
I, Ahasuerus, born to cry for ever!
banished my home, by cliffs hemmed about,
nourished in knowledge and ravaged by doubt,
sowing dry stones and fed on dry dust,
fashioned in knowledge and hollow with lust,
blessed by many, by one voice chidden,
the sanctified sower of fruit forbidden.

CHAPTER LIV

The Major was somewhat disagreeably surprised when the orderly reported that Herr Editor Esch wished to see him. Was this newspaper man an ambassador of Huguenau? an emissary of the pit and the underworld? This question made the Major almost forget that Huguenau had drawn a distinct line between himself and the presumably politically suspect Esch, and since a few moments' reflection suggested nothing decisive he said at last:

" Well, it doesn't matter . . . tell him to come in."

Esch certainly looked like neither an emissary from hell, nor a politically suspect individual; he was embarrassed and confused, like a man who was already regretting the step he had taken:

" Herr Major, my business is . . . Herr Major, in short, your article made a deep impression on me. . . ."

Major von Pasenow told himself that he must not allow himself to be taken in by hypocritical speeches, gratifying as it might be to believe that his words had had an effect.

" And if by the devil who must be driven out, the Herr Major meant me . . ."

Whereupon the Major found it necessary to make clear that a Biblical quotation implied no personal point or insinuation, for that would indeed be a degradation of the Bible, and that at every turning-point of our lives, if it was for the better, we had to put behind us a part of the devil. So that if Herr Esch had come to demand explanation or satisfaction, he could rest content with this statement.

While the Major was speaking Esch had regained his composure:

" No, Herr Major, that was not what I came about. I would even take that about the devil on my own shoulders, but not because my paper has been confiscated repeatedly," he made a disdainful gesture, " no, Herr Major, I can't be reproached for ever having run my paper less decently than I do now. I've come with another request."

And he demanded no more and no less than that the Major should point out the way of salvation to him and his friends, or the brethren, as in his excitement he called them.

As he stood there before the Major's desk, his hat in his hands, a red flush of excitement showing on each cheek-bone, a red that ebbed into the brownish hollows beneath, Esch reminded the Major of his estate steward. What right had a steward to talk about religion? and the Major had the feeling that concern with religious questions was a prescriptive right of landowners. Pictures of the religious life he knew rose up in him, he saw the church to which he and his family drove in the high-wheeled coach over the dusty summer roads, in the low sledge well covered with furs during winter; he saw himself holding the usual Bible service for his children and the servants at Christmas and at Easter, saw the Polish maids walking in their red head-cloths and wide skirts to the Catholic Church in the neighbouring village, and as that church reminded him that Herr Esch belonged to the Roman Catholic persuasion, Esch was thus brought into an unpleasantly close relationship with the Polish land-workers and that disturbing atmosphere of unreliability with which, partly from personal experience, partly because of their politics, partly out of pure prejudice, he was accustomed to accredit the Polish nation. And as it is a fact that questions of conscience in a fellow-man very often throw us into embarrassment, as though he were exaggerating something that is not nearly so important to him as he makes out, the Major, while inviting Esch to be seated, did not make any reference to the theme he had opened, but merely inquired after the well-being of the paper.

Esch, however, was not a man to be so easily deflected from his purpose. " For the sake of the paper itself, Herr Major, you must listen to me"—and in answer to the Major's questioning look—" . . . yes, you, Herr Major, have prescribed a new policy for the *Kur-Trier Herald* . . . even though I've always said myself that order must be made in the world and that even an editor must do his part in it, that is, if he doesn't want to be an anarchist and a conscienceless swine . . . Herr Major, everybody seeks salvation, everybody is afraid of evil poison, everybody is waiting for redemption to come and injustice to be destroyed."

He had begun to shout and the Major looked at him in surprise. Esch pulled himself together again: " You see, Herr Major, Socialism is only one sign among many others . . . but since your article in the new issue . . . Herr Major, it's freedom and justice in the world that's at stake . . . one mustn't take human life lightly, something must happen, otherwise all the sacrifice will have been in vain."

" All the sacrifice in vain . . ." repeated the Major as though out of an old memory. But then he collected himself. " Perhaps you want,

Herr Esch, to steer the paper back into the Socialist stream? And do you actually expect me to support you in that?"

Esch's bearing was contemptuous and disrespectful:

"It's not a question of Socialism, Herr Major . . . it's a question of the new life . . . of decency . . . of searching together for the faith . . . my friends and I have started a Bible class . . . Herr Major, when you wrote your article you meant every word of it in your heart, and you can't reject us now."

It was clear: Esch was presenting an account, even although only a spiritual one, and the Major could not but think again of his steward sitting opposite him in the office with his accounts, and he thought too of the Polish farm-labourers, who were always trying to get the better of him. Was this man not threatening him with his Socialism? Perhaps it was something long forgotten that he repeated when he said:

"Someone always rejects us, Herr Esch."

Esch had got up and, yielding to habit, had begun to walk with awkward strides up and down the room. The sharp vertical folds at either side of his mouth were still deeper than usual; how careworn he looks, thought the Major, incredible that this earnest man should be a tavern frequenter or a visitor to disreputable resorts, an emissary from the underworld. Can he be such a hypocrite? It was as impossible to imagine as that underworld itself.

Esch planted himself directly in front of the Major:

"Herr Major, to put it quite frankly . . . how can I fill my position when I'm not even clear whether our path might not be made plainer by accepting the Protestant faith. . . ."

Now the Major could of course have responded that it was not one of an editor's duties to solve theological problems,—but he was too much alarmed by Esch's direct question to find any answer at all: it was not so unlike Huguenau's entreaties to be given the army printing, and for a moment the figures of the two men seemed about to blend together again. The Major put up his hand to the Iron Cross on his breast and his bearing became official: was it fitting that he, an officer in a prominent position, should make proselytes? The Catholic Church counted after all as a sort of ally, and he would not have taken it upon him to induce an Austrian or a Bulgarian or a Turk to give up the ties binding him to his own state in favour of Germany. It was really annoying, the way that this Esch insisted on his pound of flesh, and yet again it was flattering and alluring; in this appeal to him was there not something of the faith that for ever renews and regenerates religion? But the Major still resisted, and begged to point out that, himself a Protestant, he did not feel competent to counsel a Catholic in matters of belief.

Esch once more made a disdainful gesture with his hand,—that was beside the question: in the Major's article it said that Christian must stand by Christian—so there was no difference between Catholic and Protestant Christianity, and the town priest paid little enough attention to such scruples.

The Major did not reply. Was it really a net made out of his own words that was being drawn round him? with which this man wished to drag him down into the darkness and the pit? And yet it was as though a gentle hand were stretched out to lead him forth to the peaceful banks of quiet waters. He could not help thinking of the baptism in Jordan, and almost against his will he said:

" There's no rule in matters of faith, Herr Esch; faith is a natural fountain that springs up, as we are told in the Bible," and then he added reflectively, " every one must come to know divine grace by himself."

Esch had turned his back discourteously on the Major; he stood at the window with his forehead pressed against the window pane. Now he turned round: his expression was grave, almost imploring:

" Herr Major, it isn't a question of rules . . . it's a question of trust . . ." and after a little: " otherwise it would be . . ." he could not find the right word, " otherwise the paper would be no better than all the other papers . . . a corrupt Press . . . eyewash for demagogues . . . but you, Herr Major, wanted something different. . . ."

Once more Major von Pasenow felt the sweetness of yielding, of being carried away; it was as though a silvery cloud sought to catch him up, floating over the spring streams. The security of trust! No, that man standing so seriously before him was no adventurer, no traitor, no unreliable Pole, not a man to carry your confidence over to the other side and there shamelessly and openly expose it. So at first hesitatingly, but becoming warmer as he went on, the Major began to speak of Luther's teaching, in following which nobody need despair, nobody, Herr Esch! for everyone carried the divine spark somewhere in his soul, and—the strength with which Major von Pasenow felt this he was unable even to express—no one was shut out from grace, and everyone who was granted grace might go forth to preach redemption. And any man who looked deeply into his own heart would recognize the truth and the way; and Esch too would find his way to the light and follow it. " Be comforted, Herr Editor," he said, " it will all turn out for the best." And he would be glad to talk to Herr Esch again if Herr Esch should desire it and his own scanty leisure permitted—the Major had risen and reached Esch his hand across the desk—besides he would be coming presently to have a look over the publishing office of the *Kur-Trier Herald*. He nodded to Esch. Esch remained irresolutely standing, and the Major feared a speech of thanks. But he received no thanks, for Esch asked almost roughly: " And my friends? " The Major once more became slightly official: " Later, Herr Esch, later perhaps." And Esch bowed awkwardly and retired.

Nevertheless for a man so radically impetuous as Esch there was no hanging back after this. When a few days later—to the astonishment of everybody who heard of it, and that was presently the whole town— he joined the Protestant Church, it seemed to his ardent soul an act of homage to the Major at the same time.

CHAPTER LV

DISINTEGRATION OF VALUES (7)

Historical Excursus.

That criminal and rebellious age known as the Renaissance, that age in which the Christian scheme of values was broken in two halves, one Catholic and the other Protestant, that age in which with the falling asunder of the medieval organon a process of dissolution destined to go on for five centuries was inaugurated and the seeds of the modern world planted, that age at once of sowing and of first blossoming cannot be comprehensively subsumed either under its Protestantism or its individualism or its nationalism or its joyous sensuousness, or even under its revival of humanism and natural science: if that age, which in its style presented such an obvious appearance of unity, and is now regarded as a coherent whole, possessed a homogeneous spirit commensurable with that unity and producing that style, it is certainly not to be found in any one phenomenon selected from its various manifestations, not even in a phenomenon of such profound revolutionary force as Protestantism; rather must all these phenomena be referred to a common denominator, they must all possess a common root, and that root must have lain in the logical structure of thought itself, in that specific logic which penetrated and informed all the activities of the epoch.

Now it may be asserted with some confidence that a sweeping revolution in the style of thinking—and the revolutionary aspect of all these phenomena entitles us to infer such a complete revolution in thinking—invariably results from the fact that thought has reached its provisional limit of infinity, that it is no longer able to resolve the antinomies of infinity by the old methods, and so is compelled to revise its own basic principles.

We have before our own eyes a very clear example of such a process in the research into first principles of modern mathematics, which, starting from the antinomies of infinity, has achieved a revolution of mathematical method whose extent cannot yet be estimated. True, it is impossible to decide whether here we are dealing with a new revolution in thought, or with the final and definitive liquidation of medieval logic (probably with both). For not only has a residue of medieval values survived right up to our time, giving room for the assumption that its concomitant ways of thinking have also survived; it is to be remarked as well that the paradox of all antinomies and the very essence of the antinomies of infinity is the fact that they derive from the deductive method: but that means that they derive from theological method, for there is no world system of theology that is not deductive, in other words that does not seek by reason to deduce all phenomena from a supreme principle, from God; and in the last resort every form of Platonism is thus deductive theology. So even if the Platonic-theological content in the system of modern mathematics is not immediately visible, and perhaps must even remain invisible while mathematics remains an adequate expression of the logic that prevails over mathematics as well as over everything else, yet there is a striking affinity between the antinomies of infinity postulated by mathematics and those of medieval scholasticism. The medieval discussion of the infinite, of course, did not take place on the mathematical plane (or only parenthetically, in cosmic speculations), but the "ethical" infinite, as one may venture to call it, such as is implied in the perennial problem of the infinite attributes of God, includes all the questions about actual and potential infinity and posits the same structural limitations that puzzle modern mathematics and provide its antinomies. In both cases the substance of the antinomy arises from the absoluteness with which logic is applied, an absoluteness that cannot be avoided so long as logic prevails, and that can be recognized only when the antinomian limits are reached. Among the scholastics this misleading absolutism found expression chiefly in the interpretation of symbols: the concreteness of the Church in its earthly and finite form that nevertheless claimed to be absolute could not but draw in its train a finite limitation of all symbolic forms, and though the result was a system of marvellous symbol-mirages, a system rising from symbol to symbol, overshadowed and bound in a magical unity by the heavenly-earthly, infinite-finite symbol of the Eucharist, yet it could not stave off inevitable collapse; for at its antinomian limits of infinity scholastic thought had to break down, to turn back and solve once more through dialectic the now finite Platonic idea, that is to say, to prepare the reaction towards Positivism, and to enter on that automatic development whose beginnings were already visible in the Aristotelian formation of the Church, and whose further progress, in spite of manifold attempts by the scholastics to hold it up (the theory of twofold truth, the quarrel between nominalists and realists, Occam's new formulation of the theory of knowledge) could no longer be checked; scholastic thought had to founder on its own absolutism, its own antinomies of infinity,—its logic was abrogated.

But thought corresponds to reality only for so long as its logicalness remains undisputed. This applies to all thinking, not merely to deductive dialectic (all the more as it is impossible to distinguish how much deduction is inherent in any act of thinking). It would be wrong, however, to say that deduction became suspect because people had suddenly learned to look at facts with different and better eyes; the exact reverse is the case: things are only regarded with different eyes once dialectic has broken down, and that breakdown occurs not at the point where thought interprets reality, since reality would go on indefinitely submitting itself to such interpretation, but anterior to that, in thought's own province of logic, namely in face of the problems raised by infinity. The patience with which mankind suffers the authority of logic is simply inexhaustible and can be compared only to the imperturbable patience with which it submits to the art of medicine: and just as the human body confides itself to the most nonsensical medical cures, and is actually cured by them, so reality submits to the erection of the most impossible theoretic structures,—and so long as the theory does not itself declare its bankruptcy it will be supported with confidence, and reality will remain tractable. Only after bankruptcy has been openly declared does man begin to rub his eyes and look once more at reality; only then does he seek the source of knowledge in living experience instead of in ratiocination.

These two phases of spiritual revolution can be clearly perceived in the declining years of the Middle Ages: the bankruptcy of scholastic dialectic, and thereafter the—truly Copernican—rotation of attention to the immediate object. Or, in other words, it is the change from Platonism to Positivism, from the speech of God to the language of things.

Yet with this change from the centralization of an ecclesiastical organon to the multifariousness of direct experience, with this transition from the Platonic pattern of medieval theocracy to the positivist contemplation of the empirically given and endlessly shifting world, with this atomizing of a former whole, there had to be a concurrent atomizing of value-systems in so far as these were related to object-systems. In short, values are no longer determined by a central authority, but take their colouring from the object: what matters is no longer the conservation of Biblical cosmogony, but the " scientific " observation of natural objects and the experiments that can be carried out on them; the politician is no longer concerned to model a divine state, but to manage a newly autonomous political unit that makes inevitable the emergence of new and efficient political methods in the shape of Machiavellianism; the warrior is no longer concerned with absolute war, such as took concrete shape in the Crusades, but with earthly squabbles carried on with new-fangled and unchivalrous weapons, such as fire-arms; no longer is it Christendom as a whole that is in question, but only certain empirical groups of men held together by the external bond of national language; nor is it man as the member of an ecclesiastical organon that the new individualism studies, but man as an individual in himself with his individual significance; and lastly the aim of art is no longer solely and finally the glorification of the community of saints, but the faithful observation of the external world, that faithfulness of representation which constitutes the naturalism of the Renaissance. Yet worldly as this obsession with the immediate object may seem, even purely pagan as it perhaps struck people at the time, so pagan that the newly discovered ancients were joyfully invoked as confederates, the inner object forced itself upon men's attention with no less violence than the outer, indeed the immediacy of experience in the

Renaissance is perhaps most immediate of all in its introspection: with this inward turning of the eye, with this discovery of the divine spark in the soul, God, who hitherto had been allowed to manifest Himself only through the medium of an ecclesiastical Platonic hierarchy, now became the object of immediate mystical apprehension, the re-won assurer of divine grace,—and this extraordinary juxtaposition of the most extreme pagan worldliness with the most unconditional inwardness of Protestant mysticism, this co-existence of the most disparate tendencies within the same province of style, would certainly be quite inexplicable were it not that it can be referred to the common denominator of immediacy. Like all other phenomena of the Renaissance, and perhaps in still greater measure than the others, Protestantism is a phenomenon of immediacy.

But yet another and very decisive characteristic of that epoch may here find its determining cause: the glorification of " action," the phenomenon of the "deed," which is so conspicuous in all expressions of life in the Renaissance, and not least in Protestantism; that nascent contempt for the word which tries to confine the function of language as far as possible to its autonomous realms of poetry and rhetoric, refusing it access to other spheres and substituting for it as sole operating factor the man who acts; that movement towards a dumbness which was to prepare the way for the dumbness of a whole world : all this stands in a relation which cannot be ignored to the disintegration of the world into separate value-systems, and follows from that changing-over to the language of things which, to keep the metaphor, is a dumb language. It is almost like a testimony to the fact that any understanding between the separate value-systems was superfluous, or as though such an understanding might falsify the severity and singleness of the language of things. The two great rational vehicles of understanding in the modern world, the language of science in mathematics and the language of money in book-keeping, both find their starting-point in the Renaissance, both arise from that single and exclusive concentration on a single value-system, from that esoteric theory of expression, which might be called ascetic in its severity. Yet such an attitude had little in common with the asceticism of Catholic monks, for unlike the latter it was not a means to an end, not a device for summoning ecstatic " aid," but sprang from the singleness of action, of that " action " which was thenceforth accounted the sole unambiguous language and the sole determining

force. So Protestantism also by its origin and its nature is an " action ";
it presupposes a religiously active man, seeking God, finding God, a
man endowed with the same positive activity as the new scientific
researcher, or, indeed, the new type of soldier or politician. Luther's
religion was through and through that of a man of action, and at bottom
anything but contemplative. But even in the heart of the action, at the
core of this matter-of-fact sense of actuality, there lay the same severity,
the same categorical imperative of duty, the same exclusion of all other
value-systems; that literally iconoclastic asceticism of a Calvin which
one might almost call an epistemological asceticism, and which drove
Erasmus to the point of insisting that music should be excluded from
the service of God.

Yet the Middle Ages too had recognized the force of action. And no
matter how violently the new positivism recoiled from Platonic scholasticism, in referring the individual to the solitary authority of his ego it also
laid bare the " positivist roots " of Platonism. The new Christianity did
not merely protest, it reformed as well, it looked upon itself throughout
as a Renaissance of the Christian idea; and although at first it had no
theology, it developed later, on a more autonomous and restricted basis,
a purely Platonic and idealistic theology: for that is what Kantian philosophy amounts to. So the orientation of values, the ethical imperative
directing action, remained the same as in the Middle Ages, and indeed
could not have changed, for value consists only in the effective will to
value and to unconditionality—there are no values save absolute values.
What had changed was the delimitation of the value-producing action:
hitherto the intensity of human aspiration towards the absolute had been
concentrated on the total value of the Christian organon; now, however,
all the radicality of a self-dependent logic, all the severity of autonomy,
was directed to each system of values separately, each value-system was
raised to an absolute value of its own, and that vehemence was engendered
which was to maintain these absolute values side by side in isolation
without reference to each other, that vehemence which gives the age
of the Renaissance its characteristic colouring.

Of course it could be objected that the general style of the age embraced
indifferently all the disparate value-systems, that the personality of Luther,
for instance, was by no means ascetically limited to one single system,
but strikingly united in a characteristic fashion both religious and worldly
impulses. In return it could be just as reasonably asserted that we are

dealing here with the mere beginnings of a movement that needed five hundred years for its full development, that the age was still full of yearning for the medieval synthesis, and that it was precisely a personality like Luther's, a personality subsuming in itself the most disparate tendencies, not by force of logic but by virtue of its human breadth, that met the needs of the age half way, and dominated and influenced it to an incomparably greater degree than the more " logical " Calvin. It is as if the age were still full of fear in face of the new " severity " and the approaching dumbness of the world, as if it wanted to shout down that dreadful approaching dumbness, and for this reason, perhaps, had to bring to birth the new language of God, the new polyphonic music. But these are assumptions that cannot be proved. On the other hand it can be taken for granted that this uncertain state of the age, this confusion of inchoate impulses, made possible the Counter-reformation; that the fear of approaching loneliness and isolation opened the way for a movement which promised to regain the lost unity. For the Counter-reformation took upon itself the gigantic task of gathering in again the value-systems excluded by the narrow and ascetic religiousness of Protestantism, of attempting a new synthesis of the world and all its values, and, under the guidance of the new Jesuit scholasticism, of once more striving towards the lost medieval wholeness, so that, enthroned as the supreme value, the Platonic unity of the Church might maintain for ever its divine position above all other values of the world.

CHAPTER LVI

The watchmaker Samwald often came out to the hospital now. He lingered at the places where his brother had been tended, and, wishful to show his gratitude, not only regulated the clocks of the hospital free of cost, but also offered to repair gratis the inmates' watches. And then he went to see Gödicke of the Landwehr.

Gödicke looked forward to these visits. Since the funeral many things had become clearer and less disturbing to him: the earthly part of his life had become more solid, and yet it seemed to be growing loftier and airier, without losing any of its stability. He knew now quite clearly that he need no longer be terrified at the looming darkness behind which stood that other Gödicke, or more precisely the many Gödickes of yore, for that dark barrier was nothing but the period during which he had lain in the grave. And should anyone come up and try to remind him of what was on the other side, of what had happened before his burial, he need no longer have any fear, but could, as it were, dismiss it with a shrug of the shoulders, knowing that it had ceased to be of any consequence. All that he had to do was to bide his time, for he need not dread the life that was condensing round him now, even when it pressed quite close upon him; for he had already put death behind him, and everything that came would simply serve to build the scaffolding yet higher. True, he still did not utter a word, nor did he listen when the sisters of his ward-mates addressed him; but his deafness and dumbness were now far less a defence of his ego and his solitude than an advertisement of his contempt for those who disturbed his peace. The watchmaker Samwald was the only one he tolerated, indeed he looked forward to his coming.

Samwald certainly made things easy for him. Even though Gödicke walked with his body bent, leaning on his two sticks, he could look down on the little watchmaker; but that was not what mattered most. More important was the fact that Samwald, as though he knew whom he was dealing with, made not the slightest attempt to question him or to remind him of anything that he, Ludwig Gödicke, did not like. In truth Samwald was not a great talker at any time. As they sat together on a seat in the garden he would show Gödicke a watch that he had taken over for repair, making the cover fly open so that one could see the works, and trying to explain where the defect lay. Or he would speak of his dead brother, who, so he said, was to be envied, for he had got over his troubles and was now in a happier land. But when the watchmaker Samwald went on to speak of Paradise and its heavenly joys, on the one hand that was to be discountenanced, for it pertained to the confirmation class attended by a long-discarded Ludwig Gödicke, yet on the other hand it was a sort of homage to the man Gödicke, like a question addressed to one who was already on the farther side and knew all about it. And when Samwald spoke of Bible gatherings which he was in the custom of attending and from which he derived much enlightenment, when he maintained that the misery of this war must finally lead to a brighter day of salvation, Gödicke did not bother to listen; yet it was vaguely a kind of corroboration of his new-won life, and a challenge to take up in that life a fitting and as it were a post-mortem position. The little watchmaker seemed to him then like one of the lads or women who carried the hods of bricks to the wall, and whom one never talked to civilly but merely ordered about, yet whom one needed nevertheless. This too may have been the reason why he once interrupted the little watchmaker in his stories with the order: " Bring me a beer," and when the beer did not promptly arrive he stared in front of him in incomprehending indignation. For many days he was angry with Samwald and refused to look at him, and Samwald racked his brains trying to find some way of propitiating Gödicke again. That was difficult enough. For Gödicke did not himself know that he was angry with Samwald, and he suffered a great deal from the fact that under the compulsion of an unknown decree he had to turn his face away whenever Samwald appeared. And it was not that he regarded Samwald as the originator of the decree; but he blamed him most bitterly for the fact that the decree was not rescinded. It was a sort of laborious search for each other that arose between the two men, and it was almost an inspiration of the watch-maker's when one day he seized Gödicke by the hand and led him away.

It was a fine warm afternoon, and the watchmaker Samwald led Gödicke the one-time bricklayer by the sleeve of his tunic, cautiously, step by step, taking care to avoid the jagged flint-stones on the road. Sometimes they rested. And when they had rested for a while Samwald tugged at Gödicke's sleeve, and Gödicke got up and they went on again. In this way they arrived at Esch's house.

The ladder leading up to the editorial office was too steep for Gödicke, so Samwald deposited him on the bench in front of the garden and ascended alone: he came back presently with Esch and Fendrich. " This is Gödicke," said Samwald. Gödicke made no sign. Esch led them towards the summer-house. But in front of the two forcing frames, whose glass covers were open, for Esch had been sowing for the autumn crop, Gödicke remained standing, gazing into their depths at the bottom of which lay the brown mould. Esch said: " Well? " But Gödicke still went on staring into the frames. So they all remained standing, bareheaded and in their dark suits, as though they were gathered round an open grave. Samwald said: " It was Herr Esch who started the Bible class . . . we are all seeking guidance from Heaven." Then Gödicke laughed, he did not laugh scornfully, it was only perhaps a somewhat noisy laugh, and he said: " Ludwig Gödicke, arisen from the dead," he did not say it very loudly, and he looked triumphantly at Esch, more, he straightened himself from his humble and bowed posture and was almost as big as Esch. Fendrich, who carried the Bible under his arm, regarded him with the feverish eyes of a consumptive, and then he softly touched Gödicke's uniform, as though he wished to make certain that Gödicke was really present in the flesh. But for Gödicke that seemed to finish the matter, he had done his part, it had not even been a very great strain, he could afford to rest now, and so he simply let himself down on the wooden edge of the frame, waiting for Samwald to sit down beside him. Samwald said: " He's tired," and Esch went with long strides back into the courtyard and shouted up to Frau Esch at the kitchen window to bring some coffee. Then Frau Esch brought out coffee, and they fetched Herr Lindner too from the printing-shed to drink coffee with them, and they stood round Gödicke while he sat on the edge of the frame, and gazed at him sipping his coffee. And none of them saw what Gödicke saw. And after Gödicke had been refreshed by the coffee Samwald once more took him by the hand, and they set out on their way back to the hospital. They went cautiously, and Samwald saw to it that Gödicke did not step on the jagged flints. Sometimes they rested. And when Samwald smiled at his companion, Gödicke no longer turned his eyes away.

CHAPTER LVII

Yes, Huguenau was in a very bad humour. The printed appeals for the Iron Bismarck had been wretchedly botched. That the printing-office did not possess a block of Bismarck's head was perhaps excusable, but not even a proper Iron Cross with laurel wreath complete was to be found in the place, and so there had been nothing for it but to embellish each of the four corners of the appeal with one of the little Iron Crosses usually employed to mark the death notices of soldiers killed in the war. He wouldn't have gone personally with the miserable sheet to the Major at all if he hadn't had a piece of good news as well: a firm of carvers in Giessen, whose advertisement he had discovered and to whom he had immediately wired, were prepared to supply a Bismarck statue within two weeks. But naturally enough the Major must have been deeply disappointed by the tasteless appeal; at first he had not even listened to Huguenau, and had dismissed his excuses with an ill-humoured and indifferent: " It doesn't matter." And even though he had finally condescended to fix his visit for to-day, yet he had spoilt it immediately by inquiring after Esch. That was all the more unjust, seeing that Esch himself was to blame for the lack of decent blocks in the printing-office.

His hands in his trousers-pockets, Huguenau strolled up and down the courtyard and waited for the Major. As for Esch, he had manœuvred him out of the way quite nicely. It had been quite a sly move to dissuade him the day before from going out to the paper factory—and then to-day one found that it had been a mistake after all, and that strangely enough there was a shortage of paper, and so the Herr Editor had just had to go. Unfortunately the lout had considered it necessary to take his bicycle, and if the Major put off coming for very much longer the whole manœuvre would be up the spout, and the two of them would meet after all.

It was a warm sultry day. Huguenau looked now and then at his watch, then he went into the garden, surveyed the fruit, which hung on the branches still unripe, and estimated the crop. Well, in these times things would never be allowed to ripen; long before that everything would be stolen. One fine morning Esch would find his garden cleared out. It wouldn't be long either; on the sunny side the plums were already reddening, and Huguenau put up his hand and tested the fruit between his fingers. Esch should put barbed wire round his garden; but the crop was certainly not worth so much expense. After the war barbed wire would be cheap enough.

Waiting is like barbed wire stretched inside one. Huguenau looked once more up into the branches, blinked up at the grey clouds; where the sun should be they brightened to a dazzling white. He whistled for Marguerite several times; but she did not appear and Huguenau became annoyed; of course she was down at the river again with those boys. He felt inclined to go and fetch her. But he had to wait for the Major.

Suddenly—he was just on the point of whistling for her again—Marguerite stood before him. He said severely: " Where have you been hiding again? There's visitors coming." Then he took her hand, and crossing the courtyard they went through the entry hall to the street and kept watch for the Major. I sent Esch off too soon, Huguenau could not help telling himself again and again.

At last the Major appeared round the corner; he was accompanied by the aged commissariat officer, who also filled the rôle of adjutant to the Town Commandant. Although Huguenau had reckoned on having the Major to himself, he felt nevertheless flattered that the visit should take such an official form. Really it had been stupid to let Esch go, the whole staff should have formed up in line and Marguerite in a white dress should have presented a bouquet of flowers. In some way or other Esch was responsible for this omission too, but there it was, anyhow, and Huguenau's ceremonial fervour had to be confined to a few low bows when the two officers stopped in front of the house.

Fortunately the commissariat officer said good-bye at the door, so that the occasion ceased to be official and became private, and when the Major crossed the threshold Huguenau fairly shone with affability and devotion. "Marguerite, make a curtsy," he commanded. Marguerite stared into the strange man's face. The Major ran his fingers through her black curls: "Well, won't you say how do you do, little Tartar?" Huguenau apologized: "It's Esch's little girl. . . ." The Major raised Marguerite's chin: "So you're Herr Esch's daughter?" "She's only staying here—a sort of foster-child," Huguenau said. The Major stroked her curls again: "Little black Tartar," he repeated as they passed through the entry to the courtyard. "French by birth, Herr Major . . . Esch intends to adopt her eventually . . . but that's unnecessary, she has an aunt in any case . . . wouldn't Herr Major like to see the printing-office straight away? please step this way, to the right. . . ." Huguenau ran in front. "Very well, Herr Huguenau," said the Major, "but I should like to say good-day to Herr Esch first." "Esch will be here in a few minutes, Herr Major, I thought that the Herr Major would like to look over the printing-shop first without being disturbed." "Herr Esch does not disturb me in the least," said the Major, and Huguenau was dashed by his somewhat sharp tone. Esch must have been intriguing somehow . . . well, he would soon get on his track yet and then there would be a full-flavoured secret report number 2. And because such a report was a certainty, Huguenau felt reassured, for no one can endure this inner stream of events to be held up or dammed by external forces. And so Huguenau said formally: "Herr Esch unfortunately had to go to the paper factory . . . I had to make sure that the paper would be delivered . . . but perhaps the Herr Major would like to inspect the printing-shop meanwhile."

The press was set in motion in honour of the Major, and in honour of the Major Huguenau quite gratuitously had a section of the appeal for "The Moselle Memorial Association" run off. He still held Marguerite by the hand, and when Lindner drew off the first sheets of the appeal, Huguenau lifted the uppermost one and held it out to the Major. He felt compelled to apologize once more: "It's a very simple make-up,

I'm afraid; at the very least it should have had a proper Iron Cross
with a laurel wreath . . . in a matter under the immediate patronage of
the Herr Major."

The Major had put up his hand to the Iron Cross at his buttonhole
and seemed reassured to find it still hanging there. " Oh, the Iron Cross
—you don't need another, surely that would be superfluous." Huguenau
bowed: " Yes, the Herr Major is quite right, in such difficult times a
modest make-up will have to do, I can only agree with the Herr Major
there, but a modest little block wouldn't have added much to the outlay
. . . of course that's a matter of indifference to Herr Esch." The Major
did not seem to have heard. But after a while he said: " I think, Herr
Huguenau, that you do Herr Esch an injustice." Huguenau smiled
politely and a little scornfully. But the Major was not looking at him,
but at Marguerite: " I would have taken her for a Slav, this little black
Tartar girl." Huguenau felt called upon to mention once more that the
child was French by birth. " She only comes here." The Major bent
down to Marguerite: " I've a little girl like you at home too, she's a
little bigger, it's true, fourteen . . . and not as black as a little Tartar
either . . . her name is Elisabeth . . ." and after a while he said: " So,
a little French girl." " She can only speak German," said Huguenau,
" she's forgotten everything." The Major asked: " And do you love
your foster-parents very much ? " " Yes," said Marguerite, and Huguenau
was astonished that she could tell such a lie, but as the Major seemed
absent-minded he repeated distinctly: " She stays with her relations."
The Major said: " Driven from home . . ." that really sounded somewhat absent-minded, he was an old gentleman after all, and Huguenau
said in corroboration: " Quite true, Herr Major, the right phrase, driven
from home. . . ." The Major looked at Marguerite attentively. Huguenau
said alluringly: " The case-room, Herr Major, you haven't seen the
case-room yet." The Major passed his hand over the child's brow:
" You mustn't look so cross, you mustn't wrinkle up your brow like
that . . . " the child considered earnestly and then said: " Why not? "
The Major smiled, passed his fingers lightly over her eyelids, under
which the hard eyeballs rested, smiled and said: " Little girls mustn't
have furrows on their brows . . . that's a sin . . . hidden and yet visible,
that's what sin always is." Marguerite recoiled and Huguenau remembered how she had broken away from Esch; she was quite right, he
thought. The Major now passed his hand over his own eyes: " Well, it

doesn't matter . . ." and Huguenau felt that the Major too was struggling to break away, though with feeble powers, and he was actually glad when he saw Esch on his rather too low bicycle, which made him look bandy-legged, riding into the courtyard and springing off by the outside ladder.

They all went into the courtyard to greet Esch; the Major stood between Huguenau and the little girl.

Esch leant his bicycle against the wall beneath the ladder and went slowly up to the group. He showed no trace of surprise at finding the Major there, so little surprise did he show and so calmly did he greet the guest, that Huguenau began to suspect that this lean schoolmaster already knew of the visit. So he gave vent to his ill-humour:

" What do you say to this unexpected honour? Aren't you even surprised? "

" I'm very glad," said Esch.

The Major said:

" I'm very glad that you've returned in time, Herr Esch."

Esch said gravely:

" Perhaps at the eleventh hour, Herr Major."

Huguenau said:

" It isn't so very late yet . . . would the Herr Major like to see the other offices too? the ladder, I'm afraid, is a little awkward."

Esch said:

" It was a long way."

The child said:

" He came on his bicycle."

The Major said dreamily:

" A long way . . . and he is not yet at the goal."

Huguenau said:

" We've the worst already behind us . . . we've two pages of advertisements already . . . and if we could secure the orders of the military authorities as well . . ."

Esch said:

" It's not a question of advertisements."

Huguenau said:

" We haven't even a block of an Iron Cross—I suppose you think that doesn't matter either! "

The child pointed at the Major's chest:

" There's an Iron Cross."

The Major said:

" The true badge of honour is always invisible, only sin is visible."

The child said:

" Lying is the greatest sin."

Esch said:

" The invisible is at our backs, we come out of falsehood, and if we do not find the way we must lose ourselves in the darkness of the invisible."

The child said:

" Nobody hears you when you tell a lie."

The Major said:

" God hears it."

Huguenau said:

" Nobody hears a deserter, nobody recognizes him, even if all he says is right."

Esch said:

" Nobody can see another in the darkness."

The Major said:

" Visible, and yet hidden from each other."

The child said:

" God doesn't hear it."

Esch said:

" He will hear again the voices of His children."

Huguenau said:

" It's best for nobody to hear one, one must fight one's way by oneself . . . we'll bring it off yet."

The Major said:

" We have forsaken Him and He has left us to ourselves . . . so alone that we can no longer find each other."

Esch said:

" Imprisoned in our loneliness."

The child said:

" No one will be able to find me."

The Major said:

" The one we forsake we must seek for ever."

Huguenau said:

" Do you want to hide? "

" Yes," said the child.

The milky grey sky began to break up; in several places it became blue. Barefooted and inaudible, the little girl had flitted away. Then the men went too. Each in a different direction.

Well, they were with me again yesterday, Nuchem and Marie, and we sang together. At my suggestion we sang first of all the hymn:

> To battle out we march elate,
> Firm faith our dauntless gage,
> We do not fear the Devil's hate,
> And laugh at all his rage.
> Our banner proudly waves before
> And fills our souls with might;
> Still in the forefront as of yore,
> It leads us to the fight.
>
> *Chorus*
> We will be faithful to our King,
> Till death we will be true,
> And follow on through everything
> Our flag gold, red and blue.

We sang it to the air of Andreas Hofer's song, Marie accompanied it on the lute, Nuchem hummed and beat time with his soft smooth hands. During the singing they exchanged glances a few times, but it may have been that I only fancied so, for Dr Litwak's talk had made me suspicious. At any rate I bawled out the song as loud as I could, and that for various reasons. For on the one hand I wanted to reassure Nuchem's family, who doubtless were assembled outside my door by this time: the children in the very front, probably, with their ears pressed against the door panel, then the white-bearded grandfather with his body bent forward, his hand forming an ear-trumpet, while the women kept more in the background, perhaps one of them weeping quietly to herself, the whole bunch gradually drawing nearer, yet not daring to open the door,—yes, on the one hand I wanted to reassure them, but on the other hand it was a sadistic pleasure to me to know that they were out there, and to allure and repulse them at the same moment. But by bawling so loudly I wished also to say to Nuchem and Marie: don't stand on ceremony, my children, you see that I'm occupied with myself and my voice, unbutton your frock-coat, Nuchem, lift the tails of your coat and make a bow to the lady, and you, Marie, throw off your prudishness, lift your skirt with two fingers, and dance, both of you, dance to Jerusalem, dance in my bed, make yourselves at home. And so I no longer even sang Marie's words to the air, but my own, the authentic ones: " To Mantua in chains was led, Brave Hofer leal and true," unfortunately that was all I knew, but I modulated these lines to the tune and found that they went beautifully.

At last, however, Marie concluded the song with the flourish that always rounds off songs sung to the lute, and she said:

" We did that splendidly, now as a reward we'll have a little prayer too."

And already she had slipped down on her knees before her chair, raised her clasped hands to her face, and begun the hundred and twenty-second psalm:

" I was glad when they said unto me, Let us go into the house of the Lord. Our feet shall stand within thy gates, O Jerusalem. Jerusalem is builded as a city that is compact together: Whither the tribes go up, the tribes of the Lord, unto the testimony of Israel, to give thanks unto the name of the Lord."

I could not have stopped her except by smashing the lute over her head. So I knelt down too, stretched my arms out and prayed: " Let us make tea for the daughters and young men of Israel, let us pour rum into the tea, war-rum, hero's rum, synthetic rum, that we may forget our loneliness, for our loneliness is too great, whether it be in Zion or in the holy city of Berlin." But while I was uttering these words and beating my breast with my fists, Nuchem had got up: he planted himself before me, he turned his bottom to me, and with his praying countenance fixed on the open window, at which the greasy and torn curtains fluttered in the night breeze like a faded gold, red and blue army banner, he set his swaying body in motion. Oh, that was indecent, that was indecent of Nuchem, who after all was my friend.

I sprang to the door, tore it open and shouted:

" Come in, Israel, drink tea with us, behold the obscene postures of my friend and the unveiled face of the lady."

The lobby, however, the lobby was empty. They had slipped away, they had scattered into their rooms, the women tumbling over the children, the rheumatic grandfather, who could not straighten himself, along with them.

"Splendid," said I, closing the door and turning once more to my familiar spirits, "splendid, my children, now give each other the kiss of Zion."

But the two of them stood there with their arms hanging, and did not dare to seize each other or to dance; smiling sheepishly they simply stood there. And finally we sat down and drank tea.

CHAPTER LIX

THE SYMPOSIUM OR DIALOGUE ON REDEMPTION

Incapable of communicating himself to others, incapable of breaking out of his isolation, doomed to remain the mere actor of his life, the deputy of his own ego—all that any human being can know of another is a mere symbol, the symbol of an ego that remains beyond our grasp, possessing no more value than that of a symbol; and all that can be told is the symbol of a symbol, a symbol at a second, third, nth remove, asking for representation in the true double sense of the word. Therefore it will raise no difficulty for anyone, and will at least make for brevity, if we imagine that Herr and Frau Esch together with the Major and Herr Huguenau find themselves in a scene on the stage, involved in a performance which no human being can escape: that of play-acting.

At the table in ESCH'S *summer-house are sitting* FRAU ESCH, *on her right the* MAJOR, *on her left* HUGUENAU, *opposite her (with his back to the audience)* HERR ESCH. *The evening meal is over. On the table are the bread and the wine, the latter of which* HERR ESCH *has procured from a vineyard proprietor who advertises in his paper.*

Darkness is beginning to fall. In the background the contours of the mountains can still be discerned. Two candles burn within glass globes to protect them from the breeze: moths flutter round them. The jerky asthmatic pounding of the printing-press can be heard.

ESCH: May I fill your glass again, Herr Major?

HUGUENAU: Tip-top wine, no doubt about it . . . we Alsatians must take a back seat after this when our wine is mentioned. Does the Herr Major know our Alsatian wine?

MAJOR (*absently*): I don't think so.

HUGUENAU: Well, it's a harmless wine . . . we Alsatians are altogether harmless . . . an honest tipple you could call it, all frank and aboveboard (*he laughs*) and all it does to you is to make you simply and naturally tight . . . you go to sleep when you've had enough, that's all.

ESCH: To be drunk is never natural, it's a poisoned state.

HUGUENAU: Well, well, I can remember occasions when you were quite willing to take a glass or two over the score . . . for instance . . . well, may I mention the Palatine Tavern, Herr Esch? . . . besides (*he regards* ESCH *attentively*) you don't strike me as being so free from poison as all that.

MAJOR: Your attacks on our friend Esch are very regrettable, Herr Huguenau.

ESCH: Don't mind him, Herr Major, he's not in earnest.

HUGUENAU: Yes, I am in earnest . . . I always say straight out what I think . . . our friend Esch is a wolf in sheep's clothing . . . yes, I stick to that . . . and, by your leave, he has his little orgies in private.

ESCH (*contemptuously*): No wine has ever upset my applecart yet. . . .

HUGUENAU: That's you all over, Herr Esch, trying to keep sober so that you don't give yourself away.

ESCH: . . . now and then I may take a drop too much, yes, and then the world becomes so simple that you would think it was made of nothing but truth . . . as simple as in a dream . . . simple and yet brazenly full of false names . . . the right names for things aren't to be found. . . .

HUGUENAU: You'd better drink consecrated wine, then you'd soon find those names of yours . . . or the future Socialist State, if that's what you're after.

MAJOR: One shouldn't blaspheme even in jest . . . even wine and bread are symbols of the divine.

(HUGUENAU *notices his mistake and reddens.*)

FRAU ESCH: Oh, Herr Major, it's always like this when Herr Huguenau and my husband are together . . . chaff may be a sign of friendship, but sometimes it's really past endurance, the way he drags in the mud everything that is holy to my poor husband.

HUGUENAU: Holy! Pure sham! (*He has once more regained his composure and ceremoniously relights his cigar which has gone out.*)

ESCH (*possessed by his train of thought*): The truth that comes to you in dreams walks on crutches . . . (*he strikes on the table*) the whole world goes on crutches . . . a hobbling monstrosity . . .

HUGUENAU (*interested*): An invalid?

ESCH: . . . if there is even one single error in the world, if at any point at all the false passes for true, then . . . yes, then the whole world is false . . . then everything becomes unreal . . . diabolically conjured away. . . .

HUGUENAU: Abracadabra, it's gone. . . .

MAJOR (*without paying any attention to* HUGUENAU): No, friend Esch, it's the opposite way about: there need be only one righteous man among a thousand sinners . . .

HUGUENAU: . . . the great magician Esch. . . .

ESCH (*rudely*): What do you know about magic? (*shouts at him*) I should think you're more like a conjurer, a juggler, a knife-thrower. . . .

HUGUENAU: Herr Esch, you are in company, remember yourself.

ESCH (*more calmly*): Magic and juggling are devil's work, they're the real evil, they make the confusion still worse . . .

MAJOR: Where knowledge fails, that is where evil begins. . . .

ESCH: . . . but first the man must come who will blot out every error and bring order, who will take upon him the sacrificial death, that the world may be redeemed to a new innocence, so that from the dead new life may arise. . . .

MAJOR: The one who will take the penance upon him . . . (*with assurance*) but He has already come: it was He who destroyed false knowledge and drove out the magicians . . .

ESCH: . . . the darkness still remains, and in the darkness the world is collapsing . . . nailed to the cross and in the hour of final loneliness pierced by the spear. . . .

HUGUENAU: Hm, very unpleasant.

MAJOR: A dreadful darkness was round Him, a half-light of heavy uncertainty, and no one approached Him in His loneliness to help Him . . . yet He took man's sin upon Him, He redeemed the world from sin . . .

ESCH: . . . there has been nothing until now but murder and countermurder, and order will only come when we awaken. . . .

MAJOR: We must take the penance upon us, we must be awakened out of our sin . . .

ESCH: . . . nothing is decided yet, we are still in prison and we must wait . . .

MAJOR: . . . we are encompassed by sin, and our light is darkness . . .

ESCH: . . . we are waiting for the Judgment, we still have a respite and can still begin a new life . . . evil has not yet triumphed . . .

MAJOR: . . . when we are delivered from the darkness, delivered by grace . . . then evil will vanish as if it had never been . . .

ESCH: . . . like an evil magic, a corrupt magic . . .

MAJOR: . . . evil is always outside the world, outside its frontiers: only the man who steps over the world's frontiers and steps out of the truth can fall into the abyss of evil.

ESCH: . . . we are standing on the edge of the abyss . . . on the edge of the dark gully . . .

HUGUENAU: That's too deep for us, what, Frau Esch?

(FRAU ESCH *smooths her hair back, then lays a finger on her lips as a sign to* HUGUENAU *to be silent.*)

ESCH: Many must still die, many must sacrifice themselves, so that room may be made for the son who shall build the house anew . . . only then will the mists thin away and the new life will come, radiant and innocent.

MAJOR: The evil we see is only an illusion, it takes many shapes, but it is never really there itself . . . a symbol of nothingness—only divine grace is real.

HUGUENAU (*who does not intend to be relegated to the part of a silent listener*): Well, if robbery or child-rape or desertion or embezzlement are only illusions, it's a very cheerful outlook.

MAJOR: Evil is non-existent . . . divine grace has redeemed the world from evil.

ESCH: The harder the tribulation, the deeper the darkness, the sharper the whizzing knives, the nearer is the kingdom of redemption.

MAJOR: Only the good is real and true . . . there is only one sin: not to desire the good, not to desire knowledge, not to have good-will. . . .

HUGUENAU (*eagerly*): Yes, Herr Major, that's right . . . myself for instance, I'm certainly no angel . . . (*reflectively*) . . . there's this to be said, in that case one couldn't punish anyone . . . a deserter, for instance, who had good-will couldn't be shot simply to make an example of him.

ESCH: No one stands so high that he dare judge his fellows, and no one is so depraved that his eternal soul can lose its claim to reverence.

HUGUENAU: Quite right.

MAJOR: The man who desires evil can desire good at the same time, but the man who does not desire good has made divine grace bankrupt . . . it is the sign of obstinacy, inertia of feeling.

ESCH: It's not a matter of good or bad works. . . .

HUGUENAU: I beg your pardon, Herr Major, but that doesn't seem quite to fit the case . . . once I lost six hundred marks in Reutlingen through a man going bankrupt, a tidy sum of money, and why? because the man was mad, he had religious mania, of course I wasn't to know that . . . and right enough, he was acquitted and stuck in a lunatic asylum. But my money was gone.

ESCH: What do you want to infer from that?

HUGUENAU: Why, there you have a good man, and yet he did evil works . . . (*grinning*) and if you were to do me in, Herr Esch, you would be acquitted on the plea of religious mania, but if I were to do you in I would lose my head . . . what do you say to that, Herr Esch, with your sham piety? Hm? (*He glances at the* MAJOR, *seeking approval.*)

MAJOR: The madman is like the dreamer; his truth is a false truth . . . he curses his own child . . . nobody can be the mouthpiece of God without suffering for it . . . he is singled out. . . .

ESCH: He lives in a false reality . . . we are all still living in a false reality . . . by rights we should all be madmen, mad in our loneliness.

HUGUENAU: Yes, but I'll be shot and he won't! I beg your pardon, Herr Major, but that's just where he shows his hypocrisy . . . (*becoming heated*), ah, merde, la sainte religion et les curés à faire des courbettes auprès de la guillotine, ah, merde, alors. . . . I'm an enlightened man, but that's a bit too much for me!

MAJOR: Come, come, Herr Huguenau, this Moselle seems to be dangerous to a man of your temperament (HUGUENAU *makes an apologetic gesture*) . . . to take the penance and the chastisement voluntarily upon us, as we have had to take the war, because we have sinned . . . that isn't hypocrisy.

ESCH (*absently*): Yes, to take men's sins upon you . . . in the final hour of loneliness. . . .

The printing-machine stops: the pounding falls silent; the chirping of the crickets can be heard. A wind stirs the leaves of the fruit-trees. Round the moon a few white irradiated clouds can be seen. In the sudden silence the conversation falls away and ceases.

FRAU ESCH: How good the silence is.

ESCH: Sometimes it seems as if the world were only one huge dreadful machine that never stops . . . the war and everything . . . it runs by laws that we don't understand . . . impudent self-assured laws, engineers' laws . . . every man must do what is prescribed for him, without turning his head to right or left . . . every man is a machine that one can only see from outside, a hostile machine . . . oh, the machine is the root of evil and the Evil One is the machine. Their order is the void that must come . . . before Time can begin again. . . .

MAJOR: Not evil, a symbol of evil. . . .

ESCH: Yes, a symbol.

HUGUENAU (*listening complacently to the sounds from the printing-shop*): Lindner is putting in fresh paper now.

ESCH (*in sudden fear*): Oh, God, is there no possibility of one human being reaching another? is there no fellowship, is there no understanding? Must every man be nothing but an evil machine to his fellows?

MAJOR (*lays his hand comfortingly on* ESCH'S *arm*): But, Esch . . .

ESCH: Oh, God, who is there that doesn't think evilly of me?

MAJOR: Anyone who knows you, my son . . . only knowledge can overcome estrangement.

ESCH (*his hands covering his face*): God, let it be by Thee that I am known.

MAJOR: Only to him who has knowledge will knowledge be given, only he who sows love will reap it.

ESCH (*his hands still clasped before his face*): Since I acknowledge Thee, oh, God, Thou wilt not be angry with me any more, for I am Thy beloved son, rescued by Thee from orphanhood. . . . He who submits himself to death has found love . . . only he who flings himself into a dreadful intensification of estrangement and death . . . will find unity and understanding.

MAJOR: And the divine grace will descend on him and take away his fear, the fear that he is wandering on the earth without meaning or purpose, and must go to the grave unenlightened and helpless and without meaning or purpose. . . .

ESCH: So knowledge will grow to love, and love to knowledge, and every soul that is chosen as the vessel of grace will be inviolable; uplifted by love to join the communion of souls, where each is inviolable and alone and yet united in knowledge—the highest law of knowledge not to wound a living creature: if I have known Thee, God, then I shall live eternally in Thee.

MAJOR: Let mask fall after mask until your heart
　　　　And face are open to the eternal breath. . . .

ESCH: I will become an empty vessel drained
　　　　Of all desire and solace, I will take
　　　　The chastisement upon me, plunge myself
　　　　In nothingness and die, but oh, the fear
　　　　Is terrible!

MAJOR: 　　　　　Fear is the fruitful sign
　　　　Of heavenly grace, fear is God's word inscribed
　　　　Upon the gate that leads to your salvation,—
　　　　Step through.

ESCH: 　　　　　Accept me, Lord, in my great need.
　　　　When the fore-dream of death descends upon me,
　　　　A wanderer in life's dream, the fear of death
　　　　Leaps on me, I am helpless and alone,
　　　　And doomed to die alone, forsaken by all.

(HUGUENAU *listens incomprehendingly and* FRAU ESCH *fearfully to her husband's words.*)

MAJOR: You are not alone, even though you die alone,
　　　　Released from evil, fear will leave you too,
　　　　You shall decrease that His will may increase,
　　　　And as you are known, so also you shall know
　　　　The mighty world arisen and manifest.

ESCH: If I could know Thee, Lord, in love through Him
　　　　Who knew me in His love, the waste would turn
　　　　Into a garden of eternal light,
　　　　Boundless the meads, the sun would never set. . . .

MAJOR: Garden of grace encircling all the world,
　　　　Basking in soft spring zephyrs, home where all
　　　　Fears shall have ceased.

ESCH: 　　　　　　　I have been a sinner,
　　　　Sinful and evil, evil in conscious fear,
　　　　Knowing the false way, skirting the edge of the pit,
　　　　Face and hands withered, hounded through wastes and gorges,
　　　　Fleeing in terror from the dagger's point,
　　　　With at my back Ahasuerus' fear,
　　　　And in my feet Ahasuerus' dread,

And in my eyes Ahasuerus' lust
For One whom I have lost time and again,
For One I never saw, One I betrayed
And yet who chose me broken and tempest tossed
In the icy tempest of the starry legions,
And sank His grace into me, where it grew,
Grew to redemption, set me free. . . .

MAJOR: Oh, be my brother, the brother that I lost,
Be as a brother to me. . . .

(*The two of them chant in antiphony, somewhat in the style of the Salvation Army. The* MAJOR *in baritone,* HERR ESCH *in bass.*)

Lord God of Sabaoth,
Take, oh, take us to Thine altar,
Bind us all in one firm band,
Lead us on with Thine own hand,
Lord God of Sabaoth,
Guide our feet lest we may falter,
Lead us to the Promised Land,
Lord God of Sabaoth.

(HUGUENAU, *who until now has beaten time on the table, strikes in* (*tenor*)):

Keep us safe from axe and halter,
Keep us safe from wheel and brand,
Lord God of Sabaoth.

ALL THREE: Lord God of Sabaoth.

FRAU ESCH (*strikes in* (*no voice at all*)):

Thou hast given me food and shelter,
All is Thine, if Thou command,
Lord God of Sabaoth.

ALL TOGETHER (HUGUENAU *and* ESCH *beating time on the table*):

Lord God of Sabaoth,
Save my soul, my spirit,
Save my soul from utter death,
Let not torment sear it,
Let it be in grace baptized,
Nor in sin be e'er chastised,
Keep it whole in merit,

Fan its spark with Thine own breath,
Till it flame in burning faith,
Lord God of Sabaoth,
Save, oh, save Thou me from death.

(*The* MAJOR *has laid his arm round* ESCH'S *shoulder.* HUGUENAU, *his drumming fists still on the table, now slowly lets them fall. The candles have burned down.* FRAU ESCH *pours the last of the wine into the men's glasses, being careful that each receives the same share; the final tiny residue she pours into her husband's glass. The moon is somewhat overcast, and out of the dark landscape the wind blows more coolly now, as though out of a cellar door. Now too the printing-machine once more resumes its pounding, and* FRAU ESCH *touches her husband's arm*): " Shouldn't we go to bed now? "

TRANSFORMATION

Before ESCH'S *house. The* MAJOR *and* HUGUENAU

Huguenau, jerking his thumb towards the window of the Eschs' bedroom:

" Now they're getting into bed. Esch could very well have stayed with us a little longer . . . but she knows what she's after. . . . Hm, will the Herr Major permit me to accompany him for a few steps? A little exercise does one good."

They go through the silent medieval streets. The house entries are like black holes. In one of them, pressed against the door, stand a pair of lovers, from another a dog detaches itself and runs on three legs up the street; at the corner it vanishes. Behind some of the windows a faint light is still burning—but what is happening behind the unlighted ones? perhaps a dead man is lying there, stretched out on his bed, his peaked nose in the air, and the coverlet makes a little tent over his upward-pointing toes. Both the Major and Huguenau gaze up at the windows, and Huguenau would like to ask the Major if he too cannot help thinking of dead men,—but the Major walks on in silence, almost as though he were troubled; probably his thoughts are with Esch, Huguenau tells himself, and he is indignant that Esch should go to bed with his wife and so trouble the good old chap's mind. But devil take it, why should the Major be troubled at all? he makes friends with Esch on the spot instead of keeping that officious hypocrite at arm's-length! A nice friendship, that, between the two of them, between these two fine gentlemen who evidently have forgotten that without him they would never have met each other; who was it, then, that had a prior right to the Major? and if the Major was troubled now, it served him right. More than that, according to his deserts he should be a good deal more troubled, and along with his beloved Herr Esch the Herr Major ought to suffer richly for his treachery. . . . Huguenau stopped short—a daring and seductive idea had arisen before him with clairvoyant lucidity: the idea of entering into a new and venturous relation with the Major that would enable him in a manner of speaking to betray Esch, at present lying with his wife, with the Major, and to land the Major himself in a humiliating situation! yes, a brilliant, a promising idea, and Huguenau said:

" The Herr Major will remember my first report in which I described my visit to the ki . . ." Huguenau clapped his hand over his mouth, " pardon, the public brothel. Herr Esch is sleeping respectably in his matrimonial bed now, but he made one of the party that night, all the same. Since then I've been investigating the matter further, and I think I've found a clue. I would like to have another glance into the place . . . if the Herr Major is interested in the matter and in, how shall I put it, the most interesting milieu, I would most respectfully suggest that he should make a visit of inspection."

The Major let his gaze run once more over the window fronts, over the house doors, which looked like entries to black cellar-caves, and then, to Huguenau's surprise, he said without further ado: " Let us go."

They turned back, for the house lay in the opposite direction and outside the town. The Major again strode on in silence beside Huguenau, he looked perhaps even more troubled than before, and Huguenau, greatly as he longed for a light and confidential tone, dared not even risk starting a conversation. But a still worse disappointment awaited him: when they reached the house, over whose portal a great red lantern shone, the Major abruptly said " No " and held out his hand. And when Huguenau stared at him dumbfounded, he gave a forced smile: " I think you'd better make your researches by yourself to-night." The old man turned back once more towards the town. Huguenau gazed after him in rage and bitterness; but then he remembered Esch, shrugged his shoulders, and opened the door.

He left the house in less than an hour. His spirits had improved; the fear that had weighed upon him was gone, he had put something right, and although he could not have given it a name, yet he felt definitely that he had retrieved his personality and his clear common sense. The others could do what they liked, they could give him the cold shoulder, he snapped his fingers at them. He stepped out vigorously, a Salvation Army song that he must have heard somewhere came into his mind, and with every step he beat time with his walking-stick on the ground to the words: " Lord God of Sabaoth."

CHAPTER LX

Victory Celebration of " The Moselle Memorial Association " in the beer-hall " Stadthalle " in commemoration of the Battle of Tannenberg

Jaretzki was prowling about in the garden of the " Stadthalle." In the big hall they were dancing. Of course one could dance even lacking an arm, but Jaretzki felt shy. He was glad to find Sister Mathilde standing at one of the doors of the dancing-hall:

" So you're not dancing either, Sister? "

" Of course I'm dancing; shall we have a try, Lieutenant Jaretzki? "

" Until I get that thingummy-jig, that artificial arm, there's nothing much I can do . . . except drinking and smoking . . . will you have a cigarette, Sister Mathilde? "

" Why, what are you thinking of? I'm here on duty."

" I see, it's duty that makes you offer to dance. Then duty bids you take pity on a poor one-armed cripple . . . do sit down and bear me company for a little."

Jaretzki sat down somewhat heavily at the nearest table.

" Do you enjoy all this, Sister? "

" Yes, it's very nice."

" Well, I don't like it."

" But the crowd are enjoying themselves, one mustn't grudge them their pleasure."

" Look here, Sister, perhaps I'm a little muzzy as it is . . . but that doesn't matter. . . . I tell you that this war can never stop . . . or what do you think? "

" Why, it must stop some time or other. . . ."

" What shall we do with ourselves then, when there's no more war . . . when no more cripples are turned out for you to nurse? "

Sister Mathilde considered:

"After the war . . . well, you know yourself what you're thinking of doing then. You told me of some job you've been offered. . . ."

"With me it's different . . . I've been at the Front . . . I've killed people . . . forgive me, it sounds a bit confused perhaps, but it's quite clear to me all the same . . . for me it's all over . . . but there are all those others . . ." he waved his hand towards the garden, "they must all face the music yet . . . the Russians are supposed to be forming women's battalions already. . . ."

"The things you say are quite terrifying, Lieutenant Jaretzki."

"Me? not at all . . . I'm finished with the whole business. . . . I'll go back home . . . find myself a wife . . . night after night the same one . . . no more philandering . . . I'm afraid I must be a little drunk, Sister, . . . but you see it isn't good for a man to be alone, it isn't good for a man to be alone . . . it says so in the Bible. And you think a great deal of the Bible, Sister, what?"

"What do you say, Lieutenant Jaretzki, wouldn't you like to go back to the hospital now? Some of our people are wanting to leave . . . you could go with them. . . ."

She felt his alcoholic breath on her face:

"I tell you this, Sister, that the war can't stop because every man out there has found himself alone . . . because one after another, they all find themselves alone . . . and every man who is all alone must kill some other man . . . you think I've drunk too much, Sister, but you know I can carry a lot . . . no reason at all for sending me to bed . . . but it's true, what I've been telling you."

He got up:

"Funny music, what? . . . God knows what kind of dancing this is, but shall we watch it for a little?"

Dr Ernst Pelzer, the volunteer from the trench mortar division, ran slap into Huguenau in one of the hall doorways:

"Hey, look out, Herr Grand Master of Ceremonies . . . you're a regular whirlwind . . . chasing the ladies, as usual?"

Huguenau did not listen at all; with beaming importance he indicated two gentlemen in dress-suits who had just come into the garden:

"The Burgomaster has arrived!"

"Aha—flying after higher game . . . well, good hunting to you, tally-ho! and yoicks! and all the rest of it, my noble sportsman. . . ."

"Thanks, thanks, Herr Doctor"; Huguenau, who had not heard a word, cried his thanks over his shoulder and was already getting into position for the official speech of welcome.

Surgeon-Major Kühlenbeck should really have been sitting at the table of honour. But he did not remain there long.

"Let joy be unconfined," he said, "we are mercenaries in a conquered town."

He steered for a group of young girls. He carried his head high, his beard stuck almost horizontally into the air. As he passed Fusilier Kneese, who was leaning, sad and bored, against a tree, he clapped him on the shoulder: "Well, mourning still for your appendix? You're fine soldiers, I must say, you're here to get the women with child. . . . I'm ashamed of such milksops . . . forward, my lad!"

"Very well, sir," said Kneese, standing to attention.

Kühlenbeck hooked himself on to Berta Kringel, squeezing her arm to his ribs:

"I'll dance a round with you all . . . the one that dances best will get a kiss."

The girls shrieked. Berta Kringel tried to free herself. But when he enclosed her stub-fingered hand in his soft masculine fist, he felt her fingers growing weak and nestling into his.

"So you won't dance . . . you're all afraid of me, that's what it is . . . all right, I'll take you over to the tombola . . . children like to play at such games."

Lisbeth Wöger cried:

"You're only poking fun at us again, Herr Kühlenbeck . . . a Surgeon-Major doesn't dance."

"Well, Lisbeth, you'll come to know me better yet."

And Surgeon-Major Kühlenbeck captured Lisbeth too by the arm.

While they were standing at the tombola-table, Frau Paulsen the wife of the apothecary Paulsen approached, took her stand beside Dr Kühlenbeck, and whispered with pale lips:

"Aren't you ashamed . . . with these callow creatures. . . ."

The huge man gazed at her a little apprehensively from behind his glasses; then he laughed;

" Oh, dear lady, I promise the first prize to you."

" Thanks," said Frau Paulsen, taking herself off.

Lisbeth Wöger and Berta stuck their heads together:

" Did you see how green she was with jealousy ? "

Although Heinrich's presence had to a certain degree broken through her hermit existence, Hanna Wendling had not come to the celebration willingly. But as one of the town's prominent citizens and also as an officer, Advocate Wendling had felt it his duty to attend. So they had driven over with Röders.

They sat in the dancing-hall; Dr Kessel kept them company. At the upper end of the room stood the table of honour, gleaming with napery and decked with flowers and festoons of leaves; there presided the Burgomaster and the Major, and Herr Editor Huguenau had also his place there. When he caught sight of the newcomers he steered his way across to them. That he was on the committee could be seen from the badge in his buttonhole, but still more clearly was it written on his brow. No one could fail to remark Herr Huguenau's dignity. Huguenau had known of course for a long time who this lady was: he had noticed her several times in the town, and a very little inquiry had discovered that she was Frau Advocate Wendling.

He made straight for Dr Kessel:

" May I beg you, Herr Doctor, to do me the great favour of introducing me to your friends ? "

" Yes, with pleasure."

" A great honour, a great honour," said Herr Huguenau, " a great privilege; the gracious lady lives in such retirement, and if it were not for the great good fortune of her husband being here on furlough I feel sure that we wouldn't have had the pleasure of welcoming her in our midst to-night."

The war had made her rather shy of people, replied Hanna Wendling.

" That's the wrong way to take it, dear lady. It's just in such grave times that one needs cheering up. . . . I hope that you're both staying for the dance."

" No, my wife is a little tired, so unfortunately we must go soon."

Huguenau was honestly hurt:

" But, Herr Advocate, you and your charming wife must really grant us the honour for once, our festivities really must be graced by such a beautiful lady . . . and it's for a philanthropic object, so won't the Herr Lieutenant close one eye and put mercy before justice?"

And although Frau Hanna Wendling was perfectly aware of the shallowness of these flatteries, her face opened and she said:

"Well, as a favour to you, Herr Editor, we'll stay for a little longer."

In the middle of the garden a long table had been set up for the soldiers, and "The Moselle Memorial" had presented them with a small cask of beer, which stood on its two trestles beside the table. The beer had been finished long ago, but a few of the men still loitered round the empty table. Kneese had joined them, and now he was drawing designs with a finger-tip in the pools of beer on the wooden boards:

"The Surgeon-Major says that we're to give them children."

"Who?"

"The girls here."

"Tell him he must lead the way."

Guffaws.

"He's doing that as it is."

"It would be more sense if he let us go home to our wives."

The lamps swayed in the night wind.

Jaretzki wandered alone through the garden. When he met Frau Paulsen he bowed:

"So lonely, dear lady?"

Frau Paulsen said:

"You seem to be lonely too, Herr Lieutenant."

"Doesn't mean anything in my case, I'm finished with everything."

"Come, shall we try our luck at the tombola, Herr Lieutenant?" Frau Paulsen attached herself to Jaretzki's sound right arm.

Huguenau met Surgeon-Major Kühlenbeck walking with Lisbeth and Berta under the trees.

Huguenau exclaimed in greeting:

"A happy evening, Herr Surgeon-Major, a happy evening, young ladies."

And he was gone.

Dr Kühlenbeck was still holding stub-fingered bourgeoise hands in his great warm paws:

" Well, do you like that elegant young fellow? "

" No . . ." the two girls tittered.

" Indeed? Why not? "

" There's others better than him."

" I see. Who, for instance? "

Berta said:

" There's Lieutenant Jaretzki walking with Frau Paulsen over there."

" Leave them to themselves," said the Surgeon-Major. " I'm going to stick to you."

The band blew a flourish. Huguenau stood beside the conductor on the platform, which on one side projected into the hall, on the other, in the form of a pavilion, into the garden.

Making a speaking trumpet with his hands, Huguenau shouted over the tables standing in the garden:

" Silence."

In the garden and the hall there was dead silence.

" Silence," crowed Huguenau once more into the stillness.

Captain von Schnaack of Room VI.—he had a shot wound in the lung which was now healed—stepped up beside Huguenau on the platform and now unfolded a sheet of paper :

" Victory at Amiens. 3700 English prisoners, 3 enemy aeroplanes shot down, two of them by Captain Blöcke, who thus achieves his twenty-third air victory."

Captain von Schnaack raised his arm: " Hip, hip, hooray! " The band struck up the national anthem. All rose to their feet; the most of them joined in the singing. When it had died away again, someone shouted from a shadowy corner:

" Hurrah, hurrah, hurrah, long live the war! "

Everybody turned and looked.

There sat Lieutenant Jaretzki. A bottle of champagne was standing before him, and he was trying to embrace Frau Paulsen with his sound arm.

The walls of the dancing-hall were decorated with portraits of the allied generals and rulers decked with oak-leaves and paper garlands and hung with banners. The patriotic and ceremonious part of the celebration was now over, and Huguenau could dedicate himself to pleasure. He had always been a good dancer, had always been able to flatter himself that in spite of his stoutness and short stature he cut a good figure; but to-night more was at stake, to-night more was in question than the elasticity and agility of a stout little man; here under the eyes of the military commanders the dance became a celebration of victory.

The dancer is removed beyond the reach of this world. Wrapped in the music, he has renounced his freedom of action, and yet acts in accordance with a higher and more lucid freedom. In the rigorous security of the rhythm that guides him he is safely sheltered, and a great relief comes to him from that security. Thus music brings unity and order into the confusion and chaos of life. Cancelling Time it cancels death, and yet resurrects it anew in every beat of the rhythm, even in the rhythm of that dreary and endless potpourri which, calling itself *A Selection of Music from All Countries*, is now being played, and consists of a particoloured assortment of German folk-songs and enemy dances such as the cake-walk, the matchiche and the tango. The dancer's partner hums, then, growing more ardent, she sings. And her emotional and unschooled voice sings the barbarous words of these melodies, all of which she knows without exception, her soft zephyr-like breath brushing his cheek when he bends over her in the tango. But soon he straightens himself again, his warlike spirit reawakened he gazes fixedly and sternly through his eye-glasses, gazes into the distance, and dauntlessly he and his partner defy hostile powers when the music breaks triumphantly into an heroic march; but now with the changing rhythm they fall into the artful contortions of the one-step, and shuffle with curious swayings on one spot, almost without progressing, until the long waves of the tango once more roll up and their movements once more become catlike and soft, with a yielding suppleness of leg and body. Should they pass the table of honour, behind whose flower-filled vases the Major sits side by side with the Burgomaster, then with a sweep of the arm the dancer snatches up a glass from the board—for he himself belongs to this table—and without interrupting the dance, like a tight-rope dancer who carelessly and smilingly devours a succulent meal while still high up in the air, he drinks to the seated company.

He scarcely guides his partner now; one hand, gallantly enveloped in his pocket-handkerchief, rests delicately beneath the low-cut back of her dress, but his left arm hangs carelessly by his side. Only when the music changes over to a waltz do they join their free hands; stiffly, in reciprocal tension, they brace their outstretched arms, and with their fingers locked the pair whirl round the hall. Glancing round the hall, he sees that the ranks of dancers have thinned. Only one other pair is still dancing, they come nearer, almost brush him, recede, glide away again along the walls. The others have withdrawn among the spectators; unequal to the alien dance rhythms, they stand and admire. Should the music cease, the spectators and dancers alike clap their hands, and it begins once more. It is almost like a trial of strength. Huguenau scarcely sees his partner, who with head flung back in surrender has resigned herself to his strong and yet hardly visible guidance; he does not know that the music has released in his partner a more delicate and disciplined artistry of sex, a bacchantic feminine power which will remain for ever unknown to her husband, to her lover, even to herself, nor does he see the ecstatic smile with which the other lady hangs in her partner's arms; he sees only his rival, sees only the other hostile dancer, a lean wine-agent in evening clothes with a black tie and an Iron Cross on his chest, who in elegance and military distinction outshines himself in his plain blue suit. So might Esch himself, with his long lank limbs, dance here, and therefore, to filch the lady from him, Huguenau holds her with his eye as she glides past with her partner, and he keeps on doing this until she returns his gaze, gives herself to him with her glances, so that he, Wilhelm Huguenau, now possesses both the women, possesses them without desiring them, for it is not the favour of women that matters to him, though he may be competing for it now—the pleasures of love do not matter to him; on the contrary this celebration and this spacious hall concentrate ever more exclusively around the white-decked table over there, and his thoughts are directed more and more unconditionally on the Major who sits, white-bearded and beautiful, behind the flowers watching him, him, Wilhelm Huguenau in the middle of the floor; he is a warrior dancing before his chieftain.

But the Major's eyes were filling with growing horror. This hall with these two men shamelessly shuffling, shamelessly hopping, more shameless even than the women with whom they were coupled; it was like a house of ill fame, it was the pit of corruption itself. And that a war could be accompanied by such celebrations of victory turned war itself into a bloody caricature of corruption. It was as though the world were becoming featureless, featureless every face, a pit where nothing could be distinguished, a pit from which there was no longer any rescue. Seized with horror, Major von Pasenow caught himself wishing that he, a Prussian officer, could tear the banners from the walls, not because they were desecrated by the festive abominations, but because they were incomprehensibly bound up with these abominations and this diabolical display, in an incomprehensibility behind which all the unchivalry of unchivalrous weapons, treacherous friends and broken pledges was concealed. And as he sat in a strange icy immobility, the dreadful desire arose in him to destroy this demoniacal rabble, to exterminate them, to see them lying crushed at his feet. But motionless and gigantic as a towering mountain range, as the shadow of a mountain range on the wall, there rose grave and solemn above the rabble the image of a friend, perhaps it was that of Esch, and to Major von Pasenow it seemed that it must be for this friend's sake that the Evil One had to be crushed and cast into nothingness. Major von Pasenow longed for his brother.

Sister Mathilde was searching for Dr Kühlenbeck. She found him among a crowd of prominent business men. Kringel the merchant, Quint the hotelkeeper and pork-butcher, Herr Salzer the architect, and Herr Westrich the postmaster, were all sitting there. And their wives and daughters were sitting beside them.

" A moment, Herr Surgeon-Major."

" Another woman that's cocked her eye at me."

" Just one moment, sir."

Kühlenbeck got up:

" What's wrong, my child ? "

" We must get Lieutenant Jaretzki out of here. . . ."

" Yes, I fancy he's had about enough."

Sister Mathilde smiled in agreement.

" I'll come and see to him."

Jaretzki's sound arm was lying on the table, his head was resting on it, and he was asleep.

The Surgeon-Major looked at his watch:

" Flurschütz is relieving me. He should be arriving at any moment now with the car. He can take Jaretzki back with him."

" Can we leave him here asleep like this, sir? "

" There's nothing else for it. War is war."

Dr Flurschütz blinked through somewhat inflamed eyes at the lighted garden. Then he went into the dancing-hall. The Major and the other guests of honour had already left. The long table had been removed and the whole room set free for the dancing, which proceeded on its crowded, steaming, sweating, shuffling course.

It was some time before he caught sight of his chief; with grave expression and upward-pointing beard Kühlenbeck was revolving with Frau Chemist Paulsen in a waltz. Flurschütz waited for the dance to end, and then he reported himself.

" Well, here at last, Flurschütz: you see what childish follies you have driven your worthy superior officer to with your lateness . . . but now there's no excuse for you; when the chief dances, the next in command must dance too."

" Insubordination, sir, I refuse to dance."

" And this is the younger generation . . . it seems to me that I'm younger than the lot of you . . . but now I must go, I'll send the car back for you. Bring Jaretzki with you; he's blind to the world for the moment . . . one of the sisters will return with me, you bring the other."

In the garden he unearthed Sister Carla:

" Sister Carla, I'll take you back with me, I can manage four wounded men too. Round them up, will you, but be quick."

Then he packed in his passengers. Three men were got into the back seat, Sister Carla and another man in the front seat, and he himself took his place beside the chauffeur. Seven crutches stared into the dark air (the eighth lay somewhere in the car), stars hung in the black tent of the sky. The air smelt of petrol and dust. But from time to time, particularly at the turns of the roads, one felt the nearness of the woods.

Lieutenant Jaretzki got up. He had a feeling as though he had fallen asleep in a railway carriage. Now the train was stopping at one of the bigger stations; Jaretzki resolved to visit the buffet. There were a great many people and a great many lights on the platform. " Sunday traffic " Jaretzki told himself. He had got quite cold. Round about the region of the stomach. Something warm would do him good. Suddenly his left arm was missing. Must have left it lying on the luggage-rack. He steered his way through tables and people. At the tombola counter he halted.

" A grog," he commanded.

" It's a good thing that you're here," said Sister Mathilde to Dr Flurschütz, " it won't be an easy job to deal with Jaretzki to-night."

" We'll manage it all right, Sister . . . enjoyed yourself? "

" Oh yes, it was quite jolly."

" Isn't it a little spectral to you too, Sister? "

Sister Mathilde tried to understand, and did not answer.

" Well, could you have pictured anything like this to yourself years ago? "

" It reminds me somewhat of our annual fair."

" A somewhat hysterical fair."

" Well, perhaps, Dr Flurschütz."

" Empty forms that still live . . . looks like a fair, but the people in it don't know any longer what's happening to them."

" It will all soon come right again, Herr Doctor."

She stood before him, straight and sound.

Flurschütz shook his head:

" Nothing has ever come right yet . . . least of all on the Judgment Day . . . doesn't this look a little bit like it? what? "

" The ideas you have, Doctor! . . . but we must get our patients together."

The volunteer Dr Pelzer caught up Jaretzki in his wandering course near the music pavilion.

" You seem to be looking for something badly, Herr Lieutenant."

" Yes, a grog."

" That's a famous idea, Herr Lieutenant, winter is coming, I'll fetch you a grog . . . but sit down . . . until I get it." He rushed away and Jaretzki sat down on a table, swinging his legs.

Dr Wendling and his wife, just leaving, passed by. Jaretzki saluted:

" Allow me, Herr Lieutenant, I'm Second Lieutenant Jaretzki, Hessian Light Infantry Battalion No. 8, Army of the Crown Prince, lost left arm as result of gas-poisoning at Armentières, beg to introduce myself."

Wendling looked at him in astonishment:

" Delighted," he said. " Lieutenant Dr Wendling."

" Diploma engineer Otto Jaretzki," Jaretzki now felt obliged to add, this time standing to attention before Hanna, so as to show that the introduction also included her.

Hanna Wendling had already encountered a great deal of admiration during the evening. She said graciously:

" But that's horrible, about your arm."

" Quite right, gracious lady, horrible but just."

" Come, come, Herr Comrade," said Wendling, " one can't talk of justice in such things."

Jaretzki raised one finger:

" It isn't legal justice that I mean, Herr Comrade . . . we've been given a new kind of justice, a man doesn't need so many members when he's alone . . . you'll agree with that, I'm sure, gracious lady."

" Good-evening," said Wendling.

" A pity, a horrible pity," said Jaretzki, " but of course everyone is pledged to his loneliness . . . good-evening." And he returned to his table again.

" Queer man," said Hanna Wendling.

" Drunken fool," replied her husband.

The volunteer Pelzer passing with two glasses of grog stood to attention.

Huguenau hurried out of the ballroom. He wiped the sweat from his brow, and tucked his handkerchief inside his collar.

Sister Mathilde stopped him:

" Herr Huguenau, you could help us by gathering the patients together."

" A great honour, gracious lady, shall I order a flourish to be blown? "
—and he turned at once towards the band.

" No, no, Herr Huguenau, I don't want any fuss, we can manage without that."

" As you please . . . been a splendid evening, hasn't it, gracious lady? The Herr Major has expressed his pleasure in the most gracious terms."

" Certainly, a lovely evening."

" The Herr Surgeon-Major seemed to be very pleased too . . . he was in splendid spirits . . . may I beg you to give him my humble regards . . . he left us so suddenly that I couldn't see him off."

" I wonder, Herr Huguenau, if you would let the soldiers in the ballroom know that Dr Flurschütz and myself are waiting for them at the door."

"It shall be done, it shall be done at once . . . but it isn't right of you, gracious lady, to leave us so soon . . . not a sign, I hope, that you haven't enjoyed yourself . . . well then, I shan't regard it as that."

His handkerchief tucked inside his collar, Huguenau hastened back into the ballroom.

"What about the officers, Sister?" asked Flurschütz.

"Oh, we don't need to bother about them, they've made arrangements themselves for being driven back."

"Good, then everything seems to be coming right after all . . . but we've still got Jaretzki on our shoulders."

Jaretzki and Dr Pelzer were still sitting in the garden beneath the music pavilion. Jaretzki was trying to look at the illuminations through his brown grog-glass.

Flurschütz sat down beside them:

"How about going to bed, Jaretzki?"

"I'll go to bed if I can find a woman, if I can't find a woman I won't go to bed . . . the whole thing began with the men going to bed without women and the women going to bed without men . . . that was a bad arrangement."

"He's right there," said the volunteer.

"Possibly," said Flurschütz, "and that's only occurred to you now, Jaretzki?"

"Yes, this very moment . . . but I've known it for a long time."

"Well, you'll certainly save the world with that idea."

"It would be enough if he saved Germany," said the volunteer Pelzer.

"Germany . . ." said Flurschütz, looking round the empty garden.

"Germany . . ." said Pelzer, "when it began I volunteered straight off for the Front . . . now I'm glad to be sitting here."

"Germany . . ." said Jaretzki, who had begun to weep, "too late . . ." he wiped his eyes, "Flurschütz, you're a nice fellow, I love you."

"That's good of you, I love you too . . . shall we go home now?"

"We haven't a home to go to, Flurschütz . . . I'll have a shot at getting married."

"It's too late for that too, at this time of day, I fancy," said the volunteer.

"Yes, it's rather late, Jaretzki," said Flurschütz.

"It's never too late for that," bawled Jaretzki, "but you've cut it off, you swine."

"Come, Jaretzki, it really is time now that you wakened up."

"If you cut mine off, I'll cut yours off . . . that's why the war must go on for ever . . . have you ever tried to do it with a hand-grenade . . . ? " he nodded gravely, ". . . now I, I have . . . fine eggs, the hand-grenades . . . rotten eggs."

Flurschütz took him under the arm:

"Well, Jaretzki, probably you're quite right . . . yes, and probably it's actually the only way left of coming to a mutual understanding . . . but now come along, my friend."

At the outside door the soldiers were already assembled round Sister Mathilde.

"Pull yourself together, Jaretzki," said Flurschütz.

"Righto! " said Jaretzki, and as he appeared before Sister Mathilde he straightened himself to attention and reported: "A lieutenant, a medical officer and fourteen men present . . . I beg to report that he has cut it off . . ." he made a short pause for effect, and then drew the empty sleeve out of his pocket and waved it to and fro under Sister Mathilde's long nose: "Chaste and empty."

Sister Mathilde cried:

"Those who want to drive back can do so; I am going on foot with the others."

Huguenau came rushing out:

"I hope everything has gone all right, gracious lady, and that we're all here . . . may I wish you a safe journey home? "

He shook hands with Sister Mathilde, with Dr Flurschütz, with Lieutenant Jaretzki, and with each of the fourteen soldiers, being careful to introduce himself in each case as "Huguenau."

CHAPTER LXI

STORY OF THE SALVATION ARMY GIRL IN BERLIN (10)

What really do I want of Marie? I invite her here, I ask her to sing, I couple her in all chastity with Nuchem, the Talmudist, the renegade Talmudist, I suppose I should say, and I let her go away again, let her disappear within the walls of her grey hostel. What do I want of her? and why does she lend herself to this game? is she resolved to save my soul, is she resolved to take on the endless, the ultimately impossible task of capturing the Talmudist soul of this Jew and leading it to Jesus? What does Nuchem think about it anyway? Here I am with these two human beings apparently in the hollow of my hand, and yet I know nothing about them, not even what they are thinking and what they will eat this evening; man is such an isolated creature that nobody, not even God Who created him, knows anything about him.

The whole thing disturbed me extraordinarily, especially as I had never been able to look upon Marie except as a creature filled to the brim with hymns and Bible texts, and in my uneasiness I set out for the hostel.

I had to go there twice before I found her. She was out on a round of sick-visiting, and did not return until the evening. So I sat and waited in the common-room, contemplated the Bible texts on the walls, contemplated the portrait of General Booth, and once more considered all the various possibilities. I recalled to my mind my first meeting with Marie, also her first chance encounter with Nuchem, I made myself visualize everything that had happened since, I impressed all this very thoroughly on my mind, not even excepting my situation at the moment; I examined the common-room with the greatest attention, walking about in the slowly increasing dusk, for the sky had darkened; outside heavy raindrops were falling, hastening the twilight. I asked myself whether the two old men who were also sitting in the room like myself were to be included in my memory, and I included them—best to make certain. They were very feeble, their thoughts were impenetrable, I was empty air to them.

It was quite late when Marie arrived. Meanwhile the two old men had been led out, and I had been almost afraid that I would be treated in the same way. In the barely lit room she did not recognize me at once; she said: " God send you His blessing," and I responded: " That is only a symbolic figure of speech." Recognizing me now she replied on her side: " It isn't a figure of speech, may God send you His blessing." Now I said for my part: " With us Jews everything is a symbol." Thereupon she replied: " You aren't a Jew." To which I answered: " The bread and the wine are only symbols, none the less; besides, I live among Jews." She said: " The Lord is our eternal home." That was completely in character, that was just as I had imagined it to myself, a sacred text for every eventuality; now she was delivered once more into my hand, and raising my voice I said: " I forbid you ever to enter my Jewish home again," but it had an empty sound in that place. I must have her in my flat again, it seemed, if I was to talk reasonably to her; so I laughed and said: " A joke of mine, *nebbich*, a joke." Yet though with that Yiddish word I may have been seeking to take refuge from my own speech in that of an alien, an utterly alien people, and to shelter myself under the ægis of a God alien to me, it was of no avail, I did not recover my assurance. It may be that I was really too broken by my long wait, grown old like the two old men who had finally been led out of the waiting-room; I had been humiliated by my wait, a creature instead of a creator, a disthroned God. Almost humbly I had to bring out: " I wanted to save you from scandal, Dr Litwak has been pointing out the danger to me." Now that was of course a distortion of the case, for Litwak had feared the danger simply for Nuchem's sake. And to call in such a ridiculous half-baked Freethinker as a confederate! truly I could not have given a more painful wound to my self-respect. And simple as was the retort which she found in reply, it was a reproof: " When your heart is filled with the joy of the Lord, you're safe from scandal." My patience gave under this humiliation, and I did not notice that now I was actually serving the old grandfather's and Dr Litwak's purposes: " You mustn't carry on any more with the young Jew; he has a fat wife and a swarm of children." Oh, could I have read in her soul, could I have known whether with these words I had hurt and wounded her, torn that heart which gave out that it was filled with the joy of the Lord, —but there was no sign of that, perhaps she had not even understood what I said. She merely said: " I'll come to see you. We'll sing together." I acknowledged myself beaten. " We can go now," I said with a last remnant of hope that I might still manage to decide her course. She replied: " I would love to, but I must go back to my sick patients."

So I was compelled to set off for home again with everything still unsettled. Only a soft rain was falling now. In front of me marched a very young pair of lovers; they were clasping each other and their free arms swung to the rhythm of their march.

CHAPTER LXII

DISINTEGRATION OF VALUES (8)

Religions arise out of sects and in their decadence lapse again into sects, returning to their original status before falling into complete dissolution. At the beginning of the Christian era there were the several Christ- and Mithras-cults, at its close we find the grotesque American sects and the Salvation Army.

Protestantism was the first great sect-formation in the decay of Christianity. A sect, not a new religion. For it lacked the most important characteristic of a new religion, that new theology which binds together into a new harmony the new experience of God and a new cosmogony. Protestantism, by its very nature undeductive and untheological, refused to venture beyond the sphere of the autonomous inward religious experience.

Kant's attempt to establish a retrospective Protestant theology did indeed wrestle with the task of transferring the substance of religious Platonism to the new positivistic science, but it was far from seeking to set up a universal theological canon of values on the Catholic pattern.

The defence of Catholicism against a progressive disintegration into sects was organized by the Jesuits of the Counter-reformation in a draconic, even a military, centralization of values. That was the time when even the survivals of heathenish folk-customs were pressed into the service of the Church, when folk-art received its Catholic colouring, when the Church of the Jesuits blossomed into an unheard-of splendour, aspiring towards and achieving an ecstatic unity which was no longer, indeed, the mystic symbolical unity of the Gothic, but none the less was its heroic-romantic counterpart.

Protestantism has had to dispense with that kind of defence against sectarianism. It does not absorb the non-religious values, it only tolerates them. It despises extraneous " aids," for its asceticism insists on the radical inwardness of religious experience. And although it acknowledges ecstasy to be the source and the crown of religion, yet it exacts that the ecstatic value shall be independently wrested from the sphere of pure religion, remaining absolutely uncontaminated, uncompromised, and autonomous.

This attitude of severity is what governs the relationship of Protestantism to the non-religious social values, and what it depends on also to ensure its own stability as a Church on earth. In its exclusive and single-minded devotion to God it must of necessity fall back on the sole extant emanation of God's spirit on earth, the Holy Scriptures,—and so fidelity to the Scripture becomes the highest earthly duty of the Protestant, and all the radicality, all the severity of the Protestant method is applied to maintaining it.

The most characteristically Protestant idea is the categorical imperative of duty. It is in complete opposition to Catholicism: the extraneous values of life are neither subsumed in a creed nor included in a theological canon, but are merely strictly and somewhat bleakly supervised on the authority of Scripture.

If Protestantism had chosen to follow the other line of development, the Catholic, in order to achieve in its turn an organic system of Protestant values, such as Leibniz envisaged, for example, it would perhaps have preserved itself not less successfully than Catholicism against a further splitting-up into sects; but it would have been compelled to lose its essential character. It found itself—and still finds itself—in the situation of a revolutionary party that runs the danger, once it has risen to power, of being forced to identify itself with the old order it has been opposing. The reproach of disguised Catholicism levelled against Leibniz was not quite without foundation.

There is no severity that may not be a mask for fear. But the fear of lapsing into sectarianism would be much too insignificant a motive to account for the severity of Protestantism. And the flight to punctilious fidelity, to the written word, is pregnant with the fear of God, that fear which comes to light in Luther's *pœnitentia*, that " absolute " fear of the " ruthlessness " of the Absolute which Kierkegaard experienced and in which God " is enthroned in sorrow."

It is as if Protestantism by clinging to the Scripture wished to preserve the last faint echoes of God's Word in a world that has fallen silent, a world where only things speak dumbly, a world delivered over to the silence and ruthlessness of the Absolute,—and in his fear of God the Protestant has realized that it is his own goal before which he cowers. For in excluding all other values, in casting himself in the last resort on an autonomous religious experience, he has assumed a final abstraction of a logical rigour that urges him unambiguously to strip all sensory trappings from his faith, to empty it of all content but the naked Absolute, retaining nothing but the pure form, the pure, empty and neutral form of a " religion in itself," a " mysticism in itself."

There is a striking correspondence between this process and the structure of the Jewish religion: perhaps the Jews have carried to a still more advanced stage the neutralization of religious experience, the stripping of all emotional and sensory elements from mysticism, the elimination of the " external " aids to ecstasy; perhaps they have already got as near to the coldness of the Absolute as the ordinary man can bear —but they too have preserved the utmost rigour and severity of the Law as the last vestige of a bond with religious life on the earthly plane.

This correspondence in the process of intensification, this correspondence in the form of religious structure, which is asserted to extend even to the point of causing a corresponding similarity of character between orthodox Jews and Swiss Calvinists or British Puritans, this correspondence could, of course, be attributed also to a certain similarity in the external circumstances of these religions: Protestantism being a revolutionary movement, and the Jews an oppressed minority; they are both in opposition; and it could even be alleged that Catholicism itself when driven into a minority, as for instance in Ireland, exhibits the same characteristics. Yet a Catholicism of that stamp has as little in common with the Catholicism of Rome as the original Protestant faith has with the Romanizing tendencies of the High Church. They have simply inverted their distinguishing signs. And however these empiric facts are expounded, their explanatory value is but little, since the facts would not be available at all were it not for the determining religious experience behind them.

Is it this radical religiosity, dumb and stripped of ornament, this conception of an infinity conditioned by severity and by severity alone, that determines the style of our new epoch? Is this ruthlessness of the divine principle a symptom of the infinite recession of the focus of plausibility? Is this immolation of all sensory content to be regarded as the root-cause of the prevailing disintegration of values? Yes.

The Jew, by virtue of the abstract rigour of his conception of infinity, is the really modern, the most " advanced " man *kat' exochen*: he it is who surrenders himself with absolute radicality to whatever system of values, whatever career he has chosen; he it is who raises his profession, even though it be a means of livelihood taken up by chance, to a hitherto unknown absolute pitch; he it is who, unconditionally and ruthlessly following up his actions without reference to any other system of values, attains the highest summit of spiritual enlightenment or sinks to the most brutal absorption in material things: in good as in evil a creature of extremes—it looks as though the current of the absolute Abstract which for two thousand years has flowed through the ghettoes like an almost imperceptible trickle beside the great river of life should now become the main stream; it is as if the radicality of Protestant thought had inflamed to virulence all the dread ruthlessness of abstraction which for two thousand years had been sheltered by insignificance and reduced to its minimum, as if it had released that absolute power of indefinite extension which inheres potentially in the pure Abstract alone, released it explosively to shatter our age and transform the hitherto unregarded warden of abstract thought into the paradigmatic incarnation of our disintegrating epoch.

Apparently a Christian can only decide between two alternatives: either to seek the still available protection of the Catholic harmony of values, in the literally motherly bosom of the Church, or courageously to accept the absolute Protestantism which involves abasement before an abstract God,—and wherever this decision has not been taken, fear of the future lies like an oppression. And in fact it is the case that in all countries where men are still undecided this fear is latent and constantly active, though it may find expression merely in a fear of the Jews, whose spirit and mode of living are felt, if not recognized, to be a hateful image of the future.

In the idea of a Protestant organon of values there certainly exists a desire for the reunion of all Christian churches, the kind of reunion envisaged by Leibniz, and that Leibniz, who comprehended completely the values of his age, was bound to think of it can now be seen as almost inevitable; but it was equally inevitable that a man like him, a man centuries ahead of his time, who foresaw the *lingua universalis* of logic, must have also envisaged in that final reunion the abstraction of a *religio universalis*, an abstraction of a coldness that perhaps he alone was capable of enduring, being as he was the most profound mystic of Protestantism. But the Protestant line of development postulated first the immolation of life; so it was Kant's philosophy, not Leibniz's, that engendered Protestant theology; and the rediscovery of Leibniz was reserved, significantly enough, for Catholic theologians.

The numerous sects that have split off one after another from Protestantism, and have been treated by it with that ostensible tolerance which is peculiar to every revolutionary movement, have all developed in the same direction; they are all a rehash, a whittling away and levelling down of that old idea of a Protestant organon of values; they are all on the side of the " Counter-reformation ": for instance, to leave out of account the grotesque American sects, the Salvation Army not only resembles the Jesuit movement of the Counter-reformation in its military organization, but also exhibits very clearly the same tendency to centralize all values, to draw everything into its net, to show how popular art of every kind, down to the street song, may be reclaimed for religion and reinstated as " ecstatic aids." Pathetic and inadequate expense of spirit.

Pathetic and inadequate expense of spirit, deceptive hope, to think of saving the Protestant idea from the horror of the Absolute. It is a touching cry for help, a cry summoning all the resources of a religious community, even though that may be seen only as the pale reflection of what was once a great fellowship. For at the door in rigid severity stand silence, ruthlessness and neutralization, and the cry for help mounts more and more urgently from the lips of all those who are not capable of accepting what is bound to come.

CHAPTER LXIII

On the Sunday afternoon following the celebration in the Stadthalle, Major von Pasenow, to his own surprise, decided to avail himself of Esch's invitation to visit the Bible class. It came about in the following way: actually he had not been thinking of Esch at all, and what turned the scale was perhaps simply the walking-stick which he suddenly saw leaning in the hall-stand, a walking-stick with a white ivory crook-handle, which in some way had got smuggled in among his other things and evidently must have been hidden until now in some cupboard. Of course he remembered the stick quite well, nevertheless it was strange to him. For a moment it seemed to Major von Pasenow as though he must change into mufti and visit one of those ambiguous pleasure resorts which an officer is not allowed to enter in uniform. And so to speak as a concession, he did not buckle on his sword, but took the stick in his hand and left the hotel. He remained standing hesitatingly for a little in front of the hotel, then set out in the direction of the river. He walked slowly, supporting himself on the stick, somewhat like a wounded or an invalid officer at a health resort,—and he could not help remembering vaguely that the indiarubber bulb at the point of the old stick needed to be replaced. So at a moderate pace he reached the outskirts of the town, and he had the slight agreeable sense of freedom that a man has who can turn back at any moment, like an officer on furlough. And in fact he presently did turn back—it was like a happy and reassuring, yet disconcerting return to one's home—and as though remembering an urgent promise which he had to redeem at once, he took the shortest way to Esch's dwelling.

Since the number of Esch's disciples had increased, and as during the summer months there was no need in any case for a heated room, the meetings were held in one of the empty store-rooms opening on the courtyard. A carpenter who belonged to the circle had provided rude benches; a little table with a chair behind it stood in the middle of the room. As there was no window the door was left open, and the Major, entering the courtyard, knew at once what direction to take.

Now that the Major appeared framed in the doorway and paused for a little to accustom his eyes to the twilight, everybody stood up; it almost gave the impression of an expected visit of inspection by a superior officer on his rounds, and this impression was strengthened by the uniforms of the soldiers present. This transformation, even though merely figurative, of his unusual situation into the dignified terms of the office to which he was accustomed, mitigated the shock of it for the Major; it was as though a light and yet firm hand had held him back from stepping down dark ways, it was a fleeting intimation of a danger overcome, and he raised his hand in salute.

Esch had sprung up along with the others, and now he escorted the guest to the chair behind the table. He himself remained standing beside it, rather like a guardian angel allotted to the Major. And the Major had somewhat that feeling about it, more, it was as though the object of his visit were already fulfilled, as though he were surrounded by an atmosphere of security, a simplified area of life which was waiting to receive him, the returned wanderer. Even the silence that surrounded him was like an end in itself, it might have endured as it was for ever; no one spoke a word, the room, filled with the silence, strangely emptied by the silence, seemed to extend beyond its own walls, and the yellow sunlight outside the open door flowed past like an eternal immeasurable river on whose banks they were sitting. Nobody knew how long this silent motionless state lasted, it had as it were the frozen timelessness of those seconds when men are faced with death, and although the Major knew that it was Esch who stood beside him, he felt to the full the fraternal presence of death, felt its menace as a sweet support. And when he made to turn round to Esch, it required all the effort which one needs when one awaits something decisive, knowing at the same time that one must maintain one's calm to the very last instant. With a great effort he turned round to him and said: " Please continue."

But nothing at all happened, for Esch gazed down on the Major's white hair-parting, he heard the Major's low voice, and it was as though the Major knew all about him, as though he knew all about the Major, like two friends who know each other well. He and the Major were there as on an uplifted and radiant stage, they were seated in the places of honour, the audience were still as though a bell had commanded silence, and Esch, who dared not lay his hand on the Major's shoulder, leaned on the back of the chair, although that too was undeniably pre-sumptuous. He felt strong, steadfast and firm, as strong as in the best days of his youth, at once secure and gentle, as though he were delivered from all the works of man, as though the room were no longer made of bricks laid one on another, the door no longer of sawn planks of wood, as though all were the work of God and the words in his mouth were God's words.

He opened the Bible and read from the sixteenth chapter of the Acts of the Apostles:

" And suddenly there was a great earthquake, so that the foundations of the prison were shaken: and immediately all the doors were opened, and every one's bands were loosed.

" And the keeper of the prison awaking out of his sleep, and seeing the prison doors open, he drew out his sword, and would have killed himself, supposing that the prisoners had been fled.

" But Paul cried out with a loud voice, saying, Do thyself no harm: for we are all here."

Clearing his throat cautiously, Esch waited, his finger between the pages of the closed book. He waited for the foundations of the house to tremble, he waited for a great revelation now to manifest itself, he waited for One to give the command that the black flag should be hoisted, and he thought: I must make way for him who shall create time anew. He thought all this and waited. But for the Major the words he had heard were like drops which turned to ice while they fell; he kept silence and all kept silence with him.

Esch said:

" All flight is meaningless, of our own free will we must accept our imprisonment . . . the invisible shape with the sword stands behind us."

As the Major saw very clearly for a moment, Esch had interpreted the sense of the passage in part correctly, in part in the most obscure and fantastic way; but the old man did not linger over this reflection, and it was blotted out by an emerging picture which, though resembling a memory, was yet scarcely a memory, for it presented everything corporeally before him; the old reservists of the Landsturm and the young recruits were changed into apostles and disciples, members of a community met together in some greengrocer's cellar or dark cave, speaking a strange dark language that was yet as comprehensible as a language one had known in childhood, and over them shone a celestial silvery cloud—and the disciples, like himself, were gazing up to heaven with trust and resolute ardour.

" Let us sing," said Esch, and he began:

> " Lord God of Sabaoth,
> Take, O take us to Thine altar,
> Bind us all in one firm band,
> Lead us on with Thine own hand,
> Lord God of Sabaoth."

With the sole of his boot Esch beat time; many of the others did the same, rocking themselves in time and singing. The Major may have joined in the singing, but he did not know it, the singing seemed rather to be inside him, a singing behind his closed eyes, like a crystalline drop that falls singing from a cloud. And he heard the voice say: " Do thyself no harm: for we are all here."

Esch let the singing die away, and then he said:

" It is of no avail to flee from the darkness of the prison, for we flee only into outer darkness . . . we must build the house anew when the time has come."

A voice began again:

> " Fan its spark with Thine own breath,
> Till it flame in burning faith,
> Lord God of Sabaoth."

" Shut up," said another voice.

A neighbouring voice responded:

> " Baptize us, Jesus, with thy fire,
> Let the fire descend!
> To fiery baptism we aspire,
> Let the fire descend!
> O Lord our God, of Thee we crave
> Let the fire descend!
> Nothing else can bless and save.
> Let the fire descend! "

" Shut up," repeated the other voice, a slow voice, but resonant as a vaulted crypt, and it was the voice of a man in Landwehr uniform, a man with a long beard who stood up leaning on two sticks. And despite the effort it cost him, he went on to say: " Anyone who hasn't been dead should shut up . . . whoever has been dead is baptized, but not the others."

But the first singer had also sprung to his feet and his voice rang out again, singing:

> " Save, O save my soul from death,
> Lord God of Sabaoth."

" Let the fire descend," added the Major at this moment in a low voice that was yet audible enough to make Esch bend down towards him. It was in a sense an incorporeal approach, at least the Major felt it to be so; there was an element of assurance in it, both reassuring and disconcerting, and the Major studied the ivory crook of his stick that was lying before him on the table, studied the white cuff that projected a little beyond the sleeve of his uniform coat,—it was in a sense an incorporeal serenity, a kind of etherealized, luminous, almost white serenity that expanded in the dark room and spread over the confusion of voices, like a network of tinkling glass in a strangely abstract simplification. The stream of sunlight shimmered outside like a sharp fiery sword; they were safe as in a haven of refuge, in a cave, a cellar, a catacomb.

Perhaps Esch was expecting the Major to say something more, for the Major twice lifted his hand in time with the measure of the song as if desiring to make some acknowledgment,—Esch held his breath, but the Major let his hand sink again. Then Esch said, as though to quicken into life something that was dead:

" The torch of liberty . . . the blaze of illumination . . . the torch of true freedom."

But for the Major everything was so fused and blended into one experience that he could not have told whether he actually saw the fiery crests of torches or heard the voice of the man who was continually intoning " Let the fire descend," or whether it was Esch's voice or the wailing of Samwald the little watchmaker that rose in a thin piping from the background:

> " Illumine our darkness, lead us into the joys of paradise."

But the Landwehr man, gasping as he drew himself upright, waved one of his sticks and emitted hoarse sounds, bawling:

" Arisen from the dead . . . anyone who hasn't been buried must shut up."

Esch showed his strong teeth and laughed:

" Shut up yourself, Gödicke."

These were rude words: Esch himself could not help laughing so loudly that the laughter somehow stuck in his throat and hurt him, as if he were laughing in his sleep. The Major, indeed, perceived neither the rudeness of the words nor Esch's overloud laugh, for in his clearer knowledge he saw through the surface coarseness without even remarking it; indeed it seemed to him that Esch would be able with a light touch to set everything right, that Esch's features, almost unrecognizable in the dusk, were blending with the whole room into a strangely dim, blurred landscape, and through the resonant laughter he saw the glimmer of a soul leaning out of a neighbouring window with a smile, the soul of a brother, yet not an individual soul, nor yet in actual proximity, but a soul that was like an infinitely remote homeland. And he gave Esch a smile. That knowledge, however, filled Esch too, and he too understood that the smile they exchanged raised them together to a high peak; it was as if he had come whirling from a remote distance on the wings of a roaring wind that swept away all the dead past, as if he had come in a fiery red chariot to an appointed goal, a high pinnacle on which it no longer mattered by what name a man was called or whether one figure blended with another, a goal where there was no longer any to-day or to-morrow,—he felt the breath of liberty stir on his forehead, a dream within a dream, and Esch, unbuttoning his waistcoat, stood there drawn up to his full height as if he were about to set his foot on the outer stairway of the castle.

Yet in spite of it all he had not been able to cow Ludwig Gödicke, who now hobbled forward almost up to the table and screamed pugnaciously:

" You can't say anything till you've crawled under the ground . . . down there . . ." he bored the point of his stick into the earthen floor, ". . . down there . . . crawl down there yourself first."

Esch had to laugh again. He felt strong, steadfast and robust, firm on his legs, a fine fellow whom it was worth anyone's while to do in. He stretched his arms out like a man waking from sleep or nailed on a cross:

" Are you maybe thinking of knocking me down, eh? . . . with your crutches . . . you and your crutches, you misbegotten object."

There was some shouting that he was to leave Gödicke alone, Gödicke was a holy man.

Esch made a gesture of sweeping denial:

" No one is holy . . . there's no one holy but the son who will build the house."

" I build all kinds of houses," roared Gödicke the bricklayer, " all kinds of houses have I built . . . higher and higher . . ." and he spat contemptuously.

" Skyscrapers in America, I suppose," sneered Esch.

" He can build skyscrapers too," wept Samwald the watchmaker.

" Scraper yourself . . . scraping down walls is all he's fit for."

" From the earth beneath to the very skies. . . ."

Gödicke had raised his arms in the air with his two sticks; he looked menacing and powerful, " . . . arisen from the dead! "

" Dead! " screamed Esch, " the dead believe that they're powerful . . . yes, powerful they are, but they can't awaken life in the dark house . . . the dead are murderers! Murderers, that's what they are! "

He stopped abruptly, scared by the echo of murder that was now fluttering in the air like a dark butterfly, but scared and silenced no less by the Major's behaviour: for the Major had risen to his feet with a queer, stiff jerk, and had repeated the word, had woodenly repeated " murderers," and now was gazing at the open door and the courtyard outside as if he were expecting something dreadful to appear.

All the men fell silent and stared at the Major. He did not move but went on gazing spellbound at the door, and Esch also turned his eyes towards it. There was nothing there out of the ordinary; the air quivered in the sunlight, the house wall on the other side of that sunny flood— the wall of a quay, the Major could not help thinking—was a blinding white rectangle standing out against the brown box of the doorway and the two wings of the door. But the illusion began to lose its intoxicating immediacy, and when Esch, seizing his opportunity in the silence, read again from the Bible: " and immediately all the doors were opened " the door became for the Major once more an ordinary barn door, and nothing remained except that the ordinary courtyard outside bore a far-off resemblance to his old home and the great farmyard among the byres and stables. And when Esch concluded: " Do thyself no harm, for we are all here " even the serenity vanished, leaving only fear, the fear that in a world of illusion and semblances nothing but evil could take on bodily form. " We are all here," repeated Esch, and the Major could not believe it, for these were no longer apostles and disciples before his eyes, only men of the Landsturm and recruits, men of the rank and file, and he knew that Esch, lonely as he himself, was like him staring in terror at the door. So they stood side by side.

And then it happened that in the depths of the dark box, in the frame of the doorway, a figure came into sight, a round, thickset figure that advanced over the white gravel of the yard without causing the sun to darken. Huguenau. With his hands linked behind him, a passer-by taking an amiable stroll, he walked across the courtyard and paused in the doorway, blinking as he peered in. The Major and Esch were still standing immovably, for although it seemed an eternity to them it was only a matter of a few seconds, and as soon as Huguenau had ascertained what was going on he took off his hat, entered on tiptoe, bowed to the Major and sat down modestly at the end of a seat. "The devil incarnate," murmured the Major, "the murderer . . ." but perhaps he did not say it, for his throat was drawn together and he looked at Esch almost as if imploring help. Esch, however, smiled with a hint of sarcasm, although he himself felt Huguenau's intrusion as a treacherous attack or an assassination, as a blow bringing the inevitable death that one yet longs for, even when the arm holding the dagger is merely that of a despicable agent,—Esch smiled, and, since the man who faces death is released into freedom and all is permitted to him, he touched the Major's arm: "There's always a traitor among us." And the Major answered in an equally low voice: "He should get out . . . get out . . ." and as Esch shook his head he added: " . . . naked and exposed . . . yes, naked and exposed are we on the other side," and then he said finally : " . . . well it doesn't matter . . ." for in the wave of disgust that he felt suddenly rising within him there was a broad and dominant current of indifference, of weariness. And wearily and heavily he lowered himself again into his seat by the table.

Esch, too, would have liked to hear and see no more. He would have liked to dismiss the meeting. But he could not let the Major depart in such an inharmonious frame of mind, and so, somewhat indecorously, he banged the Bible on the table and announced:

"We shall read again in the Scriptures. Isaiah, chapter forty-two, verse seven: To open the blind eyes, to bring out the prisoners from the prison, and them that sit in darkness out of the prison house."

"Amen," responded Fendrich.

"It is a fine allegory," said the Major.

"An allegory of redemption," said Esch.

" Yes, an allegory of redemption through repentance," said the Major, and drew himself up with a little jerk, as if on parade, " a fine allegory . . . shall we now bring the service to a close for to-day? "

" Amen," said Esch, and buttoned up his waistcoat.

" Amen," said the congregation.

As they left the barn and were still standing irresolutely in quiet conversation in the courtyard, Huguenau pushed his way through the groups till he reached the Major, but was taken aback by that officer's discouraging aloofness. Still, he was unwilling to abandon the encounter, all the more as he had a joke ready to fire off: " So the Herr Major has come to assist at our fine new minister's first celebration? " The curt, aloof nod with which he was answered informed him that their relationship was under a cloud, and this became still more obvious when the Major turned round and said with loud emphasis: " Come along, Esch, you and I will take a walk outside the town." Huguenau was left standing in a state of mingled incomprehension, wrath and vaguely questioning guiltiness.

The other two took the path through the garden. The sun was already inclining towards the western heights. That year it seemed as if the summer were never coming to an end: days of shimmering golden stillness followed each other in equal radiance, as if by their sweetness and peace they wanted to make the war, now in its bloodiest period, appear doubly insensate. As the sun dipped behind the chain of mountain peaks, as the sky paled into tenderer blue, as the road stretched away more peacefully and all life folded in upon itself like the breathing of a sleeper, that stillness grew more and more accessible and acceptable to the human soul. Surely that Sabbath peace lay over the whole of the German fatherland, and in a sudden uprush of yearning the Major thought of his wife and children whom he saw walking over the sunset fields. " I wish this were all over and done with," and Esch could not find any word of comfort for him. Hopeless and dreary this life seemed to both of them, its sole meagre return a walk in the evening landscape which they were both contemplating. It's like a reprieve, thought Esch. And so they went on in silence.

CHAPTER LXIV

It would be false to say that Hanna longed for the end of Heinrich's furlough. She feared it. Night after night this man was her lover. And her daytime life, that even hitherto had been only a blurring and fending-off of consciousness, a darkening directed towards evening and towards bed, was now much more unambiguously directed to that end, with a lack of ambiguity that was startling and could scarcely be attributed to love, with such hardness, such unsentimentality, was it all dominated by the knowledge that she was a woman and he a man: it was a rapture that did not smile, a literally anatomical rapture that was in part too godlike for a lawyer and his wife and in part too base.

Her life was certainly a fading into darkness. Yet this obscuration proceeded only by layers, so to speak; it never deepened into complete unconsciousness, but rather resembled a too-vivid dream in which one is painfully aware that one's will is paralysed; and the more helplessly she was committed to it, the wilder the flora and fauna she accepted, the more did that layer of consciousness awaken which lay immediately above the dream. Only it could not be put into words, not because shame prevented it, but rather because words can never penetrate to the ultimate nakedness that arises from action as the night arises from the day,—her words, too, had fallen into layers, as it were, into at least two layers of language, a night-language closely bound to the event, stammering in its utterance, and a day-language that was detached from the event and went round it in a wide circle, closing in upon it circuitously—the method that the rational always follows until it finally surrenders itself in the screaming and sobbing of despair. And often this day-language was a feeling and seeking for the ultimate cause of the disease that afflicted her. " When the war's over," Heinrich would say almost every day, " everything will be different again . . . the war has made us all more primitive somehow." " I can't understand it," was Hanna's usual answer to that, or: " One simply can't think it out, it's all so inconceivable." These rejoinders were ultimately a refusal to discuss things with Heinrich as if he were on the same level; he was a guilty party and ought to defend himself instead of surveying things from above. Therefore she said as she stood before the mirror and loosened the light tortoiseshell comb from her fair hair: " That queer man in the Stadthalle talked about our loneliness." Heinrich dismissed him: " The fellow was drunk." Hanna combed her hair and could not help thinking that her breasts were drawn up more tightly when her arms were raised. She could feel them under the silk of her chemise, on which they were outlined like two small pointed tents. She could see them in the mirror that was lit on each side by a small electric candle under a softly patterned pink shade. Then she heard Heinrich say: " It's as if we had been shaken through a sieve . . . crumbled to dust." She said: " In a time like this no children should be born." She thought of the boy who looked so like Heinrich, and it seemed unimaginable to her that her blonde body should be fashioned to receive a man's seed, to be a woman. She had to shut her eyes. He said: " It's possible that a new generation of criminals is growing up. . . . There's no guarantee that we mightn't have a flare-up at any moment just like Russia . . . well, we'll hope not . . . but our only comfort lies in the extra-ordinary vitality of inherited tradition. . . ." Both of them felt that the conversation was tailing off into irrelevancy. It was almost as if a prisoner in the dock were to say: " Lovely weather to-day. A spacious court-room," and Hanna relapsed into silence for a moment, letting herself go on that wave of hatred which made her nights more sordid, more pro-found and more lustful. Then she said: " We'll have to wait and see . . . it has certainly some connection with the war . . . but not in that way . . . it's as if the war were only the second thing." " How the second thing? " asked Heinrich. Hanna made a furrow between her eyebrows: " We are the second thing and the war is the second thing . . . the first thing is something invisible, something that we have given off. . . ." She remembered how she had longed for the end of their honeymoon to come, so that—as she then believed—she might fling herself with enthusiasm into the arrangement of their home. Their present situation was not so unlike that; a honeymoon is a kind of furlough too. What she had felt then must have really been a premonition of approaching isolation and loneliness,—perhaps, it dawned on her now, perhaps loneliness was that first thing, perhaps loneliness was the root of the disease! And seeing that it had begun immediately after her wedding—Hanna sent her thoughts back: yes, it had begun even while they were in Switzerland—and seeing that everything fitted in, she felt her suspicion grow keener that Heinrich in those days must have committed some irreparable mistake in his relation to her, some injustice or other that could never be undone but only made greater, a gigantic injustice that had helped in some way to let the war loose. She had applied her face-cream and carefully rubbed it in with her fingers, and now she examined her face in the mirror with jealous attention. The girlish face of those days had vanished, had turned into a woman's face through which that of the young girl now only glimmered. She did not know why all these things were connected, but she concluded her silent train of thought, saying: " The war is not the cause, it's only a secondary thing." And then she realized: the war is a second face, a night face. It was a disintegration of the world, a night face crumbling into cold and bodiless ash, and it was the disintegration of her own face, that disintegration she felt when Heinrich kissed her in the hollow of her shoulder. He said: " Why, certainly, the war is only the result of our mistaken policy," and perhaps he might actually have been able to understand that even policy is only a secondary matter in so far as there is a cause which lies deeper. But he was content with his explanation and Hanna, as she sprayed herself sparingly with the French perfume, now irreplaceable, and sniffed its fragrance, was no longer listening: she had bent her head for a kiss on the nape where the faint silvery hairs grew, and she obtained it. " Another," she said.

CHAPTER LXV

Esch was a man of impetuous moods. So any trifle was capable of provoking him to self-sacrifice. His desire was for simple directness: he wanted to create a world so strong in its simplicity that his own loneliness could be bound fast to it as to an iron stake.

Huguenau was a man who had braved many winds; even when he came into a stuffy room he was braving winds.

There was a man who fled from his own loneliness as far as India and America. He wanted to solve the problem of loneliness by earthly methods; but he was an æsthete, and so he had to kill himself.

Marguerite was a child, a child engendered by a sexual act, burdened with original sin and left alone to sin: someone might happen to give her a nod and ask what her name was—but such fleeting sympathy could not avail to save her.

There is no symbol that does not necessitate a further symbol,—does the immediate experience stand at the beginning or at the end of the series of symbols?

In a medieval poem the series of symbols begins in God and returns to God again—it is poised in God.

Hanna Wendling wanted things to be ordered so that in their poised equilibrium symbols would return to themselves again as in a poem.

One says Farewell, the other deserts—but they all desert from chaos; yet only he who was never bound can escape being shot.

There is nothing more despairing than a child.

He who is mentally lonely can always escape into romanticism, and from spiritual loneliness there is always a way of escape into the intimacy of sex—but for ultimate loneliness, for immediate loneliness, there is no longer any escape into symbols.

Major von Pasenow was a man who yearned passionately for the familiar assurance of home, for an invisible assurance in visible things. And his yearning was so strong that layer by layer the visible sank for him into the invisible, but the invisible, on the other hand, layer by layer became visible.

" Ah," says the romantic, drawing on the cloak of an alien value-system, " ah, now I am one of you and am no longer lonely." " Ah," says the æsthete, drawing on the same cloak, " I am still lonely, but this is a lovely cloak." The æsthete is the serpent in the romantic Garden of Eden.

Children are intimate at once with everything: the thing is both immediate and at the same time a symbol. Hence the radicality of children.

When Marguerite wept it was only from rage. She did not sympathize even with herself.

The lonelier a man becomes, the more detached he is from the value-system in which he lives, the more obviously are his actions determined by the irrational. But the romantic, clinging to the framework of an alien and dogmatic system, is—it seems incredible—completely rational and unchildlike.

The rationality of the irrational: an apparently completely rational man like Huguenau cannot distinguish between good and evil. In an absolutely rational world there would be no absolute value-system, and no sinners, or at most, mere detrimentals.

The æsthete too does not distinguish good from evil: in that lies his fascination. But he knows very well what is good and what evil, he merely chooses not to distinguish them. And that makes him depraved.

An age that is so rational that it must continually take to its heels.

CHAPTER LXVI

STORY OF THE SALVATION ARMY GIRL IN BERLIN (11)

I draw back from the Jews as much as possible, but I find myself as before compelled to go on observing them. So I cannot help wondering again at the confidence they repose in Samson Litwak, that half-free thinker. It is obvious that the man is a blockhead who was allowed to study merely because he was incapable of following a proper occupation —one has only to compare his bare unwrinkled face, that has looked out on the world from its fringe of beard for more than fifty years, with the furrowed thought-creased faces of the old Jews—and yet he seems to have a kind of oracular prestige among them which they invoke on all occasions. Perhaps it is a survival of the old belief in the half-wit as the mouthpiece of God, for it cannot be respect for scientific knowledge; they are too conscious of possessing the higher knowledge. It is hardly credible that I am mistaken. Dr Litwak, indeed, tries to put me off the scent, but he does it very badly. This tale of his " enlightenment " is pure fabrication: his reverence for the Jews' knowledge is too great, and if he gives me a friendly greeting in spite of the way I treat him, that is doubtless because I have refused to dismiss the Talmudic wisdom of the Jewish ancients as "prejudice." Obviously he has taken this as encouragement to hope that I will keep Nuchem on the right path; and so he submits to my continual snubbing of him and his attempts at familiarity.

To-day I met him on the stairs. I was going up and he was coming down. Had it been the other way about I could simply have dashed past him; it's not so easy to stop a man who is rushing down. But I was climbing up too slowly, what with the heat of the city and my half-starved condition. He barred my way jokingly with his walking-stick. Probably he wanted me to jump over it like a poodle (I catch myself in these last days becoming touchy, far too touchy; that too may be the result of semi-starvation). I raised the stick with two fingers so as to get past it.

Oh, how I loathed his grinning familiarity! He nodded to me:

"What do you say to it now? everybody's quite upset."

"Yes, it's very hot."

"If it were only the heat!"

"Well, the Austrians are held up in Transylvania."

"Who's speaking of Transylvania? . . . what do you really say to it now? he says one must have joy in the heart."

My condition makes me enter into the most idiotic discussions:

"That sounds quite like a psalm of David . . . have you any objection?"

"Objection? I only object . . . I only say the old grandfather's right, old people are always right."

"Prejudice, Samson, prejudice."

"You won't have *me* on toast!"

"Well, what does dear Grandpapa say?"

"Now listen! He says, a Jew must have joy not in the heart but here. . . ." He tapped himself on the forehead.

"In the head, then?"

"Yes, in the head."

"And what do you do with your hearts when you're joyful in the head?"

"With the heart we must serve . . . *uwchol levovcho, uwchol nawschecho, uwchol meaudecho*, that means, with all one's heart, with all one's soul, and with all one's might."

"Does Grandpapa say that too?"

"Not only the grandfather says it, it is so."

I tried to look at him pityingly, but it did not quite come off:

" And you call yourself enlightened, Herr Dr Samson Litwak? "

" Of course I'm an enlightened man . . . just as you are an enlightened man . . . of course, but is that any reason for upsetting the law? "

He laughed.

" God bless you, Dr Litwak," said I and went on climbing.

He replied: " A hundredfold," he was still laughing, " but no man can upset the law, not you, not I, not Nuchem. . . ."

I went on ascending the sordid stair. Why did I stay here? In the Army hostel I would be better accommodated. Texts on the walls instead of oleographs, for instance.

CHAPTER LXVII

STORY OF THE SALVATION ARMY GIRL IN BERLIN (12)

He said: my mule, quick-trotting, carries me
and thee together through our dream of Zion,
with jingling bells and purple bridle flying.
He said: I called to thee.
He said: my heart is open to the miracle
of the great Temple with its thousand stairs,
the city where my fathers said their prayers.
He said: we two shall build a tabernacle.
He said: till now I have waited for release
sunk in my book, waiting till I awoke.
He said: this joy I have longed for, and this peace . . .
he did not speak, it was his heart that spoke.
She too said nothing. Deep in silence lapped
so they went on, and yet their hearts were rapt.
So they went on, and yet their hearts were rapt
in silence, inner yearning, hidden glory,
so they went on and heeded not the story
of the mean streets they passed, the dens of shame.
She said: in the most secret part of me
the spark is fanned and rises into flame,
a blaze of light, a splendour without name.
He said: I thought of thee.

She said: my heart is kindled in a glow,
from me, a sinner, thou dost not turn aside.
He said: bright gleams the road to Zion that we go.
She said: for us thou once wert crucified.
They said no more: light dazzled what was said.
They did no more: the deed was perfected.

CHAPTER LXVIII

" What, are you thinking of going out at this late hour, Lieutenant Jaretzki? "

Sister Mathilde was sitting near the porch of the hospital, and Lieutenant Jaretzki, standing in the illuminated doorway, lit himself a cigarette.

" It was too hot to-day to go out . . ." he clicked his lighter shut, " a good invention, these petrol lighters . . . you know, don't you, that I'm going away next week, Sister? "

" Yes, so I heard. To Kreuznach, to a convalescent home? . . . You must be glad to get out of here at last. . . ."

" Oh, well . . . I suppose you're glad to get rid of me."

" You haven't been exactly a good patient."

Silence.

" Come for a little walk, Sister, it's cool now."

Sister Mathilde hesitated:

" I have to go in again soon . . . but, if you like, let's take a short turn."

Jaretzki said reassuringly:

" I'm quite sober, Sister."

They went out into the road. The hospital with its two rows of lighted windows lay to their right. The outline of the town beneath them was just discernible, its mass was a little blacker than the blackness of the night. A few lights were burning there, and on the hills, too, a light now and then gleamed from some solitary farmhouse. The town clocks struck nine.

" Wouldn't you like to be leaving too, Sister Mathilde? "

" Oh, I'm quite happy. . . . I have my work."

" It's really frightfully decent of you to come for a walk with a good-for-nothing down-and-out like me, Sister."

"Why shouldn't I go for a walk with you once in a way, Lieutenant Jaretzki?"

"Why not, indeed. . . ." After a while: "So you want to stay here all your life, do you?"

"Not exactly . . . not when the war's over."

"Then you're going home? . . . to Silesia?"

"How do you know that?"

"Oh, one soon finds out these things . . . and you think that it'll be a simple matter just to go home . . . as if nothing had happened?"

"I haven't really thought about it . . . things always turn out differently."

"Do you know, Sister . . . now, I'm quite sober . . . but it's my firm conviction that none of us will ever really get home again."

"But we all want to get home again, Lieutenant; what should we have been fighting for, if not for our homes?"

Jaretzki stood still.

"What have we been fighting for? What have we been fighting for . . . you'd better not ask, Sister . . . besides, just as you said, things always turn out differently in any case."

Sister Mathilde made no reply. Then she said:

"What do you mean exactly, Lieutenant?"

Jaretzki laughed:

"Well, should you ever have expected to be going for a walk with a boozing, one-armed engineer? . . . you're a Countess, aren't you?"

Sister Mathilde did not answer. She was not a Countess, but she was certainly a *von* and her grandmother was a Countess.

"Perhaps it doesn't matter a rap . . . if I'd been a Count I should just have been the same, I should have had to booze just the same . . . you see, we're all much too lonely for a thing like that to make much difference to us . . . you're not offended, are you?"

"Oh, why should I? . . ." she saw his profile against the darkness and was afraid that he might try to seize her hand. She crossed to the other side of the road.

"Time to turn back now, Lieutenant."

"You must be lonely too, Sister, or else you couldn't stick it out . . . let's be glad that the war isn't coming to an end."

They were once more at the iron gate of the hospital. Most of the windows were now dark. One could see the lowered lights in the sick wards.

"Well, now I'm going to have a drink, all the same . . . you wouldn't join me in any case, Sister."

"It's high time I was in, Lieutenant Jaretzki."

"Good-night, Sister: thank you very much."

"Good-night, Lieutenant."

Sister Mathilde felt somehow disappointed and depressed. She called after him:

"Don't be too late in coming back home, Lieutenant."

CHAPTER LXIX

Since that walk through the evening fields with Esch the Major often found himself going through Fischerstrasse after his day's work was done, indeed he often caught himself slowing down a street or two farther on, standing uncertainly for a moment, and then turning back. One could have literally affirmed that he went slinking round and round the office of the *Kur-Trier Herald*. Perhaps he would actually have gone in had he not feared an encounter with Huguenau, and he did not want to meet Huguenau; the mere prospect of meeting him in the street filled him with embarrassment. But when Esch suddenly appeared instead of Huguenau, he could not tell at first whether he had not feared this encounter even more. For there he was, the Town Commandant in full uniform, his sword at his side, standing with a newspaper civilian fellow, standing in his uniform in the open street, and he had not only offered the fellow his hand but, instead of leaving it at that, he was actually filled with happiness, forgetting all decorum, because the man showed signs of accompanying him. Still, Esch had removed his hat most respectfully, and the Major was staring at close-cropped bristling grey hair,—and it was like an assurance, like a sudden evocation of Bible classes at home, and at the same time it was the reaffirmation of that afternoon's brotherhood, bringing with it the need to say something kind to this man who was almost a friend, even if it were only that Esch might cherish a happy memory of him; he hesitated a little longer and then said: "Come along."

As a result, these walks became frequent. Not so frequent, indeed, as the Major or even Esch would have liked. For not only were the times becoming more exacting—troops were continually being billeted and withdrawn again, columns of motor transport rattled through the streets, and the Town Commandant had often to work all through the night— but Major von Pasenow could not bring himself to the point of haunting the *Herald* office again, and it was some time before Esch realized this. When he did, however, he began to make allowances; he waited discreetly near the Major's headquarters, and when practicable took Marguerite with him. " The little monkey insists on coming with me," he would say; and though the Major was not quite certain whether the child's insistence was to be considered delightful or intrusive, he accepted it kindly and stroked Marguerite's black curls. Then the three of them would wander over the fields or down the path beside the bushes on the river-bank, and often it was as if there stirred a yearning of farewell, a gentle and wistful flowing of the heart, a living ebb of resignation; it was like that certitude of the end in which every beginning has its source. But gentle as it was, it contained a trace of dejection, perhaps because Esch had no part in this farewell, perhaps because it was proper that he should be so excluded, perhaps, however, because Esch remained inscrutable on these points, persisting in a disappointing silence. That was somehow dark and secretive, for there was still a fading hope that everything could be made right and simple if Esch would only speak. Alas, it was amazingly difficult to determine precisely what he expected Esch to say; still, Esch ought to have known what it was. So they went on in silence, in the silence of the evening light and of a growing disappointment, and the radiance lying on the fields became a misleading and weary brightness. And when Esch took off his hat to let the wind blow through his short bristling hair, that gesture took on such an unseemly intimacy that the Major almost pitied the little girl for having fallen into the power of such a man. Once he said: " Little slave-girl," but that too died out in weary indifference. Marguerite, however, ran on ahead and did not concern herself about the two men.

They had climbed to the top of the valley ridge and were following the edge of the forest. The short dry grass crackled under their shoes. Stillness lay over the valley. One could hear the creaking of the carts on the road below, the stubble-fields revealed the brown soil, and the wind blew cool from the dusky depths of the foliage. The vineyards hung green on the slopes, in the rustling of the trees the silvery, metallic sharpness of autumn was already discernible, and the stiff stems by the forest edge with their black and red berries were ready to shrivel up. Over the western flanks of the hills the sun was sinking, blazing like fire in the windows of the valley houses. Each house was standing on a long carpet of shadow pointing east; one could look down on the roofs of the prison buildings, flecked with red and black, and see right into the bleak, waste courtyards where there were also gloomy sharply cut shadows.

A small field-path led down the slope and entered the main road close by the prison. Marguerite, running on ahead, had turned down it, and the Major took this as a sign from God: " We'll turn back," he said listlessly. But when they were about half-way down they both came to a stop and listened: a curious brumming noise assailed them in rhythmic jerks; it came from below, but one simply could not tell from what quarter. Nothing could be seen but a car coming speeding from the town with its engine humming in the usual way and its horn hooting every minute or so; a long cloud of dust trailed behind it. The uncanny noise had nothing to do with the car. " An ominous sound," said the Major uneasily. " Some kind of machine," said Esch, although it sounded not at all like a machine. The car followed the windings of the road and with much tooting of its horn arrived at the prison. Esch's sharper eyes observed that it was the Commandant's official car, and he became uneasy when he noted that it did not appear again on the other side of the prison buildings. But he said nothing, only hurrying his steps. The curious sound grew harder and more sharply accentuated, and when they came in sight of the prison gate they could see the car halted there among a crowd of excited people. " Something has happened," said the Major, and now they could hear welling from the barred and railed-in windows of the prison a frightful chorus beat out in bars of three phrases: " We're hungry, we're hungry, we're hungry.... We're hungry, we're hungry, we're hungry.... We're hungry, we're hungry, we're hungry . . ." and from time to time the chorus was interrupted by a conglomerate farmyard howl. The chauffeur came running to meet them: " Please, sir, it's a rebellion ... we have been looking for you everywhere . . ." then he ran back to summon the gatekeeper.

The people made way for the Major, but he had come to a stop. The air was still vibrating with the threefold chorus, and now Marguerite began to dance in time to it: " We're hungry, we're hungry, we're hungry," she carolled. The Major gazed at the building with the dreadful impenetrable windows, he gazed at the dancing child whose laughter seemed to him strangely mechanical, strangely evil, and horror overwhelmed him. Implacable destiny, inevitable trial! The chauffeur was still pulling at the iron bell and beating on the gate, but at last the grille was opened and the gate turned creaking and heavy on its hinges. The Major was leaning against a tree and his lips murmured: " This is the end." Esch moved as if to help—the Major waved him off. " This is the end," he repeated, but he drew himself up, touched the ribbon of his Iron Cross, and then, his hand on his sword-hilt, advanced quickly towards the prison gate.

He vanished inside it. Esch sat down on the small escarpment beside the road. The air was still shattered by the syncopated cries. A single shot rang out, followed by a renewed howling. Then a few last cries like the last drops from a turned-off water-tap. Then there was silence. Esch watched the gate that had closed behind the Major—" This is the end," he echoed, and went on waiting. But the end did not come, no earthquake broke out, no angel descended, and the gate was not opened. The child squatted beside him, and he would have liked to take her in his arms. Like the wings of a stage scene the prison walls towered up to the bright evening sky, like teeth with gaps between them, and Esch felt far away from himself, far away from what was happening around him, far away from everything; he shrank from changing his posture and was no longer aware how he came to be there. Beside the gate hung a notice-board that could no longer be deciphered; of course it was a list of visiting-hours, but they were only words. For even the demagogues and murderers and deformed creatures that were imprisoned would come out of their prison into a new and more enlightened community in a Promised Land. He heard the child say: " There's Uncle Huguenau," and he saw Huguenau pass by at the double, saw him and was not surprised, so soundless was everything, soundless the step of Huguenau, soundless the movements of the people by the gate, soundless as the movements of artistes and rope dancers when the music has ceased, soundless as the paling of the clear evening sky. Remote beyond recovery lay the distant horizon before the dreamer, yet he was no dreamer but an orphan seeking vainly for his home; and he was like a man whose desire has transformed itself without his knowing it, like one who has merely deadened his pain but cannot forget it. The first stars came out in the sky, and it was to Esch as if he had sat for days and years in that self-same spot, wrapped in a padded and spectral silence. Then the movements of the waiting crowd became more infrequent, more shadowy, died away completely, and there remained a soundless waiting black mass before the gate. And finally Esch was aware only of the damp grass resting against the palm of his hand.

The child had vanished; perhaps she had gone off with Huguenau; Esch did not bother, but stared at the gate. At last the Major appeared. He walked quickly with an unusually undeviating air, it almost looked as if he had a limp and were trying to conceal it. He made straight for the car. Esch had sprung to his feet. The Major was now standing in the car, he stood there drawn up to his full height and looked over Esch's head, over the heads of the crowd that were pressing in silence round the car; he looked along the white road ahead of him and over at the town, in which lights were already twinkling from the windows. In the near vicinity a red light shone out; Esch knew where that was. Maybe the Major had observed it too, for he now looked down at Esch and said, gravely holding out his hand: " Well, it doesn't matter." Esch said nothing; he shouldered his way quickly through the crowd and took the path over the fields. Had he turned round, however, and had it not been so dark, he could have seen that the Major remained standing in the car, looking after him as he vanished into the night.

After some time he heard the engine starting and saw the headlights of the car following the windings of the road.

CHAPTER LXX

Huguenau had trotted home from the prison as fast as he could, with Marguerite running behind him. In the printing-shed he bade the press be stopped: " Some important news, Lindner," and then he betook himself to his room to do some writing. When he had finished it he said " Salut," and spat in the direction of the Eschs' living-rooms. " Salut," he said again, as he passed the kitchen door, and then he handed his composition to Lindner, " Among the news of the town, in small type," he ordered. And next day the following appeared in small type among the news of the town in the *Kur-Trier Herald*:

Incident at the Prison.—Yesterday evening there were some regrettable scenes at the prison. Some of the inmates believed that they had grounds for complaint about the inferior quality of the prison fare, and the unpatriotic elements among them seized on this as a pretext for abusing the authorities and causing an uproar. The prompt intervention of the Town Commandant, Major von Pasenow, who behaved with great courage and composure, soon quelled the disturbance. The rumour that this was really an attempt to escape on the part of alleged deserters now under lock and key pending execution is, we are informed on the best authority, quite without foundation, as there are no deserters in this prison. No one was injured.

It was another of these lucid inspirations of his, and Huguenau could hardly sleep for pure joy. He kept on reckoning it all up:

firstly, that bit about the deserters would annoy the Major, but the reference to the inferior food could not leave a Town Commandant complacent either, and if there was a man who deserved to be annoyed it was the Major;

secondly, the Major would hold Esch responsible, especially because of that hint about information on the best authority; for nobody would believe that Esch knew nothing of it,—and that would certainly put an end to the walking excursions of these two gentlemen;

thirdly, when one considered how furious the skinny Esch would be, the horse-faced Reverend, it was a sweet and gratifying thought;

fourthly, it was all so law-abiding—he was the editor and could put in what he liked, and the Major would have to be grateful to him, besides, for the compliments he had worked in;

fifthly and sixthly, there was no end to the gratifying consequences, it was, in a word, a highly successful stroke, it was, in a word, a *coup*, —and besides, it would make the Major respect him: the reports of a Huguenau had the knack of striking home, even if one did despise them;

yes, fifthly and sixthly and seventhly, one could go on and on, there was ever so much more of it, although to be sure there was a suggestion of unpleasantness somewhere that it was better not to think about.

In the morning Huguenau read the article in the printing-shed and was again delighted. He looked out of the window and cast a glance up at the office, twisting his face ironically. But he did not go up there. Not, of course, that he was afraid of the Reverend. When a man was only standing on his rights he had no need to be afraid. And a man must stand on his rights when he is persecuted. Even if it should bring everything about his ears a man must stand on his rights. All a fellow wants is to be left in peace and quiet; he only wants his due. And so Huguenau went to the barber's, where he studied the *Herald* yet once more.

To be sure, his dinner remained a problem. It would be unpleasant to sit at the same table with Esch, who would in some way, although without any justification, feel himself the injured party. One knew these high and mighty looks that priests gave; enough to take away a man's appetite. And this Reverend was a Communist himself, and wanted to socialize everything, and yet always behaved as if it were the other fellow who was trying to smash up society, just because he wouldn't let himself be put upon.

Huguenau went for a walk and thought it over. But he could not hit on a good idea. It was like going to school: let one be as inventive as anything, the only final course is to sham sick. So he turned back so as to get home before Esch, and climbed the stairs to see Mother Esch (for he had recently taken to calling her that). And with every step that he mounted his indisposition became more genuine. Perhaps he was really rather unwell, and it might be better to eat nothing at all. Yet, after all, his board and lodging were included in his salary, and he needn't make Esch a present of any of it.

" Frau Esch, I'm not well."

Frau Esch looked up and was touched by Huguenau's pathetic appearance.

" I don't think I can eat anything, Frau Esch."

" But, Herr Huguenau . . . a little soup, I'll make you some nice soup . . . that never did anyone any harm."

Huguenau considered. Then he said gloomily:

" A bouillon? "

Frau Esch was startled.

" Yes, but . . . I haven't any beef in the house."

Huguenau grew gloomier.

" Oh, no beef? . . . I think I'm in a fever . . . just feel how hot I am, Mother Esch. . . ."

Frau Esch came nearer and hesitatingly laid a finger on Huguenau's hand.

Huguenau said:

" Perhaps an omelette would be the thing."

" Hadn't I better make you some herb-tea? "

Huguenau suspected economy:

" Oh, an omelette could surely be managed . . . you must have eggs in the house . . . say, three eggs."

Thereupon with dragging feet he left the kitchen.

Partly because it was the right thing for an invalid to do, partly because he had to make up for the sleep he had lost in the night, he lay down on the sofa. But there was little chance of sleep, for his excitement over the successful journalistic *coup* was still vibrating. In a kind of waking doze he looked up at the mirror above the washstand, looked at the window, listened to the noises in the house. There were the usual kitchen noises: he could hear a bit of meat being beaten—so she had swindled him after all, the fat madam, so that that blighter might have all the meat to himself. Of course she would argue she couldn't make bouillon out of pork, but a nice bit of lightly fried pork never hurt anyone, not even an invalid. Then he heard a short, sharp chopping on a board, and diagnosed it as the cutting of vegetables,—he had always been scared as he watched his mother chopping up parsley or celery with quick-cutting strokes, scared for fear she would chop off her finger-tips. Kitchen knives were sharp. He was glad when the chopping noise ended and mother wiped her unharmed fingers on the kitchen towel. If one could only go to sleep: it might be better to get into bed, and then the Esch woman could sit beside him and knit or give him hot fomentations. He felt his hand; it was really hot. The thing to do was to think of something pleasant. Women, for instance. Naked women. That was the stair creaking, someone coming up. Strange, for father wasn't usually so early. Oh, it was only the postman. Mother Esch was speaking to him. The baker used always to come up, but he never came now. That was just nonsense: it was impossible to sleep while one was hungry.

Huguenau blinked again at the window, and noted outside the chain of the Colmar mountains; the castellan of the royal castle was a Major, the Kaiser himself had appointed him. Haïssez les Prussiens et les ennemis de la sainte religion. Somebody laughed in Huguenau's ear; he heard words in Alsatian dialect. A cooking-pot boiled over; it hissed on the stove. Now someone was whispering, " we're hungry, we're hungry, we're hungry." That was too stupid. Why couldn't he have his dinner with the others? he was being treated worse and worse. Perhaps they would give his seat to the Major? The stair was creaking again—Huguenau flinched, it was his father's step. Oh, stuff, it was only Esch, the would-be Reverend.

A swine that Esch; served him right if he was annoyed. Tit for tat. You can't play with knives and not be cut. Esch had managed to turn Protestant; next thing he'd turn Jew and have himself cut, circumcised; must remember to tell the madam that. Finger-tips. Knife-tips. Best of all just to get up and go over to the office and ask him if he was thinking of turning Jew. All nonsense to be afraid of him; I'm only too lazy. But she should bring me my dinner, and be quick about it . . . before that sanctimonious blighter gets his.

Huguenau listened intently to hear if they were sitting down to table. No wonder a man grew thinner and thinner with that Esch bagging everything. But that was what he was like. A Reverend had to have a belly. Pure fraud, his parson's black coat. An executioner had a black coat too. An executioner had to eat a lot to keep up his strength. One never knew whether people were coming to lead one to the block or merely bringing one's dinner. From now on he would go to the hotel and eat meat at the Major's table. That very evening. If that omelette was much longer in coming there would be a good row. An omelette only took five minutes to make!

Frau Esch came quietly into the room and set the plate with the omelette on a chair and pushed the chair up to the sofa.

"Hadn't I better make you some tea as well, Herr Huguenau, some herb-tea?"

Huguenau looked up. His irritation had almost vanished; her sympathy did him good.

"I'm rather fevered, Frau Esch."

She ought at least to pass her hand over his forehead to feel if he had fever; he was vexed because she did not.

"I think I'll go to bed, Mother Esch."

Frau Esch, however, stood stolidly before him and insisted on giving him tea: it was a very special kind of tea, not only an ancient recipe but also a famous remedy; the herbalist, who had inherited the secret from his father and great-grandfather, had become very rich, he owned a house in Cologne, and people went to consult him from all over the country. She had seldom said so many words in one breath.

None the less Huguenau resisted:

"Some cherry-brandy, Frau Esch, would do me good."

She primmed up her face with disgust: spirits? No! Even her husband, whose health was not of the most robust, had been won over to her tea.

"That so? Does Esch drink the tea?"

"Yes," said Frau Esch.

"All right, then, for the love of God make me some too," and with a sigh Huguenau sat up and ate his omelette.

CHAPTER LXXI

Heinrich's departure had passed off with remarkable ease. In so far as physical and spiritual effects can be separated, it might have been called a purely physical experience. As Hanna came home from the station she herself felt a little like an empty house where the blinds have been drawn down. But that was all. Besides, she knew for certain that Heinrich would return unharmed from the war. And this conviction of hers, which kept the departing soldier from turning into a martyr, not only obviated the sentimental outburst she had dreaded at the station, but had the more far-reaching effect of neutralizing and displacing her wish that he might never return. When she said to her son: "Daddy will soon come back," they probably both knew what she meant.

The physical experience, for as such she was entitled to regard this six-weeks' furlough, now presented itself to her mind as a contraction of her vital powers, a contraction of her ego; it had been like a damming-in of her ego within the limits of her body, like the foaming narrowing of a river within a ravine. In the past, now that she thought of it, she had always had the feeling that her ego was not bounded by her skin and could radiate through that tenuous covering into her silken underclothing, and it had been almost as if even her gowns were informed by an emanation from her ego (that was probably why she had such infallible taste in matters of fashion), yes, it had been almost as if her ego stretched far beyond her body and enveloped rather than inhabited it, and as if she did not think in her head but somewhere outside it, on a higher watch-tower, so to speak, from which her own bodily existence, however important it might be, could be observed and regarded as a trivial irrelevancy; but during these last six weeks of physical experience, during that headlong rush through the ravine, of all that diffused spaciousness nothing had survived but a shining vapour above the tossing waters, a rainbow glitter that was in a way the last refuge of her soul. Now, however, that the kindly plain once more spread before her and she felt as if released from fetters, her feeling of relief and smoothness turned at the same time into a wish to forget the troubled narrows. This forgetfulness, however, encroached upon her only a little at a time. All her personal memories vanished with relatively great rapidity; Heinrich's bearing, his voice, his words, his walk, all that very soon disappeared; but the general memories persisted. To use a highly improper analogy: the first to disappear was his face, then his movable extremities, his hands and feet, but the unmoving, rigid body, the torso reaching from the breast-bone to the thigh, that lascivious image of the male, persisted in the depths of her memory like the statue of a god embedded in the soil or washed by the surf of a Tyrrhenian sea. And the farther this encroaching forgetfulness advanced —and that was the frightful part of it—the more that statue of the god was shortened, the more emphatic and isolated became its indecency, an indecency on which forgetfulness encroached more and more slowly, filching smaller and smaller portions—paralysed by that indecency. That is only a metaphor, and like all metaphors coarsens the real truth which is always shadowy, a play of undefined ideas, a mingled current of half-remembered memories, half-thought thoughts and half-wished desires, a river without banks, over which rises a silvery vapour, a silvery emanation that spreads to the very clouds and the black sky of stars. So the torso in the mud of the river was no mere torso, it was a hewn boulder, it was an isolated piece of furniture, household rubbish jettisoned in the stream of events, a lump abandoned to the surf: wave succeeded wave, day was woven into night and night into day, and what the days transmitted to each other was inscrutable, sometimes more inscrutable than the dreams that followed each other, and at times it included something that recognizably suggested the secret knowledge of schoolgirls yet at the same time somehow aroused a secret wish to flee from such infantile knowledge, to flee into the world of the individual and to disinter Heinrich's face once more from forgetfulness. But that was only a wish, and its fulfilment admitted of about as much possibility as the complete restoration of a Greek statue found in the soil: that is to say, it could not be fulfilled.

At first sight it might seem irrelevant whether the individual or the general prevailed in Hanna's memories. But in an age when the general is everywhere so obviously dominant, where the social bonds of humanity that are spun only from individual to individual have been loosened in favour of collective concepts of hitherto undreamed-of unities, where a de-individualized state of ruthlessness prevails such as is natural only to childhood and old age, in such a time the memory of an individual cannot escape subjection to the general law, and the isolation of a highly insignificant woman, be she ever so pretty and ever such an excellent bedfellow, cannot be explained simply as the result of an unfortunately complete deprivation of sexual intercourse, but forms a part of the whole and mirrors, like every individual destiny, a metaphysical necessity that is laid upon the world, a physical event, if one likes to call it that, and yet metaphysical in its tragedy: for that tragedy is the isolation of the ego.

CHAPTER LXXII

STORY OF THE SALVATION ARMY GIRL IN BERLIN (13)

Can this age, this disintegrating life, be said still to have reality? My passivity increases from day to day, not because I am exhausted by struggling with a reality that may be stronger than myself, but because on all sides I encounter unreality. I am thoroughly conscious that the meaning and the ethos of my life can be found only in activity, but I begin to suspect that this age no longer has time for the contemplative activity of philosophizing, which is the sole real activity. I try to philosophize—but where is the dignity of knowledge to be found to-day? Is it not long defunct? Has Philosophy itself not disintegrated into mere phrases in face of the disintegration of its object? This world without Being, this world without repose, this world that can find and maintain its equilibrium only in increasing speed of movement, this world's mad racing has become the pseudo-activity of mankind and will hurl it into nothingness—is there any resignation deeper than that of an age which is denied the capacity to philosophize? Philosophy itself has become an æsthetic pastime, a pastime that no longer really exists but has fallen into the empty detachment of evil and become a recreation for citizens who need to kill time of an evening! nothing is left us but number, nothing is left us but law!

It often seems to me as if the state I am now in, the state that keeps me here in this Jewish house, is beyond resignation and is rather a kind of wisdom that has learned to come to terms with a completely alien environment. For even Nuchem and Marie are alien to me, even these two on whom I had set my last hope, the hope that they were my creations, the sweet, unrealizable hope that I had taken their fate into my own hands and could determine it. Nuchem and Marie are not my creatures and never were so. Treacherous hope, to take the liberty of shaping the world!

Does the world have an independent existence? No. Do Nuchem and

Marie have an independent existence? Certainly not, for no being exists in itself. But the moments that determine destinies lie far beyond the range of my thinking or my powers. I myself can only fulfil my own law, supervise my own prescribed business; I am in no case to penetrate farther, and even although my love for Nuchem and Marie is not extinguished, even though I do not relax in the struggle for their souls and their fate, yet the moments by which they are determined are beyond my reach, remain hidden from me, as hidden as the white-bearded grandfather whom I meet, to be sure, now and then in the hall, but who takes on his real shape only in the living-room from which I am always excluded, and who treats with me only through his delegate Litwak; they remain as hidden from me as the white-bearded General Booth whose picture hangs in the reception-room of the hostel. And when I consider it objectively, it is not a combat that I am engaged in, neither with the grandfather nor the Salvation Army General, rather do I strive to see justice done to them, and my wooing of Nuchem and Marie applies also to them; yes, sometimes I believe that my aim is exclusively to win through my actions the love of these old men, to win their blessing so that I may not die lonely. For reality is to be found in them that have laid down the law.

Is this resignation? Is it a revulsion from all æsthetic? Where did I stand of yore? My life is darkening behind me and I do not know if I have lived or if my life was a tale told to me, so far has it sunk in remote seas. Did ships bear me to the shores of the farthest east and farthest west? was I a cotton-picker in American plantations, was I the white hunter in the elephant jungles of India? Everything is possible, nothing, not even a castle in a park, is improbable; heights and depths, all are possible, for nothing permanent has survived in this dynamic activity that exists for its own sake, this activity that is manifest in work, in quietness and serene clarity: nothing has survived—flung to the winds is my ego, flung into nothingness; irrealizable my yearning, unattainable the Promised Land, invisible the ever-brightening but constantly receding radiance, and the community that we grope for is devoid of strength yet full of evil will. Vain hope, and often groundless pride—the world has remained an alien enemy, or even less than an enemy, merely an alien entity whose surface I could explore but into which I could never penetrate, an alien entity into which I shall never penetrate, lost as I am in ever-increasing strangeness, blind in ever-increasing blindness, failing and falling asunder in yearning remembrance of the night of home, to become at last merely a vanishing breath of what has been. I have traversed many ways to find the One in which all the others are conjoined, but they have only diverged more and more from each other, and even God has not been established by me but by my fathers.

I said to Nuchem:

" You are a suspicious people, an angry people; you are jealous even of God and are constantly pulling Him up even in His own Book."

He answered:

" The law is imperishable. God is not until every jot and tittle of the Law has been deciphered."

I said to Marie:

" You are a brave but a thoughtless people! You believe that you need only be good and strike up music in order to draw God near."

She answered:

" Joy in God is God, His grace is inexhaustible."

I said to myself:

" You are a fool, you are a Platonist, you believe that in comprehending the world you can shape it and raise yourself in freedom to Godhood. Can you not see that you are bleeding yourself to death? "

I answered myself:

" Yes, I am bleeding to death."

CHAPTER LXXIII

DISINTEGRATION OF VALUES (9)

Epistemological Excursus.

Can this age be said still to have reality? Does it possess any real value in which the meaning of its existence is preserved? Is there a reality for the non-meaning of a non-existence? In what haven has reality found its refuge? in science, in law, in duty or in the uncertainty of an ever-questioning logic whose point of plausibility has vanished into the infinite? Hegel called history " the path to the liberation of spiritual substance," the path leading to the self-liberation of the spirit, and it has become the path leading to the self-destruction of all values.

Of course the question is not whether Hegel's interpretation of history has been overthrown by the World War; that had been done already by the stars in their courses; for a reality that had grown autonomous through a development extending over four hundred years would have ceased in any circumstances to be capable of submitting any longer to a deductive system. A more important question would be to inquire into the logical possibilities of this emergent anti-deductive reality, into the logical grounds for such anti-deductiveness; in short, to examine " the conditions of possible experience" in which this development of the spirit has become inevitable—but a contempt for all philosophy, a weariness of words, are themselves inherent in this reality and in this development, and it is only with a complete mistrust of the coercive suasion of words that we can pose the urgent methodological questions: what is an historical event? what is historical unity? or, to go still further: what is an event at all? what principle of selection must be followed to weld single occurrences into the unity of an event?

Autonomous life is as indissolubly and organically knit to the category of value as autonomous consciousness is knit to the category of truth,— one could find other names for the phenomena of truth and value, but as phenomena they would remain as irrefutable as *Sum* and *Cogito*, both of them drawn out of the isolated autonomy of the Self, both of them activities as well as surrounding products of that Self; thus value can be split up into the value-making activity, which in the widest sense creates worlds, and into the formed, spatially discernible and generally visible value-product, and the concept of value splits into the corresponding categories: into the ethical value of the activity and the æsthetic value of the product, the obverse and reverse sides of the same medal, and it is in combination and only in combination that these give the most general concept of value and the logical co-ordinates of all life. And, indeed, this is borne out by history: for the writing of history in antiquity was already governed by its concepts of value, the moralizing historians of the eighteenth century applied theirs with full deliberation, and in Hegel's scheme the concept of an absolute value is most clearly revealed in the ideas of a " World-spirit " and a " High Court of History." It is not surprising that the post-Hegelian philosophy of history occupied itself chiefly in considering the methodological function of the concept of value, bringing about incidentally the fateful splitting-up of the whole realm of knowledge into a philosophy of nature unaffected by values and a philosophy of spirit conditioned by values— which, if one likes, may be considered the first declared bankruptcy of philosophy, since it confined the identity of Thought and Being to the realm of logic and mathematics, allowing all the rest of knowledge to dispense with what is the main idealistic task of philosophy or to relegate it to the vagueness of intuition.

Hegel levelled against Schelling the (justified) reproach that he had projected the Absolute into the world " as if it were a bullet from a pistol." But that applies with equal force to the concept of value projected by Hegelian and post-Hegelian philosophy. Simply to project a concept of value into history and summarily to describe as " values " all that history has preserved may be permissible at a pinch for the purely æsthetic values of the creative arts, but is otherwise so sweepingly false that it drives one in contradiction to maintain that history is a conglomeration of non-values, and to deny outright that there is any value-reality in history.

First Thesis:

history is composed of values, since life can be comprehended only in the category of value—yet these values cannot be introduced into reality as absolutes, but can only be thought of in reference to an ethically-motived value-positing subject. Hegel's absolute and objectified " world spirit " was such a subject introduced into reality, but the all-embracing absoluteness of its operation could not but result in a *reductio ad absurdum*. (This is another example of the impassable limits imposed on deductive thinking.) These values are not absolutes, but only finite postulates. Where a concrete and *a priori* finite subject comes into question, that is to say, an actual person, the relativity of values, their dependence on the subject, becomes immediately clear; the biography of any person is composed of all the value-contents which have been important to him. In himself he may be a person of no value, even a destroyer of values, such as a bandit leader or a deserter, but as the centre of his own system of values he is yet a ripe subject for biography and history. And the same is true of the fictive centres of value such as a state, or a club, or a nation, or the German Hanseatic League, historically considered; indeed, even the histories of inanimate objects, as for instance the architectural history of a house, are made up from a selection of those facts which would have been important to the respective subjects if they had had a will to create values. An event without a value-positing centre dissolves into nebulosity—the battle of Kunersdorf consists not of an army list of the Grenadiers who took part in it, but of the reality-formations which were determined by the plans of the commander. Every historical unity depends on an effective or fictive centre of value; the " style " of an epoch would not be discernible unless a unifying principle of selection were assumed at its centre, or a " spirit of the age " which serves as a standard for judging the value-positing and style-creating forces in operation. Or, to fall back on a hackneyed expression, culture is a value-formation, culture can be conceived of only in terms of style, and in order to be conceivable at all it needs the assumption of a style- and value-producing " culture-spirit " at the centre of that circle of values which it represents.

Does this mean that all values are made relative? That one must abandon all hope of the logical Absolute ever manifesting itself in reality through the unifying of thought and being? that one must abandon all hope of ever even drawing near to the path that leads to the self-liberation of the spirit and of humanity?

Second Thesis:

the ripeness for history or for biography of the value-positing action is conditioned by the absoluteness of the Logos. For the actual or fictive value-positing subject can be imagined only in the isolation of its selfhood, in that inevitable, complete, and Platonic isolation whose pride it is to depend exclusively on the precepts of logic, and whose compulsion it is to state all activity in terms of logical plausibility; but this means that one must postulate, in the complete Kantian sense, not only the good will which shapes the work for the work's sake, but also the rule that all consequences must be drawn from the autonomous code of the Self, so that the work, uninfluenced by any dogma, shall spring from the pure originality of the Self and of its law. In other words, whatever does not arise purely in accordance with its own laws vanishes out of history. But however contemporary this individual force of law may be in any age, that is to say, however it may be conditioned by the spirit and style of its age, it can never be anything else than a reflection of the superposed Logos, of that Logos which is active to-day and which is thought itself, a merely earthly reflection, it is true, even in our day, but a reflection through which there gleams that which has a lasting claim to transcend all ages and alone makes it possible for stylized thinking to be projected into another ego. And this formal ultimate unity is continuously and with complete clearness revealed again and again in the narrower sphere of created work and of generally applied æsthetics, for instance in all art, but most obviously in the undying persistence of art forms.

From this we can draw the following comprehensive conclusion, the *Third Thesis:*

the world is a product [1] of the intelligible Self, for the Platonic idea has never been abandoned nor ever can be. But this product is not projected " like a bullet from a pistol," for nothing can be posited but value-making subjects, which in their turn reflect the structure of the intelligible Self and in their turn fashion their own value-products, their own world-formations: the world is not an immediate but a mediate product of the Self, it is " a product of products," " a product of products of products," and so on in infinite iteration. This process, the positing of " products of products," provides the world with its methodological organization and hierarchy, a relative organization, certainly, but yet absolute in form, since the ethical imperative postulated for the effective or fictive value-positing subjects remains undiminished in its force, together with the immanent validity of the Logos within the created product: the logic of things remains unshaken. And even though the logical advance of history must be arrested time and again whenever it reaches the limits of infinity inherent in its metaphysical construction, and though the Platonic view of the world must time and again make way for a positivistic examination of data, yet the reality of the Platonic idea remains invincible, for with every access of Positivism it merely touches its mother earth again to rise anew, upborne by the bathos of experience.

Every conceptually comprehensible unity in the world is " product of a product," every concept, every thing; and this methodological function of knowledge, of knowledge as an integrator that can comprehend a thing only by regarding it as an autonomous and value-positing subject, probably extends right into mathematics, thus abolishing the distinction between mathematical scientific abstraction and empirical abstraction. For, methodologically regarded, to define a thing as the " product of a product " is nothing else than to introduce the ideal observer into the field of observation, as has been already done long since by the empirical sciences (by physics, for example, in the Theory of Relativity) quite independently of epistemological considerations: and further, research into mathematical first principles, pursuing the questions " what is number? " and " what is unity? " has reached a point at which it has found itself compelled to accept intuition as the

[1] Product = Setzung.

only way out of its difficulties: now the principle of "product of a product" provides intuition with its logical legitimation, for the infiltration of the Self into a hypostatized value-positing subject can be justifiably termed the methodological structure of the act of intuition.

That this principle has been so long unrecognized may perhaps be explained by its obviousness, even its primitiveness. For it is indeed primitive. And the pride of man seems to find insuperable difficulty in admitting the validity of a primitive attitude. For even though this view of everything as the "product of a product" guarantees the presence of the intelligible self in every object throughout the world, yet, if one ignores for a moment this Platonic background, it amounts to a kind of animism that reanimates the whole of nature, nay, the whole of the world in its totality, an animism that introduces a value-subject into everything, into every concept however abstract, and that can be compared only to the animism of primitive peoples: it seems as if the development of logic has an ontogenesis of its own that keeps alive, even in the most highly developed logical structures, all previous and apparently obsolete thought-formations, including that of the simple animism which shortened to one link all chains of plausibility; an ontogenesis that preserves in every new advance of thought the form if not the content of primitive metaphysics—indubitably a stumbling-block for the rationalists, but a consolation to pantheistic feeling.

And yet there is consolation even for the rationalists. For if the principle of "product of products" in its dependence on the governing Logos may be interpreted as the logical structure of the intuitive act, it may also be regarded as the "condition of possible experience" for the otherwise inexplicable fact of the mutual understanding between man and man, between one isolated self and another; so it provides not only an epistemological structure that accounts for the translatableness of all languages, be they ever so different from each other, but far beyond that, infinitely far, it provides in the unity of thought a common denominator for all human speech, a warrant for the unity of mankind and of a humanity that even in its self-laceration remains the image of God—for in every thought and in every unity that man creates, the Logos, mirror of himself, shines out upon him, the Word of God shines out as the measure of all things. And even if all that is created in this world were to be annihilated, if all its æsthetic values were abolished and resolved into a function, dissolved in scepticism of all law, nay more, in the imperative duty to question and to doubt, there would yet survive untouched the unity of thought, the ethical postulate, the rigorous operation of ethical value as pure function, the real duty of its most strict observance: all these would survive and with them a continuing unity of the world, a unity of mankind, illuminating all things, still surviving and imperishable through all eternities of space and time.

CHAPTER LXXIV

Dr Flurschütz was helping Jaretzki to fit on his artificial arm. Sister Mathilde too was in attendance.

Jaretzki was jerking at the straps:

"Well, Flurschütz, aren't you heart-broken that I'm leaving you so soon . . . not to speak of Sister Mathilde!"

"Do you know, Jaretzki, I would really like to keep you here for a while longer under observation . . . you're at a highly questionable stage of your development."

"Can't say . . . wait a minute," Jaretzki endeavoured to wedge a cigarette between the fingers of the artificial hand, " . . . wait a minute, how would it do if we added a kind of cigarette-receiver to this . . . or a permanent cigarette-holder . . . that would be quite an ingenious idea . . . ?"

"Stand still just for a minute, Jaretzki," Flurschütz fastened the straps, " . . . there, how do you feel?"

"Like a newly-born machine . . . a machine at a fine stage of development . . . if the cigarettes were better it would be still finer."

"Couldn't you let this smoking of yours alone altogether . . . and the other thing too, of course."

"Love? Oh yes, like a shot."

Sister Mathilde said quite superfluously:

"No, Dr Flurschütz meant that you should give up drinking."

"Oh, I see, I didn't understand . . . when one is sober, it's so hard to understand things. . . . I'm surprised that that has never struck you, Flurschütz: it's only when people are drunk that they can understand one another."

"That's a daring attempt at self-justification!"

"But just cast your mind back, Flurschütz, and remember how gloriously drunk we all were in August 1914 . . . it seems to me as though that was the first and the last time that people felt a real sense of fellowship."

" Scheler says something like that. . . ."

" Who? "

" Scheler. *The Genius of War* . . . not much of a book."

" Oh, I see, a book . . . that doesn't count . . . but I tell you this, Flurschütz, and I say it in all seriousness: give me some other, some new drunkenness, it doesn't matter what as far as I'm concerned, morphia or patriotism or communism or anything else that makes a man drunk . . . give me something to make me feel we're all comrades again, and I'll give up drinking . . . to-morrow."

Flurschütz reflected; then he said:

" There's something in what you say . . . but if you must have intoxication and fellowship, there's a simple enough remedy: fall in love."

" Under doctor's orders, certainly . . . have you ever fallen in love under doctor's orders, Sister? "

Sister Mathilde blushed; two red patches appeared amid the freckles that covered her neck.

Jaretzki averted his eyes:

" A bad stage of development for falling in love . . . it seems to me we're all in a bad way . . . even love's no more use . . ." he tested the joints of the artificial arm, " . . . we should really be given instructions for using this thing . . . there must surely be a special joint for cuddling somewhere in it."

Flurschütz strangely enough felt shocked. Perhaps because Sister Mathilde was present. Sister Mathilde blushed still more deeply:

" What ideas you have, Herr Jaretzki! "

" How? they're quite good ideas . . . artificial limbs for making love . . . yes, quite a splendid idea, special models for staff officers, from colonels upwards . . . I'll set up a factory."

Flurschütz said:

" Must you always play the *enfant terrible*? "

" Not at all, I simply have ideas for the armament industry . . . now let's take it off." Jaretzki began to undo the straps; Sister Mathilde helped him. He straightened the joints of the metallic fingers: " There, now it only needs a glove . . . little finger, ring finger and that's the thumb that picks out the plum."

Flurschütz examined the scars on the naked arm stump.

" I think it fits quite all right, only be careful at the beginning that it doesn't rub your arm sore."

" Let the good charwomen rub and scrub . . . this one picks out the plums."

" Well, Jaretzki, as far as you're concerned at any rate, there really seems no hope of common understanding."

CHAPTER LXXV

Huguenau's dodging Esch at the dinner-hour had of course availed nothing. That very same evening there was a violent scene. Nevertheless Esch was soon disarmed, for Huguenau not only took his stand in his documented rights as a publisher, which fully authorized him to insert any article that he liked, but he also employed Esch's own arguments: " My dear friend," he jeered, " you've complained often enough about people queering your pitch when you wanted to unmask public abuses . . . but when someone else has the courage actually to do it you draw in your horns . . . of course one doesn't fling away the favour of a high and mighty Town Commandant in a hurry . . . must always trim your coat to suit the fashion, what? " Yes, Esch had to listen to things like that, and although it was a vile and cowardly attack with which the fellow had taken him in the rear, he could find nothing better as a retort but guttersnipe abuse, and after that had held his tongue.

But Huguenau had thereupon adroitly changed his tactics. He had gone to Frau Esch and complained bitterly that her husband had treated abominably a conscientious partner, simply because said partner had conscientiously and selflessly tried to do his duty. That had not been without its effect, and when next day Esch came up to his dinner he found a sulky and offended Huguenau and a wife who with conciliating words spoke up for Herr Huguenau's innocence, so that before they knew where they were they were reconciled and all supped their soup in peace together, much to the satisfaction of Frau Esch, who was anxious not to lose a patron so generous with his praise.

But perhaps Esch too was actually glad that he had avoided having to show Huguenau the door: one couldn't tell what attacks against the Major this fellow might still have in mind . . . it was best in any case not to let him out of one's sight. So Huguenau stayed where he was, although these meals were none too sociable, especially as Esch now took to glaring at Huguenau across the dishes, mustering him with suspicious eyes.

To Huguenau's credit it must be said that he did his best to brighten matters: but his efforts met with scant success. Even a week later Esch was still in his most bearish mood. And to the hesitant inquiries of his spouse he replied only in a growl: " Emigrate to America. . . ." After which nothing more was said. Finally, however, Huguenau leant back satiated, and broke the uncomfortable silence with these auspicious words:

" Mother Esch," he said, lifting one finger, " Mother Esch, I've hunted up a farmer who will deliver flour to us, maybe a gammon occasionally too."

" Indeed? " said Esch mistrustfully, " where have you picked him up? "

Of course this farmer was non-existent, but what is non-existent may one day come to life, and Huguenau was annoyed that his good will was never recognized. Yet he did not want to get into a squabble with Esch so soon again, on the contrary he wanted to say something conciliatory:

" We must lighten things a little for Mother Esch if we can . . . four mouths . . . I'm surprised that she manages it at all . . . for one must count in the kid as well."

Esch smiled:

" Yes, the little one."

Huguenau said forthcomingly:

" Where has she been hiding herself? "

Frau Esch sighed:

" You're right, nowadays it's no trifle to fill four mouths . . . it would have been better if my husband hadn't saddled us with the worry of the child."

" I refuse to listen to a word about that," Esch burst out. He looked angrily across at his wife, who sat there with a curiously frigid smile, as though conscious of guilt. Esch was somewhat mollified: " When there's no new life, everything's dead."

" That's so," said Frau Esch, " that's so."

Huguenau said:

" But she runs about the streets all day . . . with the boys; you mark my words, she'll run away yet."

" Oh, it suits her quite well to stay with us," said Frau Esch. And Esch, almost warily, almost as though he were touching a pregnant woman, gripped his wife above the elbow by the thick arm: " And I say that she likes to stay with us, do you hear? "

Huguenau was exasperated by the two of them. He said:

" It suits me too to stay with you, Mother Esch . . . wouldn't you like to adopt me as well? " He would have liked to add that Esch then would have the son that he was always raving about and that was to build the house—but for some reason incomprehensible even to himself he felt deeply indignant, and the whole business seemed to him no longer a matter for jest. If Esch had suddenly sprung up and threatened him Huguenau would not have been surprised. No doubt about it, it would be better to slip away and look for Marguerite; she would probably be down in the courtyard. The best thing would be to fly from the place and take Marguerite with him.

Frau Esch too seemed terrified by the unreasonable request that Huguenau had made to her. She felt her arm clasped by her husband's bony hand, and with her mouth open she stared at Huguenau, who meanwhile had risen; only when he had reached the door did she stammer: " And why not, Herr Huguenau? . . ."

Huguenau heard her, but it did not lessen his bitter indignation against Esch. He found Marguerite below and presented her with a whole mark. " For your travels," he said, " but you must dress yourself properly for going away . . . warm knickers . . . let me see . . . it seems to me you're almost naked . . . in autumn it's cold."

CHAPTER LXXVI

It was already past nine when Dr Kessel's door-bell rang. Kühlenbeck was sitting in the corner of the sofa smoking his cigar: " Well, Kessel, is this another patient? " " What else can it be? " replied Kessel, who had risen automatically, " what else . . . not a single night that one can sleep in peace." And he walked wearily into the next room to fetch his bag.

Meanwhile the maid had come up: " Herr Doctor, Herr Doctor, the Herr Major is below." " Who? " shouted Kessel from the next room. " The Herr Major." " It must be something for me," said Kühlenbeck. " I'm coming at once," cried Kessel, and, his black bag still in his hand, he hurried out to receive the guest.

Presently the Major appeared in the doorway; he smiled a little awkwardly:

" I knew that you two gentlemen were here together . . . and as you so kindly invited me once, Herr Doctor Kessel . . . I thought that you two gentlemen were perhaps having a musical evening."

" Well, thank God there's nothing happened. I thought something had gone wrong again," said Kühlenbeck, " . . . well, all the better."

" No, nothing has gone wrong," said the Major.

" No more revolts? " said Kühlenbeck, with his usual tactlessness, and went on: " Who really was it that put that idiotic article in the *Herald*? Esch, or that clown with the French name? "

The Major did not reply; he had been unpleasantly affected by Kühlenbeck's question. He regretted having come. Kühlenbeck however went on:

" Well, prison can't be exactly comfortable for these gentry . . . but they're safely away from the Front and that should be enough to keep them contented. They must have forgotten what a sheer stroke of luck it is to be alive, simply to live, no matter how shabbily . . . human beings have short memories."

" These newspaper people," said the Major, although it was not a real answer at all.

" I was afraid that it was another summons to a patient," said Kessel, " it's to be hoped that there won't be anybody to-night."

Kühlenbeck went on talking:

" An unheard-of luxury for the State to keep prisons going these days . . . superfluous in any case . . . the whole world is a prison . . . but it can't last for much longer . . . besides the prison here should have been evacuated long ago . . . what will we do with these people when we've all got to shift? "

" It hasn't come to that yet," said the Major, " and with God's help it won't come to that either." He said this, but he did not believe it. Only that afternoon he had received another secret order with instructions in case of the possible evacuation of the town. Orders and counter-orders were coming in pell-mell and one did not know what the next hour would bring. It was a veritable pit.

Kühlenbeck regarded his great capable surgeon's hands.

" If the French come across here . . . take my word for it, we'll strangle them with our bare hands."

Kessel said:

" Sometimes I think it a good thing that my wife is not alive

to see these times." He gazed at the photograph which hung over
the piano surrounded by a wreath of immortelles and a band of
crêpe.

The Major too gazed up at it: " Your wife was musical too? " he
asked at last. Beside the piano stood the 'cello in a grey-linen case on
whose cover a red lyre and two crossed flutes were embroidered. Why
had he come here? Why had he come to see these doctors? did he
feel ill? and he couldn't stand doctors, they were all Freethinkers and
unreliable. Had no sense of honour. There sat the Surgeon-Major with
his head laid back on the corner of the sofa, blowing smoke rings up
towards the ceiling, sticking his pointed beard into the air. It was all
unseemly. Why had he come here? yet better to be here all the same
than in the lonely hotel bedroom, or in the dining-hall where any moment
that fellow Huguenau might appear. Kessel had rung for another bottle
of Berncastler, and the Major hastily drank a glass. Then he said: " I
thought that you would be having some music."

Kessel smiled absently:

" Yes, my wife was very musical."

Kühlenbeck said:

" What do you say, Kessel? why not fetch out your 'cello for
once? . . . it will do us all good."

The Major felt that Kühlenbeck was wanting to show him a kindness,
even if it was perhaps a little too familiar of him. So he merely said:
" Yes, that would be splendid."

Kessel went over to the 'cello and with a glance at the photograph
took out the instrument. But then he stopped: " Yes, but who will play
the accompaniment for me? "

" You'll manage all right by yourself, Kessel," said Kühlenbeck,
" pluck does it." Kessel still hesitated a little: " Yes, but what shall I
play? " " Something with feeling," said Kühlenbeck, and Kessel drew
in a chair and seated himself beside the piano, as though there were
someone there accompanying him; he struck a note, ran his hand
tenderly over the strings of the bow and tuned the instrument. Then
he closed his eyes.

He played Brahms' 'cello sonata in E flat, Op. 38. His mild face had a
curious inward look, the grey moustache above his compressed lips was
no longer a moustache, but a grey shadow, the furrows in his cheeks
had altered their contours, it was no longer a face, it was almost invisible,

perhaps a grey autumnal landscape waiting for the snow to come. And even when a tear trickled down his nose, it was no longer a tear. Only the hand was still a hand, and it was as though the stroke of the bow had drawn all life into itself, rising and falling on the waves of the soft brown stream of sound which became broader and broader, flowing round and enclosing the player, so that he was cut off and very alone. He played. Probably he was only a dilettante, but that could well be a matter of indifference to him, as it was for the Major and even perhaps for Kühlenbeck: for the clamorous silence of that time, its tumult of dumb impenetrable noise raised up between one human being and another, a wall through which the human voice cannot penetrate, so that it has to falter and die—the terrifying silence of that time was cancelled, Time itself was cancelled and shaped itself into space which enclosed them all while Kessel's 'cello rang out, uprearing sound, upbuilding space, fulfilling space, fulfilling them also.

When the music had died away and Dr Kessel once more became Dr Kessel, the Major gave himself a little jerk so as to conceal his emotion under a prescribed military bearing. And he waited for Kessel now to say something comforting—surely one might say it now! But Dr Kessel merely bent his head and one could see the meagre locks—not at all like Esch's grey stiff brush of hair—that sparsely covered the top of his head. Almost with shame he put the instrument away, shoving it into its linen case, which gave one almost an unseemly impression, and Kühlenbeck from his sofa corner merely muttered " Ay." Perhaps they were all three ashamed.

At last Kühlenbeck said:

" Ay, doctors are a musical lot."

The Major searched his memory. In his youth he had had a friend, or was it a friend? who had played the violin, but he was not a doctor, although he . . . perhaps, indeed, he was a doctor or had wanted to be one. Memory stopped there, memory froze, movement froze, and the Major saw nothing but his own bare hand resting on the black cloth of his army trousers. And independently of his own will his lips said " Naked and exposed. . . ."

" I beg your pardon! " said Kühlenbeck.

The Major turned towards him: " Oh, nothing . . . these are bad times . . . I thank you, Herr Doctor Kessel."

Now Kessel said at last:

" Yes, music is a comfort in these times . . . there's not much else left in the way of comfort."

Kühlenbeck brought his hand down on the table:

" Don't whine, Kessel . . . for let the world be full of devils, we dare not despair . . . let peace only come and we'll raise our heads again."

The Major shook his head:

" Against foul treachery one is powerless." The image of Esch rose before him, that tanned brown face with the challenging smile, yes, challenging was the right word, that face which nevertheless seemed somehow to be asking for forgiveness and now had the reproachful expression of a horse that has fallen and cannot get up again.

" We Germans have always been betrayed," said Kühlenbeck, " and we're still alive in spite of it." He raised his glass: " Long live Germany! "

The Major too raised his glass, and he thought, " Germany," thought of the order and security which Germany had hitherto meant to him. He could no longer see Germany. In some way or other he held Huguenau responsible for the misfortunes of the Fatherland, for the marching through of troops, for the contradictory orders of the Army Command, for the unchivalrous weapons of this war of gas, for the growing and general disorder. And he would actually have liked the image of Esch to melt and blend into one with that of Huguenau, proving that they were both emissaries of the Evil One, both adventurers who had emerged out of that inextricable turmoil filled with business affairs and faces which one did not understand, both unreliable and contemptible, loaded with guilt, demoniacally loaded with guilt for the disastrous conclusion of the war:

Kessel said:

" I'm finished with it. . . . I'll do my duty, but I'm finished with it."

An inextricable maze was life, the net of evil lay over the world, and the dumb, stupendous din had begun again. Whoever strayed from the strict path of evangelical Christian duty was a sinner, and the hope that divine grace might fulfil itself here below had been a sinful hope, though proclaimed by the voice of the friend who had shattered the silence and rigidity that encased him and released him from his isolation in a blissful outpouring of the soul. And the Major said: " We have strayed from the path of duty and must bear the penalty."

" Well, well, Herr Major," laughed Kühlenbeck, " I don't agree with you there, but I do agree that it's time we were striking the path for home, so that our exhausted friend Kessel may get to his little bed." He had got up, his army coat hung somewhat loosely on his massive body. A disguised civilian, the Major could not help thinking—that wasn't the King's uniform. Major von Pasenow had also risen. Why had he come here, he, an officer in the King's uniform? Earthly duty was a reflection of divine ordinance, and the service of something greater than oneself obliged a man to subordinate his life to higher ideas, demanded from him that he should give up even the last thin strip of personal freedom left him, if it was necessary. Voluntary obedience, yes, that was the attitude laid down by God; all the rest was to be regarded as non-existent. The Major pulled down his coat so that it hung straight, touched the ribbon of his Iron Cross, and in the punctilious military correctness with which he took his leave he found again that serenity and security which duty and a uniform bestow on men.

Dr Kessel had escorted them downstairs. At the door the Major said with a certain formality: "I thank you, Herr Doctor Kessel, for the artistic treat which you have given us." Kessel hesitated a little in replying and then he said in a low voice: "I should thank you, Herr Major ... this is the first time since the death of my dear wife that I have touched my 'cello." The Major, however, did not hear and merely held out his hand with a certain stiffness. He went with Kühlenbeck through narrow streets, they crossed the market-place, a thin autumnal rain blew slantingly in their faces, they both wore the grey overcoat of an officer, both wore officers' caps, and yet they were not comrades in the King's uniform. The Major noted this inwardly.

CHAPTER LXXVII

STORY OF THE SALVATION ARMY GIRL IN BERLIN (14)

Perceptions which are attained through fastings and self-mortifications certainly lack a final logical sharpness. I think I may say with certainty that about this time a change took place in my perceptive states. I regarded this transformation, however, with the utmost distrust, as it went hand in hand with long-continued under-nourishment; indeed I was almost prepared to agree with Dr Litwak's diagnosis and admit that I was sick, especially as the change consisted in a feeling of great physical lucidity rather than in a sharpening of my perception of the world round me. For instance if I put the old question to myself whether my life still possessed any intelligible reality, it was this physical feeling that provided me with the answer and gave me the certitude of living in a sort of second-grade reality, giving rise to a kind of unreal reality, of real unreality, which sent through me a thrill of strange gladness. It was a state, as it were, hovering between knowledge not yet grasped and knowledge grasped, a symbol that had found another symbol for itself, a sleep-walking that led towards the light, a fear that annulled itself and yet rose reborn again from itself; it was like a hovering above the sea of death, a winged rising and falling over the waves without touching them, so light had I become,—it was an almost physical intuition by which I seized the higher Platonic reality of the world, and all my being was filled with the certainty that I needed take only a small step to transform this physical intuition into a rational one.

In this wavering reality things streamed towards me and streamed into me and I had no need to raise a finger. What had formerly looked like passivity now found its meaning. If formerly I had stayed inside to give free rein to my thoughts, to hold philosophical monologues and now and then to jot down the heads of them, now I stayed in my room like an invalid who is obedient to his doctor and his malady. Everything turned out as Dr Litwak had prophesied. He visits me now regularly, and sometimes I myself actually call him in; and when, suddenly changing his opinion, he sets out to prove to me that I am not ill at all, " You're just a little anæmic and more than half-crazy," he seems to be right in that too, for I feel as though there were very little blood in my veins. I don't want to think any longer, not, however, because I would be incapable of it; no, I don't think any longer simply because I despise thinking. It is not that I have become so very wise as all that, I make no claim whatever to have reached the final plane of knowledge, or to have surmounted knowledge—alas, I know too well that I am far below the plane of knowledge; what keeps me from thinking is rather the fear of losing this hovering state, a fear that conceals itself behind contempt for the word. Or is it the suddenly awakened conviction that the unity of thought and being can be realized only within the most modest limits? Both thought and being reduced to their minimum!

Marie sometimes visits me, brings me gifts of food as she does to her other invalids, and I accept them. Recently she arrived when Litwak and

Nuchem were with me. According to her normal custom she greeted them with a friendly " God bless you " and Litwak responded with his usual answer: " A hundredfold." Marie coughed and he put on a solicitous face: " You should be careful," he said, from which it remained uncertain whether he meant the presumable presence of lung trouble in Marie or the danger of infection to which he saw Nuchem exposed. He offered also to examine Marie free of charge, and when she declined he said: " You should at least go out walking as much as you can in the fresh air . . . and take him with you, he's anæmic." Nuchem stood about and glanced through my books. For the rest, Litwak was always prescribing new medicines for me, and when he handed me the prescription he would laugh: " You won't take it in any case, but a doctor must prescribe something." We had arrived at a kind of mutual understanding.

What was the point of contact between us? why had I to stay with these people? why had this provisory Jewish domicile become a permanency for me, which I could no longer imagine myself leaving? why did I yield so obediently to those Jews? everything was provisory, these refugees were provisory, yes, so was their whole existence, and Time itself was provisory too, as provisory as the war, which was lingering on past its own end. The provisory seems to have become the definitive; incessantly it cancels itself and yet remains. It pursues us and we come to terms with it, in a Jewish house, in a hostel. But it lifts us above the past, it holds us suspended in a happy, almost euphorian hovering state in which everything looks towards the future.

Finally I obeyed Dr Litwak and went out for walks whenever Nuchem or Marie could accompany me.

These autumn days were very beautiful and I sat with Marie under the trees. And as everything had a radiant candour, and as words were of no consequence, I asked her:

" Are you a fallen woman? "

" I was one," she replied.

" And are you chaste now? "

" Yes."

" You know that you'll never save Nuchem? "

" Yes, I know."

" Then you love him? "

She smiled.

Mirror of itself, symbol of a symbol! to what bourne can the continuous chain of symbols lead us if not to death!

" Listen, Marie, I've made up my mind to kill myself, to shoot myself or jump into the Landwehr Canal . . . but you must go with me, by myself I won't move a step."

That sounded like a joke, but it was seriously meant. She must have guessed that, for without smiling, almost matter-of-factly, she replied:

" No, I won't do that, and you mustn't kill yourself either."

" But your love for Nuchem is quite hopeless."

She was unable to draw any consequences from that; she simply fixed her eyes questioningly on me, searching for the possibility of an understanding between us. Her eyes were colourless.

It was not a very pleasant game that I was playing with her, and yet the understanding between us must have been already established, for she said:

" We are in the joy of the Lord."

I said:

" Nuchem will not kill himself, he daren't, he is under the law, but we are in the joy of the Lord . . . we can dare to do it."

Perhaps the thought that Nuchem was preserved from all danger of suicide reassured her, for now she smiled again, yes, she even crossed her legs like a lady and the superior complacency of a lady was written on her face:

" We too are under the law."

I could not take offence at her Salvation Army phrases, it may be because while one is in a provisory state every phrase loses its meaning, it may be because then it takes on a new meaning beforehand and fits the case. It may be that words too can hover between the past and the future, that they too hover between the law and the joy of the Lord, taking refuge from the contempt which is their deserved fate in a new meaning in the unstable flux.

Yet I did not want to hear anything about the law, for it had recalled me back to reality; I did not want to hear anything about the law, I wanted to maintain intact my own state of suspension, and I asked:

" You're happy, in spite of your hopeless love? "

" Yes," she said.

Irretrievably lost is our home, inaccessibly stretches the distance before us, but our grief is eased more and more, becomes more and more transparent, perhaps even invisible; nothing remains but a painful echo of what has once been. And Marie said:

" The sorrow in the world is great, but the joy of the Lord is greater."

I said:

" Oh, Marie, you have known what estrangement is and yet you are happy . . . and you know that death alone, that your last moment alone, will annul that estrangement, and yet you desire to live."

She replied:

" Whoever lives in Christ is never alone . . . come to us."

" No," I said, " I belong to my Jewish quarters, I'm going to Nuchem."

But that no longer made any impression on her.

CHAPTER LXXVIII

A man whose arms have been amputated is a torso. This thought was the bridge which Hanna Wendling was accustomed to employ when she endeavoured to find her way back from the general to the individual and the concrete. And at the end of this bridge stood not Heinrich, but, swaying a little, Jaretzki with his empty sleeve tucked into the pocket of his army coat. It took a long time before she was able to recognize this fancy clearly, and still longer before she grasped that it might in some way correspond to an actual reality. And then another considerable time passed before she summoned the decision to ring up Dr Kessel.

This extremely retarded process was certainly not caused by a particularly strong moral sense; no, it was simply that she had lost any feeling for time or tempo, it was a slowing down of the life-stream, yet not at all a damming up of it, but rather an evaporation into nothingness, an oozing away into a completely porous ground, a vanishing without remembrance of her thoughts as she thought them. And when Dr Kessel as arranged called for her in his buggy to take her to the town, it seemed to her that she had called in the doctor on account of some strange anxiety, which she could not formulate, about her son, and only with an effort did she manage to get her memory to work. Then, it is true, she asked at once in sudden apprehension, which she immediately forgot again— they were just crossing the garden—who the one-armed lieutenant in the hospital really was. Dr Kessel was at a loss for a moment, but when he had helped her into the buggy and groaning a little sat down beside her he suddenly recollected: " Of course, you mean Jaretzki, of course . . .

poor young fellow, he's to be sent to an institution for nervous cases now, I believe." With which the Jaretzki episode was finished for Hanna. She dispatched her purchases in the town, sent off a parcel to Heinrich, absolved a visit to Röders. She had asked Walter to meet her there; then they were to walk home together. Her inexplicable anxieties about Walter were all at once gone. It was a mild and peaceful autumn evening.

It would not have been surprising if Hanna Wendling had dreamt that night of a Greek torso buried in the river mud or a block of marble or—even that would have sufficed—a pebble washed by the stream. But as she remembered no such dream it would be neither honest nor relevant to express any opinion on the matter. On the other hand it is certain that she passed a restless night and often awoke and peered across at the open window, waiting for the venetian blinds to be raised and the masked head of a burglar to appear. Next morning she thought of furnishing the storeroom beside the kitchen for the use of the gardener and his wife, so that there should be at any rate a man in the house whom one could summon in case of anything happening, but she rejected the plan, for the weakly little gardener would be really no protection, and all that remained was a residue of violent indignation against Heinrich for putting the gardener's house at such a distance from the villa; also he had neglected to have bars fixed over the windows. Yet she herself had to admit that all this uneasiness had hardly anything to do with real fear; it was not so much fear as a sort of exasperation at the lonely and isolated position of the villa, and although Hanna would certainly have felt and expressed a repugnance to any house where she was in closer contact with her neighbours, yet the empty space which surrounded the villa was so empty, the dead landscape, which looked as though it had been patched together out of scraps and bits, was so dead, that it became as it were a ring of vacancy which coiled itself more and more closely round her loneliness, a ring which could be broken only by a violent stroke, by bursting it, by an assault from inside or an invasion from outside. Shortly before she had read something in the newspaper about the Russian Revolution and the soviets, under the heading " The Invasion from Below "; she had remembered this phrase during the night and it returned again and again to her mind like the refrain of a popular song. In any case it would be well to get an estimate for affixing bars to the windows from Krahl the locksmith.

The nights grew longer and the cold moon lay in the sky like a pebble.

In spite of the piercing cold Hanna could not summon up the resolution
to close the window. Still more than the appearance of a noiseless burglar
she dreaded the crash that would be made if the window panes were
forced in, and this strange tension, which was not actually fear, yet was
on the point at any moment of toppling over into panic, betrayed her into
quasi-romantic gestures. So now almost every night she leaned against
the open window and gazed out at the dead zone of the autumn,
curiously attracted, almost drawn out of herself into the vacancy of the
landscape, and her fear, which by that attraction was denuded of all
fear, became a light bubble—her heart bore itself as lightly as a flower,
and the rigidity of her isolation opened out in the released freedom of
her breathing. And that was almost like a blissful infidelity towards
Heinrich, it was a state which she experienced as the diametrical opposite
of another and past state . . . yes, but what state? and then she became
aware that it was the opposite of what she had once called the physical
experience. And the best of it was that at those moments the physical
experience was completely forgotten.

CHAPTER LXXIX

Esch's fears were destined to be realized: Huguenau got the Major
into fresh trouble. It must be admitted, however, that Huguenau's rôle
at first was a passive one.

At the beginning of October there arrived on the Major's desk one
of those lists which the Army Command issued from time to time in its
attempt to track down all soldiers missing from their regiments, including
suspected deserters; and among the names there was that of a certain
Wilhelm Huguenau from Colmar, a private in the Fourteenth Fusiliers.

The Major had already laid the list aside when he grew aware that
something was bothering him. So he picked it up once more; being
far-sighted he held it out at arm's-length, turning it to the light, and
read again: "Wilhelm Huguenau," a name that he surely had heard
before. He looked up questioningly at the orderly whose duty it was
to wait while the day's post was examined; he was just able to see that
the man, obviously expecting some order, had drawn himself up at
attention, and was just able to collect his strength sufficiently to say,
"You may go," but once he was alone he sank forward over the desk
with his face buried in his hands.

From this blank confusion he started up with the thought that the orderly was still standing by the door and that the orderly was Esch. At first he did not dare to look and see, but when he finally assured himself that there was no one there he said aloud in the empty room: "Well, it doesn't matter . . ." as if that settled it. But that did not settle it, the image of Esch still stood by the door gazing at him, gazing at him as if it had just discovered that he was a branded man. It was a stern reproachful look that rested upon him, and the Major was ashamed because he had watched Huguenau dancing. But that remembrance died away and suddenly he heard Esch's voice: "There's always a traitor among us."

"There's always a traitor among us," repeated the Major. A traitor is a dishonourable man, a traitor is a man who betrays his fatherland, a traitor is a man who is false to his fatherland, false to his fatherland and his comrades . . . a deserter is a traitor. And while in this manner his thoughts were gradually drawing closer to some veiled and hidden preoccupation, suddenly the veil was rent and all at once he knew everything, everything: he himself was the traitor, he himself, the Town Commandant, had allied himself with a deserter and had looked on while the man danced, he had allied himself with a deserter so that he might be invited into an editorial office, so that the deserter might pave the way for him into civilian affairs, into friendships with men who were not comrades . . . the Major put his hand up to the Iron Cross and tore at its ribbon: a traitor had no right to a decoration, a traitor must be deprived of his decoration, could not be buried with it on his breast . . . a deed of dishonour could be paid for only with a pistol bullet . . . one had to take the punishment on one's own shoulders . . . and the Major, rigidly immobile, with a frozen look in his eyes, said: "The unchivalrous end."

His hand was still touching the buttons of his uniform; mechanically he assured himself that they were all fastened, and that was a strange reassurance, a kind of hope that one could still return to duty, to one's own secure life, even although Esch's image had not yet vanished. It was a glittering and uncanny image, it stood in the other world and yet in this, it was both good and evil, it was bright and assured and yet had all the unreliability of the civilian, of the man who has his waistcoat open at the neck and lets his shirt be seen. And the Major, his fingers still on his uniform buttons, drew himself up, smoothed the

wrinkles out of his coat, passed his hand over his forehead and said:
" Phantasms."

He would have liked to send for Esch; Esch was the man to clear
everything up . . . he longed to do it, but that would be a fresh deviation
from the path of duty, a fresh deviation into civilian affairs. That must
not happen. Besides . . . one must decide things for oneself: all these
suspicions might prove groundless . . . and, on reflection, it was certain
that this Huguenau had always behaved in a correct and patriotic manner
. . . perhaps everything would be cleared up yet and turn out well.

With hands that still trembled a little the Major held the list again
before his eyes, then he laid it down and addressed himself to the other
letters that had come in. Yet, strong as was the effort he made to bring
his thoughts under control, it was not strong enough to master the contradictory orders and service instructions before him; he was incapable
of resolving the contradictions. Chaos was invading the world on every
side and chaos was spreading over his thoughts and over the world,
darkness was spreading, and the advance of darkness sounded like the
agony of a painful death, like a death-rattle in which only one thing was
audible, only one thing certain, the downfall of the Fatherland—oh,
how the darkness was rising and the chaos, and out of that chaos, as if
from a sink of poisonous gases, there grinned the visage of Huguenau,
the visage of the traitor, the instrument of divine wrath, the author of
all the encroaching evil.

For two whole days the Major endured the torment of an indecision
that the pressure of precipitate events kept him from realizing. In face
of the general disorder it would have been quite natural had he simply
let the matter drop, for a desertion was of little account; but it was just
as natural for the Town Commandant not even to consider the possibility of such an easy way out. For the categorical imperative of duty
cannot allow evasion to be piled upon evasion; and on the second day
the Major gave instructions for Huguenau to be summoned.

At the sight of the traitor all the Major's repressed disgust broke out
with renewed force. Huguenau's friendly greeting he countered with
official reserve, and reaching the list across the table pointed silently to
the name " Wilhelm Huguenau," which was marked with a red line.
Huguenau realized that everything was now at stake, and face to face
with imminent danger drew again upon the lucid assurance that had
hitherto preserved him. The tone that he adopted was light enough, but

behind the flashing eyeglasses the firmness of his look was an indication
to the Major that here was a man who knew very well how to defend
himself.

"I have been expecting something like this for a long time, my dear
Major, the disorder in the army, if you will allow me to say so, is daily
increasing . . . yes, you may shake your head, but so it is; I am, unfortunately, a living witness to it; when I reported at the Central Press
Office the sergeant on duty took all my papers from me, in order, as he
said, to send particulars to my regiment; I suspected at once that I
would have grave difficulties, since it isn't the thing to send a soldier
anywhere without his papers—you agree with me there, of course—
but I was reassured when they told me that they would send on the
papers after me. All that I got was a provisional travelling-permit for
Trier, you understand, I had nothing in my pocket but that permit,
otherwise I was left to my own resources! Well, and I had to give up
the permit, of course, to the military police at the station . . . that's the
whole story. Of course I must admit that I shouldn't have kept on
forgetting about it, but you know better than anyone, sir, how over-
burdened I am with work, and when the authorities are so remiss one can't
blame a simple taxpayer who's doing his best to defend his country. At
least, one would think so. But instead of setting their own house in
order they find it naturally much easier to brand a respectable man as a
deserter. If my patriotic duty did not forbid me, sir, I would gladly
expose such incredible conduct in the Press!"

All that sounded plausible; the Major was again undecided.

"If I might venture to suggest it, sir, you should take up this line;
inform the army police and the regiment—sticking to the truth—that
I am in charge here of the official newspaper for the region, and that I
shall send on as soon as possible the missing papers, which I shall
meanwhile try to procure."

The Major's ill-humour fastened on the phrase "sticking to the
truth." What language the man dared to use!

"It's not for you to prescribe to me what reports I am to make.
Besides, to stick completely to the truth: I don't believe you!"

"You don't believe me? Has it perhaps occurred to you, sir, to find
out whether the informer who laid this accusation is trustworthy?
And that it can be only the work of some informer—and a stupid and
malicious one at that—is as clear as daylight. . . ."

He stared triumphantly at the Major, who, surprised by this new attack, did not even remember that for this particular accusation no informer had been necessary. And triumphantly Huguenau continued:

"How many people, after all, know that I have had trouble about my papers? only one, so far as I know, and that one has often enough abused me as a traitor, pretending that he was speaking in joke, or symbolically, as he chooses to put it; you have only to cast your mind back, sir. . . . I know these sham-pious jokers . . . religious mania's what people call it, and a poor man like me can lose all his money because of it, not to speak of his head. . . ."

The Major interrupted him with unexpected suddenness; he even rapped on the table with the paper-knife:

"Will you have the goodness to leave Herr Esch out of the question? He is an honourable man."

Perhaps it was not wise of Huguenau to persist in hanging on, for his house of cards threatened every minute to collapse. He knew that, but something within him said "va banque" and he could not do otherwise:

"I beg respectfully, sir, to point out that it is you and not I who mention Herr Esch by name. So I'm not mistaken, and he's the fine informer, is he? Ah, if that's the way the wind's blowing, and it's to please Herr Esch that you do his dirty work for him, then all I ask, my dear sir, is to be arrested."

This shaft went home. The Major pointed a finger at Huguenau and stammered with difficulty:

"Out you get . . . out you get . . . I'll have you thrown out."

"As you please, Herr Major . . . quite as you please. I know what I have to expect from a Prussian officer who adopts such means to remove a witness of his defeatist speeches in communistic gatherings; it's all very well to trim your sails to the wind, but it's not my habit to denounce the trimmer. . . . Salut."

These last words, which were really sheer nonsense and only added by Huguenau to embellish his rhetoric, were not even heard by the Major. He kept on murmuring tonelessly: "Out you get . . . he's to get out . . . the traitor" long after Huguenau had left the room and disrespectfully banged the door behind him. It was the end, the unchivalrous end! he was branded for ever!

Was there still a way of escape? no, there was none . . . the Major drew his army revolver from the drawer of his desk and laid it before him.

Then he took a sheet of letter-paper and laid it also before him; it was to be his petition for a successor to relieve him. He would have preferred simply to ask to be cashiered in disgrace. But the punctual performance of official duties must go on. He would not leave his place until he had handed everything over in a regular manner.

Although the Major believed that he was doing all this with prompt and soldier-like dispatch, his actions were extremely slow and every movement cost him a painful effort. And it was with an intense effort that he began to write: he wanted to write with a firm hand. Perhaps the very intensity of the strain he put upon himself prevented him from getting further than the first words: "To the . . ." he had traced upon the paper, in letters that seemed unrecognizable even to himself, and there he stuck —the pen-nib was splintered, it had torn the paper and made an ugly splutter. And firmly, even convulsively, clutching the pen-handle the Major slowly crumpled up, no longer a Major but a worn old man. He attempted again to dip the broken nib into the ink but without success, he only knocked over the inkpot, and the ink ran in a narrow stream over the top of the desk and trickled on to his trousers. The Major paid no attention to it. He sat there with ink-stained hands and stared at the door through which Huguenau had vanished. But when some time later the door opened and the orderly appeared he managed to sit up and stretch out his arm commandingly: "Get out," he ordered the somewhat flustered man, "get out . . . I am staying at my post."

CHAPTER LXXX

Jaretzki had gone off with Captain von Schnaack. The sisters were still standing in front of the gate waving after the carriage that was taking both men to the station. When they turned to re-enter the house Sister Mathilde looked peaked and old-maidish. Flurschütz said:

" It was really terribly decent of you to take him under your wing last night . . . the fellow was in an awful state . . . where on earth did he get hold of the vodka? "

" An unfortunate man," said Sister Mathilde.

" Have you ever read *Dead Souls*? "

" Let me think . . . I believe I have. . . ."

" Gogol," said Sister Carla, with the pride of ready information, " Russian serfs."

" Jaretzki is a dead soul," said Flurschütz, then, after a pause, pointing to a group of soldiers in the garden, " . . . that's what they all are, dead souls . . . probably all of us, too; it's touched all of us somewhere."

" Can you lend me the book? " asked Sister Mathilde.

" I don't have it here . . . but we can get hold of it . . . as for books . . . do you know, I can't read anything now. . . ."

He had sat down on the seat beside the porch and was staring at the road, at the mountains, at the clear autumnal sky that was darkening in the north. Sister Mathilde hesitated a moment, then she too sat down.

" You know, Sister, we really need to discover some new means of communication, something beyond speech . . . all that is written and said has become quite dumb and meaningless . . . something new is needed, or else our chief is absolutely in the right with his surgery. . . ."

" I don't quite understand," said Sister Mathilde.

" Oh, it's not worth bothering about, it's just . . . I only meant that if our souls are dead there's nothing for it but the surgical knife . . . but that's just nonsense."

Sister Mathilde thought of something:

" Didn't Lieutenant Jaretzki say something like that when his arm had to be amputated? "

" Very possibly he did, he's infected with radicalism too . . . of course he couldn't be anything but radical . . . like every trapped animal. . . ."

Sister Mathilde was shocked by the word " animal ":

" I believe he was only trying to forget everything . . . he once hinted at that; and all that drinking . . ."

Flurschütz had pushed his cap back; he felt the scar on his forehead and passed his finger over it.

" Well, I shouldn't be surprised if we were entering on a time when people will do nothing but try to forget, only to forget: to sleep and eat and sleep and eat . . . just like our fellows here . . . to sleep and eat and play cards. . . ."

" But that would be dreadful, to live without ideals! "

" My dear Sister Mathilde, what you are seeing here is scarcely the war, it's only a miniature edition of the war . . . you haven't been out of this place for four years . . . and all the men keep a shut mouth even when they're wounded . . . keep a shut mouth and forget about it . . . but you can take my word for it, not one of them has brought back any ideals."

Sister Mathilde got up. The thunder-clouds were now outlined against the clear sky like a broad black wall.

" I'm going to apply for a field hospital again as soon as I can," he said.

" Lieutenant Jaretzki believes that the war is never going to come to an end."

" Yes . . . perhaps that's just why I want to get out there again."

" I suppose I ought to go out there too. . . ."

" Oh, you're doing your bit here, Sister."

Sister Mathilde looked up at the sky.

" I must bring in the deck-chairs."

" Yes, you'd better do that, Sister."

CHAPTER LXXXI

It was Saturday; Huguenau was paying out the week's wages in the printing-room.

Life had gone on in the usual manner; not for a moment had it occurred to Huguenau that as an openly advertised deserter who was already being tracked down he really should take to flight. He had simply stayed where he was. Not only because he was already too much bound up with local affairs, not only because a business conscience cannot bear to see any enterprise abandoned in which a considerable sum of money has been invested, whether one's own or another's—it was rather a feeling of general indefiniteness that kept him where he was and prevented him from admitting defeat, a feeling that compelled him to assert his reality against that of the others. And though it was somewhat nebulous, yet it resolved itself into a very definite idea: that the Major and Esch would get together behind his back and sneer at him. So he stayed where he was, only making an agreement with Frau Esch that meals he did not consume were to be made up to him, thus enabling him to avoid without material loss the hateful midday dinners.

Of course he knew that the trend of affairs was not favourable to the taking of action against a single insignificant Alsatian deserter; he felt himself relatively secure, and moreover he had positively a strangle-hold on the Major. He knew that, but he preferred not to know it. On the contrary he played with the thought that the luck of war might take another turn, that the Major might again be a power in the land, and that the Major and Esch were only waiting until then to crush him. It was for him to foil them in good time. Maybe it was sheer superstition, but he could not afford to fold his hands, he had to use every minute of his time, he had far too many urgent things to settle; and although he could not have told precisely whither this urgency was driving him, yet he consoled himself with the reflection that it was only their own fault if he laid counter-mines against his enemies.

Now he was paying out the wages. Lindner regarded the money, counted it over again, looked at it once more and left it lying on the table. The apprentice compositor was standing by, equally silent. Huguenau was puzzled:

"Well, Lindner, why don't you pick up your money?"

Finally, with obvious reluctance, Lindner brought out the words:

"The Union rate's ninety-two pfennings."

That was something new. But Huguenau was not at a loss:

"Yes, yes, in large printing-works . . . but not in a tight squeeze like this . . . you're an old, experienced workman and you must know the condition we're in. With enemies on every hand, nothing but enemies . . . if I hadn't set the paper on its legs again there wouldn't be any wages at all to-day . . . that's all the thanks I get. Do you imagine I wouldn't be glad to give you twice as much . . . but where am I to get it from? Perhaps you think we're a Government paper bolstered up with subsidies . . . then, of course, there would be some sense in your joining the Union and asking for Union rates. I would join it myself; I'd be much better off."

"I haven't joined the Union," muttered Lindner.

"How do you know the Union rate, then?"

"One soon gets to hear of it."

Huguenau had meanwhile considered the matter. Of course Liebel was at the bottom of this with his workshop propaganda. So he was an enemy too. But Liebel was a man to keep in with for the present. He said therefore:

"Well, we'll manage some arrangement . . . let's say, from November the new rate, and until then we'll see what can be done."

Both men professed themselves content.

In the evening Huguenau went to the Palatine Tavern to look for Liebel. The Lindner affair was really only a pretext. Huguenau was not at all ill-natured; he looked with clear eyes at the world; only a man has to know who are his enemies so that he can make a change of front when necessary. Oh, he knew well enough who his enemy was. They had managed to shut down the brothel and two outlying pubs . . . but when he offered to help them in their fight with the real subversive elements the Major had turned tail. Well, to-morrow he would butter the old man up again in the newspaper, this time for having closed the brothel. And Huguenau hummed to himself: " Lord God of Sabaoth."

In the Palatine he found Liebel, Doctor Pelzer, who had volunteered as a private, and a few more. Pelzer asked at once:

" And where have you left Esch? we never see him at all nowadays."

Huguenau grinned:

" Bible class for the Holy Sabbath . . . he'll be getting himself circumcised next."

They all roared with laughter, and Huguenau swelled with pride. But Pelzer said:

" All the same, Esch is a fine chap."

Liebel shook his head:

" It's almost incredible, the stuff that people swallow. . . ."

Pelzer said:

" It's just in times like these that everyone has his own ideas. . . . I'm a Socialist, and so are you, Liebel . . . but that's just why, all the same, Esch is a fine chap. . . . I like him very much."

Liebel's forehead, which rose up not unlike a tower, reddened, and the vein running over it stood out:

" In my opinion that kind of thing just makes people besotted and should be stopped."

" Quite right," said Huguenau, " destructive ideas."

Someone at the table laughed:

" O Lord, how even the big capitalists are changing their tune! "

Huguenau's eyeglasses flashed at the speaker:

" If I were a big capitalist I wouldn't be sitting here, but in Cologne, if not in Berlin."

" Um, you're not exactly a communist either, Herr Huguenau," said Pelzer.

" Nor that either, my dear Herr Doctor . . . but I know what's just and what's unjust . . . who was the first to expose the state of things in the prison? eh? "

" Nobody denies the services you've rendered," conceded Pelzer, " where would we have got such a fine Iron Bismarck but for you? "

Huguenau became genial; he clapped Pelzer on the shoulder:

" Pull your grandmother's leg, my dear fellow! "

But then he proceeded to let himself go:

The services he had rendered were neither here nor there. Of course he had always been a good patriot, of course he had acclaimed the victories of his Fatherland, and would anybody venture to blame him for that? but he had always known very well that that was the only way of rousing the bourgeoisie, who kept a tight hand on their ill-gotten gains, to do something for the children of the poor proletarian victims of the war; as far as he remembered it was he who had managed that! but what thanks had he got? it wouldn't surprise him to find that secret police orders were already out against him! but he wasn't afraid, let them do their worst, he had friends who would get him out of prison if necessary. This secret service work must in any case be put a stop to. " A man disappears, nobody knows how, and the next thing you hear is that he's been buried in the prison yard; God only knows how many are still languishing in prison! No, we don't get justice, we get only police justice! and the worst of it all is the sham piety of these police butchers; they have their Bibles always in their hands, but only to hit people over the head with. And they say grace before and after meat, but other people can starve to death, grace or no grace. . . ."

Pelzer had listened approvingly, but now he interrupted:

" Seems to me, Huguenau, you're an *agent provocateur*."

Huguenau scratched his head:

" And do you imagine that I haven't had offers of that kind made to me? if I could only tell you . . . well, never mind. . . . I was always an honest man and I'll remain an honest man if it should cost me my head . . . only I can't stand that sham hypocrisy."

Liebel said in agreement:

" This Bible stuff is only a stunt . . . the masters simply love to see the people fed on Bible texts."

Huguenau nodded:

" Yes, first a text and then a bullet . . . there are plenty who had a hand in the shooting affair in the prison . . . well, I'd better say nothing. But I'd rather go to quod than to one of their Bible classes."

So Huguenau aligned his position in the struggle then beginning between the upper and lower orders. And although Bolshevist propaganda was a matter of complete indifference to him, and he would have been the first to call for help if his own possessions had been in danger, although indeed it was only with great uneasiness that he reported in the *Kur-Trier Herald* the increasing number of inroads on property, yet he said now with honest conviction:

" The Russians are great fellows."

And Pelzer said:

" I believe you, my boy."

As they left the inn Huguenau shook his finger at Liebel:

" You're another of these sham-pious Johnnies . . . egging on my good old Lindner against me, and yet I'm only working for the people . . . and you know it, too. Well, I suppose we'll come to an understanding yet."

CHAPTER LXXXII

An eight-year-old child has resolved to wander alone out into the world.

She walks along the narrow strip of grass between the wheel-ruts and sees the pale purple of fading clover-heads that have strayed there, dried cakes of cow-dung, hoary with age, that have grass growing in their cracks, and the prickly burrs that cling to her stockings. She sees many other things too, the meadow-saffron growing in the fields and two dun cows grazing on the valley slopes, and since she cannot be always looking at the landscape she looks also at her frock and sees the little wild roses printed on its black cotton: over and over again a fully opened flower and a bud together on one bright green stalk between two small green leaves; in the middle of the opened rose there is a yellow point. She wishes that she had a black hat in which a rose with a bud and two leaves could be pinned—that would go well with the frock. But she has only a grey woollen cloak with a hood.

As she wanders along the river like this, one hand on her hip and the other clutching a mark to defray her expenses, she is in well-known country. She is not afraid. She walks through the landscape as a house-wife might walk through her dwelling, and if the pleasant feeling in her big toe induces her to kick a stone off the strip of grass, that is only a kind of tidying up. All around her everything is clear. She can see the clumps of trees that stand clearly modelled in the transparent air of the early autumn afternoon, and the landscape has no mystery for her:

behind the transparent air is the bright blue sky, among the transparent
green leafage there appears from time to time, as if it could not be otherwise, a tree with yellow leaves, and often, although there is not a breath
of wind, a yellow leaf comes fluttering from somewhere and slowly
circling settles on the path.

When she turns her eyes to the right, yonder where the willows and
bushes fringe the shore of the river, she can see the white boulders in
the river-bed, she can even see the water; for the foliage of the bushes
has thinned out with the autumn and reveals the brown branches, it is
no longer the impenetrable green wall of summer. But if she turns her
eyes to the left she sees the marsh-meadow: uncanny and malicious it
lies there, and if one sets a foot in its grass the water plashes up and
seeps into one's shoes; one dare not try to cross a marsh like that, for
who knows? one might sink and be smothered in the bog.

Children have a more restricted and yet a more intense feeling for
nature than grown-ups. They will never linger at a beautiful prospect
to absorb the whole of a landscape, but a tree standing on a distant hill
can attract them so strongly that they feel as if they could take it in
their mouths and must run to touch it. And when a great valley spreads
before their feet they do not want to gaze at it, but to fling themselves
into it as if they could fling their own fears in too; that is why children
are in such constant and often purposeless movement, rolling in the grass,
climbing trees, trying to eat leaves, and finally concealing themselves
in the top of a tree or deep in the dark security of a bush.

Much, therefore, of what is generally ascribed to the sheer inexhaust-
ibility of a youth's unfolding powers and to its purposeless yet purposeful
exuberance is really nothing else than the naked fear of the creature that
has begun to die in realizing its own loneliness; a child rushes to and fro
because in so many senses it is wandering about at the beginning of its
course; the laughter of a child, so often censured by adults as idle, is the
laughter of one who sees himself surprised and mastered by loneliness:
so it is not only comprehensible that an eight-year-old may decide
to go out into the world in an extraordinary, one might almost say, an
heroic and final attempt to concentrate her own loneliness and conquer
within that the greater loneliness, to challenge infinity by unity and unity
by infinity—not only is that comprehensible, but it is also comprehensible
that in an enterprise of this kind the motives influencing her will be
neither ordinary nor weighed by ordinary standards; a mere butterfly,

that is to say a thing of such little weight that it cannot come into consideration at all, may have a determining influence on the whole course of her adventure—for instance, let the butterfly that has fluttered for some time ahead of her suddenly leave the path to vanish across the marshes, and it is only in the eyes of an adult that that will seem irrelevant, for adults cannot see that it is the soul of the butterfly, not the butterfly itself, and yet itself, that has deserted the child. She comes to a stop; she takes her hand from her hip and with a wild swoop doomed beforehand to failure she tries to catch the creature that is already far away.

She does, indeed, continue on her original path for some time. She comes almost to the great iron bridge that carries across the river the main road from the east towards the town. The path by the shore which she has been following would here climb up the road embankment and cross it to descend on the other side. But the child does not get so far as that. For in face of the familiar bridge with its grey lattice-work that cuts the black pine-forest into multitudinous black rectangles when one looks through it, a sight that has always terrified her, and of the surprising and apparently unending familiarity of the country, she now quite suddenly decides to leave the valley. No sooner thought than done. And even although when she wandered off from home she may have hoped that what was familiar and homelike would vanish only gradually, merging almost painlessly, as it were, into what was strange, yet the painfulness of this sudden farewell to the valley is drowned in her strong desire to cross to the other side of the marsh, to where the butterfly vanished.

It is only a moderately high bluff that rises over there, but it is high enough for the child to see nothing of the house on its summit save the roof, and nothing of the trees that grow there save their tops. Perhaps her most sensible course would be simply to tackle the ascent from the main road. But her impatience is too great: under the bright blue sky, that cool-warm sky of the Indian summer, under the rays of the sun that burn her back, she begins to run; she runs along the edge of the marsh looking for a ford or a raised path, the narrowest of paths will do; but while she is searching she has run right round the marsh and is already at the foot of the hill, just as if the hill had run to meet her like a camel and was kneeling down for her to climb up on it. This twofold haste, her own and that of the hill, is a little uncanny, and she really hesitates now that she is about to set foot on the imperceptible swell that marks the transition from the flat marshland to the steep hill. If she now lifts her head the farmhouse up there has quite vanished from sight and only a few tree-tops are visible. But the higher she clambers the more the little settlement up there grows to meet her eye, first the trees in their rich green as if spring were calling to her, then the roof from which the chimney rises like a candle, and finally the white walls of the house gleam through the trees: it is some kind of farmhouse set in a very green garden, and the last slope, so steep that she scrambles up on all-fours, is likewise so green that she advances her arms until she is stretched flat on her belly, her face in the grass, and only then slowly lets her knees follow.

Now that she is really at the top and the farmyard dog barks and tugs at his chain, the springtime she hoped to find is wanting. The landscape, indeed, is strange and unfamiliar, and even the valley, into which she now casts a glance, even that is no longer the valley out of which she came. A twofold transformation! a transformation that is certainly heightened by melancholy, but none the less is not decisive, for the transformation can be attributed to the change in the light: with that swiftness peculiar to autumn the clear purity of the light has become opaque and milky, and the whitening shield of the sky looks down on another sky, for the valley is beginning also to fill with cloud that is equally white. It is yet afternoon, ah, yet afternoon, but the evening of strangeness has already invaded it. Far into the infinite distance stretches the road on which the farm is set, and in the quickly mounting cold the butterflies droop and die. And that is decisive! She is suddenly aware that there is no fixed goal for her, that her casting about and seeking for a goal has been in vain, that only the infinite distance itself can be a goal. The child does not formulate this thought, but she answers with her actions the question she has not posed, she flings herself into the strangeness, she flees along the road, she flees along the road that stretches without end, she loses her wits and cannot even weep in her breathless race that is like a suspension of movement between the moveless masses of cloud. And when the evening really steals upon her through the clouds, when the moon becomes a bright patch in the cloudy roof, when the clouds are then washed away by some noiseless force and all the stars are vaulted above her, when the stillness of dusk is superseded by the immobility of night, she finds herself in an unknown village, stumbling through silent alleys in which here and there a cart is standing without its horses.

It is almost a matter of no account how far Marguerite will penetrate, whether she will ever be brought back or whether she will fall a prey to some wandering tramp—the sleepwalking of the infinite has seized upon her and never more will let her go.

CHAPTER LXXXIII

STORY OF THE SALVATION ARMY GIRL IN BERLIN (15)

O autumn year, O new year of starvation,
O gentle stars that warmed the autumn leaves,
O agony of the long day! agony of barren sheaves,
O agony of farewell, when in sad resignation
they said farewell, and in their eyes, grief-stricken,
was nought but tearless seeking to hold fast
that moment of farewell, the very last:
then in the city where hooting motors thicken
they lost each other's traces, one by one,
each other's hearts, and anguish veiled the sun
and turned the moon to stone, yet was not fear;
for old men's wisdom, shining silver-clear,
illumined them until their anguish grew
into the richest dower that they knew.
Was it not anguish drew them first of all
together, like tired leaves upon the way?
And their love's anguish, was it not a ray
from Heaven's own anguish, beneath whose purple pall
His glances in their silvery radiance play?
The shy dove spreads its wings and flies abroad
across the rolling billows of the sullen flood,
bringing the covenant o'er the waters grey:
in anguish God is throned, is throned in desolation,
in Him love turns to anguish, and anguish is love's motion,
a covenant between Time and Time in earth's duress,
a covenant between loneliness and loneliness—
the anguish God sent down with deepest love was fraught,
and God's own anguish changed His being into Thought.

CHAPTER LXXXIV

The Bible readings were now badly attended. The urgency of external events drew men's attention away from what was happening in their own souls, and that applied especially to strangers, who lent a ready ear to every rumour that conveyed the possibility of their imminent return home. The townsmen were more constant; the Bible class had already become for them a part of the established order which they wished to preserve independently of war or peace, and in some corner of himself each of them was secretly disturbed rather than pleased by the rumours of peace.

Fendrich and Samwald were natives of the town and were amongst the most faithful. Huguenau, indeed, asserted that Fendrich only came because Frau Esch had always milk in the house; he even went so far as to complain that he was skimped of his breakfast coffee because Frau Esch wanted to save the milk for the pious Fendrich. And he said this not only behind her back; but Frau Esch laughed at him: " Fancy being so jealous as that, Herr Huguenau," and Huguenau retorted: " You just look out, Mother Esch, or your husband's canting crew will eat you out of house and home." Huguenau's reproaches, however, were unjust; Fendrich would have come even without the milk-coffee.

In any case there they were again in the kitchen, both Samwald and Fendrich. Huguenau, who had just made ready to go out, stuck his nose in at the door: " Having a good guzzle? " Frau Esch answered for them: " Oh, I haven't a thing in the house." Huguenau eyed them both to see if they were chewing, and glanced at the table, but on assuring himself that there was no food set out he was quite satisfied. " Then I can leave you with a good conscience," he said, " you're in the best of company, Mother Esch." Yet he did not go; he was anxious to find out what she was saying to them. But they were all silent, so he began to talk himself: " Where's your friend to-day, Herr Samwald? the one with the sticks? " Samwald indicated the window which was rattling in the wind: " When the weather's bad he has aches and pains . . . he feels it beforehand." " Oh, la la," said Huguenau, " rheumatism; yes, that's a trial." Samwald shook his head: " No, he feels changes beforehand . . . he knows lots of things beforehand." Huguenau was only half listening: " Of course, it might be gout." Fendrich shivered a little: " I can feel it too

in all my bones . . . in our factory there are more than twenty down with
'flu . . . old Petri's daughter died yesterday . . . there have been some
deaths in the hospital, too. Esch say it's the plague . . . the lung plague."
Huguenau was disgusted: " He should be more careful with his defeatist
arguments. . . . Plague! That would be a fine thing, indeed." Samwald
said: " As for Gödicke, even the plague couldn't touch him . . . he has
been raised from the dead." Fendrich had still more to add on the subject:
" According to the Bible all the plagues of the Apocalypse are bound to
come now . . . the Major prophesied that too . . . so did Esch." " Merde,
I've had enough of this," said Huguenau, " I wish you a very merry
meeting. Salut."

On the stairway he met Esch: " Two of your jolly companions are
sitting waiting for you up there . . . if the whole town starts babbling of
the plague it'll be your fault . . . you and your canting crew will send the
whole world crazy, you're just making people besotted." Esch showed
his strong teeth and waved his hand airily, which provoked Huguenau:
" There's nothing to grin at, Sir Reverend." To his surprise Esch became
serious at once: " You're right, this is no time for laughing . . . the two
up there are quite right." Huguenau felt uncomfortable: " How are they
right? . . . about the plague, for instance? " Esch said quietly: " Yes, and
it would be better for you, yes, for you, my dear sir, if you were to realize
at last that we're in the midst of fear and tribulation. . . ." " I'd like to
know what good that could do me," said Huguenau, and began to continue his way downstairs. Esch had his schoolmastering voice: " I could
soon enlighten you on that, but you don't want to find out . . . you're
afraid to find out. . . ." Huguenau turned round. Esch was standing two
steps above him and looked hugely powerful; it was annoying to have to
look up at him like that, and Huguenau hopped up a step again. Suspicion
was awakening in him again. What was it that Esch was keeping to himself? What could he know? But when Esch went on: " Only he who is
in tribulation will partake of grace . . ." Huguenau stopped him: " Here,
I want to listen to no more of that. . . ." Again Esch displayed his abomin-
able sarcastic grin: " Didn't I tell you? it doesn't suit your new change
of front . . . in fact, it has never suited you."

And he turned to continue his ascent.

There was a lightning flash behind Huguenau's eyeglasses:

" One moment, Herr Esch. . . ."

Esch paused.

"Yes, Herr Esch, I've something to say to you . . . of course that
drivel doesn't suit me . . . grin if you like, it never has suited me. . . . I've
always been a Freethinker and never made any secret of it. . . . I've never
interfered with your canting piety, so you'll kindly leave me to find
happiness in my own fashion . . . you can call it a new change of front
for all I care, and you can come nosing behind me too if you like, as
you've evidently been doing, and I'm no demagogue either like you,
and I don't make people into besotted fools as you do, I'm not ambitious,
but when I hear what's being said, not by your hypocrites upstairs, of
course not, but by other people, then I think it's likely that things will
take a very different turn from what you expect, Herr Reverend. . . . I
mean, you're going to see strange things, and you'll see some people
strung up on lamp-posts too . . . if the Major hadn't taken it into his
head to be angry with me I would give him a friendly warning, I'm a
decent chap, I am . . . he's got his back up against you, too, the doddering
old fool, but all the same I'm giving you the chance of passing on the
warning. You see, I play with all my cards on the table: I don't stab
people in the back like some others I know."

And with that he turned at last to go and tramped whistling down
the stairs. Afterwards he was annoyed with himself for having been so
good-natured—there was no reason why he should feel that he owed
anything to the Herren Pasenow and Esch—why on earth had he warned
them, and of what?

Esch stood still for a moment. He felt for some reason struck to the
heart. Then he said to himself: " A man who sacrifices himself must be a
decent chap." And although one couldn't put it past Huguenau to commit
any abomination, yet so long as he blustered so much it was all right:
dogs that bark don't bite. Let him jaw in the public-houses as much as
he liked, it wouldn't hurt anybody, least of all the Major. Esch smiled,
he stood firm and strong on his feet, and then he stretched his arms like
one who awakes from sleep or is nailed on a cross. He felt strong,
firm and robust, and as if it were an entry settling the world's account
he repeated: "A man who sacrifices himself must be a decent chap,"
then he pushed open the door of the kitchen.

CHAPTER LXXXV

" No one can see another in the darkness."

Events of 3rd, 4th and 5th November 1918.

What Huguenau had prophesied actually came to pass: one did see strange things, and these strange things took place on the 3rd and 4th of November.

On the morning of the 2nd of November a small demonstration was made by the workers from the paper factory. It proceeded, as such processions always do, towards the Town Hall, but this time, really for no particular reason, the windows were smashed in. The Major called out the half-company which still remained at his disposal, and the demonstrators dispersed. Nevertheless the ensuing calm was only on the surface. The town was filled with rumours; the collapse of the German front was known, but nobody could ascertain if there were any negotiations for an armistice, and terrible things hung in the air.

So the day passed. In the evening a red glare could be seen in the west and it was said that all Trier was in flames. Huguenau, who regretted now that he had not long since sold the paper to the communists, resolved to run off a special edition, but his two workers were nowhere to be found. During the night there was firing in the neighbourhood of the prison. The rumour went that it had been a signal inciting the prisoners to a revolt. Later the information was divulged that a prison warder had let off several alarm shots on account of a misunderstanding; but nobody believed it.

Meantime morning had come, cold, foggy and winter-like. Already by seven the town council had assembled in the unheated, faintly lit, panelled council-chamber; the arming of respectable citizens was universally demanded—but on the objection, which became stronger and stronger, that this might be interpreted as a provocative step against the workers, the formation of a Civil Guard which should include workers and middle class alike was decided upon. There arose certain difficulties with the Town Commandant regarding the giving out of rifles from the stock in the munition stores, but finally—almost over the Major's head—the arms were requisitioned. Naturally there was no time left for a systematic levy, and so a committee under the chairmanship of the Burgomaster was chosen, which was to be responsible for the distribution of arms. That morning rifles were already being given out to all those who could prove that they were citizens of the town and could use a gun, and as things had reached that stage the Town Commandant could no longer refuse the collaboration of the military with the Civil Guard; the allocation of posts was already being made from the Commandant's office.

Esch and Huguenau had reported as a matter of course. Esch, resolved above all to remain near the Major, asked urgently to be employed within the town. He was put on night service, while Huguenau had to stand guard on the bridge during the afternoon.

Huguenau sat on the stone parapet of the bridge and shivered in the November fog. His rifle with its bayonet fixed leant beside him. Grass grew between the stone blocks of the parapet, and Huguenau occupied himself in plucking it out. One could also unloosen ancient pieces of mortar from between the stones and then let them drop into the water. He was intensely bored and found the whole affair stupid. The upturned collar of his recently purchased overcoat chafed roughly against his neck and chin and gave no warmth. Out of pure boredom he satisfied the calls of nature, but that also was presently over, and he merely sat there again. It was stupid to sit there with the silly green band on one's sleeve, and cold besides. And he considered whether he should not step over to the brothel—for the Major's order closing it had not had the slightest effect; it now ran a secret trade.

He was just picturing to himself that the old dame in the brothel must have put on the fires by this time and that it would be beautifully warm in there, when Marguerite appeared before him. Huguenau was glad to see her:

"Tiens," he said, "what are you doing here. . . . I thought you had run away . . . what have you done with the mark I gave you?"

Marguerite did not reply.

Huguenau felt he would be happier in the brothel:

"You're no use to me . . . you're not fourteen yet . . . see that you get safely home."

Nevertheless he took her on his knee; it was warmer. After a while he asked: "Have you got on your warm knickers?" When she said yes he felt reassured. They snuggled closely to each other. The Town Hall clock rang through the fog; five o'clock, and how dark it was already.

" Short days," said Huguenau, " another year going past already."

A second clock followed with four and then five strokes. Huguenau grew more and more melancholy. What was the use of all this? what was he doing here? over there across the fields lay Esch's place, and Huguenau spat in a wide arc in its direction. But then a sudden fear clutched him; he had left the door of the printing-shed wide open, and if there should be any looting that day they would smash his machine to pieces.

" Get down," he said roughly to Marguerite, and when she hesitated he boxed her ears. Hastily he searched his pockets for the printing-shed key. Should he himself return or should he send Marguerite with the key to Frau Esch?

He was almost on the point of deserting his post and betaking himself home when he shrank back, for now there came a real terror that pierced him to the marrow; on the edge of the forest there was a dazzling flash, followed the next moment by a frightful detonation. He was just able to realize that it came from the barracks of the trench mortar company where some fool must have exploded what remained of the ammunition, but he at once instinctively flung himself down and was wise enough to remain lying on the ground to await further explosions. Right enough, two more violent detonations followed at short intervals and then the din subsided into a sporadic crackle.

Huguenau peered cautiously over the stone parapet and saw the walls of the munition-sheds red and smouldering with the fire inside, and the roof of the barracks burning. " So it's begun," he told himself, stood up, and removed the dirt from his new winter overcoat. Then he looked round for Marguerite and whistled for her several times, but she had run away—home, he hoped. He had little time to deliberate, for already a crowd of men were coming running down towards him from the barracks with sticks, stones and some even with rifles in their hands. And to Huguenau's astonishment Marguerite was running along beside them.

Their objective was the jail, that was clear. Huguenau grasped that in an instant, and he felt like a chief of staff whose commands were being exactly carried out to the minute. " Fine fellows," said something within him, and he found it the most natural thing in the world that he should join them.

They reached the prison at the double, shouting and yelling. The gate was shut. A hail of stones rattled against it and then a direct attack was attempted. With the butt end of his rifle Huguenau crashed the first blow against the oaken panels. Someone had got hold of a crowbar, they had not to employ it very long, a breach was soon made, the door sprang open and the crowd surged into the courtyard. It was deserted, the staff had hidden themselves somewhere; well, they would soon be smoked out, these fellows—but from the cells rang a wild chorus: "Hurrah for freedom! Hurrah for freedom! Hip, hip, hooray!"

When the first detonation came Esch was sitting in the kitchen. With one bound he was at the window, but started back when at the second explosion the loosened window together with the window frame flew at his head. Was it an air raid? His wife crouched on her knees among the splintered glass and babbled a Paternoster. For one second he gaped at her in open-mouthed amazement; all her life she had not prayed! then he jerked her to her feet. "Into the cellar, air raid." Meanwhile from the top of the stairs he saw the munition store in flames, and heard the crackle of explosions coming from it. So it had begun. And his next thought was: "The Major!" To push his whimpering wife back into the room—her lamenting voice imploring him not to leave her still rang in his ears—to seize his rifle and rush downstairs was the work of a moment. The street was full of yelling people. From the market-place came a trumpet call. Esch panted up the street. Behind him a pair of harnessed horses were being led forward at a trot; he knew that they were intended for the fire brigade and it did him good to think that a remnant of order still remained intact. The fire-engine was already standing in the market-place, it had been drawn out, but the crew had not yet arrived in full force. The bugler climbed on to the driver's seat and blew the summons again and again, but as yet only six men had turned up. From the other side of the market-place a troop of soldiers came running and the captain was sensible enough to put them at the disposal of the fire brigade; the fire-engine rolled away with a full complement.

In the Town Hall all the doors were open. Nobody to be found : the Commandant's headquarters empty. That was a relief to Esch; for at least they would not find the old man here if they came. But where was he? When Esch came out again he at last caught sight of a soldier and shouted at him asking whether he had seen the Commandant. Yes, the Commandant had called out the Civil Guard and was either at the barracks or the prison . . . which apparently had been stormed.

To the prison, then! Esch broke into an awkward, heavy trot.

While the crowd pushed their way into the prison buildings Huguenau had remained standing in the courtyard. It had been a success, without doubt it was a success—Huguenau made the sarcastic grimace that he could now manage quite well. The Major would get a nice surprise if he were to see him here, and Esch ditto. No doubt about it, it was a brilliantly triumphal success! nevertheless Huguenau felt uncomfortable—what next? he regarded the courtyard, the burning barracks gave a splendid light, but it was nothing so extraordinary after all, the courtyard looked just as he had always expected it to look. And he had had enough of this crowd too.

Suddenly he heard piercing screams. They had hunted out a warder and were dragging him out into the courtyard. When Huguenau came up the man was lying as though crucified on the ground, except that one rigid leg jerked convulsively and rhythmically in the air. Two women had thrown themselves upon him, and the man with the crowbar was standing with hobnailed boots on one of the poor wretch's hands and bringing the iron bar down with a thud on his tortured limbs. Huguenau felt that he was about to vomit. With panic in his belly and heart he shouldered his rifle and ran back to the town.

The town lay sharply outlined with its pointed gables in the glare of the burning barracks, the black contours of the houses surmounted by the towers of the Town Hall and the churches. From these the clocks struck the half-hour serenely, as though a still deeper peace hovered over this human community. And the familiar strokes of the bells, the familiar sight of the houses, all the peace that was still there while round about everything was burning, turned Huguenau's choking fear into a wild longing for human proximity. He ran straight across the fields, sometimes stopping to recover his breath. Then he caught a smell of cooked meat and once more the thought transfixed him that the door of the printing-shed was not locked, that the burglars and housebreakers would be streaming out of the prison now, and with redoubled fear, with redoubled resolution, he struggled on towards home.

Hanna Wendling was lying in bed with a high fever. At first Dr Kessel had tried to lay the blame for it on her keeping her bedroom window open every night; but later he had had to admit that it was Spanish influenza.

When the explosion took place and the window panes came crashing into the room Hanna was not in the least surprised: it was not she who was responsible for the closing of the windows, it had been forced upon her, and as Heinrich had neglected to have bars put on them, of course the burglars would climb in now. Almost with satisfaction she mentally noted: " The invasion from below," and waited for what would follow next. But when a more deafening crash ensued she came to her senses and jumped out of bed with the sudden knowledge that she must go to her son.

She held fast to the bed-post and tried to marshal her thoughts; the boy was in the kitchen, yes, now she remembered that she had sent him downstairs to be out of the reach of infection. She must go down to him.

A strong draught blew through the room, blew through the whole house. All the windows and doors were driven out of their frames and on the first floor the panes of the whole glass frontage had been burst in, for at this high-lying part of the valley the air-pressure was particularly violent. The next detonation swept half of the tiled roof off with a great clatter. If the house had not been centrally heated a conflagration would have been unavoidable. Hanna, however, did not feel the cold, she scarcely noticed even the clattering din, she did not understand what had happened, nor did she try in the least to understand: passing the screaming housemaid, whom she met in the dressing-room, she hastened to the kitchen.

In the kitchen it struck her that she must have been cold before, for here it was cosy. The windows down here had not suffered. The cook was crouching in a corner with the sobbing trembling child on her lap. The cat was lying peacefully in front of the stove. Also the curious smell of burning fireworks had vanished; this place smelt clean and warm. One had the feeling of having been rescued. Then she discovered that with incomprehensible presence of mind she had brought her bed-quilt with her. She wrapped herself in the quilt and sat down in the corner farthest from her son; she must take care that he did not catch the influenza from her, and she waved him away when he made to go over to her. The housemaid had followed her, and now the gardener and his wife arrived too: " The barracks are on fire . . . look there." The gardener pointed towards the window, but the women did not dare to go across to it, but remained sitting where they were. Hanna felt perfectly clear in the head. She said: " We must wait for it to end," and wrapped herself more firmly in her quilt. Suddenly for some reason the electric light went out. The house-maid screamed again, Hanna repeated in the darkness: " We must wait for it to end," and then she fell again into a vague doze. The boy had fallen asleep in the cook's arms. The housemaid and the gardener's wife sat on the coal bunker, the gardener leaned against the fireplace. The windows still rattled, and from time to time another row of tiles fell from the roof. They sat in darkness, they all gazed at the lighted windows, they gazed without moving, and they grew more and more motionless.

Esch hastened along the road that led downwards to the prison—his rifle had slid down from his shoulder, and he held it in his hands like a charging soldier. About half-way to the prison he heard the shouting of an approaching crowd. He flung himself into the bushes until they should have gone past. There were some two hundred men, a very mixed rabble, convicts among them, recognizable by their grey uniforms. Some of them were trying to sing the *Marseillaise*, others the *Internationale*. A man with a sergeant's voice kept shouting perpetually: " Form fours," but nobody paid any attention. At the head of the procession, above the heads of the marchers, swayed a puppet; it was the stuffed uniform of a prison warder hung from a cross-bar, from a sort of gallows—apparently they had stripped someone naked for this purpose; to the puppet's chest a white placard was fastened, and in the flickering light of the burning depot Esch could make out the words " Town Commandant." They actually had a child with them, perched on one of the men's shoulders, a little girl who reminded one somewhat of Marguerite, but Esch had no time to think of such things; he waited until the procession passed and then, to avoid any stragglers, he kept to the fields adjoining the road and ran on.

The lights of a motor-car suddenly appeared in front of him. Esch's blood ran cold—it could only be the Major! the Major, blindly rushing into the arms of the rebels. He must be stopped! stopped at any cost! Esch slithered down the bank and stationed himself in the middle of the road, waving his arms and shouting at the top of his voice. But the occupants of the car did not notice him or did not want to notice him, and if he had not leapt to the side he would have been run over. He had just time to make sure that it was actually the Major's car, and that besides the Major three soldiers were in it, one of them standing on the footboard. He stared helplessly after the car, then he ran for all he was worth behind it, he ran in terrible fear, expecting every moment to see something dreadful happening. And already in front of him there were several reports; they were followed by a crashing blow somewhat like an explosion, then came shouts and a general hubbub. Esch rushed up the bank again.

The crowd was standing beside the first houses of the town; the neighbourhood was still lighted up by the fire. Taking cover behind the bushes Esch reached the first garden fence and creeping behind it could now draw near. The car had fallen on its side and lay burning on the opposite bank of the road. From all appearances the driver had lost control over the car and run into the bank when he saw the crowd, or he may have been hit by a stone. Half-doubled up in front of a tree on which he had split his skull, he was still groaning, while one of the soldiers lay outstretched on the road. Another, a sergeant, who appeared to have escaped with a whole skin, was surrounded by the raving mob. Under the fists and cudgels of the rioters he was making feeble and imploring gestures, saying something which could not be heard amid the noise: then he too sank down. Esch considered whether he should open fire on the crowd, but at that moment a blue flame burst from the bonnet of the car and someone shouted: " The car is exploding ! " The crowd retreated, became silent and waited for the explosion. But when nothing happened, and the car merely went on quietly burning, cries arose of " To the Commandant's quarters ! " " To the Town Hall," and the mob rolled on again towards the town.

But where was the Major? Suddenly Esch knew; he was beneath the car and in danger of being burned alive. Goaded by fear Esch clambered over the wooden fence, rushed up to the car, and tugged at the wreckage; a dry sobbing overcame him when he saw clearly that he would not be able to lift it by himself. He stood in despair in front of the burning car, and burned his helpless hands with fresh attempts. Then a man came up. It was the third soldier and he was unhurt, for he had been flung right over the road bank and fallen in a field. Together they managed to raise one side of the car. Esch crawled underneath, supporting the body of the car on his back, and the soldier pulled out the Major. Thank God ! But still they were not out of the wood, they must get out of reach of the perilously burning car as quickly as possible, and so they carried the unconscious Major up the bank and laid him down behind a few bushes on the grass.

Esch knelt down beside the Major and gazed into his face; it was a peaceful face, and his breathing was regular, though feeble. His heart also was beating quietly and rhythmically—Esch had torn open the Major's overcoat and tunic—and with the exception of a few burns and abrasions no external wound was to be found. The soldier stood by: "There's the others too. . . ." Esch straightened himself with difficulty. All at once he felt that he could hardly drag even himself along, nevertheless he pulled himself together once more, and they carried the wounded sergeant also to safety. The bodies of the dead soldier and the dead chauffeur they laid at the side of the road.

When it was finished Esch flung himself down on the grass beside the Major: "Must take a breath for a minute. . . . I'm done in." He was so exhausted that when flames suddenly flared over the roofs of the town and the soldier shouted: " The fools have set fire to the Town Hall! " he scarcely paid any attention.

In the hospital there had been chaos and confusion.

At first everybody had rushed into the garden without regard to the patients who were unable to move; nobody listened to their lamentations.

Kühlenbeck had had to exert all his authority to restore order again. He had single-handed shifted the gravest cases to the basement; he carried the patients like children in his arms, his voice boomed through the corridors, and he cursed at everybody like a bargee, including even Flurschütz and Sister Mathilde, if his commands were not executed on the spot. Sister Carla had disappeared and could not be found.

Finally things began to look ship-shape again. The beds were carried down from the devastated upper floor, and by twos and threes the patients reappeared. Some were missing. They were in the garden, or perhaps had strayed still farther, into the woods or somewhere.

Flurschütz and an attendant set out to look for them. One of the first that they discovered outside the garden was Gödicke; he had not got very far and was standing on the hillside, which he had chosen as a coign of vantage, his two sticks uplifted towards the heavens.

One would have thought that he was exulting.

And in fact when they came nearer they heard him laughing with that barking, animal laughter for which all the inmates had been waiting for months.

He paid no attention to the two of them when they shouted to him, and when they came nearer and made as though to lead him back he shook his sticks threateningly.

Flurschütz felt somewhat at a loss:

"But, Gödicke, do come along. . . ."

Gödicke pointed with his sticks at the flames and bawled in delight: "The Judgment Day . . . arisen from the dead . . . arisen from the dead . . . you must go to hell if you don't rise from the dead . . . the devil will get you all . . . he'll get you all now. . . ."

What was to be done with the man! But after they had stared at him for a while the attendant found the right words:

"Ludwig, it's the dinner-hour, come down from the scaffolding."

Gödicke fell silent; he gazed suspiciously at them out of his bearded face, but finally he hobbled after them.

Breathless and trembling Huguenau crossed the garden and reached the printing-shed. For a moment he did not know what had led him there. Then he remembered. The printing-press!

He entered. The dark room was fitfully illumined from outside and lay in Sabbath-like order and neatness. Huguenau, his rifle between his knees, sat down in front of the press. He felt disappointed; the machine did not repay his exertions; cold and impassive it stood there and merely threw restless shadows which made him feel uncomfortable. If the convict rabble came it would serve the bloody machine jolly well right if they smashed it to pieces. Although it was a beautiful little machine . . . he laid his hands on it and was angry because the iron felt so cold. Merde, why should he get angry about that? Huguenau shrugged his shoulders, gazed out into the courtyard, across at the barn where the Sunday meetings were held. Would Esch be preaching there again next Sunday? Haïssez les ennemis de la sainte religion. Pious hypocrites. An empty barn, that was all their stock in trade . . . what had a man like that to lose! A man like that should have his bones broken for him. He had no worries . . . preached on Sunday, and now he was sitting upstairs with his wife and they were comforting each other, while a fellow had to sit down here beside this bloody machine.

Once more he forgot why he had come. He leant his rifle against the printing-press. Standing in the courtyard he sniffed: again a smell of meat cooking was wafted to him. To-night of course there would be no supper, but upstairs they would be having something all right—she would see that Esch didn't want.

When he reached the landing above he started back, for the door of his room was lifted out of its hinges. That wasn't as it should be. The door was jammed too, only with a great effort was he able to push it open, and inside in his room things looked still more desolate: the mirror no longer hung above the washing-table, but lay on the top of the broken crockery. A wilderness. Incomprehensible and disturbing, it reminded one of splintered bones. Huguenau sat down on the sofa, he wanted to realize what had happened but he did not want to think . . . someone should come to explain it all to him and comfort him . . . stroke his hair.

Then it occurred to him that he must summon Frau Esch in any case to show her the damage . . . otherwise she would finish by holding him responsible for it . . . he had no intention of paying for damage that he had not caused. But just as he was about to call to her she rushed into his room, having heard his footsteps: " Where is my man? "

A spacious, blissful and deeply moving sense of comfort descended on Huguenau at the sight of a familiar face. He smiled to her frankly and cordially: " Mother Esch . . ." he literally beamed upon her . . . now all will be well, she'll put me to bed. . . . Meanwhile she did not seem even to see him: " Where is my man? " The stupid question disturbed him—what did the woman want Esch for now? if he wasn't there, it was surely all the better . . . he replied roughly: " How should I know where he's loafing about? He'll come back for his supper all right."

Perhaps she had not even listened, for she stepped up to him, seized him by the shoulders, and almost screamed at him:

" He's gone, he's gone with his rifle. . . . I've heard firing."

A hope rose in Huguenau: Esch was shot! but why in that case did the woman have such a lamenting voice? why did she have the wrong reaction? He wanted her to comfort him, and instead of that he must keep her here and comfort her, and all on account of Esch too! She was still beseeching him: " Where is he? " and she was still clutching him by the shoulder. Both embarrassed and furious he stroked her thick arm as if she were a weeping child, he would even have gladly shown her some kindness, he ran his hand up and down her arm, but his mouth spoke unkind words: " What are you snivelling about Esch for? haven't we all had enough of the schoolmaster? . . . after all, you've got me . . ." and only while he was saying this did he himself become aware that he was making a more brutal demand on her . . . as a sort of substitute for what she had failed to give him. Now she too guessed what he was after: " Herr Huguenau, for God's sake, Herr Huguenau. . . ." And already almost bereft of will-power, she made scarcely any further resistance to his panting urgency. Like a criminal trying to save the hangman trouble she undid her underclothes, and without even a kiss he fell with her on the sofa.

Afterwards her first words were: " Save my man! " Huguenau felt indifferent about that; Esch could live now as long as he liked. But the next moment she broke out into shrill screams: the window was suddenly illumined a blood red, orange-yellow flames shot up, the Town Hall was burning. She sank to the floor, a shapeless lump . . . she, she was to blame for everything: " Jesus Maria, what have I done, what have I done . . ." she crept over to him, " . . . save him, save him. . . ." Huguenau had stepped to the window. He felt annoyed; now trouble was beginning here too. He had had enough of it out there already, more than enough. And what did this woman want from him? it was Esch that was finally responsible . . . he could burn out there with the Major if he liked, holy men had always been burned. And now there would be looting on the top of everything else . . . and he had forgotten again to lock up the printing-shed . . . he took the opportunity of escaping with credit: " I'll look after him." If he should meet Esch now, he reflected as he went out, he would fling him down the stairs.

But in the printing-shed everything was neat and orderly as before. His rifle leant there and the machine threw its restless shadows. Red, black, yellow and orange-coloured, the sheaves of fire from the Town Hall shot up into the sky, while the barracks and the munition depot on the other side were still smouldering, a dirty brown. The bare branches of the fruit-trees were stiffly outlined. Huguenau contemplated the spectacle and found all at once that it was as it should be . . . everything was as it should be, and the printing-machine too pleased him once more . . . everything was as it should be, everything had been put right, he had been given back his customary nature and his clear common sense . . . now all that was needed was to put the final touch to the business and all would be well!

He softly climbed the stairs again, peeped cautiously into the devastated kitchen, stole over to the bread cupboard and cut himself a good slice, and as he could find nothing more returned to the printing-shed, settled himself comfortably, took the rifle between his outstretched legs, and began slowly to eat . . . one would manage somehow or other to settle the looters too.

Esch and the soldier knelt beside the Major. They were trying to bring him back to consciousness and rubbing his chest and hands with the damp grass. When at last he opened his eyes, they moved his arms and legs up and down, and it proved that nothing was broken. But he responded to none of their appeals, he remained lying outstretched on his back, and only his hands had grown restless, clutching at the damp earth, burrowing in the earth, seeking for clods and crumbling them to pieces.

It was clear that they must get him away as quickly as possible. To summon help from the town was out of the question; so they would have to manage by themselves. The wounded sergeant had meantime gathered his strength sufficiently to sit up—one could therefore leave him by himself for a little, and they decided first of all to carry the Major across the fields to Esch's house; it would have been too risky to take him by the main road.

As they were debating over the best way to set about it, the Major made signs as though he wished to speak: clutching a fragment of earth in his fingers he raised his hand, and his lips opened and pushed themselves forward, but his hand fell again and again to the ground and no sound could be caught. Esch put his ear quite close to the Major's mouth and waited: at last he made out the words: " Fell with my horse . . . an easy obstacle, fell all the same . . . the right foreleg broken. . . . I'll shoot him myself . . . wipe out dishonour with a bullet . . ." and then more distinctly and as though he were seeking for assent: " . . . with a bullet, not with unchivalrous weapons. . . ." " What did he say? " asked the soldier. Esch replied softly: " He thinks that he's fallen from his horse . . . but now we must go . . . if only it wasn't so damned light . . . we'll better take our rifles with us in any case."

The Major had closed his eyes again. They raised him cautiously, and every now and then resting and exchanging places, they carried him across the sodden rain-soaked fields, whose miry soil clung persistently and heavily to their shoes. The Major opened his eyes once, saw the conflagration in the town, and looking straight at Esch, commanded: "Gas bombs . . . go and put them out." Then he sank back again into somnolence.

Arrived in his courtyard Esch dismissed the soldier; he was to go back at once to his comrades—Esch himself would follow later, he would easily find someone in the house to help him to carry the Major upstairs. So for the time being they laid him on the bench in front of the garden. But when the soldier was gone Esch went quietly into the house, leant his rifle against the wall and opened the trap-door to the cellar. Then he took the Major on his back and carried him in, cautiously feeling his way down the steps leading into the cellar, and when he reached the bottom laid him on a heap of potatoes, which he first carefully covered with a woollen rug. Then he lighted the paraffin lamp fastened to the dingy wall and stopped up the chinks in the cellar with boards and rags, so that no ray of light might pierce through and be seen from outside. Finally he scribbled a note which he stuck into the Major's clasped hands: "Herr Major, you were knocked unconscious in an accident to the motor-car. I shall come back soon. Yours faithfully Esch." He examined the lamp once more to see whether there was enough oil in it; perhaps he would not be able to return for a long time. The ladder leading up to the cellar door had only three steps: before Esch opened it he turned round for a last time, regarded almost with misgiving the low-vaulted roof and the man lying motionlessly outstretched: but for the smell of paraffin one might have taken it for a tomb.

Slowly he climbed out. At the foot of the house stairs he listened for a little for any sound from above. Nothing moved—well, his wife would have calmed down by now . . . the wounded man outside the town was more important at present. He shouldered his rifle and stepped out into the street.

But his thoughts were with the man who lay in the cellar, the paraffin lamp at his head. When the light expires the Redeemer is near. The light must expire so that the debt of time might be paid.

Huguenau had just finished his slice of bread and was considering how he could get hold of further nourishment, when in the sharp light outside he caught sight of a figure in the garden. He seized his rifle, but recognized at the same moment that it was Esch himself, carrying a sort of sack on his shoulders. So the Herr Reverend had actually joined the looters! of course that wasn't surprising; well, he would soon make sure, and he waited curiously for Esch to come nearer with his burden. Esch's footsteps approached slowly and heavily through the courtyard; it was quite a long time before he was visible through the window. But then Huguenau became almost breathless with astonishment—Esch was carrying a man! Esch was carrying the Major out there! there was no possible mistake about it, it was the Major that Esch was carrying. Huguenau stole on tiptoe to the door and stuck out his head through the opening—no doubt about it, it was the Major—and he saw Esch disappearing with his burden through the cellar door.

Huguenau was intensely excited while he waited to see how things would develop further. And when Esch once more appeared and stepped out into the street, Huguenau too shouldered his rifle and followed at a safe distance.

The streets running in the direction of the Town Hall were fully illumined by the glare, but in the side-streets the houses threw sharp flickering shadows. Not a human being was to be seen. Everybody had rushed to the market-place, from which came a vague sound of tumult. Huguenau could not help thinking that in these deserted streets anyone could loot to his heart's delight; and if he himself were to force his way into some house now and carry out whatever he liked, no one would seek to prevent him—though of course what was there of any value that one could lift from such hovels, and the phrase " better game " came into his mind. Esch turned round the next corner; so he wasn't going to the Town Hall, the sanctimonious villain. Two youths ran past; Huguenau clutched his rifle in his hands, ready to strike. From a side-street a man leading a bicycle reeled towards him; he held the handle-bar convulsively with his left hand, the right arm dangled by his side as though broken; Huguenau gazed with horror into a smashed and battered face, from which one of the eyes still stared unseeingly into vacancy. Caring for nothing save to keep hold of his bicycle, as though he were resolved to take it with him into the next world, the stricken man reeled past. Face bashed in with a rifle butt, Huguenau told himself, and he clutched his rifle more firmly. A dog detached itself from a house door, ran sniffing behind the wounded man and licked the drops of blood as they fell. Esch was no longer to be seen. Huguenau quickened his steps. At the next street-crossing he caught again the glint of Esch's fixed bayonet. He followed more quickly.

Esch marched straight on, looking neither to the right nor the left; even the burning Town Hall did not seem to arouse his interest. Now his footsteps echoed no longer on the uneven pavement, for it came to a stop out here, and presently he turned into a narrow lane which ran along the town walls. Huguenau began to walk fast; he was now some twenty paces behind Esch, who calmly continued on his way: should he knock him over the head with the rifle butt? no, that would only be silly, what was needed was something that would end the business for good. And then it overwhelmed him like an illumination—he lowered his rifle, reached Esch with a few feline tango-like leaps, and ran the bayonet into his angular back. To the murderer's great astonishment Esch went on calmly for a few steps more, then he fell forward on his face without a sound.

Huguenau stood beside the fallen man. His foot touched Esch's hand, which lay across a wheel-track in the sticky mire. Should he stamp on it? no doubt about it, the man was dead. Huguenau felt grateful to him— all was well now! he crouched down and looked into the sidewards-turned face with its unshaven stubble of hair. When he failed to find in it the jeering expression that he feared he was satisfied and clapped the dead man benevolently, almost tenderly, on the shoulder.

All was well.

He exchanged the rifles, leaving his own bloodstained one with the dead man, assuredly a superfluous piece of caution on such a day, but he liked to do everything methodically and in order. And after that he set out on his return journey. The town wall was brilliantly lighted up by the burning buildings, the shadows of the trees were outlined on it, a last orange-yellow shower of sparks shot up from the roof—Huguenau could not help remembering the man in the picture in Colmar soaring up into the opening heaven, and would have liked to shake him by the uplifted right hand, so light and happy did he feel—then the Town Hall tower crashed in and the conflagration ebbed to a brownish smoky red.

"Rose Cottage," half-wrecked, still lay dark and silent in the night breeze which blew up there.

In the kitchen nothing had changed. In rigid immobility the six people still sat petrified in their places, still sat there motionless, more motionless perhaps even than before, as if bound and fettered in the stretched wires of expectation. They neither slept nor watched, nor did they know how long this state had already lasted. Only the child slept. The quilt had slipped from Hanna's shoulder, but she did not feel cold. Once she said into the silence: " We must wait for it to end," but the others probably did not even hear. And yet they listened, listened into vacancy, listened for the voices which came to them from outside. And though in Hanna's ear the words " The invasion from below " kept perpetually repeating themselves, and though she could no longer attach any meaning to them, meaningless words, meaningless sounds, yet she listened to see whether it was not these meaningless words that people were shouting outside there. The water-tap dripped monotonously. None of the six moved. Perhaps the others also heard the words she was listening to, for in spite of the wide social differences between them, in spite of their isolation and estrangement, they had all become a unified whole; a magic ring was cast round them, a chain whose links were themselves and which could not be broken through without grave injury. And in this enchantment, in this collective state of trance, it is comprehensible enough that for Hanna the cry of invasion should become more and more distinct, more distinct than she could ever have apprehended it with her physical hearing; the cry came to her as though winged by the power of their collective listening, it was borne on the current of that power, which was nevertheless a powerless power, power merely to accept and to hear, and the cry was very loud, the voice grew mightier and mightier and was like a rushing wind sweeping through the world. The dog whined in the garden and several times started barking. Then the dog too fell silent, and she heard nothing more save the voice. And at the voice's command she stood up; the others did not seem to notice it, not even when she opened the door and left the room; she went in her bare feet, but she did not know it. Her bare soles went over a stretch of concrete, that was the passage, they went up five stone steps, went over linoleum, that was the office, went over parquet-flooring and carpeting, that was the hall, went over very dry coconut-matting, over splintered tiles, over the paving of a garden-path. In such an undeviating advance as this, which may almost be called a march, only the footsoles know the way, for the eyes see only the goal—and as she stepped out of the door she saw it, she saw the goal! at the end of the endlessly stretching paved path, stretching like a long bridge, there, with one leg swung over the garden fence, was the invader, the housebreaker, there, clambering over the parapet of the bridge—a man in grey convict's clothes; like a grey block of stone he clung there. And did not move. With her hands outstretched before her she stepped on to the bridge, she let the quilt fall, her nightgown billowed in the wind, and thus she strode towards the motionless man. But whether it was that the others in the kitchen had after all noticed her leaving, or that they were drawn in a magical chain after her, the gardener appeared, followed by the housemaid, followed by the cook, followed by the gardener's wife, and, though in faint and subdued voices, they called now to their mistress.

It was no doubt the weirdness of this procession led by the white lady with the ghostly robes that made the hair bristle on the housebreaker's head and paralysed him so completely that he was scarcely capable of swinging his leg back over the fence again. And when he had done so he gaped for a while longer at the spectral apparition, and then he ran from the place and vanished in the darkness.

Meanwhile Hanna went on her way, and when she reached the fence she stuck her hand through the railings as through the bars of a window, and seemed to be waving good-bye to someone. From the town came the glare of the conflagration, but the explosions had ceased and the spell was broken. And even the wind had fallen. She sank to sleep against the bars of the fence and was carried back into the house by the gardener and the cook, where they prepared a bed for her in the storeroom next to the kitchen.

(There next day Hanna Wendling succumbed to a severe attack of influenza complicated by pneumonia.)

Huguenau marched back. Before a house a sobbing child was standing, it was certainly not more than three at most. Where could Marguerite be hiding? he wondered. He lifted up the child, pointed out to it the beautiful fireworks sending their light over from the market-place; and he imitated the crackling and hissing of the flames and the crashing of the falling beams, his-s-ss whish-sh-sh-sh bang! until he made the child laugh. Then he carried it into the house and informed the mother that she shouldn't leave a small child out in the street in times such as these without someone to look after it.

When he reached the house he leant his rifle against the wall of the entrance hall just as Esch had done, then lifted the trap-door and climbed down to the Major.

Since Esch left the Major had not changed his position; he was still lying on the heap of potatoes, the note between his fingers; but his blue eyes were open and staring at the flame of the cellar lamp. Nor did he turn his eyes away from it when Huguenau entered. Huguenau cleared his throat, and when the Major gave no sign he felt offended. This wasn't a time to continue keeping up a childish quarrel. He pulled in the stool which Frau Esch used when she picked the potatoes, and with a polite bow seated himself opposite the Major:

"Herr Major, I can understand of course that you have reasons for not wanting to see me, but that's ancient history by now, and besides events have ended by justifying me, and I can't keep silent about the fact that you have seen me in a quite false light; don't forget, Herr Major, that I have been the victim of a miserable intrigue, one shouldn't speak ill of the dead, but only think of the contempt that that canting parson treated me with from the very beginning, Herr Major. And never a word of thanks! Has the Herr Major ever given me a word of recognition for all the functions I've arranged in honour of the Herr Major? no, never more than ' I thank you '—but for the rest: you keep your distance and I'll keep mine. But I don't want to be unjust, once you did give me your hand quite spontaneously, that time the Iron Bismarck was unveiled: you see, Herr Major, that I've cherished in my memory every act of kindness you've shown me, but even then the Herr Major's lips had an ironical expression on them. If you only knew how I hated it when Esch put on that expression. I was always shut out, if I may be permitted to say so. And why? simply because I didn't happen to belong to the town from the beginning . . . a foreigner, so to speak, an interloper, as Esch so kindly put it. That was no reason for jeering at me and slighting me; I had always to decrease, that was another of his expressions—I had always to decrease, so that our Reverend Parson might increase and cut a great figure before the Herr Major. I saw that all right, and I can assure Herr Major that that hurts a man's feelings; and the insinuations you used to throw out about ' evil,' all pointing at me, ah yes, I understood them quite well too, just try and remember, Herr Major, for a whole evening you talked about evil, no wonder if a man who gets such things said to him should end by becoming really evil. I admit too that the facts seemed to support it, and that the Herr Major would perhaps call me a blackmailer or a murderer to-day. And yet it's only a matter of appearance, in reality it's all quite different, only one can't express it exactly, so to speak; besides, it looks as though you haven't the slightest desire to know what it really is. Yes, Herr Major, you talked a great deal about love that evening too, and Esch has been drivelling about love ever since—his drivel always made me sick, in any case, but when one is continually talking about love one might at least try to understand a fellow-creature. Oh, Herr Major, I know of course that I can't ask for that, and that a man in Herr Major's position would never condescend to have such feelings for a man like me, after all nothing better than a common deserter, though I would like to be allowed to say that Esch wasn't such a great deal better than myself. . . . I don't know whether the Herr Major quite understands what I mean, but I beg the Herr Major to have patience. . . ."

Polishing his eyeglasses he gazed at the Major, from whom there still proceeded neither movement nor sound:

" I beg the Herr Major most urgently not to imagine that I am keeping him imprisoned in this cellar for the purpose of forcing him to listen to me; frightful things are happening out there in the town, and if the Herr Major were to go out the Herr Major would be strung up to a lamp-post. The Herr Major will be able to convince himself of that to-morrow with his own eyes; for God's sake, put some trust in me for once. . . ."

So Huguenau spoke on to the living and motionless puppet, until he saw at last that the Major did not hear him. But even then he did not want to believe it:

" I beg pardon, the Herr Major is exhausted and here I am talking. I'll fetch something to eat."

He hastily rushed upstairs. Frau Esch sat humped together on one of the kitchen chairs, sobbing to herself, her body shaking convulsively. When he entered she started up:

" Where is my man? "

" He's all right, he'll be here presently. Have you anything to eat? I need it for a wounded man."

" Is my man wounded? "

" No, I told you he'll be here presently. Give me something to eat. Could you make an omelette? No, that would take too long. . . ."

He went into the living-room; a plate with a slice of sausage stood on the table. Without asking he seized it and stuck it between two slices of bread. Frau Esch had followed him and in a voice shrill with anxiety cried:

" Let that be, that belongs to my man."

Huguenau had the uncomfortable feeling that one dared take nothing belonging to the dead; perhaps too it would bring the Major ill luck if he ate the food of the dead. Besides, sausage wasn't the right sort of thing for him in any case. He reflected for a moment:

" Right, but surely you must have some milk . . . you always have milk in the house."

Yes, she had some milk. He filled a milk-jug and carried it carefully down to the cellar.

" Herr Major, here's milk, lovely rich new milk! " he cried in a brisk voice.

The Major did not move. Obviously milk wasn't the right thing either; Huguenau was annoyed at his mistake: perhaps I should have brought him wine instead? that would have roused and strengthened him . . . still he seems to be very feeble . . . well, now we'll try him with it all the same! And Huguenau bent down and lifted the old man's head, and the Major let him do it without making any resistance and even obediently opened his lips when Huguenau put the beak of the milk-jug to them. And when the Major accepted and swallowed the slowly trickling milk Huguenau felt happy. He ran upstairs to fetch a second jugful; at the door he glanced back, saw that the Major had turned his head to see where he was going, and nodding back kindly he waved a hand: " I'll be back at once." And when he descended once more the Major was still gazing at the cellar door and greeted him with a little smile, indeed it was more like a faint laugh. But he drank only a few drops more. Holding Huguenau by the finger he had fallen asleep.

With his finger in the Major's hand Huguenau sat on. He read the note which was still lying on the Major's breast and put this piece of evidence in his pocket. Of course he wouldn't need it, for if he found himself in a tight corner he would say in any case that the Major had been given into his keeping by Esch: all the same, best to make doubly sure. From time to time he tried cautiously to free his finger, but then the Major wakened, smiled vaguely and without releasing the finger fell asleep again. The stool was very hard and uncomfortable. Thus they passed the rest of the night.

Towards morning Huguenau managed to free himself. No joke to sit all night on a stool. He climbed out to the street. It was still dark.

The town seemed to be quiet. He went across to the market-place. The Town Hall, gutted to the very ground, was smouldering and smoking. The military and the fire brigade had set sentries round it. Two houses in the market-place had also caught fire, and house furniture lay piled up in confusion in front of them. Now and then the hose was again set in action to damp down some new smouldering outbreak. Huguenau was struck by the fact that men in convict uniform were also helping to work the hose and eagerly taking part in the work of clearing up the mess. He spoke to a man who like himself was wearing a green armlet, and asked what had happened since last evening, for he himself had been occupied elsewhere. The man was glad to talk: the collapse of the Town Hall, he said, had really finished the whole business. After that they had all stood round the fire looking pretty foolish, friend and foe alike, and had their work cut out to save the neighbouring houses. A few ruffians, it was true, had tried to force their way into the houses, but when their own comrades heard the women screaming they had fallen on the looters. One or two of them had got their skulls caved in, and that was all to the good, for after that nobody had thought of looting any more. Just a few minutes ago the wounded had been taken over to the hospital—it was high time too, for their shrieks and groans were almost past endurance. Of course the authorities in Trier had been rung up straight away, but there was chaos and rioting there too, naturally, and two car-loads of soldiers had only arrived a little while ago, when all was over. It was said too that the Town Commandant was missing. . . .

No need to worry about the Commandant, said Huguenau, he himself had got him in safe keeping; and the Major had been in a pretty tight corner too, really he himself deserved a medal for lifesaving, for now the old man was being well looked after, and as he said before, quite safe.

He raised his fingers to his hat in salute, turned back the way he had come, and set out at a trot for the hospital. The dawn was already breaking.

Kühlenbeck was not to be found at first, but presently he appeared, and when he caught sight of Huguenau, bawled at him: " What do you want here, you clown? " Huguenau put on his most offended expression: " Herr Doctor Kühlenbeck, I have to report to you that Herr Esch and myself had to hide the Herr Town Commandant, who is gravely wounded, in our premises all night . . . will you be so good as to give instructions for him to be removed at once." Kühlenbeck rushed to the door:

"Doctor Flurschütz," he thundered down the corridor. Flurschütz came. "Take a car—the cars have returned now, haven't they?—and drive to the newspaper place, take two attendants with you . . . you know where it is, I suppose . . . but it's all one," he barked at Huguenau, "for you're going with them." Then he seemed to soften: he actually gave Huguenau his hand and said: "Come, it was very nice of you both to look after him. . . ."

When they reached the cellar the Major was still peacefully sleeping on his heap of potatoes, and still asleep he was carried out. Meanwhile Huguenau had run across to the editorial office. There wasn't much ready cash in the place, it was true, only the petty cash and some stamps; the rest he carried upon him, except for what he had sent to Cologne and put in the bank; but it would be a pity to leave the stamps . . . one never knew what might happen . . . perhaps there might be some more looting after all! When he returned the Major was already installed in the car, a few people were standing round it asking what had happened, and Flurschütz was preparing to drive off. It was like a blow in the face to Huguenau; they were about to take the Major away without him. And suddenly he saw clearly that he himself dared not in any circumstances stay behind, he hadn't the slightest wish to be present when Esch's body was brought home.

"Wait for me, I'm coming immediately, Doctor," he cried, "immediately!"

"How? Do you want to come with us, Herr Huguenau?"

"But of course! I've got to give my report on the whole business . . . just one minute, please."

He rushed upstairs. Frau Esch was praying on her knees in the kitchen. When Huguenau appeared in the doorway she made towards him, still on her knees. He did not listen to her appeals, but dashed past her into his room, seized such of his possessions as he could lay hands on—and he did not possess much—rammed them into his fibre suitcase, sat upon it until the lock snapped to, and then flew back. "Ready," he shouted to the chauffeur, and they drove off.

At the hospital Kühlenbeck was standing in front of the door, his watch in his hand:

"Well, what's the matter with him?"

Flurschütz, who had got out first, gazed across at the Major with his somewhat inflamed eyes:

" Perhaps concussion . . . perhaps something more serious. . . ."

Kühlenbeck said:

" This place is a pure madhouse already . . . and it calls itself a hospital . . . well, we'll see. . . ."

The Major, who during the drive had begun to blink up at the pallid morning sky, was now wide awake. As he was being lifted out of the car he became excited; he flung himself about, and it was obvious that he was looking for something. Kühlenbeck stepped across and bent over him:

" Come, this is a nice way to behave, Herr Major! "

But at that the Major became quite furious. Whether it was that he recognized Kühlenbeck, or that he did not recognize him, at any rate he seized him by the beard, tugged at it fiercely, gnashing his teeth, and only with difficulty could be got under control. But he became peaceable and docile at once as soon as Huguenau stepped up to the stretcher. He took hold of Huguenau's finger again, Huguenau had to walk alongside the stretcher, and he would only submit to be examined so long as Huguenau sat by his side.

Kühlenbeck, however, broke off his examination very soon:

" It has no object," he said, " we'll give him an injection and then we'll just have to send him away . . . this place will have to be evacuated in any case . . . so get him off to Cologne as quickly as possible . . . but how? I can't spare anybody here, the order to evacuate the hospital may arrive at any moment. . . .

Huguenau stepped forward:

" Perhaps I could take the Herr Major to Cologne . . . as a voluntary ambulance attendant, if I may put it like that . . . the gentlemen can see for themselves that the Herr Major is satisfied with my attendance."

Kühlenbeck reflected:

" With the afternoon train? . . . no, that's far too uncertain now. . . ."

Flurschütz had an idea:

" But there must be a motor-van going to Cologne to-day . . . couldn't one arrange somehow or other for it to take him? "

" To-day anything can be arranged," said Kühlenbeck.

" Then may I ask you to give me a permit to proceed to Cologne? "
said Huguenau.

And so it happened that Huguenau, furnished with authentic military
documents, on his sleeve a red-cross armlet which he had extracted from
Sister Mathilde, was given official charge of the Major, and conducted
him to Cologne. They fixed up the stretcher in the van, Huguenau took
up his post beside it on his fibre case, and the Major seized his hand and
did not let it go again. After a while Huguenau too was overcome by
fatigue. He settled himself as well as he could beside the stretcher, pushed
his case under his head, and lying side by side, hand in hand, they slept
like two friends. And so they arrived at Cologne.

Huguenau delivered the Major at the hospital according to orders,
waited patiently by his bed until an injection had banished all danger of
a new outbreak, and then he was able to steal away. From the hospital
authorities he actually engineered a permit to return to his Colmar home,
whereupon he lifted from the bank the remainder of the balance credited
to the *Kur-Trier Herald*, and next day he departed. His war Odyssey,
his lovely holiday was at an end. It was the 5th of November.

CHAPTER LXXXVI

STORY OF THE SALVATION ARMY GIRL IN BERLIN (16)

Who can be more light-hearted than an invalid? there is nothing to
force him into the struggle for life, he is quite at liberty even to die if he
likes. He is not obliged to draw inductive conclusions from the events
of the day in order to orient his behaviour; he can remain wrapped in
the cocoon of his own thoughts,—wrapped in the autonomy of his own
knowledge he is free to think deductively, to think theologically. Who
can be happier than the man who is at freedom to think out his
religion!

Sometimes I go out by myself. I walk along slowly, my hands in my
pockets, and gaze into the faces of the passers-by. They are finite faces,
but often, indeed always, I can manage to discover the infinite behind
them. These are, so to speak, my inductive escapades. The fact that
during these roving expeditions, which certainly never take me very far
—only once did I get as far as Schöneberg, and that made me very tired—
I have never encountered Marie, that among all the faces hers has never

emerged, that she has so completely vanished from my ken, hardly even disappoints me, for the times are uncertain, and she was always expecting to be sent away on foreign missionary service. I am quite happy without her, as it is.

The days have grown short. And as electric current is expensive and a man wrapped in the cocoon of his own autonomy can easily dispense with light, I have long nights. Nuchem often sits with me. Sits in the darkness and says little. His thoughts no doubt are with Marie, but he has never mentioned her.

Once he said:

" The war will stop now."

" Indeed," I said.

" Then there will be a revolution," he went on.

I saw a chance of pouncing upon him:

" Then they will put an end to religion."

I heard him laughing silently in the darkness:

" Is that said in your books? "

" Hegel says: it is infinite love that makes God identify Himself with what is alien to Him so as to annihilate it. So Hegel says . . . and then the absolute religion will come."

He laughed again, a vague shadow in the darkness:

" The law remains," he said.

His obduracy was unshakable: I said:

" Yes, yes, I know, you're the eternal Jew."

He said softly:

" We'll go back to Jerusalem now."

I had talked too much in any case and let the matter drop there.

CHAPTER LXXXVII

The broad keel of the ship whose port is never found
Cleaves heavy furrows in the phantom waves
That die far off in shoreless watery graves:
O sea of sleep, whose spindrift rings our void around!
Dream heavy with blind freightage! dream of founts unsealed,
Dream seeking for Another on that swift bark,
Dread longings! far more dreadful through the stark
Law by which far from land their soundless knell is pealed:

No dream has ever found another's dream,
Lonely the night, even though Thy mighty breath
Wraps it, a deep from whence suspires our faith
That we some time transfigured and raised on high
May face each other in the radiant beam
Of grace, may face each other and yet not die.

CHAPTER LXXXVIII

DISINTEGRATION OF VALUES (10)

Epilogue.

All was well.

And Huguenau, furnished with an authentic military permit, had
returned to his home in Colmar at the army's expense.

Had he committed a murder? had he done a revolutionary deed? he
had no need to reflect upon it, nor did he do so. Had he done so, however,
he might simply have said that his procedure had been quite reasonable
and that any one of the town's prominent citizens, among whom, after
all, he had a right to range himself, would have done exactly the same.
For there was a firm line of demarcation between what was reasonable
and what was unreasonable, between reality and unreality, and Huguenau
would have conceded at most that in less warlike or less revolutionary
times he would have left the deed undone, which would have been a
pity. And he would probably have added judiciously: " There's a time
for everything." But the opportunity did not arise, for he never gave a
thought to that deed, nor was he ever to think of it again.

Huguenau did not think of what he had done, and still less did he
recognize the irrationality that had pervaded his actions, pervaded them
indeed to such an extent that one could have said the irrational had burst
its bounds; a man never knows anything about the irrationality that
informs his wordless actions; he knows nothing of " the invasion from
below " to which he is subject, he cannot know anything about it, since
at every moment he is ruled by some system of values that has no other
aim but to conceal and control all the irrationality on which his earth-
bound empirical life is based. The irrational, as well as consciousness, is,
in the Kantian sense, a vehicle that accompanies all categories—it is the
absolute of Life, running parallel, with all its instincts, conations and

emotions, to the other absolute of Thought: irrationality not only supports every value-system—for the spontaneous act of positing a value, on which the value-system is based, is an irrational act—but it informs the whole general feeling of every age, the feeling which assures the prevalence of the value-system, and which both in its origin and in its nature is insusceptible to rational evidence. And the powerful apparatus of cognitive interpretation which is erected around all atomic facts to make their content plausible has the same function as that other and not less powerful apparatus of ethical interpretation which makes human conduct plausible; both of them consist of bridges thrown out by reason, crossing and recrossing at different levels, for the sole purpose of leading earthly existence out of its essential irrationality, out of " evil," by way of a higher and " reasonable " meaning up to that ultimate metaphysical value which by its deductive structure helps man to assign a fitting relevance to his own actions, to all things and to the world, but at the same time enables him to find himself again so that his vision ceases to be erratic and transient. In circumstances like these it is not surprising that Huguenau knew nothing about his own irrationality.

Every system of values springs from irrational impulses, and to transform those irrational, ethically invalid contacts with the world into something absolutely rational becomes the aim of every super-personal system of values—an essential and radical task of " formation." And every system of values comes to grief in the endeavour. For the only method that the rational can follow is that of approximation, an encircling method that seeks to reach the irrational by describing smaller and smaller arcs around it, yet never in fact reaches it, whether the irrational appears as an irrationality of one's inner feelings, an unconsciousness of what is actually being lived and experienced, or as an irrationality of world conditions and of the infinitely complex nature of the universe—all that the rational can do is to atomize it. And when people say that " a man without feelings is no man at all," they say so out of some perception of the truth that no system of values can exist without an irreducible residue of the irrational which preserves the rational itself from a literally suicidal autonomy, from a "super rationality " that is, if anything, still more objectionable, still more " evil " and " sinful " from the standpoint of the value-system, than the irrational: for, in contradistinction to the plastic irrational, the pure Ratio, arising through dialectic and deduction, becomes set and incapable of further formation when it grows autonomous, and this rigidity annuls its own logicality and brings it up against its logical limit of infinity,—when reason becomes autonomous it is thus radically evil, for in annulling the logicality of the value-system it destroys the system itself; it inaugurates the system's disintegration and ultimate collapse.

There is a stage in the development of every system of values during which the mutual interpenetration of the rational and the irrational reaches its maximum, a kind of saturated condition of equilibrium in which the elements of evil on both sides become ineffective, invisible and harmless—and these are the times of culminating achievement and of perfect style! for the style of an epoch could almost be defined in terms of this interpenetration: when such a stage of culminating achievement is reached the rational may penetrate through countless pores into life, but it remains subject to life and to the central will to value; and the irrational may flow through countless veins of the value-system, but is as it were canalized, and even in its most minute ramifications subserves and assists the central will to value,—the irrational by itself has no style, the rational by itself has no style, or rather they are both liberated from style, the one in the freedom of Nature, the other in the freedom of mathematics; but when they are combined, when they mutually restrain each other, the result of this restrained and rational life of the irrational is the phenomenon that may be described as the peculiar style of a value-system.

But this condition of equilibrium is never permanent, it is only a transitional stage; the logic of facts drives the rational towards the super-rational, and drives the super-rational towards its limits; it initiates the process of disintegration, the splitting up of the whole value-system into partial systems, a process which ends in complete dissociation, with free and autonomous Reason on the one hand, and free and autonomous Life on the other. For a time, of course, the partial systems are still penetrated by reason and even led by reason to their own independent autonomy, to the limits of their own autonomous infinity; but the play of reason within a partial system is restricted to its immediate environment. So there arises a specific commercial kind of thinking, or a specific military kind of thinking, each of which strives towards ruthless and consistent absoluteness, each of which constructs a deductive *schema* of plausibility to suit itself, each of which has its " theology," or its " private theology," if one may call it so—and the degree of success attained by such a military or commercial theology in constructing a specific and diminished organon of its own is precisely determined by the proportion of irrational elements which have been retained in its partial system: for the partial systems also are reflections of the Self and of the total system, and they too pass through or strive towards a phase of equilibrium which gives them style, so that it is possible to speak of a military or a commercial style of living. The smaller the system becomes, however, the more restricted is its power of ethical expansion and its ethical will, the more hardened and indifferent does it become to evil, to the super-rational and to the irrational that is still alive within it, the smaller grows the number of forces at its disposal and the greater the number of those to which it is indifferent, relegating them to the individual as his private concern: the further the breaking-up of the total system proceeds, the more the reason in the world becomes detached, the more visible and effective does the irrational become. The total system of a religion makes the world that it dominates a rational world, and in the same way the independent sovereignty of reason must liberate all that is irrational and mute.

The final indivisible unit in the disintegration of values is the human individual. And the less that individual partakes in some authoritative system, and the more he is left to his own empiric autonomy—in that respect, too, the heir of the Renaissance and of the individualism that it heralded—the narrower and more modest does his " private theology " become, the more incapable is it of comprehending any values beyond its immediate and most personal environment: whatever comes from beyond the limits of its narrow circle can be accepted only in a crude and undigested state, in other words accepted as dogma—and so arises that empty and dogmatic play of conventions, that is to say of super-rationalities reduced to the smallest dimensions, which is typical of the average Philistine (a term which undeniably fits Huguenau), a play of unconflicting interaction between a living vitality sunk in the irrational and the empty form of a super-rationality that functions in a vacuum and subserves nothing but the irrational; both of them unrestrained and without style, associated in an incongruity that is incapable of creating any further value. The man who is thus outside the confines of every value-combination, and has become the exclusive representative of an individual value, is metaphysically an outcast, for his autonomy presupposes the resolution and disintegration of all system into its individual elements; such a man is liberated from values and from style, and can be influenced only by the irrational.

Huguenau, a man liberated from values, was nevertheless still a member of the commercial system; he was a man who had a good reputation in provincial business circles; he was a conscientious and prudent agent, and he had always fulfilled his commercial duties wholly and completely, even with radical thoroughness. His murder of Esch, moreover, while it hardly came within the province of his duty as a business man, was not an infringement of the business code. It had been a kind of holiday deed, committed at a time when even the commercial system of values was temporarily suspended and only individual motives remained. On the other hand it was quite in accordance with business ethics, to which Huguenau had now reverted, when in consideration of the depreciation of the mark after the conclusion of peace he addressed the following letter to Frau Gertrud Esch:

DEAR MADAM,

Hoping that this finds you well as it leaves me at present, I take the opportunity of reminding you that according to our contract of 14.5.1918 I am in control of 90 per cent. of the shares of the " Kur-Trier Herald," including, to be correct, 30 per cent. belonging to various gentlemen of that town, whose representative however I have the honour to be, so that without my knowledge and consent the business cannot be carried on nor any fresh commitments undertaken, and I must hold you and these gentlemen wholly and completely responsible for all possible losses arising out of any such infringement of my rights. Should you and these gentlemen, however, be continuing to issue the paper, I must beg you to remit immediately a statement of accounts and the profits accruing to my group of shareholders, amounting to 60 per cent. of the whole (see contract § 3), and courteously reserve to myself the right of taking further action.

On the other hand, with my customary loyalty, of which you are already aware, I admit frankly that the force majeure of the war collapse has prevented me from remitting at the proper time the two remaining instalments due from me on behalf of my group, amounting in all to 13.400 marks, of which 8000 marks fall to you as heir of the late Herr August Esch. With the same frankness, however, I must point out that you, as you must admit, have neglected to send to me, as business manager of the paper, a demand note properly registered claiming the payment of these instalments before a duly fixed date, so that now, should you present the said demand note, I am merely bound to pay you that sum of money plus deferred interest in order to settle all legal claims between us.

But since I am anxious to avoid having any dispute in a law-court with the amiable wife of my late respected friend Herr August Esch, even although the property in question lies in occupied territory and my French nationality would give me the greatest advantage in any such dispute, and since moreover I prefer to have things settled out of hand, I beg to propose that we should compound our affair by mutual agreement, which would be all to your advantage, considering the legal position.

The simplest way of doing this would be for you to buy back from me, acting on behalf of my group, our 60 per cent. of shares in the business, and I am ready to sell them on the most favourable conditions; and without prejudice, unless I can dispose of them meanwhile on better terms, I offer them to you for the half of the original price, reckoned in francs at par. The total price was 13.400 marks—at par about 16,000 francs—so that I am giving you exceptionally favourable terms if I offer them at 8000 francs (eight thousand French francs), with the reminder that I have not taken into consideration at all either the sums of money I expended privately on the business, or my current expenses, or the time and labour I sacrificed on its behalf, although these alone have increased the value of the business to considerably more than when I took it over. And in adopting this generous attitude and offering you such exceptionally favourable terms, my only motive is to make things easy for you and bring about a convenient settlement, all the more as you can easily raise the money by a mortgage on your freehold, if you do not have it at hand.

Finally I take the liberty of pointing out that with my group's 60 per cent. of shares in addition to your own existing 10 per cent. you will have an overwhelming majority of 70 per cent. under your control, with which you can easily squeeze out the other minority group, and I am convinced that you will shortly find yourself sole proprietor of a flourishing business, and in this connection I cannot refrain from adding that the advertising department, after the way in which I flatter myself that I organized it, is a gold mine in itself, and that I put myself gladly at your disposal to assist you further with it by word and deed.

Under these circumstances you can quite well see that I am sacrificing my own interests in making you this offer, merely because it would be difficult for me to manage the paper from here, but I am convinced that I could get a

considerably better offer from other clients, which would not redound to your
advantage, and so I beg you to send me an affirmative answer within 14 days,
in default of which I shall put the matter in the hands of my lawyers.

In the pleasant conviction that you will appreciate my friendly and generous
proposal, so that we shall come to a complete and final settlement, I take the
liberty of informing you that business in our district is extremely satisfactory
and that I am doing very well, and remain

Yours respectfully

WILH. HUGUENAU.

Registered. (*André Huguenau and Co.*)

That was an ugly and oppressive proceeding, but it did not appear in
that light to Huguenau; it violated neither his private theology nor that
of the commercial value-system; indeed, not one of Huguenau's fellow-
citizens would have found it objectionable; for no exception could have
been taken to the letter on legal or commercial grounds, and even Frau
Esch accepted its legality as a fate to which she could submit with a better
grace than to a confiscation by communists, for instance. Huguenau
himself regretted afterwards that he had been so unnecessarily modest
in his demands—the half of what it had cost him!—only one must never
put on the screw too much, and the 8000 francs, when they actually
arrived, made a welcome contribution to the firm in Colmar, and more
than that: they were the final liquidation of his war adventures, the final
seal set upon his return home, and perhaps, although only perhaps, that
gave him a twinge of sorrow. For now his holiday was definitely at an
end. And in so far as human life, running its insignificant course, can be
said to contain anything worthy of comment, nothing of the kind occurred
during the rest of Huguenau's life. He had taken over his father's business,
and he carried it on in the spirit of his forefathers, solidly and with an
eye to profit. And since a bachelor's life is no life for a prosperous business
man, and the tradition of his family, that had determined his own
existence, required him to marry some worthy woman, both for the sake
of having children and because her dowry could be used in consolidating
the family business, he set about taking the necessary steps to that end.
And since the franc meanwhile had begun to depreciate, while the
Germans had established a gold currency, it was only natural and not
worth commenting on that he should look for his bride on the right bank
of the Rhine. And since it was in Nassau that he eventually found a girl

with a suitable dowry, and Nassau is a Protestant district, it was not surprising that love and financial advantage combined should persuade a Freethinker to change his religion. And since the bride and her family were stupid enough to attach some weight to the question, he did adopt the evangelical creed to please them. And when one or another of his fellow-citizens shook a disapproving head over such a step, Huguenau the Freethinker pointed out that it was a meaningless formality, and as if to emphasize the fact voted, in spite of his Protestantism, for the Catholic Party when it formed a political alliance in the year 1926 with the communists. And since the Alsatians, like most of the Alemanni, are often whimsical people and many of them have a slate loose somewhere, they did not wonder for very long over Huguenau's eccentricities, which were really not eccentricities at all, for Huguenau's life flowed peacefully on between sacks of coffee and bales of cloth, between sleeping and eating, between business deals and games of cards. He became the father of a family, his elastic plumpness grew rounder and in time became a little flabby; his upright walk, too, visibly degenerated into a waddle; he was courteous to his customers, and to his subordinates a strict master and a model of industry; he was out and about early every morning, he indulged in no holidays, his pleasures were few and his æsthetic enjoyments either non-existent or dismissed with contempt; his obligations left him barely time even to go for a walk on Sundays with his wife and children, so how could he visit the Museum?—he didn't care for pictures anyhow. He rose to municipal honours, his feet were again on the path of duty. His life was the same life that his physical forbears had led for two hundred years, and his face was their face. They all resembled each other strongly, the Huguenaus, fat and complacent and serious in their folds of solid flesh, and it was hardly to be suspected that one of them should develop an ironically sarcastic expression. But whether this peculiarity was the result of mixed blood, or was merely a freak of nature, or marked a certain maturity in this descendant of the Huguenaus, a maturity that detached him from the family tree, it is difficult to determine, and in any case it was not considered important by anybody, least of all by Huguenau. For many things had become indifferent to Huguenau, and whenever his war adventures came into his mind they shrank into smaller and smaller compass, until at last all that remained was a single entry of 8000 francs in which they were symbolized and which was their final balance; and all that he had experienced at that time faded into a mere silhouette, into the delicate half-tones of the French banknotes that Huguenau the business man had been handling ever since. The soft grey shadow of dream-like and silvery sleep drew a veil over all that had happened; it grew more and more vague, more and more shadowy, as if a darkened glass had been set before it, and in the end he could not tell whether he had lived that life or whether it was a tale someone had told him.

It could perhaps be argued that all this fading away and forgetting was merely symptomatic of a state of resignation induced by the fact that the bourgeois system of values had been set up again in Alsace, including Colmar, of course, with the help of the victorious French bayonets, although the land itself, thanks to the wrongs it had had to suffer for centuries from right and left alike, was still as full of revolutionary spirit as any other frontier region, and even in Huguenau rebellion was still raising its head. It could be argued in any case that irrational forces once liberated are unwilling to submit themselves again to any old system of values, and that if they are compelled to submission they must necessarily diffuse a blight of deadness over the community and the individual alike. And out of that arises the problem of what happens to the irrational forces liberated by the disintegration of values: are they really nothing but fighting forces in the struggle between the several value-systems? are they really nothing but means for mutual destruction? are they really nothing but murder? and when the disintegration of values has gone as far as it can go in a reduction to the final indivisible units, to a struggle between one individual and another, must these guerrilla forces inevitably provoke a general dissension, a struggle of all against all? Or, to confine the question to Huguenau's particular case: can a partial value-system, such as the commercial one to which Huguenau reverted, possess a sufficient power of cohesion without external help from bayonets or police truncheons to combine the dissociated irrational impulses into a new organon, and to provide a new focus for the equally dissociated will-to-value?

Epistemologically, of course, these questions are inadmissible, since they make assumptions regarding the nature of the irrational. By the mere use of the word " forces " they assume a mechanistic theory and an anthropomorphic and voluntarist metaphysic; in short, they give a meaning to the irrational, and the irrational invalidates any meaning attached to it. In its original and undifferentiated condition the irrational admits of no theorizing and no interpretation beyond the simple affirmation of its anonymous existence, even although its living inarticulateness provides all the material for rational value-formations. This recalcitrance of the irrational is fully recognized by the total system superimposed upon it, that is to say by the religious system, the system of the Church. The Church recognizes only one value-system, her own, because her Platonic origin compels her to acknowledge only one Truth, only one Logos: her wholly rational alignment rules out any tolerance of the illogical, and compels her *a priori* to deny to the irrational and its hypothetical " attributes " any epistemological or even ethical significance. For the Church the irrational is simply the bestial, and all that can be said about it is that it is there and must be subsumed in the category of evil. From this point of view the irrational presents no problem for consideration, except in relation to the question of how evil can possibly exist within a world created by God; and the alleged capacity of the irrational to construct systems is not even considered except in reference to the possible ways in which evil can become manifest. True, these are questions which the Church has never ignored nor ever can ignore; the existence of evil is a necessary presupposition for the *ecclesia militans*, and since the progressive disintegration of values releases continuous manifestations of evil, the Church is constantly forced to stigmatize as evil whatever causes the disintegration; in other words, the Church has to discard the superrational and relegate it to the category of evil along with the irrational. But since the Church on the one hand knows as well as any private person that every manifestation is the " product of a product," knowing perhaps even more clearly than any private person that the condition of possible experience for all manifestations is determined by some " value," and since on the other hand she must regard her own value-structure as the only admissible one, she is bound to maintain that irrational evil, while incapable of constructing a system, is yet capable of aping the form of an existent system in order to manifest itself, and whatever its manifestations, she will regard them merely as imitations of her own structure; she is bound to maintain that evil, while it cannot think rationally, is yet capable of an empty aping of thought, a thought without true content (evil as the *privatio* of good), an empty, super-rational and dogmatic play of conventions, a kind of sophistry led astray by the irrational, subserving only the irrational, perverting the ethical will into an empty echo of moral maxims; but a sophistry that ultimately swells to the dimensions of a total system and raises evil from the Philistine level to the dignity of an Antichrist. For the Church the more completely evil establishes itself in the world, the more completely is Christ menaced by the mock Antichrist, the more menacing becomes the value-system of the Antichrist, which has to be a total system simply because the system of the Church is already a total system; so the Church sees evil spreading itself and becoming indivisible and homogeneous like the opposing truth which it imitates. Such a total system of evil as conceived by the Church throws into the shade all partial systems, and the most outstanding expression of the disintegration of values, the Protestant idea, acquires in the eyes of Catholicism a preponderant significance among the phenomena of disintegration, being regarded as the main idea, the *leit-motif*, in that fateful and irrational process, although Protestantism and all other partial systems are looked upon as merely distorted reflections of the true value, preliminary stages for the menacing total system of Antichrist which is to come. This estimate of Protestantism not only accords with the Church's special point of view, but has some foundation in objective fact, in the fact, for instance, that Protestantism displays a remarkable affinity with every other partial system of whatever kind: let it be capitalist or nationalist or what you will, every partial system can be brought under the same " revolutionary " anti-Catholic denominator as Protestantism; from the Church's point of view, that is to say, they all belong to the criminal category in which the irrational value-destroying forces of heresy are manifest. And although the Church often makes external concessions and, preferring the lesser evil to the greater, appears to tolerate this or the other separatist movement, such as a nationalist movement, as a nucleus of conservation against the more radical and purely revolutionary sects, yet she will never abandon the severity of her attitude towards the fundamental problem of how to align the irrational forces: for her it means either Christ or Antichrist, either a return into the bosom of the Church or the downfall of the world in the complete disintegration of values caused by the internecine struggle.

Every partial system, considered as a value-system, must imitate the structure of the total system, whether it be a simple reflection of that or its distorted perversion, and in so far as the tenets of the original system are based on formal principles, they must be reproduced and confirmed in the smaller sect; substantive differences, however, in the interpretation of these tenets, differences which are inevitable because no system can admit that it is " evil," must arise from a different orientation towards the irrational. The logical genesis, the logical basis of every partial system compels it to be revolutionary: a nationalist movement, for instance, following its logical development towards an absolute, sets up an organon in which the National State takes the central place of God, and in thus relating all values to the idea of the State, in thus subordinating the individual and his spiritual freedom to the power of the State, it not only finds itself in a revolutionary anti-capitalist position, but is even more stringently propelled in an anti-religious, anti-ecclesiastical direction which leads by a plain, undeviating path to the absolute revolutionary disintegration of values, and so, of course, to the ultimate supersession of the partial system itself. If a partial system, therefore, is to secure its continued existence in this process of disintegration, if it is to be able to bridle its own Ratio which hurries it towards ultimate extinction, it must take refuge in an alliance with the irrational. Thus arises that remarkable ambiguity characterizing every partial system, an ambiguity which amounts to dishonesty, epistemologically speaking: on the one hand the partial system adopts the attitude of a total system towards the process of advancing disintegration and stigmatizes the irrational as rebellious and criminal, while on the other hand it is compelled to distinguish among the homogeneous mass of irrationality and anonymous wickedness a group of " good " irrational forces which are needed to help it in checking further disintegration and in establishing its own claim to survival. Every half-way revolution, and in this sense all partial systems are half-way revolutions, bases its case on irrational assumptions, on mass feeling, on the dignity of an " irrational inspiration " that is exploited to discredit the radical logic of complete revolution; every partial system must expressly acknowledge a residue of " unformed " irrationality, which it maintains, so to speak, as a private preserve exempt from reason, in order to keep itself stable in the flux of disintegration.

For revolutions are insurrections of evil against evil, insurrections of the irrational against the rational, insurrections of the irrational masquerading as extreme logical reasoning against rational institutions complacently defending themselves by an appeal to irrational sentiment: revolutions are struggles between unreality and unreality, between tyranny and tyranny, and they are inevitable once the release of the super-rational has drawn in its train the release of the irrational, once the disintegration of values has advanced to its last integral unit, the individual;

for the individual, isolated and autonomous, stripped of all prejudice, is defenceless before the invasion of the irrational. Revolution is the breaking through of the irrational, the breaking through of the autonomous, the breaking through of life, and the isolated human being, stripped of values, is its instrument; and since the human outcast is the first to suffer the extremes of human misery and loneliness, the proletarian, for instance, victimized by hunger, or the soldier in the trenches victimized by intensive artillery fire, and since these literal outcasts must be the first to achieve freedom from values, they must also be the first to hear the voice of murder that drowns the muteness of the irrational with its clangour as of iron ringing upon iron. And it is always the adherent of the smaller value-system who slays the adherent of the larger system that is breaking up; it is always he, unfortunate wretch, who assumes the rôle of executioner in the process of value-disintegration, and on the day when the trumpets of judgment sound it is the man released from all values who becomes the executioner of a world that has pronounced its own sentence.

Huguenau had committed a murder. He forgot it afterwards; it never came into his mind again, while every single business *coup* that he had successfully brought off (his letter to Frau Esch!) remained accurately imprinted on his memory. And that was only natural: for none of our actions remains alive except those that consort with our reigning system of values, and Huguenau had reverted once more to the commercial system. And in exactly the same way, had circumstances been more favourable, he could have become as staunch a supporter of revolution as he was now of commerce, even although he was heir to a flourishing family business. For the proletarian who supports a revolution is not essentially the " revolutionist " he thinks himself; there is no difference, for instance, between the crowd that exulted in the quartering of Damien, the man who attempted a King's assassination, and the crowd that thronged thirty-five years later around the guillotine of a King, Louis XVI. —the revolutionist as an independent figure does not exist, he is merely the exponent of something greater than himself, the exponent in this case of the European spirit. The individual man may be sunk in a Philistine life, he may even be set in the mould of an old partial system; like Huguenau he may land in the commercial system; or he may attach himself to a preliminary revolutionary movement or to the definitive revolution; but none the less the spirit of positivistic disintegration is spread over all the Occidental world, nor is its visible expression restricted to the materialism of the Russian proletariat, which is merely one variation of the positivism into which the whole of Western philosophy, in so far as it can still be called philosophy, has resolved itself. Compared with this greater unity dissensions about the distribution of wealth sink into the background, although even there the distinction between Americanized methods of organization and communist methods is becoming less and less noticeable: our thought-patterns are moving with increasing urgency towards a common conclusion, a conclusion that makes it irrelevant whether the stamp of this or the other political party is affixed to it, since its whole significance, fundamentally speaking, lies solely in the fact that it is capable of becoming a total system and of once more combining the insurgent forces of the irrational. That is why a preliminary revolution based on the irrational does not matter in the long run, whether it is abortive or not; for it cannot prevent the definitive rational revolution into which it must inevitably be drawn, although as a temporary phenomenon it may be useful in revealing what a more complete system cannot reveal: that there are irrational forces, that they are effective, and that their very nature impels them to attach themselves to a new organon of values, to a total system which in the eyes of the Church can be no other than that of Antichrist. This judgment of the Church is not based on the appearance of such subordinate symptoms as the fanatical anti-Platonism of the communists, or the rationalist propaganda of Marxist or bourgeois Freethinkers; that kind of atheism, sinful as it may be, is too insignificant, indeed too pathetic, in the eyes of the Church, to be named in the same breath as the evil of Antichrist: what concerns the Church is the whole spirit of Europe, the " heretical " spirit of immediacy, of positivism, in face of which it does not really matter whether Protestantism is the progenitor of revolutionary nationalism by way of Fichte or, more obviously, of Marxian communism by way of Hegel; and although the Church, with the unfailing intuition of hatred, the hatred of heresy, can identify Protestantism in its remotest offshoots, and for that very reason denounces communism with an intransigence otherwise inexplicable, since she could quite well accept the primitive Christian conceptions underlying it, yet for all that the concrete phenomenon of communism is not yet the final formal elaboration of Antichrist, but merely a preliminary phase. It is not yet a total system in itself, even although it displays a regular Marxist theology derived from the Protestant theology of Kantianism, and a strictly expounded doctrine with a fixed ontology and an unassailable ethic; even although, indeed, it is provided with all the concomitants of a regular theology organized into what looks like a visible church, and although that church is deliberately setting itself up as an anti-church with machines as the apparatus of its cult and engineers and demagogues as its priesthood; it is not yet a total system as such, it is not yet Antichrist, but a preliminary phase, an indication of the approaching disintegration of the Christian-Platonic world. And in this dogmatic structure, in this uprearing of a Marxist anti-church with an ascetic and severe conception of the State, it is already possible clearly to discern— and no one discerns it more clearly than the Catholic Church—the gigantic contour of a spirit that rises far beyond Marxism, far beyond the apotheosis of the State, a spirit that is so far ahead of revolutionary doctrine of any kind that it makes even Marxism look like a circuitous advance: it is the contour of a churchless " Church in itself," the ontology of an abstract natural science without substance, an abstract ethic without dogma; in short, an organon of that severe and logical ultimate abstraction which is attained when the point of plausibility has receded into the infinite, and in which all the radicality of Protestantism is evident. It is the positivism that characterized Luther and the whole Renaissance, the same double affirmation of the given world and of the need for ascetic severity, a doctrine that is now fulfilling its essential implications and tending towards a new unity of Thought and Being, towards a new unity of ethical and material infinity. It is the unity which informs every system of theology and which must endure even if the attempt is made to deny the reality of Thought, but which takes on a new lease of life when the scientific point at which things are assumed as true coincides with the point at which things are believed to be true, so that the double truth once more becomes single and unambiguous. For at the end of the infinite line of inquiry which leads to this point there stands the pure deed-in-itself, the idea of a pure organon of abstract duty, the idea of a rational belief without a God; there stands the unyielding Law of an abstract religion devoid of content, perhaps even the rational immediacy of an abstract mysticism whose wordless asceticism and unornamented religiosity, governed by austerity and by austerity alone, points the way to the last goal of this completely Protestant revolution: the unaccented vacuum of a ruthless absoluteness in which is throned the abstract Spirit of God, God's Spirit, not Himself and yet Himself, reigning in sorrow amid the terror of dreamless, unbroken silence that constitutes the pure Logos.

In this predicament of the European spirit Huguenau was scarcely involved at all, but he was involved in the prevailing uncertainty. For the irrational in man has an affinity with the irrational in the world; and although the uncertainty in the world is, so to speak, a rational uncertainty, often, indeed, merely an economic uncertainty, yet it springs from the irrationality of the super-rational, from an independent reason that strives towards infinity in every province of human activity, and so, reaching the super-rational limits of its infinity, overthrows itself and becomes irrational, passing beyond comprehension. Currency hitherto accepted becomes incalculable, standards fluctuate, and, in spite of all the explanations that can be adduced to account for the irrational, what is finite fails to keep pace with the infinite and no reasonable means avail to reduce the irrational uncertainty of the infinite to sense and reason again. It is as though the infinite awakens to a concrete and independent life of its own, informed and drawn out by the Absolute that glimmers on the farthest horizon in this hour between downfall and uprising, in this magical hour of death and birth. And Huguenau, although he might avert his eyes from that distant dawn and refuse to acknowledge anything of the kind, could not but feel the icy breath sweeping over the world, freezing it to rigidity and withering all meaning out of the things of the world. And when Huguenau followed each morning the chronicle of events in his newspaper he did so with the uneasiness of all newspaper readers who greedily clutch at the facts presented to them, especially those facts that are supplemented by illustrations, in the daily and renewed hope that the mass of facts may fill the emptiness of a world that has fallen silent, the emptiness of a soul that has fallen silent. They read their newspapers and in their hearts is the terror that comes from awakening every morning to loneliness, for the speech of the old community life has failed them and that of the new is too faint for them to hear. They sustain, indeed, a pose of understanding and clear-sightedness by sharply criticizing the political and social situation or the working of the legal system, and they even exchange opinions on these subjects during the course of the day; but in reality they are without a language, standing mutely between what has been and what is not yet; they give no credence to words and require them to be confirmed by pictures, they have even ceased to believe in the adequacy of their own utterances, and thus caught

between an end and a beginning they know only that the logic of facts is
ruthless and that the Law remains unassailable: there is no soul, however
degenerate, however base, however Philistine and devoted to the tritest
dogmas, that can avoid this knowledge and this terror,—like a child surprised and overwhelmed by loneliness, a prey to the terror of the creature
that has begun to die, man must go seeking the fordable passage that
shall at last assure his life and his safety. Nowhere does he find help. And
it is in vain that he strives continuously to find a haven in some partial
system; in vain he may expect to be sheltered from uncertainty in old
romantic structures, or hope that in a partial revolution all that is known
and familiar to him will yield only with the utmost slowness, in a kind
of painless transition, to what is inexorably alien,—he can get no help,
for he finds himself cozened by the false glamour of a sham communal
life, and the deeper, more secret relationship he is groping for flutters
from the hand that thought to grasp it; and even if in his disappointment
he takes refuge in the monetary-commercial system still he cannot escape
disappointment: even that most characteristic mode of the bourgeois
existence, that partial system which is hardier than all others because it
promises an unshakable unity in the world, the unity that man needs to
reassure his uncertainty—two marks are always more than one mark and
a sum of eight thousand francs is made up of many francs and yet is a
whole, a rational organon in terms of which the world can be reckoned
up—even that hardy and enduring growth, in which the bourgeois desires
so strongly to believe even while all currencies are tottering, is beginning
to wither away; the irrational cannot be kept out at any point, and no
vision of the world can any longer be reduced to a sum in rational addition.
And even Wilhelm Huguenau, now a prosperous business man risen to
municipal honours, a man whose first inquiry about everything in life
usually concerned its price and the profit it might yield, even Wilhelm
Huguenau, although he thought it quite rational in such times of financial
insecurity to show a more suspicious face to the world, even he found
himself at times ironically shrugging off something, or with a sweeping
gesture trying to brush away something that, strangely enough, he could
not account for at all; and then in sudden perplexity he would ask " What
is money? " and sometimes even refuse credit to a customer, after mustering him with a sharp, suspicious look, simply because he took a dislike
to the man or objected to something in his expression, a sarcastic twitch
of the lips, perhaps—and whether this capriciousness served him well or

ill, whether it drove a potentially good customer into the arms of a rival or got rid of a bad customer at the right moment, quite apart from all practical considerations it was an abrupt method, though, perhaps, a lucid one, that resulted from a kind of short-circuiting; it was in any case unusual in business dealings, undoubtedly irrational, and probably largely responsible for the gulf that imperceptibly began to widen between Huguenau and his fellow-citizens as if he were isolated in a dead zone of silence. Huguenau had but the vaguest inkling of its existence, yet its outlines became less vague and almost palpable as soon as he found himself in any social gathering, in a cinema, or in a beer-hall where young people were dancing, or at banquets celebrating the anniversary of the French triumph: on such occasions Huguenau, himself a probable future Burgomaster, would sit among the other notables at the flower-decked table and watch the dancers with a serious, vacant, boyish gaze behind his thick eyeglasses, and although he was by no means of an age to re-nounce dancing, yet he could hardly believe it himself when he whispered to his neighbour (as he never omitted to do) that at one time he had been a good enough dancer. For whether he was sitting in such a patriotic assembly or strolling on Sundays with his eldest boy along the Strass-burger Allee to watch the bicycle races, he found himself falling irresistibly into a strange state of uneasiness, so that he even began to attend social gatherings merely to put himself to the test; it was an uneasiness in which things imperceptibly moved out of their places and in which every social gathering, although it ought to have presented an integral aspect, began to disintegrate into something that was disconcertingly multifarious, something that somebody or other, by means of decorations, garlands and banners, had combined into an artificial unity, against his own better judgment. And if Huguenau had not shied off from such out-of-the-way thoughts he would undoubtedly have discovered that there is not a single idea, not a single name, that has a corresponding concrete unity under-lying it; he would certainly have discovered that the unity of any event and the integrity of the world are guaranteed merely by enigmatic, although visible, symbols, which are necessary because without them the visible world would fall asunder into unnameable, bodiless, dry layers of cold and transparent ash—and so Huguenau would have perceived the curse of the casual, of the fortuitous, that spreads itself over things and their relations to each other, making it impossible to think of any arrange-ment that would not be equally arbitrary and fortuitous: would not the racing bicyclists have to scatter to the four winds if they were no longer combined by a common uniform and a common club badge? Huguenau did not ask such a question, for it exceeded the grasp of what might be called, not without reason, his private theology; yet the unasked question irritated him no less than the elusiveness of the experiences that worried him, and his irritation might, for instance, discharge itself in boxing his child on the ear for no reason at all on the way home. Having relieved his feelings in this manner, however, he found it easy to come back to sober reality, thus confirming Hegel's maxim: " Real freedom of will is a harmony between the theoretical and the practical spirit." In the best of tempers he would march back into the town, past the various churches out of which the congregations were just emerging, humming merrily to himself as he went and beating time with his stick, and whenever he met an acquaintance he would greet him and say " Salut."

For everything ultimately depends on one's relation to freedom, and even the pettiest and narrowest theology that extends merely far enough to make plausible the meanest actions of an empirical ego, in other words even the private theology of a Huguenau, is enlisted in the service of freedom, and regards freedom as the real centre of its deductions, its real mystic centre (and that was true for Huguenau at least from the day on which he deserted his trench in the grey dawn, thus following out an apparently irrational but none the less highly rational course of action in the service of freedom, so that everything he had striven towards since that day and everything he was yet to strive for in his life could be taken as a repetition of his actions in that first high-day and holiday mood): indeed it is almost as if freedom were in a lofty category by itself, soaring high above all that is rational and irrational, like an end and a beginning, resembling the Absolute with which its light is blended and yet which it surpasses, as if it were an ultimate, serene ray shining beyond the fiery caverns of the opening heavens. The irrational could never attach itself to the rational, nor the rational diffuse itself in the harmony of living feeling, were they not both partakers in an overarching and majestic Being which is at once the highest reality and the profoundest unreality: it is only in this conjunction of reality and unreality that the wholeness of the world and its form can be apprehended; it is the idea of freedom that justifies the continued rebirth of humanity, for it can never be realized on earth and the road that leads to it must ever be trodden anew. Oh, agonizing compulsion towards freedom! terrible and ever-renewed revolution of knowledge! which justifies the insurrection of Absolute against Absolute, the insurrection of life against reason—justifying reason when, apparently at variance with itself, it unleashes the absolute of the irrational against the absolute of the rational, justifying it by providing the final assurance that the unleashed irrational forces will once more combine into a value-system. There is no value-system that does not subordinate itself to freedom; even the most reduced system is groping towards freedom, even the outcast victim of all earthly loneliness and detachment, the man who achieves no more than the freedom to commit a murder, the freedom to enter prison, or at most the freedom of a deserter, even he, the man stripped of all values, on whom all earthly compulsions press—there is no man exposed to the breath of the Eternal who does not once see the star of freedom rising in the night of his isolation: each man must fulfil his dream, unhallowed or holy, and he does so to have his share of freedom in the darkness and dullness of his life. And so Huguenau often had the feeling that he was sitting in some pit or dark cavern looking out over a cold zone that lay like a girdle of loneliness around his station, while life streamed in distant pictures over the dusky firmament, and then he had a great yearning to creep out of his pen and share in the freedom and loneliness outside, the existence of which he vaguely guessed at as if it were a vision blown in from somewhere or other upon him alone; it was like a knowledge of the deepest community of the spirit into which that most profound loneliness must inevitably change, but it never got beyond the dull conviction that out there it would be somehow or other possible to compel people to be warm and friendly, to compel them by threats of murder or violence, or at least by a box on the ear, to accept him and to listen to his truth, which he was yet incapable of articulating. For even although he was scarcely distinguishable from others in his actions and his mode of life, even although he ran more and more surely on the lines that had been laid down for him in youth, and that he never thought of leaving again, even although it was an utterly carnal, yes, a solid life that was advancing in him towards death, yet in a certain sense it grew more lofty and airy as he felt himself daily more cut off and isolated while ceasing to suffer from the isolation: cut off from the world and yet in it, he saw men receding from him into regions ever more remote and more longed-for, but he made no attempt to explore that far country; and in thus resigning himself he again showed his complete likeness to all other mortals. For every man knows that human life does not stretch far enough for a journey to the end of the path that mounts like a spiral road to higher and higher reaches, the path on which all that has vanished behind one's back rises again in front on a loftier level, only to fade into the distant haze with every fresh step one takes: that endless course of the closed circle and of fulfilment, that lucid reality in which things fall asunder and recede to the poles, to the uttermost limits of the world where all that has been sundered is again joined into one, where distance is again annulled and the irrational takes on its visible shape, where fear no more becomes longing and longing no more turns into fear, where the freedom of the self is received again into the Platonic freedom of God; that endless course of the closed circle and of fulfilment that can be trodden only by him who has fulfilled his nature—unattainable for any man.

Unattainable for any man! And even if Huguenau had landed in a revolutionary instead of in a commercial system he would still have been barred from entering on the path of fulfilment. For murder remains murder, evil remains evil, and the Philistinism of a value-system whose field is restricted to the individual and his irrational impulses, that last product of every disintegration of values, remains the point of absolute degeneracy; the point, so to speak, of an invariant absolute zero that is common to all scales of value and all value-systems without reference to their mutual relativity, and that must be common to all of them since no value-system can be conceived unless in its idea and logical nature it observes the " condition of possible experience," the empirical draft of a logical structure common to all systems and of an *a priori* immutability that is bound up with the Logos. And it almost seems like an outcrop of the same logical necessity that the transition from any value-system to a new one must pass through that zero-point of atomic dissolution, must take its way through a generation destitute of any connection with either the old or the new system, a generation whose very detachment, whose almost insane indifference to the suffering of others, whose stark denudation of values provides an ethical and so an historical justification for the ruthless rejection in times of revolution of all that is humane. And perhaps it must be so, since only such a silent and self-contained generation is able to endure the sight of the Absolute and the rising glare of freedom, the light that flares out over the deepest darkness, and only over the deepest darkness: the earthly reflection of the Absolute is like an image in a dark pool, and the earthly echo of its silence is the iron clangour of murder, which yet sends mute vibrations rolling like an impenetrable wall of deafening silence between man and man, so that no voice can rise beyond it or through it, and man must tremble. Dread reflection, dread echo of the Ratio bursting its way through to the Absolute! its ruthlessness finds an earthly counterpart in violence and mute force, and the rational immediacy of its divine end becomes on earth the immediacy of the irrational that forces men to reluctant yet dumb obedience; its endless chain of inquiry is reduced on earth to the single link of the irrational that asks no more questions but merely acts, setting out to destroy a community of life that has ceased to justify its existence, a so-called community devoid of force but filled with evil will, a community that drowns itself in blood and chokes in its own poison-gases. What a lonely death is the earthly counterpart of divine isolation! Man, exposed to the horror of unrestrained reason, bidden to serve it without comprehending it, caught in the toils of a process that develops far over his head, caught in the toils of his own irrationality, man is like the savage who is bewitched by black magic and cannot see the connection between means and effect, he is like the madman who cannot find his way out of the tangle of his Irrational and Super-rational, he is like the criminal who cannot find his way into the value-realities of the community he desires to enter. Irrevocably the past escapes him, irrevocably the future flees from him, and the droning of machines gives him no indication of the path to his goal that rises unattainable and formless in the haze of the infinite, bearing aloft the black torch of the Absolute. Dread hour of death and of birth, dread hour of the Absolute sustained by a generation that has extinguished itself, a generation that knows nothing about the infinite into which it is driven by its own logic—inexperienced, helpless, and insensate, the men of this generation are delivered to the icy hurricane, they must forget in order to live and they do not know why they die. Their path is the path of Ahasuerus, their duty is his duty, their freedom is the freedom of the hunted creature and their aim is forgetfulness. Lost generation! as non-existent as Evil itself, featureless and traditionless in the morass of the indiscriminate, doomed to lose itself temporally, to have no tradition in an age that is making absolute history! Whatever the individual man's attitude to the course of the revolution, whether he turns reactionary and clings to outworn forms, mistaking the æsthetic for the ethical as all conservatives do, or whether he holds aloof in the passivity of egoistic knowledge, or whether he gives himself up to his irrational impulses and applies himself to the destructive work of the revolution:

he remains unethical in his destiny, an outcast from his epoch, an outcast from Time,

yet nowhere and never is the spirit of the epoch so strong, so truly ethical and historical as in that last and first flare-up which is revolution, that act of self-elimination and self-renewal, the last and greatest ethical achievement of the old disintegrating system and the first achievement of the new, the moment when time is annulled and history radically formed in the pathos of the absolute zero!

Great is the anguish of the man who becomes aware of his isolation and seeks to escape from his own memory; he is obsessed and outcast, flung back into the deepest animal anguish, into the anguish of the creature that suffers violence and inflicts violence, flung back into an overwhelming loneliness in which his flight and his despair and his stupor may become so great that he cannot help thinking of inflicting violence on himself so as to escape the immutable law of events. And in his fear of the voice of judgment that threatens to issue from the darkness, there awakens within him a doubly strong yearning for a Leader to take him tenderly and lightly by the hand, to set things in order and show him the way; a Leader who is nobody's follower and who will precede him on the un-trodden path of the closed circle and lead him on to ever-higher reaches, to an ever-brighter revelation; the Leader who will build the house anew that the dead may come to life again, and who himself has risen again from the multitude of the dead; the Healer who by his own actions will give a meaning to the incomprehensible events of the age, so that Time can begin anew. That is his yearning. Yet even if the Leader were to come the hoped-for miracle would not happen; his life would be an ordinary life on earth; and just as belief has taken on the disguise of provisional assumption, and assumption that of belief in rational religion, so the healer walks in the most unlikely guise and may even be the casual passer-by now crossing the street—for wherever he walks, whether in the turmoil of city streets or in the light of evening fields, his road is the road to Zion and yet the road we must all take; his journey is a search for the fordable passage between the evil of the irrational and the evil of the super-rational, and his freedom is the anguished freedom of duty, is sacrifice and expia-tion for the past; even for him the way is the way of trial, determined by austerity, and his isolation is that of a lost child, is that of the lost son

whose bourne fades into the unattainable since he has been abandoned
by his father. And despite all that: the mere hope of wisdom from a
Leader is wisdom for us, the mere divination of grace is grace, and un-
availing as may be our hope that in a Leader's visible life the Absolute
will one day fulfil itself on earth, yet our goal remains accessible, our
hope that a Messiah will lead us to it remains imperishable, and the
renascence of values is fated to recur. And hemmed in as we may be by
the increasing muteness of the abstract, each man a victim of the iciest
necessity, flung into nothingness, his ego flung to the winds—it is the
breath of the Absolute that sweeps across the world, and from our dim
inklings and gropings for truth there will spring up the high-day and
holiday assurance with which we shall know that every man has the divine
spark in his soul and that our oneness cannot be forfeited; unforfeitable
the brotherhood of humble human creatures, from whose deepest anguish
there shines unforfeitable and unforfeited the anguish of a divine grace,
the oneness of all men, gleaming in all things, beyond all Space and all
Time; the oneness in which all light has its source and from which springs
the healing of all living things—symbol of a symbol, image of an image,
emerging from the destiny that is sinking in darkness, welling up out of
madness and dreamlessness like the gift of maternal life wrested from
the unknown and rewon as a heritage, the prototype of all imagery rising
in the insurrection of the irrational, blotting out the self and transcending
its confines, annulling time and distance; in the icy hurricane, in the
tempest of collapse all the doors spring open, the foundations of our
prison are troubled, and from the profoundest darkness of the world,
from our bitterest and profoundest darkness the cry of succour comes
to the helpless, there sounds the voice that binds all that has been to all
that is to come, that binds our loneliness to all other lonelinesses, and it
is not the voice of dread and doom; it falters in the silence of the Logos
and yet is borne on by it, raised high over the clamour of the non-existent;
it is the voice of man and of the tribes of men, the voice of comfort and
hope and immediate love: " Do thyself no harm! for we are all here ! "

Vienna, 1928–31.

Biographical Note

Hermann Broch was born on 1 November 1886 of Jewish parents from the textile quarter of Vienna. The family background – his father was a wholesale textile merchant from Moravia, his mother the daughter of a Viennese wholesale leather dealer – singled him out, as the first of two sons, for a career in the family firm. Between 1904 and 1906 he studied at the city's Technical College for Textile Manufacture and at the Spinning and Weaving College at Mühlhausen (Mulhouse, Alsace) in preparation for running the Brochs' textile concern at Teesdorf near Vienna. The following year he went on a fact-finding mission to the USA to study methods of cotton production and patented a cotton-mixing machine of which he was co-inventor. Volunteering in 1909 for service in the Austro-Hungarian Imperial Army, he was obliged to discontinue his training with the artillery in Zagreb because of ill health. Later the same year he joined the board of directors of the family spinning works. Having been declared unfit for military service during the First World War, he acted as director of a Red Cross convalescent home for soldiers within the grounds of the Teesdorf factory, while continuing to manage the family business. Broch once self-deprecatingly referred to himself as a 'captain of industry', yet his organizational skills and the constructive paternalism with which the Teesdorf plant treated its work-force had come to the attention of the Austrian business establishment and he was invited to serve in the Arbitration Section of the Austrian Trades Court and the State Anti-Unemployment Bureau.

By the age of forty, Broch had established a reputation not just as a successful industrialist, but also as a formidable autodidact with growing interests in modernist literature and philosophy. Even before the outbreak of the First World War he had begun publishing essays in the prestigious Viennese journal *Der Brenner*; his first work of fiction, the 'Methodological Novella' (later to become part of his 1950 novel *The*

309

Guiltless), had appeared in Franz Blei's *Summa* (1918); and he had a string of literary, philosophical and cultural essays and reviews to his credit by the mid 1920s. These, together with the fact that he began moving in Viennese *Kaffeehaus* circles, brought him to the attention of Stefan Zweig, Karl Kraus and Robert Musil. Between 1925 and 1930, he enrolled for courses in philosophy, mathematics and psychology at the University of Vienna. His decision to sell the family firm in 1927 and devote himself to intellectual pursuits came as a shock to his family. Broch was no doubt primarily responding to the economic warning signals of the time, but the coincidence of this radical *volte-face* with his intensive work on the first draft of *The Sleepwalkers* suggests that what he called the 'terrible strain' of his 'double existence' had also been instrumental in bringing about the biggest change of direction in his entire life.

The next decisive event in his life was not to be of Broch's own making. In 1938 Hitler's forces invaded Austria and Broch found himself on a Gestapo list. Whether this was because of his Jewishness or his politics remains unclear. His postman is rumoured to have denounced him on account of a subscription to the Moscow journal *Das Wort*, but Broch's voluminous international correspondence with leading pacifists and socialists on behalf of his proposed 'League of Nations Resolution' would have been equally incriminating. Broch spent three weeks in 'protective custody' before being released and instructed to report to the Viennese authorities. He was astute enough to evade further Gestapo attention before successfully fleeing to Scotland where, thanks to the good offices of his English translators Willa and Edwin Muir, he eventually obtained a US visa. Broch arrived in New York in October 1938 and was destined to stay in the United States until he died of a heart attack in May 1951.

'One thing at least I have in common with Kafka and Musil', Broch once remarked, is that 'none of us has an actual biography; we lived and wrote, nothing more.' Certainly, by the time Broch arrived in the United States he was inclined to identify his life exclusively with his writing. He had successfully completed the transition from man of industry to internationally acclaimed writer, mentioned alongside Joyce, Gide, Musil, Huxley and Thomas Mann. *The Sleepwalkers* had enjoyed instant recognition in the early 1930s, although an unfortunate combination of adverse economic circumstances and National Socialist pressures meant that the novel would now be more helpful to him in his new host country than in Europe. Although he had written a number of other works since the appearance of the *Sleepwalkers* trilogy in 1931–2 – including *The Unknown Quantity* (1933), a complex of stories that would become the core of *The Guiltless* (1950), as well as drafts of *The Spell* and *The Death of Virgil* – his principal calling-card was still his first novel; MGM and Paramount were interested in film rights to it, people of the stature of Albert Einstein, Thornton Wilder, Aldous Huxley and T. S. Eliot thought highly of the trilogy, and its theoretical sections on the disintegration of values would, it was hoped, help Broch gain a post at one of the Ivy League universities. However, like many exiles of his generation, he was to remain on the margins of academe. A number of awards (from the Bollingen, Guggenheim and Rockefeller Foundations) enabled him complete his *magnum opus*, the novel *The Death of Virgil*, as well as a long cultural essay on *Hugo von Hofmannsthal and His Times* and, most important of all, to continue working on his Theory of Mass Hysteria, the major project of his final years. While the parallel German and English publication of *The Death of Virgil* in 1945 had benefited from a highly favourable reception, for the following six years Broch was to resume his intolerable 'double existence': having to devote himself – now reluctantly – once more to literary work (above all, his two incomplete novels *The Guiltless* and *The Spell*) in order to placate his publishers and re-establish himself in Europe, while struggling against the passage of time and various illnesses to complete his project on mass hysteria. Broch died, in the eyes of the outside world as the author of two literary masterpieces, but in his own view as someone whose main sociological, political and humanitarian work remained unfinished.

John White

READ MORE IN PENGUIN

In every corner of the world, on every subject under the sun, Penguin represents quality and variety – the very best in publishing today.

For complete information about books available from Penguin – including Puffins, Penguin Classics and Arkana – and how to order them, write to us at the appropriate address below. Please note that for copyright reasons the selection of books varies from country to country.

In the United Kingdom: Please write to *Dept. EP, Penguin Books Ltd, Bath Road, Harmondsworth, West Drayton, Middlesex UB7 ODA*

In the United States: Please write to *Consumer Sales, Penguin Putnam Inc., P.O. Box 12289 Dept. B, Newark, New Jersey 07101-5289*. VISA and MasterCard holders call 1-800-788-6262 to order Penguin titles

In Canada: Please write to *Penguin Books Canada Ltd, 10 Alcorn Avenue, Suite 300, Toronto, Ontario M4V 3B2*

In Australia: Please write to *Penguin Books Australia Ltd, P.O. Box 257, Ringwood, Victoria 3134*

In New Zealand: Please write to *Penguin Books (NZ) Ltd, Private Bag 102902, North Shore Mail Centre, Auckland 10*

In India: Please write to *Penguin Books India Pvt Ltd, 11 Community Centre, Panchsheel Park, New Delhi 110017*

In the Netherlands: Please write to *Penguin Books Netherlands bv, Postbus 3507, NL-1001 AH Amsterdam*

In Germany: Please write to *Penguin Books Deutschland GmbH, Metzlerstrasse 26, 60594 Frankfurt am Main*

In Spain: Please write to *Penguin Books S. A., Bravo Murillo 19, 1° B, 28015 Madrid*

In Italy: Please write to *Penguin Italia s.r.l., Via Benedetto Croce 2, 20094 Corsico, Milano*

In France: Please write to *Penguin France, Le Carré Wilson, 62 rue Benjamin Baillaud, 31500 Toulouse*

In Japan: Please write to *Penguin Books Japan Ltd, Kaneko Building, 2-3-25 Koraku, Bunkyo-Ku, Tokyo 112*

In South Africa: Please write to *Penguin Books South Africa (Pty) Ltd, Private Bag X14, Parkview, 2122 Johannesburg*

BY THE SAME AUTHOR

The Romantic

In this first volume of *The Sleepwalkers* trilogy, Broch explores the dilemma between the demands of the spirit and the flesh. His tormented, neurotic hero is Joachim von Pasenow, an officer in the Guards from an aristocratic family. When he unexpectedly finds himself the heir to a great estate, he must make his choice between the chorus-girl he loves and the conventional, pallid woman of rank his parents approve of. With its visionary depiction of humanity, flawed and unpredictable, Stephen Spender called *The Sleepwalkers* 'one of the few really great original and thoughtful novels of this century'.

'Broch performs with an impeccable virtuosity' Aldous Huxley

The Anarchist

The second in Broch's masterly trilogy, *The Sleepwalkers*, *The Anarchist* follows the destiny of August Esch, who faces an uncertain future after he is wrongfully dismissed from his job as a book-keeper. He becomes enmeshed in the attempt to avenge Martin, a political activist, imprisoned by the authorities; but his personal battle is with his own lust, which he seeks to channel into marriage with Frau Hentjen. *The Anarchist* is a brilliant depiction of German society as it approached the First World War.

'In this new way of seeing man ... Broch in *The Sleepwalkers* prefigures ... the future possibilities of the novel' Milan Kundera

The Death of Virgil

Hermann Broch, an Austrian Jew imprisoned by the Nazis who managed to escape to America in 1938, became obsessed with literature's tendency to prettify suffering, and its impotence in the face of political terror. Broch explores these themes through the story of the dying Virgil, his relations with the Emperor Augustus and his desperate decision to burn the manuscript of his unfinished *Aeneid*. *The Death of Virgil* ranks among the boldest and most powerful attempts to confront the horrors of the twentieth century.

'One of the most extraordinary and profound experiments ever to have been undertaken with ... the novel' Thomas Mann